VIRAGO
MODERN CLASSICS
537

Charlotte Anna Perkins

Charlotte Anna Perkins (1860–1935) was born in Hartford, Connecticut. At the age of twenty-four she married and in the following year her only child, Katharine, was born. In 1887 she separated from her husband. *The Yellow Wallpaper* was published in *The New England Magazine* in 1892 and a book of verse, *In This Our World*, was published in the following year. Charlotte Perkins Stetson spent the years between 1895 and 1900 lecturing. It was in this period that she produced the bulk of her work that centred on the oppression of women, including *Women and Economics* (1898). She edited *The Forerunner* periodical in this century. In 1900 she married George Houghton Gilman. He died in 1934 and suffering from inoperable cancer, Charlotte Perkins Gilman committed suicide a year later. Her autobiography, *The Living of Charlotte Perkins Gilman*, was published posthumously.

THE YELLOW WALLPAPER AND SELECTED WRITINGS

Charlotte Perkins Gilman

Introduced by Maggie O'Farrell

virago

VIRAGO

First published in Great Britain in 2009 by Virago Press

11 13 15 14 12

Introduction copyright © Maggie O'Farrell 2009

The moral right of the author has been asserted.

A CIP catalogue record for this book
is available from the British Library.

ISBN 978-1-84408-558-3

Typeset in Goudy by M Rules
Printed and bound in Great Britain by
Clays Ltd, St Ives plc

Papers used by Virago are from well-managed forests
and other responsible sources.

MIX
Paper from
responsible sources
FSC® C104740

Virago
An imprint of
Little, Brown Book Group
Carmelite House
50 Victoria Embankment
London EC4Y 0DZ

An Hachette UK Company
www.hachette.co.uk

www.virago.co.uk

CONTENTS

CONTENTS

INTRODUCTION

At the close of the nineteenth century, a Boston physician was so enraged by the publication of a certain story that he wrote the following complaint: 'The story can hardly, it would seem, give pleasure to any reader . . . such literature contains deadly peril. Should such stories be allowed to pass without severest censure?'

It's a pretty powerful claim, that a work of literature places the reader in danger or 'deadly peril'. There is, of course, no shortage of books that have in the past been labelled dangerous, but usually for reasons of morality. There aren't many that have been considered capable of robbing you of your mental stability, even your life, as the Boston doctor is suggesting.

The story that got him in such a lather was Charlotte Perkins Gilman's 'The Yellow Wallpaper'. First published in *The New England Magazine* in 1892, it is an account by a nameless young woman of a summer spent in a large country house. She is, she tells you on the first page, 'sick' with a 'temporary nervous depression – a slight hysterical tendency'. Her husband, a doctor, confines her to a top-floor room to rest: '[I] am absolutely forbidden to "work" until I am well again. Personally, I disagree with their ideas. Personally, I believe that congenial work, with excitement and change, would do me good. But what is one to do?'

In that last clause, you have the crux, the terrible essence of the story. The answer is that there is nothing for her to do. Kept from 'society and stimulus', denied the freedom to write (she must hide any pages from the watchful eyes of her husband and her sister-in-law), forbidden any kind of mental activity at all, she is quite literally bored out of her mind. Slowly suffocating under the wrong kind of care, she is forced to dwell on the only things in front of her: the room; the grim bars on the windows; the bed, screwed to the floor; and the peculiar repetitions of the patterned, yellow wallpaper.

I can clearly remember the first time I encountered 'The Yellow Wallpaper'. I was sixteen and I had asked for *The Oxford Book of Gothic Tales* as a Christmas present. It was, I think, the first hardback I'd ever owned. It came with a dark, winter-green cover, decorated with ivy, and a dim painting of a woman surrounded by gloom and poppies.

It was late on Christmas night, a storm was hurling itself off the sea, and I settled down in bed with my new book. I read Wadham, Poe, Hawthorne, and just as I was about to shut the book and go to sleep, I noticed this opening sentence: 'It is very seldom that mere ordinary people like John and myself secure ancestral halls for the summer.'

Something in that frank, intimate, urgent voice must have struck me, because I read on. And when I got to the end and raised my head, I remember being amazed to find myself back in my own life, in the present, not in the top floor of an old house, the floor littered by torn hunks of sulphurous yellow wallpaper.

I had never read anything like it before. I hadn't known it was possible to write in such a clean, insouciant style; I hadn't known it was possible to write about oppression, illness, madness, marriage. It was one of those moments you often have as a teenager, when the world suddenly shifts on its axis and everything looks sharp with potential.

I learned later, when I studied 'The Yellow Wallpaper' as an undergraduate, that it is a closely autobiographical work, and that the writing of it was fuelled by indignation at the treatment Gilman herself received under the doctor who is directly named – as a threat to the narrator – in the text.

Gilman was born Charlotte Anna Perkins on 3rd July 1860 in Connecticut, to Mary and Frederick Beecher Perkins (Harriet Beecher Stowe, author of *Uncle Tom's Cabin*, was her great aunt). Her childhood appears to have been a strange, insecure one. She had an older brother, Thomas Adie, but there were two other siblings who died in infancy. In her autobiography, Gilman makes the devastating claim that as a little girl, her mother only showed her affection when she thought she was asleep.

Mary Perkins was told by a doctor that if she had more children she might die; soon after this, Frederick left. With no means of financial support, Mary Perkins and her two children were left in poverty, condemned to the existence of poor relations, moving from the house of one sympathetic relative to the next.

In 1878, aged eighteen, Charlotte began attending the Rhode Island School of Design, supporting herself by making trade cards. In 1884, she married the artist Charles Walter Stetson; the marriage proved to be a fraught one and would, unusually for the time, end in divorce. Gilman had a child with Stetson, Katharine Beecher Stetson, whose birth prompted a severe bout of what would now be diagnosed as post-natal depression.

Motherhood did not sit easily with Gilman. Her autobiography reveals that she felt no happiness holding her baby, only pain. In 1887, after what Gilman herself describes as 'a severe and continuous nervous breakdown tending to melancholia – and beyond', she consulted the expert Dr Silas Weir Mitchell. He diagnosed nervous exhaustion or neurasthenia (a catch-all diagnosis popular at the time) and prescribed the rest cure. This was a controversial treatment that Weir Mitchell pioneered and favoured above all others. Its tenets were complete bed rest, total isolation from family and friends, and overfeeding on a diet rich in dairy produce to increase fat on the body. The patient was forbidden to leave her bed, read, write, sew, talk or feed herself.

Just typing that list makes me shudder in horror. And worse is to come, because Gilman survived a month under Weir Mitchell and was sent home with the following instructions: 'live as domestic a life as possible. Have your child with you all the time . . . Lie down an hour after each meal. Have but two hours' intellectual life a day. And never touch pen, brush or pencil as long as you live.'

For a woman of Gilman's intelligence and drive, it can only be imagined what torture such a 'life' was. She tried to follow Weir Michell's advice, but the result of this unliveable situation was a near collapse – and 'The Yellow Wallpaper'.

Despite its utter control, its exquisite poise, 'The Yellow Wallpaper' is an angry story. You can feel the fury crackling off the page, driving each carefully chosen word; you sense it inhabiting the white spaces around the text. But it is a right-eous, directed, measured anger. Gilman goes after Weir Mitchell with a single-minded focus, and every paragraph, every full-stop, every line of dialogue dismantles him and his treatments, bit by precise bit.

In an article she later wrote for her magazine, *Forerunner*, entitled 'Why I Wrote "The Yellow Wallpaper"' she explains that the rest cure brought her 'so near the borderline of utter mental ruin that I could see over'. She attributes her recovery to casting 'the noted specialist's advice to the winds' and going to work again. That work was 'The Yellow Wallpaper', a copy of which she sent 'to the physician who so nearly drove me mad. He never acknowledged it.'

The article goes on to record her delight and pride that the story 'has to my knowledge saved one woman from a similar fate – so terrifying her family that they let her out into normal activity and she recovered.' And that 'many years later I was told that the great specialist had admitted to friends of his that he had altered his treatment of neurasthenia since reading "The Yellow Wallpaper".' This was never corroborated by Weir Mitchell who, unsurprisingly, refused to be drawn on the subject. But for an anecdote, it has the unmistakable ring of truth. I myself would pay untold sums for a time machine so that I could go back to Weir Mitchell's study, to watch his face as he read the manuscript

To look at 'The Yellow Wallpaper', however, solely in auto-biographical terms, or those of historical or medical interest, is to diminish its value. 'The Yellow Wallpaper' is a great work of literature, the product of a questing, burning intellect.

The mad woman has been used as a trope for centuries by writers, but more often as a walk-on part: we are allowed short, horrifying glimpses of the mad Ophelia and the hallucinating Lady Macbeth; before they are hurried to their deaths; Bertha Rochester escapes her attic prison to cause fires and havoc, and is then put back before she, too, is sent to death. What 'The Yellow Wallpaper' does is give the mad woman pen and paper, and ultimately a voice of her own. We hear from her, directly and in detail.

'The Yellow Wallpaper' is a cry, not so much of defiance, but of demand. A demand to be heard, a demand to be understood, a demand to be acknowledged. You hear echoes of this cry in later books: in Jean Rhys' *Wide Sargasso Sea*, in Janet Frame's *An Angel at My Table* – in particular at that moment when a writing prize saves her from an impending lobotomy. You can hear it in Sylvia Plath, in Antonia White, in Jennifer Dawson, in Susannah Kaysen. All we can do is listen.

Maggie O'Farrell, Edinburgh, 2008

STORIES

THE YELLOW WALLPAPER

It is very seldom that mere ordinary people like John and myself secure ancestral halls for the summer.

A colonial mansion, a hereditary estate, I would say a haunted house, and reach the height of romantic felicity – but that would be asking too much of fate!

Still I will proudly declare that there is something queer about it.

Else, why should it be let so cheaply? And why have stood so long untenanted?

John laughs at me, of course, but one expects that in marriage.

John is practical in the extreme. He has no patience with faith, an intense horror of superstition, and he scoffs openly at any talk of things not to be felt and seen and put down in figures.

John is a physician, and *perhaps* – (I would not say it to a living soul, of course, but this is dead paper and a great relief to my mind) – *perhaps* that is one reason I do not get well faster.

You see he does not believe I am sick!

And what can one do?

If a physician of high standing, and one's own husband, assures friends and relatives that there is really nothing the matter with one but temporary nervous depression – a slight hysterical tendency – what is one to do?

My brother is also a physician, and also of high standing, and he says the same thing.

So I take phosphates or phosphites – whichever it is, and tonics, and journeys, and air, and exercise, and am absolutely forbidden to 'work' until I am well again.

Personally, I disagree with their ideas.

Personally, I believe that congenial work, with excitement and change, would do me good.

But what is one to do?

I did write for a while in spite of them; but it *does* exhaust me a good deal – having to be so sly about it, or else meet with heavy opposition.

I sometimes fancy that in my condition if I had less opposition and more society and stimulus – but John says the very worst thing I can do is to think about my condition, and I confess it always makes me feel bad.

So I will let it alone and talk about the house.

The most beautiful place! It is quite alone, standing well back from the road, quite three miles from the village. It makes me think of English places that you read about, for there are hedges and walls and gates that lock, and lots of separate little houses for the gardeners and people.

There is a *delicious* garden! I never saw such a garden – large and shady, full of box-bordered paths, and lined with long grape-covered arbors with seats under them.

There were greenhouses, too, but they are all broken now.

There was some legal trouble, I believe, something about the heirs and coheirs; anyhow, the place has been empty for years.

That spoils my ghostliness, I am afraid, but I don't care – there is something strange about the house – I can feel it.

I even said so to John one moonlight evening, but he said what I felt was a *draught*, and shut the window.

I get unreasonably angry with John sometimes. I'm sure I never used to be so sensitive. I think it is due to this nervous condition.

But John says if I feel so, I shall neglect proper self-control; so I take pains to control myself – before him, at least, and that makes me very tired.

I don't like our room a bit. I wanted one downstairs that opened on the piazza and had roses all over the window, and such pretty old-fashioned chintz hangings! but John would not hear of it.

He said there was only one window and not room for two beds, and no near room for him if he took another.

He is very careful and loving, and hardly lets me stir without special direction.

I have a schedule prescription for each hour in the day; he takes all care from me, and so I feel basely ungrateful not to value it more.

He said we came here solely on my account, that I was to have perfect rest and all the air I could get. 'Your exercise depends on your strength, my dear,' said he, 'and your food somewhat on your appetite; but air you can absorb all the time.' So we took the nursery at the top of the house.

It is a big, airy room, the whole floor nearly, with windows that look all ways, and air and sunshine galore. It was a nursery first and then playroom and gymnasium, I should judge; for the windows are barred for little children, and there are rings and things in the walls.

The paint and paper look as if a boys' school had used it. It is stripped off – the paper – in great patches all around the head of my bed, about as far as I can reach, and in a great place on the other side of the room low down. I never saw a worse paper in my life.

One of those sprawling flamboyant patterns committing every artistic sin.

It is dull enough to confuse the eye in following, pronounced enough to constantly irritate and provoke study, and when you follow the lame uncertain curves for a little distance they suddenly commit suicide – plunge off at outrageous angles, destroy themselves in unheard of contradictions.

The color is repellent, almost revolting; a smouldering unclean yellow, strangely faded by the slow-turning sunlight.

It is a dull yet lurid orange in some places, a sickly sulphur tint in others.

No wonder the children hated it! I should hate it myself if I had to live in this room long.

There comes John, and I must put this away, – he hates to have me write a word.

We have been here two weeks, and I haven't felt like writing before, since that first day.

I am sitting by the window now, up in this atrocious nursery, and there is nothing to hinder my writing as much as I please, save lack of strength.

John is away all day, and even some nights when his cases are serious.

I am glad my case is not serious!

But these nervous troubles are dreadfully depressing.

John does not know how much I really suffer. He knows there is no *reason* to suffer, and that satisfies him.

Of course it is only nervousness. It does weigh on me so not to do my duty in any way!

I meant to be such a help to John, such a real rest and comfort, and here I am a comparative burden already!

Nobody would believe what an effort it is to do what little I am able, – to dress and entertain, and order things.

It is fortunate Mary is so good with the baby. Such a dear baby!

And yet I *cannot* be with him, it makes me so nervous.

I suppose John never was nervous in his life. He laughs at me so about this wallpaper!

At first he meant to repaper the room, but afterwards he said that I was letting it get the better of me, and that nothing was worse for a nervous patient than to give way to such fancies.

He said that after the wallpaper was changed it would be the heavy bedstead, and then the barred windows, and then that gate at the head of the stairs, and so on.

'You know the place is doing you good,' he said, 'and really, dear, I don't care to renovate the house just for a three months' rental.'

'Then do let us go downstairs,' I said, 'there are such pretty rooms there.'

Then he took me in his arms and called me a blessed little goose, and said he would go down to the cellar, if I wished, and have it whitewashed into the bargain.

But he is right enough about the beds and windows and things.

It is an airy and comfortable room as any one need wish, and, of course, I would not be so silly as to make him uncomfortable just for a whim.

I'm really getting quite fond of the big room, all but that horrid paper.

Out of one window I can see the garden, those mysterious deepshaded arbors, the riotous old-fashioned flowers, and bushes and gnarly trees.

Out of another I get a lovely view of the bay and a little private wharf belonging to the estate. There is a beautiful shaded lane that runs down there from the house. I always fancy I see people walking in these numerous paths and arbors, but John has cautioned me not to give way to fancy in the least. He says that with my imaginative power and habit of story-making, a nervous weakness like mine is sure to lead to all manner of excited fancies, and that I ought to use my will and good sense to check the tendency. So I try.

I think sometimes that if I were only well enough to write a little it would relieve the press of ideas and rest me.

But I find I get pretty tired when I try.

It is so discouraging not to have any advice and companionship about my work. When I get really well, John says we will ask Cousin Henry and Julia down for a long visit; but he says he would as soon put fireworks in my pillowcase as to let me have those stimulating people about now.

I wish I could get well faster.

But I must not think about that. This paper looks to me as if it _knew_ what a vicious influence it had!

There is a recurrent spot where the pattern lolls like a

broken neck and two bulbous eyes stare at you upside down.

I get positively angry with the impertinence of it and the everlastingness. Up and down and sideways they crawl, and those absurd, unblinking eyes are everywhere. There is one place where two breadths didn't match, and the eyes go all up and down the line, one a little higher than the other.

I never saw so much expression in an inanimate thing before, and we all know how much expression they have! I used to lie awake as a child and get more entertainment and terror out of blank walls and plain furniture than most children could find in a toystore.

I remember what a kindly wink the knobs of our big, old bureau used to have, and there was one chair that always seemed like a strong friend.

I used to feel that if any of the other things looked too fierce I could always hop into that chair and be safe.

The furniture in this room is no worse than inharmonious, however, for we had to bring it all from downstairs. I suppose when this was used as a playroom they had to take the nursery things out, and no wonder! I never saw such ravages as the children have made here.

The wallpaper, as I said before, is torn off in spots, and it sticketh closer than a brother – they must have had perseverance as well as hatred.

Then the floor is scratched and gouged and splintered, the plaster itself is dug out here and there, and this great heavy bed which is all we found in the room, looks as if it had been through the wars.

But I don't mind it a bit – only the paper.

There comes John's sister. Such a dear girl as she is, and so careful of me! I must not let her find me writing.

She is a perfect and enthusiastic housekeeper, and hopes for no better profession. I verily believe she thinks it is the writing which made me sick!

But I can write when she is out, and see her a long way off from these windows.

There is one that commands the road, a lovely shaded winding road, and one that just looks off over the country. A lovely country, too, full of great elms and velvet meadows.

This wallpaper has a kind of sub-pattern in a different shade, a particularly irritating one, for you can only see it in certain lights, and not clearly then.

But in the places where it isn't faded and where the sun is just so – I can see a strange, provoking, formless sort of figure, that seems to skulk about behind that silly and conspicuous front design.

There's sister on the stairs!

Well, the Fourth of July is over! The people are all gone and I am tired out. John thought it might do me good to see a little company, so we just had mother and Nellie and the children down for a week.

Of course I didn't do a thing. Jennie sees to everything now.

But it tired me all the same.

John says if I don't pick up faster he shall send me to Weir Mitchell in the fall.

But I don't want to go there at all. I had a friend who was in his hands once, and she says he is just like John and my brother, only more so!

Besides, it is such an undertaking to go so far.

I don't feel as if it was worth while to turn my hand over for anything, and I'm getting dreadfully fretful and querulous.

I cry at nothing, and cry most of the time.

Of course I don't when John is here, or anybody else, but when I am alone.

And I am alone a good deal just now. John is kept in town very often by serious cases, and Jennie is good and lets me alone when I want her to.

So I walk a little in the garden or down that lovely lane, sit on the porch under the roses, and lie down up here a good deal.

I'm getting really fond of the room in spite of the wallpaper. Perhaps *because* of the wallpaper.

It dwells in my mind so!

I lie here on this great immovable bed – it is nailed down, I believe – and follow that pattern about by the hour. It is as good as gymnastics, I assure you. I start, we'll say, at the bottom, down in the corner over there where it has not been touched, and I determine for the thousandth time that I *will* follow that pointless pattern to some sort of a conclusion.

I know a little of the principle of design, and I know this thing was not arranged on any laws of radiation, or alternation, or repetition, or symmetry, or anything else that I ever heard of.

It is repeated, of course, by the breadths, but not otherwise.

Looked at in one way each breadth stands alone, the bloated curves and flourishes – a kind of 'debased Romanesque' with *delirium tremens* – go waddling up and down in isolated columns of fatuity.

But, on the other hand, they connect diagonally, and the sprawling outlines run off in great slanting waves of optic horror, like a lot of wallowing seaweeds in full chase.

The whole thing goes horizontally, too, at least it seems so, and I exhaust myself in trying to distinguish the order of its going in that direction.

They have used a horizontal breadth for a frieze, and that adds wonderfully to the confusion.

There is one end of the room where it is almost intact, and there, when the crosslights fade and the low sun shines directly upon it, I can almost fancy radiation after all, – the interminable grotesques seem to form around a common centre and rush off in headlong plunges of equal distraction.

It makes me tired to follow it. I will take a nap I guess.

I don't know why I should write this.

I don't want to.

I don't feel able.

And I know John would think it absurd. But I *must* say what I feel and think in some way – it is such a relief!

But the effort is getting to be greater than the relief.

Half the time now I am awfully lazy, and lie down ever so much.

John says I mustn't lose my strength, and has me take cod liver oil and lots of tonics and things, to say nothing of ale and wine and rare meat.

Dear John! He loves me very dearly, and hates to have me sick. I tried to have a real earnest reasonable talk with him the other day, and tell him how I wish he would let me go and make a visit to Cousin Henry and Julia.

But he said I wasn't able to go, nor able to stand it after I got there; and I did not make out a very good case for myself, for I was crying before I had finished.

It is getting to be a great effort for me to think straight. Just this nervous weakness I suppose.

And dear John gathered me up in his arms, and just carried me upstairs and laid me on the bed, and sat by me and read to me till it tired my head.

He said I was his darling and his comfort and all he had, and that I must take care of myself for his sake, and keep well.

He says no one but myself can help me out of it, that I must use my will and self-control and not let any silly fancies run away with me.

There's one comfort, the baby is well and happy, and does not have to occupy this nursery with the horrid wallpaper.

If we had not used it, that blessed child would have! What a fortunate escape! Why, I wouldn't have a child of mine, an impressionable little thing, live in such a room for worlds.

I never thought of it before, but it is lucky that John kept me here after all, I can stand it so much easier than a baby, you see.

Of course I never mention it to them any more – I am too wise, – but I keep watch of it all the same.

There are things in that paper that nobody knows but me, or ever will.

Behind that outside pattern the dim shapes get clearer every day.

It is always the same shape, only very numerous.

And it is like a woman stooping down and creeping about behind that pattern. I don't like it a bit. I wonder – I begin to think – I wish John would take me away from here!

It is so hard to talk with John about my case, because he is so wise, and because he loves me so.

But I tried it last night.

It was moonlight. The moon shines in all around just as the sun does.

I hate to see it sometimes, it creeps so slowly, and always comes in by one window or another.

John was asleep and I hated to waken him, so I kept still and watched the moonlight on that undulating wallpaper till I felt creepy.

The faint figure behind seemed to shake the pattern, just as if she wanted to get out.

I got up softly and went to feel and see if the paper *did* move, and when I came back John was awake.

'What is it, little girl?' he said. 'Don't go walking about like that – you'll get cold.'

I thought it was a good time to talk, so I told him that I really was not gaining here, and that I wished he would take me away.

'Why darling!' said he, 'our lease will be up in three weeks, and I can't see how to leave before.

'The repairs are not done at home, and I cannot possibly leave town just now. Of course if you were in any danger, I could and would, but you really are better, dear, whether you can see it or not. I am a doctor, dear, and I know. You are gaining flesh and color, your appetite is better, I feel really much easier about you.'

'I don't weigh a bit more,' said I, 'nor as much; and my appetite may be better in the evening when you are here, but it is worse in the morning when you are away!'

'Bless her little heart!' said he with a big hug, 'she shall be as sick as she pleases! But now let's improve the shining hours by going to sleep, and talk about it in the morning!'

'And you won't go away?' I asked gloomily.

'Why, how can I, dear? It is only three weeks more and then we will take a nice little trip of a few days while Jennie is getting the house ready. Really dear you are better!'

'Better in body perhaps –' I began, and stopped short, for he sat up straight and looked at me with such a stern, reproachful look that I could not say another word.

'My darling,' said he, 'I beg of you, for my sake and for our child's sake, as well as for your own, that you will never for one instant let that idea enter your mind! There is nothing so dangerous, so fascinating, to a temperament like yours. It is a false and foolish fancy. Can you not trust me as a physician when I tell you so?'

So of course I said no more on that score, and we went to sleep before long. He thought I was asleep first, but I wasn't, and lay there for hours trying to decide whether that front pattern and the back pattern really did move together or separately.

On a pattern like this, by daylight, there is a lack of sequence, a defiance of law, that is a constant irritant to a normal mind.

The color is hideous enough, and unreliable enough, and infuriating enough, but the pattern is torturing.

You think you have mastered it, but just as you get well underway in following, it turns a back-somersault and there you are. It slaps you in the face, knocks you down, and tramples upon you. It is like a bad dream.

The outside pattern is a florid arabesque, reminding one of a fungus. If you can imagine a toadstool in joints, an interminable string of toadstools, budding and sprouting in endless convolutions – why, that is something like it.

That is, sometimes!

There is one marked peculiarity about this paper, a thing nobody seems to notice but myself, and that is that it changes as the light changes.

When the sun shoots in through the east window – I always watch for that first long, straight ray – it changes so quickly that I never can quite believe it.

That is why I watch it always.

By moonlight – the moon shines in all night when there is a moon – I wouldn't know it was the same paper.

At night in any kind of light, in twilight, candle light, lamp-light, and worst of all by moonlight, it becomes bars! The outside pattern I mean, and the woman behind it is as plain as can be.

I didn't realize for a long time what the thing was that showed behind, that dim sub-pattern, but now I am quite sure it is a woman.

By daylight she is subdued, quiet. I fancy it is the pattern that keeps her so still. It is so puzzling. It keeps me quiet by the hour.

I lie down ever so much now. John says it is good for me, and to sleep all I can.

Indeed he started the habit by making me lie down for an hour after each meal.

It is a very bad habit I am convinced, for you see I don't sleep.

And that cultivates deceit, for I don't tell them I'm awake – O no!

The fact is I am getting a little afraid of John.

He seems very queer sometimes, and even Jennie has an inexplicable look.

It strikes me occasionally, just as a scientific hypothesis, – that perhaps it is the paper!

I have watched John when he did not know I was looking, and come into the room suddenly on the most innocent excuses, and I've caught him several times *looking at the paper*! And Jennie too. I caught Jennie with her hand on it once.

She didn't know I was in the room, and when I asked her in

a quiet, a very quiet voice, with the most restrained manner possible, what she was doing with the paper – she turned around as if she had been caught stealing, and looked quite angry – asked me why I should frighten her so!

Then she said that the paper stained everything it touched, that she had found yellow smooches on all my clothes and John's, and she wished we would be more careful!

Did not that sound innocent? But I know she was studying that pattern, and I am determined that nobody shall find it out but myself!

Life is very much more exciting now than it used to be. You see I have something more to expect, to look forward to, to watch. I really do eat better, and am more quiet than I was.

John is so pleased to see me improve! He laughed a little the other day, and said I seemed to be flourishing in spite of my wall-paper.

I turned it off with a laugh. I had no intention of telling him it was *because* of the wallpaper – he would make fun of me. He might even want to take me away.

I don't want to leave now until I have found it out. There is a week more, and I think that will be enough.

I'm feeling ever so much better! I don't sleep much at night, for it is so interesting to watch developments; but I sleep a good deal in the daytime.

In the daytime it is tiresome and perplexing.

There are always new shoots on the fungus, and new shades of yellow all over it. I cannot keep count of them, though I have tried conscientiously.

It is the strangest yellow, that wallpaper! It makes me think of all the yellow things I ever saw – not beautiful ones like buttercups, but old foul, bad yellow things.

But there is something else about that paper – the smell! I noticed it the moment we came into the room, but with so much air and sun it was not bad. Now we have had a week of fog and rain, and whether the windows are open or not, the smell is here.

It creeps all over the house.

I find it hovering in the dining-room, skulking in the parlor, hiding in the hall, lying in wait for me on the stairs.

It gets into my hair.

Even when I go to ride, if I turn my head suddenly and surprise it – there is that smell!

Such a peculiar odor, too! I have spent hours in trying to analyze it, to find what it smelled like.

It is not bad – at first, and very gentle, but quite the subtlest, most enduring odor I ever met.

In this damp weather it is awful, I wake up in the night and find it hanging over me.

It used to disturb me at first. I thought seriously of burning the house – to reach the smell.

But now I am used to it. The only thing I can think of that it is like is the *color* of the paper! A yellow smell.

There is a very funny mark on this wall, low down, near the mopboard. A streak that runs round the room. It goes behind every piece of furniture, except the bed, a long, straight, even *smooch*, as if it had been rubbed over and over.

I wonder how it was done and who did it, and what they did it for. Round and round and round – round and round and round – it makes me dizzy!

*

I really have discovered something at last.

Through watching so much at night, when it changes so, I have finally found out.

The front pattern *does* move – and no wonder! The woman behind shakes it!

Sometimes I think there are a great many women behind, and sometimes only one, and she crawls around fast, and her crawling shakes it all over.

Then in the very bright spots she keeps still, and in the very shady spots she just takes hold of the bars and shakes them hard.

And she is all the time trying to climb through. But nobody could climb through that pattern – it strangles so; I think that is why it has so many heads.

They get through, and then the pattern strangles them off and turns them upside down, and makes their eyes white!

If those heads were covered or taken off it would not be half so bad.

I think that woman gets out in the daytime!

And I'll tell you why – privately – I've seen her!

I can see her out of every one of my windows!

It is the same woman, I know, for she is always creeping, and most women do not creep by daylight.

I see her on that long road under the trees, creeping along, and when a carriage comes she hides under the blackberry vines.

I don't blame her a bit. It must be very humiliating to be caught creeping by daylight!

I always lock the door when I creep by daylight. I can't do it at night, for I know John would suspect something at once.

And John is so queer now, that I don't want to irritate him. I wish he would take another room! Besides, I don't want anybody to get that woman out at night but myself.

I often wonder if I could see her out of all the windows at once.

But, turn as fast as I can, I can only see out of one at one time.

And though I always see her, she *may* be able to creep faster than I can turn!

I have watched her sometimes away off in the open country, creeping as fast as a cloud shadow in a high wind.

If only that top pattern could be gotten off from the under one! I mean to try it, little by little.

I have found out another funny thing, but I shan't tell it this time! It does not do to trust people too much.

There are only two more days to get this paper off, and I believe John is beginning to notice. I don't like the look in his eyes.

And I heard him ask Jennie a lot of professional questions about me. She had a very good report to give.

She said I slept a good deal in the daytime.

John knows I don't sleep very well at night, for all I'm so quiet!

He asked me all sorts of questions, too, and pretended to be very loving and kind.

As if I couldn't see through him!

Still, I don't wonder he acts so, sleeping under this paper for three months.

It only interests me, but I feel sure John and Jennie are secretly affected by it.

*

Hurrah! This is the last day, but it is enough. John is to stay in town over night, and won't be out until this evening.

Jennie wanted to sleep with me – the sly thing! but I told her I should undoubtedly rest better for a night all alone.

That was clever, for really I wasn't alone a bit! As soon as it was moonlight and that poor thing began to crawl and shake the pattern, I got up and ran to help her.

I pulled and she shook, I shook and she pulled, and before morning we had peeled off yards of that paper.

A strip about as high as my head and half around the room.

And then when the sun came and that awful pattern began to laugh at me, I declared I would finish it today!

We go away tomorrow, and they are moving all my furniture down again to leave things as they were before.

Jennie looked at the wall in amazement, but I told her merrily that I did it out of pure spite at the vicious thing.

She laughed and said she wouldn't mind doing it herself, but I must not get tired.

How she betrayed herself that time!

But I am here, and no person touches this paper but me, – not *alive*!

She tried to get me out of the room – it was too patent! But I said it was so quiet and empty and clean now that I believed I would lie down again and sleep all I could; and not to wake me even for dinner – I would call when I woke.

So now she is gone, and the servants are gone, and the things are gone, and there is nothing left but that great bedstead nailed down, with the canvas mattress we found on it.

We shall sleep downstairs tonight, and take the boat home tomorrow.

I quite enjoy the room, now it is bare again.

How those children did tear about here!

This bedstead is fairly gnawed!

But I must get to work.

I have locked the door and thrown the key down into the front path.

I don't want to go out, and I don't want to have anybody come in, till John comes.

I want to astonish him.

I've got a rope up here that even Jennie did not find. If that woman does get out, and tries to get away, I can tie her!

But I forgot I could not reach far without anything to stand on!

This bed will *not* move!

I tried to lift and push it until I was lame, and then I got so angry I bit off a little piece at one corner – but it hurt my teeth.

Then I peeled off all the paper I could reach standing on the floor. It sticks horribly and the pattern just enjoys it! All those strangled heads and bulbous eyes and waddling fungus growths just shriek with derision!

I am getting angry enough to do something desperate. To jump out of the window would be admirable exercise, but the bars are too strong even to try.

Besides I wouldn't do it. Of course not. I know well enough that a step like that is improper and might be misconstrued.

I don't like to *look* out of the windows even – there are so many of those creeping women, and they creep so fast.

I wonder if they all come out of that wallpaper as I did?

But I am securely fastened now by my well-hidden rope – you don't get *me* out in the road there!

I suppose I shall have to get back behind the pattern when it comes night, and that is hard!

It is so pleasant to be out in this great room and creep around as I please!

I don't want to go outside. I won't, even if Jennie asks me to.

For outside you have to creep on the ground, and everything is green instead of yellow.

But here I can creep smoothly on the floor, and my shoulder just fits in that long smooch around the wall, so I cannot lose my way.

Why there's John at the door!

It is no use, young man, you can't open it!

How he does call and pound!

Now he's crying for an axe.

It would be a shame to break down that beautiful door!

'John dear!' said I in the gentlest voice, 'the key is down by the front steps, under a plantain leaf!'

That silenced him for a few moments.

Then he said – very quietly indeed, 'Open the door, my darling!'

'I can't,' said I. 'The key is down by the front door under a plantain leaf!'

And then I said it again, several times, very gently and slowly, and said it so often that he had to go and see, and he got it of course, and came in. He stopped short by the door.

'What is the matter?' he cried. 'For God's sake, what are you doing!'

I kept on creeping just the same, but I looked at him over my shoulder.

'I've got out at last,' said I, 'in spite of you and Jane. And I've pulled off most of the paper, so you can't put me back!'

Now why should that man have fainted? But he did, and right across my path by the wall, so that I had to creep over him every time!

THE UNEXPECTED

I

'It is the unexpected which happens,' says the French proverb. I like the proverb, because it is true – and because it is French.

Edouard Charpentier is my name.

I am an American by birth, but that is all. From infancy, when I had a French nurse; in childhood, when I had a French governess; through youth, passed in a French school; to manhood, devoted to French art, I have been French by sympathy and education.

France – modern France – and French art – modern French art – I adore!

My school is the *pleine-aire*, and my master, could I but find him, is M. Duchesne. M. Duchesne has had pictures in the Salon for three years, and pictures elsewhere, eagerly bought, and yet Paris knows not M. Duchesne. We know his house, his horse, his carriage, his servants and his garden-wall, but he sees no one, speaks to no one; indeed, he has left Paris for a time, and we worship afar off.

I have a sketch by this master which I treasure jealously – a pencil sketch of a great picture yet to come. I await it.

M. Duchesne paints from the model, and I paint from the model, exclusively. It is the only way to be firm, accurate, true. Without the model we may have German fantasy or English domesticity, but no modern French art.

It is hard, too, to get models continually when one is but a student after five years' work, and one's pictures bring francs indeed, but not dollars.

Still, there is Georgette!

There, also, were Emilie and Pauline. But now it is Georgette, and she is adorable!

'Tis true, she has not much soul; but, then, she has a charming body, and 'tis that I copy.

Georgette and I get on together to admiration. How much better is this than matrimony for an artist! How wise is M. Daudet!

Antoine is my dearest friend. I paint with him, and we are happy. Georgette is my dearest model. I paint from her, and we are happy.

Into this peaceful scene comes a letter from America, bringing much emotion.

It appears I had a great-uncle there, in some northeastern corner of New England. Maine? No; Vermont.

And it appears, strangely enough, that this northeastern great-uncle was seized in his old age with a passion for French art; at least I know not how else to account for his hunting me up through a lawyer and leaving me some quarter of a million when he died.

An admirable great-uncle!

But I must go home and settle the property; that is imperative. I must leave Paris, I must leave Antoine, I must leave Georgette!

Could anything be further from Paris than a town in Vermont? No, not the Andaman Islands.

And could anything be further from Antoine and Georgette than the family of great-cousins I find myself among?

But one of them – ah, Heaven! some forty-seventh cousin who is so beautiful that I forget she is an American, I forget Paris, I forget Antoine – yes, and even Georgette! Poor Georgette! But this is fate.

This cousin is not like the other cousins. I pursue, I inquire, I ascertain.

Her name is Mary D. Greenleaf. I shall call her Marie.

And she comes from Boston.

But, beyond the name, how can I describe her? I have seen beauty, yes, much beauty, in maid, matron and model, but I never saw anything to equal this country girl. What a figure!

No, not a 'figure' – the word shames her. She has a body, the body of a young Diana, and a body and a figure are two very different things. I am an artist, and I have lived in Paris, and I know the difference.

The lawyers in Boston can settle that property, I find.

The air is delightful in northern Vermont in March. There are mountains, clouds, trees. I will paint here a while. Ah, yes; and I will assist this shy young soul!

'Cousin Marie,' say I, 'come, let me teach you to paint!'

'It would be too difficult for you, Mr Carpenter – it would take too long!'

'Call me Edouard!' I cry. 'Are we not cousins? Cousin Edouard, I beg of you! And nothing is difficult when you are with me, Marie – nothing can be too long at your side!'

'Thanks, cousin Edward, but I think I will not impose on

your good nature. Besides, I shall not stay here. I go back to Boston, to my aunt.'

I find the air of Boston is good in March, and there are places of interest there, and rising American artists who deserve encouragement. I will stay in Boston a while to assist the lawyers in settling my property; it is necessary.

I visit Marie continually. Am I not a cousin?

I talk to her of life, of art, of Paris, of M. Duchesne. I show her my precious sketch.

'But,' says she, 'I am not wholly a wood nymph, as you seem fondly to imagine. I have been to Paris myself – with my uncle – years since.'

'Fairest cousin,' say I, 'if you had not been even to Boston, I should still love you! Come and see Paris again – with me!' And then she would laugh at me and send me away. Ah, yes! I had come even to marriage, you see!

I soon found she had the usual woman's faith in those conventions. I gave her *Artists' Wives*. She said she had read it. She laughed at Daudet and me!

I talked to her of ruined geniuses I had known myself, but she said a ruined genius was no worse than a ruined woman! One cannot reason with young girls!

Do not believe I succumbed without a struggle. I even tore myself away and went to New York. It was not far enough, I fear. I soon came back.

She lived with an aunt – my adorable little precisian! – with a horrible strong-minded aunt, and such a life as I led between them for a whole month!

I call continually. I bury her in flowers. I take her to the theatre, aunt and all. And at this the aunt seemed greatly surprised, but I disapprove of American familiarities. No; my wife – and wife she must be – shall be treated with punctilious respect.

Never was I so laughed at and argued with in my life as I was laughed at by that dreadful beauty, and argued with by that dreadful aunt.

The only rest was in pictures. Marie would look at pictures always, and seemed to have a real appreciation of them, almost an understanding, of a sort. So that I began to hope – dimly and faintly to hope – that she might grow to care for mine. To have a wife who would care for one's art, who would come to one's studio – but, then, the models! I paint from the model almost entirely, as I said, and I know what women are about models, without Daudet to tell me!

And this prudish New England girl! Well, she might come to the studio on stated days, and perhaps in time I might lead her gently to understand.

That I should ever live to commit matrimony!

But Fate rules all men.

I think that girl refused me nine times. She always put me off with absurd excuses and reasons: said I didn't know her yet; said we should never agree; said I was French and she was American; said I cared more for art than I did for her! At that I earnestly assured her that I would become an organ-grinder or a bank-clerk rather than lose her – and then she seemed downright angry, and sent me away again.

Women are strangely inconsistent!

She always sent me away, but I always came back.

After about a month of this torture, I chanced to find her, one soft May twilight, without the aunt, sitting by a window in the fragrant dusk.

She had flowers in her hand – flowers I had sent her – and

sat looking down at them, her strong, pure profile clear against the saffron sky.

I came in quietly, and stood watching, in a rapture of hope and admiration. And while I watched I saw a great pearl tear roll down among my violets.

That was enough.

I sprang forward, I knelt beside her, I caught her hands in mine, I drew her to me, I cried, exultantly: 'You love me! And I – ah, God! how I love you!'

Even then she would have put me from her. She insisted that I did not know her yet, that she ought to tell me – but I held her close and kissed away her words, and said: 'You love me, perfect one, and I love you. The rest will be right.'

Then she laid her white hands on my shoulders, and looked deep into my eyes.

'I believe that is true,' said she; 'and I will marry you, Edward.'

She dropped her face on my shoulder then – that face of fire and roses – and we were still.

II

It is but two months' time from then; I have been married a fortnight. The first week was heaven – and the second was hell! O my God! my wife! That young Diana to be but—! I have borne it a week. I have feared and despised myself. I have suspected and hated myself. I have discovered and cursed myself. Aye, and cursed her, and *him*, whom this day I shall kill!

It is now three o'clock. I cannot kill him until four, for he comes not till then.

I am very comfortable here in this room opposite – very comfortable; and I can wait and think and remember.

Let me think.

First, to kill him. That is simple and easily settled.

Shall I kill her?

If she lived, could I ever see her again? Ever touch that hand – those lips – that, within two weeks of marriage—? No, she shall die!

And, if she lived, what would be before her but more shame, and more, till she felt it herself?

Far better that she die!

And I?

Could I live to forget her? To carry always in my heart a black stone across that door? To rise and rise, and do great work – *alone!*

Never! I cannot forget her!

Better die with her, even now.

Hark! Is that a step on the stair? Not yet.

My money is well bestowed. Antoine is a better artist than I, and a better man, and the money will widen and lighten a noble life in his hands.

And little Georgette is provided for. How long ago, how faint and weak, that seems! But Georgette loved me, I believe, at least for a time – longer than a week.

To wait – until four o'clock!

To think – I have thought; it is all arranged!

These pistols, that she admired but day before yesterday, that we practised with together, both loaded full. What a shot she is! I believe she can do everything!

To wait – to think – to remember.

Let me remember.

I knew her a week, wooed her a month, have been married a fortnight.

She always said I didn't know her. She was always on the point of telling me something, and I would not let her. She seemed half repentant, half in jest – I preferred to trust her. Those clear, brown eyes – clear and bright, like brook water with the sun through it! And she would smile so! 'Tis not that I must remember.

Am I sure? Sure! I laugh at myself.

What would you call it, you – any man? A young woman steals from her house, alone, every day, and comes privately, cloaked and veiled, to this place, this den of Bohemians, this building of New York studios! Painters? I know them – I am a painter myself.

She goes to this room, day after day, and tells me nothing.

I say to her gently: 'What do you do with your days, my love?'

'Oh, many things,' she answers; 'I am studying art – to please you!'

That was ingenious. She knew she might be watched.

I say, 'Cannot I teach you?' and she says, 'I have a teacher I used to study with. I must finish. I want to surprise you!' So she would soothe me – to appearance.

But I watch and follow, I take this little room. I wait, and I see.

Lessons? Oh, perjured one! There is no tenant of that room but yourself, and to it *he* comes each day.

Is that a step? Not yet. I watch and wait. This is America, I say, not France. This is my wife. I will trust her. But the man comes every day. He is young. He is handsome – handsome as a fiend.

I cannot bear it. I go to the door. I knock. There is no response. I try the door. It is locked. I stoop and look through the key-hole. What do I see? Ah, God! The hat and cloak of that man upon a chair, and then only a tall screen. Behind that screen, low voices!

I did not go home last night. I am here to-day – with these!

That is a step. Yes! Softly, now. He has gone in. I heard her speak. She said: 'You are late, Guillaume!'

Let me give them a little time.

Now – softly – I come, friends. *I* am not late!

III

Across the narrow passage I steal, noiselessly. The door is unlocked this time. I burst in.

There stands my young wife, pale, trembling, startled, unable to speak.

There is the handsome Guillaume – behind the screen. My fingers press the triggers. There is a sharp double report. Guillaume tumbles over, howling, and Marie flings herself between us.

'Edward! One moment! Give me a moment for my life! The pistols are harmless, dear – blank cartridges. I fixed them myself. I saw you suspected. But you've spoiled my surprise. I shall have to tell you now. This is my studio, love. Here is the picture you have the sketch of. *I* am "M. Duchesne" – Mary Duchesne Greenleaf Carpenter – and this is my model!'

We are very happy in Paris, with our double studio. We sometimes share our models. We laugh at M. Daudet.

THE GIANT WISTARIA

'Meddle not with my new vine, child! See! Thou hast already broken the tender shoot! Never needle or distaff for thee, and yet thou wilt not be quiet!'

The nervous fingers wavered, clutched at a small carnelian cross that hung from her neck, then fell despairingly.

'Give me my child, mother, and then I will be quiet!'

'Hush! hush! thou fool – some one might be near! See – there is thy father coming, even now! Get in quickly!'

She raised her eyes to her mother's face, weary eyes that yet had a flickering, uncertain blaze in their shaded depths.

'Art thou a mother and hast no pity on me, a mother? Give me my child!'

Her voice rose in a strange, low cry, broken by her father's hand upon her mouth.

'Shameless!' said he, with set teeth. 'Get to thy chamber, and be not seen again tonight, or I will have thee bound!'

She went at that, and a hard-faced serving woman followed, and presently returned, bringing a key to her mistress.

'Is all well with her, – and the child also?'

'She is quiet, Mistress Dwining, well for the night, be sure. The child fretteth endlessly, but save for that it thriveth with me.'

The parents were left alone together on the high square porch with its great pillars, and the rising moon began to make faint shadows of the young vine leaves that shot up luxuriantly around them; moving shadows, like little stretching fingers, on the broad and heavy planks of the oaken floor.

'It groweth well, this vine thou broughtest me in the ship, my husband.'

'Aye,' he broke in bitterly, 'and so doth the shame I brought thee! Had I known of it I would sooner have had the ship founder beneath us, and have seen our child cleanly drowned, than live to this end!'

'Thou art very hard, Samuel, art thou not afeard for her life? She grieveth sore for the child, aye, and for the green fields to walk in!'

'Nay,' said he grimly, 'I fear not. She hath lost already what is more than life; and she shall have air enough soon. To-morrow the ship is ready, and we return to England. None knoweth of our stain here, not one, and if the town hath a child unaccounted for to rear in decent ways – why, it is not the first, even here. It will be well enough cared for! And truly we have matter for thankfulness, that her cousin is yet willing to marry her.'

'Hast thou told him?'

'Aye! Thinkest thou I would cast shame into another man's house, unknowing it? He hath always desired her, but she would none of him, the stubborn! She hath small choice now!'

'Will he be kind, Samuel? can he—'

'Kind? What call'st thou it to take such as she to wife? Kind!

How many men would take her, an' she had double the fortune? and being of the family already, he is glad to hide the blot for-ever.'

'An' if she would not? He is but a coarse fellow, and she ever shunned him.'

'Art thou mad, woman? She weddeth him ere we sail tomor-row, or she stayeth ever in that chamber. The girl is not so sheer a fool! He maketh an honest woman of her, and saveth our house from open shame. What other hope for her than a new life to cover the old? Let her have an honest child, an' she so longeth for one!'

He strode heavily across the porch, till the loose planks creaked again, strode back and forth, with his arms folded and his brows fiercely knit above his iron mouth.

Overhead the shadows flickered mockingly across a white face among the leaves, with eyes of wasted fire.

'O, George, what a house! what a lovely house! I am sure it's haunted! Let us get that house to live in this summer! We will have Kate and Jack and Susy and Jim of course, and a splendid time of it!'

Young husbands are indulgent, but still they have to recog-nize facts.

'My dear, the house may not be to rent; and it may also not be habitable.'

'There is surely somebody in it. I am going to inquire!'

The great central gate was rusted off its hinges, and the long drive had trees in it, but a little footpath showed signs of steady usage, and up that Mrs Jenny went, followed by her obedient George. The front windows of the old mansion were blank, but in a wing at the back they found white curtains and open doors.

Outside, in the clear May sunshine, a woman was washing. She was polite and friendly, and evidently glad of visitors in that lonely place. She 'guessed it could be rented – didn't know.' The heirs were in Europe, but 'there was a lawyer in New York had the lettin' of it.' There had been folks there years ago, but not in her time. She and her husband had the rent of their part for taking care of the place. 'Not that they took much care on't either, but keepin' robbers out.' It was furnished throughout, old-fashioned enough, but good; and if they took it she could do the work for 'em herself, she guessed – 'if *he* was willin'!'

Never was a crazy scheme more easily arranged. George knew that lawyer in New York; the rent was not alarming; and the nearness to a rising sea-shore resort made it a still pleasanter place to spend the summer.

Kate and Jack and Susy and Jim cheerfully accepted, and the June moon found them all sitting on the high front porch.

They had explored the house from top to bottom, from the great room in the garret, with nothing in it but a rickety cradle, to the well in the cellar without a curb and with a rusty chain going down to unknown blackness below. They had explored the grounds, once beautiful with rare trees and shrubs, but now a gloomy wilderness of tangled shade.

The old lilacs and laburnums, the spirea and syringa, nodded against the second-story windows. What garden plants survived were great ragged bushes or great shapeless beds. A huge wistaria vine covered the whole front of the house. The trunk, it was too large to call a stem, rose at the corner of the porch by the high steps, and had once climbed its pillars; but now the pillars were wrenched from their places and held rigid and helpless by the tightly wound and knotted arms.

It fenced in all the upper story of the porch with a knitted wall of stem and leaf; it ran along the eaves, holding up the gutter that had once supported it; it shaded every window with heavy green; and the drooping, fragrant blossoms made a waving sheet of purple from roof to ground.

'Did you ever see such a wistaria!' cried ecstatic Mrs Jenny. 'It is worth the rent just to sit under such a vine, – a fig tree beside it would be sheer superfluity and wicked extravagance!'

'Jenny makes much of her wistaria,' said George, 'because she's so disappointed about the ghosts. She made up her mind at first sight to have ghosts in the house, and she can't find even a ghost story!'

'No,' Jenny assented mournfully; 'I pumped poor Mrs Pepperill for three days, but could get nothing out of her. But I'm convinced there is a story, if we could only find it. You need not tell me that a house like this, with a garden like this, and a cellar like this, isn't haunted!'

'I agree with you,' said Jack. Jack was a reporter on a New York daily, and engaged to Mrs Jenny's pretty sister. 'And if we don't find a real ghost, you may be very sure I shall make one. It's too good an opportunity to lose!'

The pretty sister, who sat next him, resented. 'You shan't do anything of the sort, Jack! This is a *real* ghostly place, and I won't have you make fun of it! Look at that group of trees out there in the long grass – it looks for all the world like a crouching, hunted figure!'

'It looks to me like a woman picking huckleberries,' said Jim, who was married to George's pretty sister.

'Be still, Jim!' said that fair young woman. 'I believe in Jenny's ghost as much as she does. Such a place! Just look at this great wistaria trunk crawling up by the steps here! It looks for all the world like a writhing body – ringing – beseeching!'

'Yes,' answered the subdued Jim, 'it does, Susy. See its waist, – about two yards of it, and twisted at that! A waste of good material!'

'Don't be so horrid, boys! Go off and smoke somewhere if you can't be congenial!'

'We can! We will! We'll be as ghostly as you please.' And forthwith they began to see bloodstains and crouching figures so plentifully that the most delightful shivers multiplied, and the fair enthusiasts started for bed, declaring they should never sleep a wink.

'We shall all surely dream,' cried Mrs Jenny, 'and we must all tell our dreams in the morning!'

'There's another thing certain,' said George, catching Susy as she tripped over a loose plank; 'and that is that you frisky creatures must use the side door till I get this Eiffel tower of a portico fixed, or we shall have some fresh ghosts on our hands! We found a plank here that yawns like a trap-door – big enough to swallow you, – and I believe the bottom of the thing is in China!'

The next morning found them all alive, and eating a substantial New England breakfast, to the accompaniment of saws and hammers on the porch, where carpenters of quite miraculous promptness were tearing things to pieces generally.

'It's got to come down mostly,' they had said. 'These timbers are clean rotted through, what ain't pulled out o' line by this great creeper. That's about all that holds the thing up.'

There was clear reason in what they said, and with a caution from anxious Mrs Jenny not to hurt the wistaria, they were left to demolish and repair at leisure.

'How about ghosts?' asked Jack after a fourth griddle cake. 'I had one, and it's taken away my appetite!'

Mrs Jenny gave a little shriek and dropped her knife and fork.

'Oh, so had I! I had the most awful – well, not dream exactly, but feeling. I had forgotten all about it!'

'Must have been awful,' said Jack, taking another cake. 'Do tell us about the feeling. My ghost will wait.'

'It makes me creep to think of it even now,' she said. 'I woke up, all at once, with that dreadful feeling as if something were going to happen, you know! I was wide awake, and hearing every little sound for miles around, it seemed to me. There are so many strange little noises in the country for all it is so still. Millions of crickets and things outside, and all kinds of rustles in the trees! There wasn't much wind, and the moonlight came through in my three great windows in three white squares on the black old floor, and those fingery wistaria leaves we were talking of last night just seemed to crawl all over them. And – O, girls, you know that dreadful well in the cellar?'

A most gratifying impression was made by this, and Jenny proceeded cheerfully:

'Well, while it was so horridly still, and I lay there trying not to wake George, I heard as plainly as if it were right in the room, that old chain down there rattle and creak over the stones!'

'Bravo!' cried Jack. 'That's fine! I'll put it in the Sunday edition!'

'Be still!' said Kate. 'What was it, Jenny? Did you really see anything?'

'No, I didn't, I'm sorry to say. But just then I didn't want to. I woke George, and made such a fuss that he gave me bromide, and said he'd go and look, and that's the last I thought of it till Jack reminded me, – the bromide worked so well.'

'Now, Jack, give us yours,' said Jim. 'Maybe, it will dovetail in somehow. Thirsty ghost, I imagine; maybe they had prohibition here even then!'

Jack folded his napkin, and leaned back in his most impressive manner.

'It was striking twelve by the great hall clock—' he began.

'There isn't any hall clock!'

'O hush, Jim, you spoil the current! It was just one o'clock then, by my old-fashioned repeater.'

'Waterbury! Never mind what time it was!'

'Well, honestly, I woke up sharp, like our beloved hostess, and tried to go to sleep again, but couldn't. I experienced all those moonlight and grasshopper sensations, just like Jenny, and was wondering what could have been the matter with the supper, when in came my ghost, and I knew it was all a dream! It was a female ghost, and I imagine she was young and handsome, but all those crouching, hunted figures of last evening ran riot in my brain, and this poor creature looked just like them. She was all wrapped up in a shawl, and had a big bundle under her arm, – dear me, I am spoiling the story! With the air and gait of one in frantic haste and terror, the muffled figure glided to a dark old bureau, and seemed taking things from the drawers. As she turned, the moonlight shone full on a little red cross that hung from her neck by a thin gold chain – I saw it glitter as she crept noiselessly from the room! That's all.'

'O Jack, don't be so horrid! Did you really? Is that all! What do you think it was?'

'I am not horrid by nature, only professionally. I really did. That was all. And I am fully convinced it was the genuine, legitimate ghost of an eloping chambermaid with kleptomania!'

'You are too bad, Jack!' cried Jenny. 'You take all the horror out of it. There isn't a "creep" left among us.'

'It's no time for creeps at nine-thirty a.m., with sunlight and carpenters outside! However, if you can't wait till twilight for your creeps, I think I can furnish one or two,' said George. 'I went down cellar after Jenny's ghost!'

There was a delighted chorus of female voices, and Jenny cast upon her lord a glance of genuine gratitude.

'It's all very well to lie in bed and see ghosts, or hear them,' he went on. 'But the young householder suspecteth burglars, even though as a medical man he knoweth nerves, and after Jenny dropped off I started on a voyage of discovery. I never will again, I promise you!'

'Why, what *was* it?'

'Oh, George!'

'I got a candle—'

'Good mark for the burglars,' murmured Jack.

'And went all over the house, gradually working down to the cellar and the well.'

'Well?' said Jack.

'Now you can laugh; but that cellar is no joke by daylight, and a candle there at night is about as inspiring as a lightning-bug in the Mammoth Cave. I went along with the light, trying not to fall into the well prematurely; got to it all at once; held the light down and *then* I saw, right under my feet – (I nearly fell over her, or walked through her, perhaps), – a woman, hunched up under a shawl! She had hold of the chain, and the candle shone on her hands – white, thin hands, – on a little red cross that hung from her neck – *vide* Jack! I'm no believer in ghosts, and I firmly object to unknown parties in the house at night; so I spoke to her rather fiercely. She didn't seem to notice that, and I reached down to take hold of her, – then I came upstairs!'

'What for?'

'What happened?'

'What was the matter?'

'Well, nothing happened. Only she wasn't there! May have been indigestion, of course, but as a physician I don't advise any one to court indigestion alone at midnight in a cellar!'

'This is the most interesting and peripatetic and evasive ghost I ever heard of!' said Jack. 'It's my belief she has no end of silver tankards, and jewels galore, at the bottom of that well, and I move we go and see!'

'To the bottom of the well, Jack?'

'To the bottom of the mystery. Come on!'

There was unanimous assent, and the fresh cambrics and pretty boots were gallantly escorted below by gentlemen whose jokes were so frequent that many of them were a little forced.

The deep old cellar was so dark that they had to bring lights, and the well so gloomy in its blackness that the ladies recoiled.

'That well is enough to scare even a ghost. It's my opinion you'd better let well enough alone?' quoth Jim.

'Truth lies hid in a well, and we must get her out,' said George. 'Bear a hand with the chain?'

Jim pulled away on the chain, George turned the creaking windlass, and Jack was chorus.

'A wet sheet for this ghost, if not a flowing sea,' said he. 'Seems to be hard work raising spirits! I suppose he kicked the bucket when he went down!'

As the chain lightened and shortened there grew a strained silence among them; and when at length the bucket appeared, rising slowly through the dark water, there was an eager, half reluctant peering, and a natural drawing back. They poked the gloomy contents. 'Only water.'

'Nothing but mud.'

'Something—'

They emptied the bucket up on the dark earth, and then the girls all went out into the air, into the bright warm sunshine in front of the house, where was the sound of saw and hammer, and the smell of new wood. There was nothing said until the men joined them, and then Jenny timidly asked:

'How old should you think it was, George?'

'All of a century,' he answered. 'That water is a preservative, – lime in it. Oh! – you mean? – Not more than a month; a very little baby!'

There was another silence at this, broken by a cry from the workmen. They had removed the floor and the side walls of the old porch, so that the sunshine poured down to the dark stones of the cellar bottom. And there, in the strangling grasp of the roots of the great wistaria, lay the bones of a woman, from whose neck still hung a tiny scarlet cross on a thin chain of gold.

AN EXTINCT ANGEL

There was once a species of angel inhabiting this planet, acting as 'a universal solvent' to all the jarring, irreconcilable elements of human life.

It was quite numerous; almost every family had one; and, although differing in degree of seraphic virtue, all were, by common consent, angels.

The advantages of possessing such a creature were untold. In the first place, the chances of the mere human being in the way of getting to heaven were greatly increased by these semi-heavenly belongings; they gave one a sort of lien on the next world, a practical claim most comforting to the owner.

For the angels of course possessed virtues above mere humanity; and because the angels were so well-behaved, therefore the owners were given credit.

Beside this direct advantage of complimentary tickets up above were innumerable indirect advantages below. The possession of one of these angels smoothed every feature of life, and gave peace and joy to an otherwise hard lot.

It was the business of the angel to assuage, to soothe, to

44

comfort, to delight. No matter how unruly were the passions of the owner, sometimes even to the extent of legally beating his angel with 'a stick no thicker than his thumb,' the angel was to have no passion whatever – unless self-sacrifice may be called a passion, and indeed it often amounted to one with her.

The human creature went out to his daily toil and comforted himself as he saw fit. He was apt to come home tired and cross, and in this exigency it was the business of the angel to wear a smile for his benefit – a soft, perennial, heavenly smile.

By an unfortunate limitation of humanity the angel was required, in addition to such celestial duties as smiling and soothing, to do kitchen service, cleaning, sewing, nursing, and other mundane tasks. But these things must be accomplished without the slightest diminution of the angelic virtues.

The angelic virtues, by the way, were of a curiously paradoxical nature.

They were inherent. A human being did not pretend to name them, could not be expected to have them, acknowledged them as far beyond his gross earthly nature; and yet, for all this, he kept constant watch over the virtues of the angel, wrote whole books of advice for angels on how they should behave, and openly held that angels would lose their virtues altogether should they once cease to obey the will and defer to the judgment of human kind.

This looks strange to us today as we consider these past conditions, but then it seemed fair enough; and the angels – bless their submissive, patient hearts! – never thought of questioning it.

It was perhaps only to be expected that when an angel fell the human creature should punish the celestial creature with unrelenting fury. It was so much easier to be an angel than to be human, that there was no excuse for an angel's falling, even by means of her own angelic pity and tender affection.

It seems perhaps hard that the very human creature the angel fell on, or fell with, or fell to – however you choose to put it – was as harsh as anyone in condemnation of the fall. He never assisted the angel to rise, but got out from under and resumed his way, leaving her in the mud. She was a great convenience to walk on, and, as was stoutly maintained by the human creature, helped keep the other angels clean.

This is exceedingly mysterious, and had better not be inquired into too closely.

The amount of physical labor of a severe and degrading sort required of one of these bright spirits, was amazing. Certain kinds of work – always and essentially dirty – were relegated wholly to her. Yet one of her first and most rigid duties was the keeping of her angelic robes spotlessly clean.

The human creature took great delight in contemplating the flowing robes of the angels. Their changeful motion suggested to him all manner of sweet and lovely thoughts and memories; also, the angelic virtues above mentioned were supposed largely to inhere in the flowing robes. Therefore flow they must, and the ample garments waved unchecked over the weary limbs of the wearer, the contiguous furniture and the stairs. For the angels unfortunately had no wings, and their work was such as required a good deal of going up and down stairs.

It is quite a peculiar thing, in contemplating this work, to see how largely it consisted in dealing with dirt. Yes, it does seem strange to this enlightened age; but the fact was that the angels waited on the human creatures in every form of menial service, doing things as their natural duty which the human creature loathed and scorned.

It does seem irreconcilable, but they reconciled it. The angel was an angel and the work was the angel's work, and what more do you want?

There is one thing about the subject which looks a little suspicious: The angels – I say it under breath – were not very bright!

The human creatures did not like intelligent angels – intelligence seemed to dim their shine, somehow, and pale their virtues. It was harder to reconcile things where the angels had any sense. Therefore every possible care was taken to prevent the angels from learning anything of our gross human wisdom.

But little by little, owing to the unthought-of consequences of repeated intermarriage between the angel and the human being, the angel longed for, found and ate the fruit of the forbidden tree of knowledge.

And in that day she surely died.

The species is now extinct. It is rumored that here and there in remote regions you can still find a solitary specimen – in places where no access is to be had to the deadly fruit; but the race as a race is extinct.

Poor dodo!

THE ROCKING-CHAIR

A waving spot of sunshine, a signal light that caught the eye at once in a waste of commonplace houses, and all the dreary dimness of a narrow city street.

Across some low roof that made a gap in the wall of masonry, shot a level, brilliant beam of the just-setting sun, touching the golden head of a girl in an open window.

She sat in a high-backed rocking-chair with brass mountings that glittered as it swung, rocking slowly back and forth, never lifting her head, but fairly lighting up the street with the glory of her sunlit hair.

We two stopped and stared, and, so staring, caught sight of a small sign in a lower window – 'Furnished Lodgings.' With a common impulse we crossed the street and knocked at the dingy front door.

Slow, even footsteps approached from within, and a soft girlish laugh ceased suddenly as the door opened, showing us an old woman, with a dull, expressionless face and faded eyes.

Yes, she had rooms to let. Yes, we could see them. No, there was no service. No, there were no meals. So murmuring monotonously, she led the way upstairs. It was an ordinary house enough, on a poor sort of street, a house in no way remarkable or unlike its fellows.

She showed us two rooms, connected, neither better nor worse than most of their class, rooms without a striking feature about them, unless it was the great brass-bound chair we found still rocking gently by the window.

But the gold-haired girl was nowhere to be seen.

I fancied I heard the light rustle of girlish robes in the inner chamber – a breath of that low laugh – but the door leading to this apartment was locked, and when I asked the woman if we could see the other rooms she said she had no other rooms to let.

A few words aside with Hal, and we decided to take these two, and move in at once. There was no reason we should not. We were looking for lodgings when that swinging sunbeam caught our eyes, and the accommodations were fully as good as we could pay for. So we closed our bargain on the spot, returned to our deserted boarding-house for a few belongings, and were settled anew that night.

Hal and I were young newspaper men, 'penny-a-liners,' part of that struggling crowd of aspirants who are to literature what squires and pages were to knighthood in olden days. We were winning our spurs. So far it was slow work, unpleasant and ill-paid – so was squireship and pagehood, I am sure; menial service and laborious polishing of armor; long running afoot while the master rode. But the squire could at least honor his lord and leader, while we, alas! had small honor for those above us in our profession, with but too good reason. We, of course, should do far nobler things when these same spurs were won!

Now it may have been mere literary instinct – the grasping

at 'material' of the pot-boiling writers of the day, and it may have been another kind of instinct – the unacknowledged attraction of the fair unknown; but, whatever the reason, the place had drawn us both, and here we were.

Unbroken friendship begun in babyhood held us two together, all the more closely because Hal was a merry, prosaic, clear-headed fellow, and I sensitive and romantic.

The fearless frankness of family life we shared, but held the right to unapproachable reserves, and so kept love unstrained.

We examined our new quarters with interest. The front room, Hal's, was rather big and bare. The back room, mine, rather small and bare.

He preferred that room, I am convinced, because of the window and the chair. I preferred the other, because of the locked door. We neither of us mentioned these prejudices.

'Are you sure you would not rather have this room?' asked Hal, conscious, perhaps, of an ulterior motive in his choice.

'No, indeed,' said I, with a similar reservation; 'you only have the street and I have a real "view" from my window. The only thing I begrudge you is the chair!'

'You may come and rock therein at any hour of the day or night,' said he magnanimously. 'It is tremendously comfortable, for all its black looks.'

It was a comfortable chair, a very comfortable chair, and we both used it a great deal. A very high-backed chair, curving a little forward at the top, with heavy square corners. These corners, the ends of the rockers, the great sharp knobs that tipped the arms, and every other point and angle were mounted in brass.

'Might be used for a battering-ram!' said Hal.

He sat smoking in it, rocking slowly and complacently by the window, while I lounged on the foot of the bed, and watched a pale young moon sink slowly over the western housetops.

It went out of sight at last, and the room grew darker and darker till I could only see Hal's handsome head and the curving chair-back move slowly to and fro against the dim sky.

'What brought us here so suddenly, Maurice?' he asked, out of the dark.

'Three reasons,' I answered. 'Our need of lodgings, the suitability of these, and a beautiful head.'

'Correct,' said he. 'Anything else?'

'Nothing you would admit the existence of, my sternly logical friend. But I am conscious of a certain compulsion, or at least attraction, in the case, which does not seem wholly accounted for, even by golden hair.'

'For once I will agree with you,' said Hal. 'I feel the same way myself, and I am not impressionable.'

We were silent for a little. I may have closed my eyes, – it may have been longer than I thought, but it did not seem another moment when something brushed softly against my arm, and Hal in his great chair was rocking beside me.

'Excuse me,' said he, seeing me start. 'This chair evidently "walks," I've seen 'em before.'

So had I, on carpets, but there was no carpet here, and I thought I was awake.

He pulled the heavy thing back to the window again, and we went to bed.

Our door was open, and we could talk back and forth, but presently I dropped off and slept heavily until morning. But I must have dreamed most vividly, for he accused me of rocking in his chair half the night; said he could see my outline clearly against the starlight.

'No,' said I, 'you dreamed it. You've got rocking-chair on the brain.'

'Dream it is, then,' he answered cheerily. 'Better a nightmare than a contradiction; a vampire than a quarrel! Come on, let's go to breakfast!'

We wondered greatly as the days went by that we saw nothing of our golden-haired charmer. But we wondered in silence, and neither mentioned it to the other.

Sometimes I heard her light movements in the room next mine, or the soft laugh somewhere in the house; but the mother's slow, even steps were more frequent, and even she was not often visible.

All either of us saw of the girl, to my knowledge, was from the street, for she still availed herself of our chair by the window. This we disapproved of, on principle, the more so as we left the doors locked, and her presence proved the possession of another key. No; there was the door in my room! But I did not mention the idea. Under the circumstances, however, we made no complaint, and used to rush stealthily and swiftly upstairs, hoping to surprise her. But we never succeeded. Only the chair was often found still rocking, and sometimes I fancied a faint sweet odor lingering about, an odor strangely saddening and suggestive. But one day when I thought Hal was there I rushed in unceremoniously and caught her. It was but a glimpse – a swift, light, noiseless sweep – she vanished into my own room. Following her with apologies for such a sudden entrance, I was too late. The envious door was locked again.

Our landlady's fair daughter was evidently shy enough when brought to bay, but strangely willing to take liberties in our absence.

Still, I had seen her, and for that sight would have forgiven much. Hers was a strange beauty, infinitely attractive yet infinitely perplexing. I marveled in secret, and longed with painful eagerness for another meeting; but I said nothing to Hal of my surprising her – it did not seem fair to the girl! She might have some good reason for going there; perhaps I could meet her again.

So I took to coming home early, on one excuse or another, and inventing all manner of errands to get to the room when Hal was not in.

But it was not until after numberless surprises on that point, finding him there when I supposed him downtown, and noticing something a little forced in his needless explanations, that I began to wonder if he might not be on the same quest.

Soon I was sure of it. I reached the corner of the street one evening just at sunset, and – yes, there was the rhythmic swing of that bright head in the dark frame of the open window. There also was Hal in the street below. She looked out, she smiled. He let himself in and went upstairs.

I quickened my pace. I was in time to see the movement stop, the fair head turn, and Hal standing beyond her in the shadow.

I passed the door, passed the street, walked an hour – two hours – got a late supper somewhere, and came back about bedtime with a sharp and bitter feeling in my heart that I strove in vain to reason down. Why he had not as good a right to meet her as I it were hard to say, and yet I was strangely angry with him.

When I returned the lamplight shone behind the white curtain, and the shadow of the great chair stood motionless against it. Another shadow crossed – Hal – smoking. I went up.

He greeted me effusively and asked why I was so late. Where

I got supper. Was unnaturally cheerful. There was a sudden dreadful sense of concealment between us. But he told nothing and I asked nothing, and we went silently to bed.

I blamed him for saying no word about our fair mystery, and yet I had said none concerning my own meeting. I racked my brain with questions as to how much he had really seen of her; if she had talked to him; what she had told him; how long she had stayed.

I tossed all night and Hal was sleepless too, for I heard him rocking for hours, by the window, by the bed, close to my door. I never knew a rocking-chair to 'walk' as that one did.

Towards morning the steady creak and swing was too much for my nerves or temper.

'For goodness' sake, Hal, do stop that and go to bed!'

'What?' came a sleepy voice.

'Don't fool!' said I, 'I haven't slept a wink tonight for your everlasting rocking. Now do leave off and go to bed.'

'Go to bed! I've been in bed all night and I wish you had! Can't you use the chair without blaming me for it?'

And all the time I *heard* him rock, rock, rock, over by the hall door!

I rose stealthily and entered the room, meaning to surprise the ill-timed joker and convict him in the act.

Both rooms were full of the dim phosphorescence of reflected moonlight; I knew them even in the dark; and yet I stumbled just inside the door, and fell heavily.

Hal was out of bed in a moment and had struck a light.

'Are you hurt, my dear boy?'

I was hurt, and solely by his fault, for the chair was not where I supposed, but close to my bedroom door, where he must have left it to leap into bed when he heard me coming. So it was in no amiable humor that I refused his offers of assistance and limped back to my own sleepless pillow. I had struck my ankle on one of those brass-tipped rockers, and it pained me severely. I never saw a chair so made to hurt as that one. It was so large and heavy and ill-balanced, and every joint and corner so shod with brass. Hal and I had punished ourselves enough on it before, especially in the dark when we forgot where the thing was standing, but never so severely as this. It was not like Hal to play such tricks, and both heart and ankle ached as I crept into bed again to toss and doze and dream and fitfully start till morning.

Hal was kindness itself, but he would insist that he had been asleep and I rocking all night, till I grew actually angry with him.

'That's carrying a joke too far,' I said at last. 'I don't mind a joke, even when it hurts, but there are limits.'

'Yes, there are!' said he, significantly, and we dropped the subject.

Several days passed. Hal had repeated meetings with the gold-haired damsel; this I saw from the street; but save for these bitter glimpses I waited vainly.

It was hard to bear, harder almost than the growing estrangement between Hal and me, and that cut deeply. I think that at last either one of us would have been glad to go away by himself, but neither was willing to leave the other to the room, the chair, the beautiful unknown.

Coming home one morning unexpectedly, I found the dull-faced landlady arranging the rooms, and quite laid myself out to make an impression upon her, to no purpose.

'That is a fine old chair you have there,' said I, as she stood mechanically polishing the brass corners with her apron.

She looked at the darkly glittering thing with almost a flash of pride.

'Yes,' said she, 'a fine chair!'

'Is it old!' I pursued.

'Very old,' she answered briefly.

'But I thought rocking-chairs were a modern American invention!' said I.

She looked at me apathetically.

'It is Spanish,' she said, 'Spanish oak, Spanish leather, Spanish brass, Spanish—.' I did not catch the last word, and she left the room without another.

It was a strange ill-balanced thing, that chair, though so easy and comfortable to sit in. The rockers were long and sharp behind, always lying in wait for the unwary, but cut short in front; and the back was so high and so heavy on top, that what with its weight and the shortness of the front rockers, it tipped forward with an ease and a violence equally astonishing.

This I knew from experience, as it had plunged over upon me during some of our frequent encounters. Hal also was a sufferer, but in spite of our manifold bruises, neither of us would have had the chair removed, for did not she sit in it, evening after evening, and rock there in the golden light of the setting sun.

So, evening after evening, we two fled from our work as early as possible, and hurried home alone, by separate ways, to the dingy street and the glorified window.

I could not endure forever. When Hal came home first, I, lingering in the street below, could see through our window that lovely head and his in close proximity. When I came first, it was to catch perhaps a quick glance from above – a bewildering smile – no more. She was always gone when I reached the room, and the inner door of my chamber irrevocably locked.

At times I even caught the click of the latch, heard the flutter of loose robes on the other side; and sometimes this daily disappointment, this constant agony of hope deferred, would bring me to my knees by that door, begging her to open to me, crying to her in every term of passionate endearment and persuasion that tortured heart of man could think to use.

Hal had neither word nor look for me now, save those of studied politeness and cold indifference, and how could I behave otherwise to him, so proven to my face a liar?

I saw him from the street one night, in the broad level sunlight, sitting in that chair, with the beautiful head on his shoulder. It was more than I could bear. If he had won, and won so utterly, I would ask but to speak to her once, and say farewell to both for ever. So I heavily climbed the stairs, knocked loudly, and entered at Hal's 'Come in!' only to find him sitting there alone, smoking – yes, smoking in the chair which but a moment since had held her too!

He had but just lit the cigar, a paltry device to blind my eyes.

'Look here, Hal,' said I, 'I can't stand this any longer. May I ask you one thing? Let me see her once, just once, that I may say goodbye, and then neither of you need see me again!'

Hal rose to his feet and looked me straight in the eye. Then he threw that whole cigar out of the window, and walked to within two feet of me.

'Are you crazy,' he said, '*I* ask her! *I!* I have never had speech of her in my life! And *you*—' He stopped and turned away.

'And I what?' I would have it out now whatever came.

'And you have seen her day after day – talked with her – I need not repeat all that my eyes have seen!'

'You need not, indeed,' said I. 'It would tax even your invention. I have never seen her in this room but once, and then but for a fleeting glimpse – no word. From the street I have seen her often – with you!'

He turned very white and walked from me to the window, then turned again.

'I have never seen her in this room for even such a moment as you own to. From the street I have seen her often – *with you!*'

We looked at each other.

'Do you mean to say,' I inquired slowly, 'that I did not see you just now sitting in that chair, by that window, with her in your arms?'

'Stop!' he cried, throwing out his hand with a fierce gesture. It struck sharply on the corner of the chair-back. He wiped the blood mechanically from the three-cornered cut, looking fixedly at me.

'I saw you,' said I.

'You did not!' said he.

I turned slowly on my heel and went into my room. I could not bear to tell that man, my more than brother, that he lied.

I sat down on my bed with my head on my hands, and presently I heard Hal's door open and shut, his step on the stair, the front door slam behind him. He had gone, I knew not where, and if he went to his death and a word of mine would have stopped him, I would not have said it. I do not know how long I sat there, in the company of hopeless love and jealousy and hate.

Suddenly, out of the silence of the empty room, came the steady swing and creak of the great chair. Perhaps – it must be! I sprang to my feet and noiselessly opened the door. There she sat by the window, looking out, and – yes – she threw a kiss to some one below. Ah, how beautiful she was! How beautiful! I made a step toward her. I held out my hands, I uttered I know not what – when all at once came Hal's quick step upon the stairs.

She heard it, too, and, giving me one look, one subtle, mysterious, triumphant look, slipped past me and into my room just as Hal burst in. He saw her go. He came straight to me and I thought he would have struck me down where I stood.

'Out of my way,' he cried. 'I will speak to her. Is it not enough to see?' – he motioned toward the window with his wounded hand – 'Let me pass!'

'She is not there,' I answered. 'She has gone through into the other room.'

A light laugh sounded close by us, a faint, soft, silver laugh, almost at my elbow.

He flung me from his path, threw open the door, and entered. The room was empty.

'Where have you hidden her?' he demanded. I coldly pointed to the other door.

'So her room opens into yours, does it?' he muttered with a bitter smile. 'No wonder you preferred the "view"! Perhaps I can open it too?' And he laid his hand upon the latch.

I smiled then, for bitter experience had taught me that it was always locked, locked to all my prayers and entreaties. Let him kneel there as I had! But it opened under his hand! I sprang to his side, and we looked into – a closet, two by four, as bare and shallow as an empty coffin!

He turned to me, as white with rage as I was with terror. I was not thinking of him.

'What have you done with her?' he cried. And then contemptuously – 'That I should stop to question a liar!'

I paid no heed to him, but walked back into the other room, where the great chair rocked by the window.

He followed me, furious with disappointment, and laid his hand upon the swaying back, his strong fingers closing on it till the nails were white.

'Will you leave this place?' said he.

'No,' said I.

'I will live no longer with a liar and a traitor,' said he.

'Then you will have to kill yourself,' said I.

With a muttered oath he sprang upon me, but caught his foot in the long rocker, and fell heavily.

So wild a wave of hate rose in my heart that I could have trampled upon him where he lay – killed him like a dog – but with a mighty effort I turned from him and left the room.

When I returned it was broad day. Early and still, not sunrise yet, but full of hard, clear light on roof and wall and roadway. I stopped on the lower floor to find the landlady and announce my immediate departure. Door after door I knocked at, tried and opened; room after room I entered and searched thoroughly; in all that house, from cellar to garret, was no furnished room but ours, no sign of human occupancy. Dust, dust, and cobwebs everywhere. Nothing else.

With a strange sinking of the heart I came back to our own door.

Surely I heard the landlady's slow, even step inside, and that soft, low laugh. I rushed in.

The room was empty of all life; both rooms utterly empty.

Yes, of all life; for, with the love of a lifetime surging in my heart, I sprang to where Hal lay beneath the window, and found him dead.

Dead, and most horribly dead. Three heavy marks – blows –

three deep, three-cornered gashes – I started to my feet – even the chair had gone!

Again the whispered laugh. Out of that house of terror I fled desperately.

From the street I cast one shuddering glance at the fateful window.

The risen sun was gilding all the housetops, and its level rays, striking the high panes on the building opposite, shone back in a calm glory on the great chair by the window, the sweet face, down-dropped eyes, and swaying golden head.

DESERTED

Mrs Ellphalet Johnson was a very hardworking woman – even her nextdoor neighbors admitted that. Her chimney blackened the soft morning air as early as any in town; her wash fluttered white under the apple boughs long before breakfast. That is, before Ellphalet's breakfast.

Ellphalet kept store. He preferred keeping store to farming because he could sit down more. In the store it was all in the way of business. His customers sat down on every available object – the counter, the sugar barrel, the cracker box, even the cask of molasses, but not on that last until the counter and other things were full.

There were a few chairs around the store in the rear and vast political measures were discussed there – matters far beyond the reach of Mrs Johnson's busy feminine brain.

The house was over the store. The stairs connecting the two came down in the end where the store was, and when a customer came in who wanted not a seat but service Mr Ellphalet Johnson would tip back his chair a little further, open the stair door and say, 'Maria!'

Then Mrs Johnson would hurry down and attend to the customer. Mrs Johnson had a good head in a servile sort of way and usually kept the accounts. This she did after the store was closed and the children were in bed.

But in spite of all her efforts Ellphalet got into difficulties. He never fully explained to her what these difficulties were, but they were such as induced him to transfer the family bank account and business liabilities to her name.

This, he explained with lofty comprehensiveness, was merely a matter of form, and quite essential for the safety of the children.

'And Maria,' he added, seeking to bring the conversation to a more comprehensible level, 'there's a lady over at Clark's, a Miss Burton, who wants board in a private family, and I told her she could come here. I knew the spare room was suitable, and one more or less wouldn't make any difference to you.'

'But I wanted mother for a while this summer!' urged Maria. 'She'd be such a help preservin' and with the baby.'

Ellphalet grinned.

'Well, I don't want your mother,' said he: 'not by a long chalk. And this lady is to pay a dollar a day right along and you're to bank it in your name – here's the book.'

Maria took the book and looked at it. Eight hundred dollars were set down already to her credit.

'Why, 'Liphalet, where'd you get this?' she exclaimed.

'Sold the river lot,' he answered, and tipped back his chair to its farthest, looking at her with narrowed eyes from under the brim of his hat.

A dull red color rose on Mrs Johnson's faded face.

'That was my lot,' said she slowly. 'My father gave it to me when he died and I never meant to have had it sold in the world.'

'You don't know nothin' about business an' never will,' said Ellphalet. 'But now you pay 'tention to this and see if you can understand it. Here's the deeds of this house, store an' all the furniture and stock. All in your name. Now, the reason of it is that I've got creditors who might clean me out any time, but if I can tide over this year I'll get over it all right. For this year the hull property's in your name and none of my creditors can touch it. See? As to that lot 'twan't no more yours than this house was or the farm – they all come from your father, but when you married me it made 'em mine, and it ought to. A man supports the family. He's got to hold the property. But for this year it's in your name.'

The year passed slowly. Mrs Johnson grew to understand somewhat of the value of her position and to do more and more of the business.

In truth, though she never owned to her most intimate friend that 'Liphalet drinked!' this sad fact was now becoming painfully apparent.

Much had Mrs Johnson suffered in the fifteen years of her laborious marriage. She had worked, on the average, fifteen hours a day, and lost much sleep besides. She had put into the family all its real estate, and really kept the store. She had borne and reared four children and lost two, and out of all this she had learned nothing until what she thought the last straw turned out to be a blessing in disguise. That was the lady boarder. If Mr Johnson had dreamed of that worthy woman's real position he would never have placed his conservative spare chamber at her disposal.

But he did not suspect, and never learned until it was too late.

She was a lawyer, and in spite of the absolute prohibition of all brain work for three months, she had brought with her a few little calf-bound books from force of habit.

So it chanced that Mrs Johnson, in the invigorating freshness of new acquaintance, was led to read somewhat in the penal and civil codes of her native State. Moreover, the boarder, moved by a strong sense of human kindness to this struggling woman and seeing the responsibilities of life with wider reach, urged upon her a new view of her duties to her children and the world.

Wherefore, it came to pass that when Ellphalet waked up one morning very late, indeed, after a little heavier drinking than was usual to him, and called vainly, with quite advanced profanity, for his faithful wife, he found her not in attendance.

Somewhat sobered by surprise he arose and searched the house.

No wife, no child, no boarder!

And a little later, to his incredulous horror and amazement, he discovered that the house and store, stock, furniture and farm had been sold over his head, and the proceeds had disappeared with his wife.

She left him a letter, however, in which it was set forth that if he gave up drinking and became a self-supporting citizen she would gladly receive him again as a husband – on her own terms.

In the meantime she would allow him $30 a month, to be paid to him personally on application to her lawyer, whose address she enclosed.

For herself she had gone into business independently, and should do well by the children.

Ellphalet read the letter repeatedly.

The name of the lawyer confused him.

'Elizabeth!' said he. 'Elizabeth Burton! Great Scott!'

Then the deserted husband took up the burden of life. It made a new man of him.

AN UNNATURAL MOTHER

'Don't tell me!' said old Mis' Briggs, with a forbidding shake of the head; 'no mother that was a mother would desert her own child for anything on earth!'

'And leaving it a care on the town, too!' put in Susannah Jacobs, 'as if we hadn't enough to do to take care of our own!'

Miss Jacobs was a well-to-do old maid, owning a comfortable farm and homestead, and living alone with an impoverished cousin acting as general servant, companion and protegée. Mis' Briggs, on the contrary, had had thirteen children, five of whom remained to bless her, so that what maternal feeling Miss Jacobs might lack, Mis' Briggs could certainly supply.

'I should think,' piped little Martha Ann Simmons, the village dressmaker, 'that she might a saved her young one first and then tried what she could do for the town.'

Martha had been married, had lost her husband, and had one sickly boy to care for.

The youngest Briggs girl, still unmarried at thirty-six, and in her mother's eyes a most tender infant, now ventured to make a remark.

'You don't any of you seem to think what she did for all of us – if she hadn't left hers we should all have lost ours, sure.'

'You ain't no call to judge, Maria Melia,' her mother hastened to reply; 'you've no children of your own, and you can't judge of a mother's duty. No mother ought to leave her child, whatever happens. The Lord gave it to her to take care of – he never gave her other people's. You needn't tell me!'

'She was an unnatural mother!' repeated Miss Jacobs harshly, 'as I said to begin with.'

'What is the story?' asked the City Boarder. The City Boarder was interested in stories from a business point of view, but they did not know that. 'What did this woman do?' she asked.

There was no difficulty in eliciting particulars. The difficulty was rather in discriminating amidst their profusion and contradictoriness. But when the City Boarder got it clear in her mind it was somewhat as follows:

The name of the much condemned heroine was Esther Greenwood, and she lived and died here in Toddsville.

Toddsville was a mill village. The Todds lived on a beautiful eminence overlooking the little town, as the castles of robber barons on the Rhine used to overlook their little towns. The mills and the mill hands' houses were built close along the bed of the river. They had to be pretty close, because the valley was a narrow one, and the bordering hills were too steep for travel, but the water power was fine. Above the village was the reservoir, filling the entire valley save for a narrow road beside it, a fair blue smiling lake, edged with lilies and blue flag, rich in pickerel and perch. This lake gave them fish, it gave them ice, it gave the power that ran the mills that gave the town its bread. Blue Lake was both useful and ornamental.

In this pretty and industrious village Esther had grown up, the somewhat neglected child of a heart-broken widower. He had lost a young wife, and three fair babies before her – this one was left him, and he said he meant that she should have all the chance there was.

'That was what ailed her in the first place!' they all eagerly explained to the City Boarder. 'She never knew what 'twas to have a mother, and she grew up a regular tomboy! Why she used to roam the country for miles around, in all weather like an Injun! And her father wouldn't take no advice!'

This topic lent itself to eager discussion. The recreant father, it appeared, was a doctor, not their accepted standby, the resident physician of the neighborhood, but an alien doctor, possessed of 'views.'

'You never heard such things as he advocated,' Miss Jacobs explained. 'He wouldn't give no medicines, hardly; said "nature" did the curing – he couldn't.'

'And he couldn't either – that was clear,' Mrs Briggs agreed. 'Look at his wife and children dying on his hands, as it were! "Physician heal thyself," I say.'

'But, mother,' Maria Amelia put in, 'she was an invalid when he married her, they say; and those children died of polly – polly – what's that thing that nobody can help?'

'That may all be so,' Miss Jacobs admitted, 'but all the same it's a doctor's business to give medicine. If "nature" was all that was wanted, we needn't have any doctor at all!'

'I believe in medicine and plenty of it. I always gave my children a good clearance, spring and fall, whether anything ailed 'em or not, just to be on the safe side. And if there was anything the matter with 'em they had plenty more. I never had anything to reproach myself with on that score,' stated Mrs Briggs, firmly. Then as a sort of concession to the family graveyard, she added piously, 'The Lord giveth and the Lord taketh away.'

'You should have seen the way he dressed that child!' pursued Miss Jacobs. 'It was a reproach to the town. Why, you couldn't tell at a distance whether it was a boy or a girl. And barefoot! He let that child go barefoot till she was so big we was actually mortified to see her.'

It appeared that a wild, healthy childhood had made Esther very different in her early womanhood from the meek, well-behaved damsels of the little place. She was well enough liked by those who knew her at all, and the children of the place adored her, but the worthy matrons shook their heads and prophesied no good of a girl who was 'queer.'

She was described with rich detail in reminiscence, how she wore her hair short till she was fifteen – 'just shingled like a boy's – it did seem a shame that girl had no mother to look after her – and her clo'se was almost a scandal, even when she did put on shoes and stockings.' 'Just gingham – brown gingham – and *short*!'

'I think she was a real nice girl,' said Maria Amelia. 'I can remember her just as well! She was *so* nice to us children. She was five or six years older than I was, and most girls that age won't have anything to do with little ones. But she was as kind and pleasant. She'd take us berrying and on all sorts of walks, and teach us new games and tell us things. I don't remember anyone that ever did us the good she did!'

Maria Amelia's thin chest heaved with emotion; and there were tears in her eyes; but her mother took her up somewhat sharply.

'That sounds well I must say – right before your own mother that's toiled and slaved for you! It's all very well for a young thing that's got nothing on earth to do to make herself agreeable to young ones. That poor blinded father of hers never taught her to do the work a girl should – naturally he couldn't.'

'At least he might have married again and given her another mother,' said Susannah Jacobs, with decision, with so much decision in fact that the City Boarder studied her expression for a moment and concluded that if this recreant father had not married again it was not for lack of opportunity.

Mrs Simmons cast an understanding glance upon Miss Jacobs, and nodded wisely.

'Yes, he ought to have done that, of course. A man's not fit to bring up children, anyhow – how can they? Mothers have the instinct – that is, all natural mothers have. But, dear me! There's some as don't seem to *be* mothers – even when they have a child!'

'You're quite right, Mis' Simmons,' agreed the mother of thirteen. 'It's a divine instinct, I say. I'm sorry for the child that lacks it. Now this Esther. We always knew she wan't like other girls – she never seemed to care for dress and company and things girls naturally do, but was always philandering over the hills with a parcel of young ones. There wan't a child in town but would run after her. She made more trouble 'n a little in families, the young ones quotin' what Aunt Esther said, and tellin' what Aunt Esther did to their own mothers, and she only a young girl. Why she actually seemed to care more for them children than she did for beaux or anything – it wasn't natural!'

'But she did marry?' pursued the City Boarder.

'Marry! Yes, she married finally. We all thought she never would, but she did. After the things her father taught her it did seem as if he'd ruined *all* her chances. It's simply terrible the way that girl was trained.'

'Him being a doctor,' put in Mrs Simmons, 'made it different, I suppose.'

'Doctor or no doctor,' Miss Jacobs rigidly interposed, 'it was a crying shame to have a young girl so instructed.'

'Maria Melia,' said her mother, 'I want you should get me my smelling salts. They're up in the spare chamber, I believe – When your Aunt Marcia was here she had one of her spells – don't you remember? – and she asked for salts. Look in the top bureau drawer – they must be there.'

Maria Amelia, thirty-six, but unmarried, withdrew dutifully, and the other ladies drew closer to the City Boarder.

'It's the most shocking thing I ever heard of,' murmured Mrs Briggs. 'Do you know he – a father – actually taught his daughter how babies come!'

There was a breathless hush.

'He did,' eagerly chimed in the little dressmaker, 'all the particulars. It was perfectly awful!'

'He said,' continued Mrs Briggs, 'that he expected her to be a mother and that she ought to understand what was before her!'

'He was waited on by a committee of ladies from the church, married ladies, all older than he was,' explained Miss Jacobs severely. 'They told him it was creating a scandal in the town – and what do you think he said?'

There was another breathless silence.

Above, the steps of Maria Amelia were heard, approaching the stairs.

'It ain't there, Ma!'

'Well, you look in the high boy and in the top drawer; they're somewhere up there,' her mother replied.

Then, in a sepulchral whisper:

72

'He told us – yes, ma'am, I was on that committee – he told us that until young women knew what was before them as mothers they would not do their duty in choosing a father for their children! That was his expression – "choosing a father!" A nice thing for a young girl to be thinking of – a father for her children!'

'Yes, and more than that,' inserted Miss Jacobs, who, though not on the committee, seemed familiar with its workings. 'He told them—' But Mrs Briggs waved her aside and continued swiftly—

'He taught that innocent girl about – the Bad Disease! Actually!'

'He did!' said the dressmaker. 'It got out, too, all over town. There wasn't a man here would have married her after that.'

Miss Jacobs insisted on taking up the tale. 'I understand that he said it was "to protect her!" Protect her, indeed! Against matrimony! As if any man alive would want to marry a young girl who knew all the evil of life! I was brought up differently, I assure you!'

'Young girls should be kept innocent!' Mrs Briggs solemnly proclaimed. 'Why, when I was married I knew no more what was before me than a babe unborn and my girls were all brought up so, too!'

Then, as Maria Amelia returned with the salts, she continued more loudly, 'but she did marry after all. And a mighty queer husband she got, too. He was an artist or something, made pictures for the magazines and such as that, and they do say she met him first out in the hills. That's the first 'twas known of it here, anyhow – them two traipsing about all over; him with his painting things! They married and just settled down to live with her father, for she vowed she wouldn't leave him, and he said it didn't make no difference where he lived, he took his business with him.'

'They seemed very happy together,' said Maria Amelia.

'Happy! Well, they might have been, I suppose. It was a pretty queer family, I think.' And her mother shook her head in retrospection. 'They got on all right for a while; but the old man died, and those two – well, I don't call it housekeeping – the way they lived!'

'No,' said Miss Jacobs. 'They spent more time out of doors than they did in the house. She followed him around everywhere. And for open love making—'

They all showed deep disapproval at this memory. All but the City Boarder and Maria Amelia.

'She had one child, a girl,' continued Mrs Briggs, 'and it was just shocking to see how she neglected that child from the beginnin'. She never seemed to have no maternal feelin' at all!'

'But I thought you said she was very fond of children,' remonstrated the City Boarder.

'Oh, *children*, yes. She'd take up with any dirty faced brat in town, even to them Kanucks. I've seen her again and again with a whole swarm of the mill hands' young ones round her, goin' on some picnic or other – "open air school," she used to call it – *Such* notions as she had. But when it come to her own child! Why—' Here the speaker's voice sank to a horrified hush. 'She never had no baby clo'se for it! Not a single sock!'

The City Boarder was interested. 'Why, what did she do with the little thing?'

'The Lord knows!' answered old Mis' Briggs. 'She neved would let us hardly see it when 'twas little, 'Shamed too, I don't doubt. But that's strange feelin's for a mother. Why, I was so proud of my babies! And I kept 'em lookin' so pretty! I'd a-sat up all night and sewed and washed, but I'd a had my children look well!' And the poor old eyes filled with tears as she thought of the eight little graves in the churchyard, which she never failed to keep looking pretty, even now. 'She just let that young one roll round in the grass like a puppy with hardly nothin' on! Why, a squaw does better. She does keep 'em done up for a spell! That child was treated worse'n an Injun! We all done what we could, of course. We felt it no more'n right. But she was real hateful about it, and we had to let her be.'

'The child died?' asked the City Boarder.

'Died! Dear no! That's it you saw going by; a great strappin' girl she is, too, and promisin' to grow up well, thanks to Mrs Stone's taking her. Mrs Stone always thought a heap of Esther. It's a mercy to the child that she lost her mother, I do believe! How she ever survived that kind of treatment beats all! Why that woman never seemed to have the first spark of maternal feeling to the end! She seemed just as fond of the other young ones after she had her own as she was before, and that's against nature. The way it happened was this. You see they lived up the valley nearer to the lake than the village. He was away, and was coming home that night, it seems, driving from Drayton along the lake road. And she set out to meet him. She must a walked up to the dam to look for him; and we think maybe she saw the team clear across the lake. Maybe she thought he could get to the house and save little Esther in time – that's the only explanation we ever could put on it. But this is what she did; and you can judge for yourselves if any mother in her senses *could* ha' done such a thing! You see 'twas the time of that awful disaster, you've read of it, likely, that destroyed three villages. Well, she got to the dam and see that 'twas givin' way – she was always great for knowin' all such things. And she just turned and ran.

Jake Elder was up on the hill after a stray cow, and he seen her go. He was too far off to imagine what ailed her, but he said he never saw a woman run so in his life.

'And, if you'll believe it, she run right by her own house – never stopped – never looked at it. Just run for the village. Of course, she may have lost her head with the fright, but that wasn't like her. No, I think she had made up her mind to leave that innocent baby to die! She just ran down here and give warnin', and, of course, we sent word down valley on horseback, and there was no lives lost in all three villages. She started to run back as soon as we was 'roused, but 'twas too late then.

'Jake saw it all, though he was too far off to do a thing. He said he couldn't stir a foot, it was so awful. He seen the wagon drivin' along as nice as you please till it got close to the dam, and then Greenwood seemed to see the danger and whipped up like mad. He was the father, you know. But he wasn't quite in time – the dam give way and the water went over him like a tidal wave. She was almost to the gate when it struck the house and her, – and we never found her body nor his for days and days. They was washed clear down river.

'Their house was strong and it stood a little high, and had some big trees between it and the lake too. It was moved off the place and brought up against the side of the stone church down yonder, but 'twant wholly in pieces. And that child was found swimmin' round in its bed, most drowned, but not quite. The wonder is, it didn't die of a cold, but it's here yet – must have a strong constitution. Their folks never did nothing for it – so we had to keep it here.'

'Well, now, mother,' said Maria Amelia Briggs. 'It does seem to me that she did her duty. You know yourself that if she hadn't give warnin' all three of the villages would a' been cleaned out – a matter of fifteen hundred people. And if she'd stopped to lug that child, she couldn't have got here in time. Don't you believe she was thinkin' of those mill-hands' children?'

'Maria 'Melia, I'm ashamed of you!' said old Mis' Briggs. 'But you ain't married and ain't a mother. A mother's duty is to her own child! She neglected her own to look after other folks – the Lord never gave her them other children to care for!'

'Yes,' said Miss Jacobs, 'and here's her child, a burden on the town! She was an unnatural mother!'

THREE THANKSGIVINGS

Andrew's letter and Jean's letter were in Mrs Morrison's lap. She had read them both, and sat looking at them with a varying sort of smile, now motherly and now unmotherly.

'You belong with me,' Andrew wrote. 'It is not right that Jean's husband should support my mother. I can do it easily now. You shall have a good room and every comfort. The old house will let for enough to give you quite a little income of your own, or it can be sold and I will invest the money where you'll get a deal more out of it. It is not right that you should live alone there. Sally is old and liable to accident. I am anxious about you. Come on for Thanksgiving – and come to stay. Here is the money to come with. You know I want you. Annie joins me in sending love. ANDREW.'

Mrs Morrison read it all through again, and laid it down with her quiet, twinkling smile. Then she read Jean's.

'Now, mother, you've got to come to us for Thanksgiving this year. Just think! You haven't seen baby since he was three months old! And have never seen the twins. You won't know him – he's such a splendid big boy now. Joe says for you to

78

come, of course. And, mother, why won't you come and live with us? Joe wants you, too. There's the little room upstairs; it's not very big, but we can put in a Franklin stove for you and make you pretty comfortable. Joe says he should think you ought to sell that white elephant of a place. He says he could put the money into his store and pay you good interest. I wish you would, mother. We'd just love to have you here. You'd be such a comfort to me, and such a help with the babies. And Joe just loves you. Do come now, and stay with us. Here is the money for the trip. – Your affectionate daughter,

JEANNIE.'

Mrs Morrison laid this beside the other, folded both, and placed them in their respective envelopes, then in their several well-filled pigeon-holes in her big, old-fashioned desk. She turned and paced slowly up and down the long parlor, a tall woman, commanding of aspect, yet of a winningly attractive manner, erect and light-footed, still imposingly handsome.

It was now November, the last lingering boarder was long since gone, and a quiet winter lay before her. She was alone, but for Sally; and she smiled at Andrew's cautious expression, 'liable to accident.' He could not say 'feeble' or 'ailing,' Sally being a colored lady of changeless aspect and incessant activity.

Mrs Morrison was alone, and while living in the Welcome House she was never unhappy. Her father had built it, she was born there, she grew up playing on the broad green lawns in front, and in the acre of garden behind. It was the finest house in the village, and she then thought it the finest in the world.

Even after living with her father at Washington and abroad, after visiting hall, castle and palace, she still found the Welcome House beautiful and impressive.

If she kept on taking boarders she could live the year

through, and pay interest, but not principal, on her little mortgage. This had been the one possible and necessary thing while the children were there, though it was a business she hated.

But her youthful experience in diplomatic circles, and the years of practical management in church affairs, enabled her to bear it with patience and success. The boarders often confided to one another, as they chatted and tatted on the long piazza, that Mrs Morrison was 'certainly very refined.'

Now Sally whisked in cheerfully, announcing supper, and Mrs Morrison went out to her great silver tea-tray at the lit end of the long, dark mahogany table, with as much dignity as if twenty titled guests were before her.

Afterward Mr Butts called. He came early in the evening, with his usual air of determination and a somewhat unusual spruceness. Mr Peter Butts was a florid, blonde person, a little stout, a little pompous, sturdy and immovable in the attitude of a self-made man. He had been a poor boy when she was a rich girl; and it gratified him much to realize – and to call upon her to realize – that their positions had changed. He meant no unkindness, his pride was honest and unveiled. Tact he had none.

She had refused Mr Butts, almost with laughter, when he proposed to her in her gay girlhood. She had refused him, more gently, when he proposed to her in her early widowhood. He had always been her friend, and her husband's friend, a solid member of the church, and had taken the small mortgage on the house. She refused to allow him at first, but he was convincingly frank about it.

'This has nothing to do with my wanting you, Delia Morrison,' he said. 'I've always wanted you – and I've always wanted this house, too. You won't sell, but you've got to mortgage. By and by you can't pay up, and I'll get it – see? Then maybe you'll take me – to keep the house. Don't be a fool, Delia. It's a perfectly good investment.'

She had taken the loan. She had paid the interest. She would pay the interest if she had to take boarders all her life. And she would not, at any price, marry Peter Butts.

He broached the subject again that evening, cheerful and undismayed. 'You might as well come to it, Delia,' he said. 'Then, we could live right here just the same. You aren't so young as you were, to be sure; I'm not, either. But you are as good a house-keeper as ever – better – you've had more experience.

'You are extremely kind, Mr Butts,' said the lady, 'but I do not wish to marry you.'

'I know you don't,' he said. 'You've made that clear. You don't, but I do. You've had your way and married the minister. He was a good man, but he's dead. Now you might as well marry me.'

'I do not wish to marry again, Mr Butts; neither you nor anyone.'

'Very proper, very proper, Delia,' he replied. 'It wouldn't look well if you did – at any rate, if you showed it. But why should-n't you? The children are gone now – you can't hold them up against me any more.'

'Yes, the children are both settled now, and doing nicely,' she admitted.

'You don't want to go and live with them – either one of them – do you?' he asked.

'I should prefer to stay here,' she answered.

'Exactly! And you can't! You'd rather live here and be a grandee – but you can't do it. Keepin' house for boarders isn't any better than keepin' house for me, as I see. You'd much better marry me.'

'I should prefer to keep the house without you, Mr Butts.'

'I know you would. But you can't, I tell you. I'd like to know what a woman of your age can do with a house like this – and no money? You can't live eternally on hens' eggs and garden truck. That won't pay the mortgage.'

Mrs Morrison looked at him with her cordial smile, calm and non-committal. 'Perhaps I can manage it,' she said.

'That mortgage falls due two years from Thanksgiving, you know.'

'Yes – I have not forgotten.'

'Well, then, you might just as well marry me now, and save two years of interest. It'll be my house, either way – but you'll be keepin it just the same.'

'It is very kind of you, Mr Butts. I must decline the offer none the less. I can pay the interest, I am sure. And perhaps – in two years time – I can pay the principal. It's not a large sum.'

'That depends on how you look at it,' said he. 'Two thousand dollars is considerable money for a single woman to raise in two years – *and* interest.'

He went away, as cheerful and determined as ever; and Mrs Morrison saw him go with a keen light in her fine eyes, a more definite line to that steady, pleasant smile

Then she went to spend Thanksgiving with Andrew. He was glad to see her. Annie was glad to see her. They proudly installed her in 'her room,' and said she must call it 'home' now.

This affectionately offered home was twelve by fifteen, and eight feet high. It had two windows, one looking at some pale gray clapboards within reach of a broom, the other giving a view of several small fenced yards occupied by cats, clothes and children. There was an ailanthus tree under the window, a lady ailanthus tree. Annie told her bow profusely it bloomed. Mrs

Morrison particularly disliked the smell of ailanthus flowers. 'It doesn't bloom in November,' said she to herself. 'I can be thankful for that!'

Andrew's church was very like the church of his father, and Mrs Andrew was doing her best to fill the position of minister's wife – doing it well, too – there was no vacancy for a minister's mother.

Besides, the work she had done so cheerfully to help her husband was not what she most cared for, after all. She liked the people, she liked to manage, but she was not strong on doctrine. Even her husband had never known how far her views differed from his. Mrs Morrison had never mentioned what they were.

Andrew's people were very polite to her. She was invited out with them, waited upon and watched over and set down among the old ladies and gentlemen – she had never realized so keenly that she was no longer young. Here nothing recalled her youth, every careful provision anticipated age. Annie brought her a hot-water bag at night, tucking it in at the foot of the bed with affectionate care. Mrs Morrison thanked her, and subsequently took it out – airing the bed a little before she got into it. The house seemed very hot to her, after the big, windy halls at home.

The little dining-room, the little round table with the little round fern-dish in the middle, the little turkey and the little carving-set – game-set she would have called it – all made her feel as if she was looking through the wrong end of an opera-glass.

In Annie's precise efficiency she saw no room for her assistance; no room in the church, no room in the small, busy town, prosperous and progressive, and no room in the house. 'Not enough to turn round in!' she said to herself. Annie, who had grown up in a city flat, thought their little parsonage palatial. Mrs Morrison grew up in the Welcome House.

She stayed a week, pleasant and polite, conversational, interested in all that went on.

'I think your mother is just lovely,' said Annie to Andrew.

'Charming woman, your mother,' said the leading church member.

'What a delightful old lady your mother is!' said the pretty soprano.

And Andrew was deeply hurt and disappointed when she announced her determination to stay on for the present in her old home. 'Dear boy,' she said, 'you mustn't take it to heart. I love to be with you, of course, but I love my home, and want to keep it as long as I can. It is a great pleasure to see you and Annie so well settled, and so happy together. I am most truly thankful for you.'

'My home is open to you whenever you wish to come, mother,' said Andrew. But he was a little angry.

Mrs Morrison came home as eager as a girl, and opened her own door with her own key, in spite of Sally's haste.

Two years were before her in which she must find some way to keep herself and Sally, and to pay two thousand dollars and the interest to Peter Butts. She considered her assets. Here was the house – the white elephant. It *was* big – very big. It was profusely furnished. Her father had entertained lavishly like the Southern-born, hospitable gentleman he was; and the bedrooms ran in suites – somewhat deteriorated by the use of boarders, but still numerous and habitable. Boarders – she abhorred them. They were people from afar, strangers and interlopers. She went over the place from garret to cellar, from front gate to backyard fence.

The garden had great possibilities. She was fond of garden-ing, and understood it well. She measured and estimated.

'This garden,' she finally decided, 'with the hens, will feed us two women and sell enough to pay Sally. If we make plenty of jelly, it may cover the coal bill, too. As to clothes – I don't need any. They last admirably. I can manage. I can *live* – but two thousand dollars – *and* interest!'

In the great attic was more furniture, discarded sets put there when her extravagant young mother had ordered new ones. And chairs – uncounted chairs. Senator Welcome used to invite numbers to meet his political friends – and they had delivered glowing orations in the wide, double parlors, the impassioned speakers standing on a temporary dais, now in the cellar; and the enthusiastic listeners disposed more or less com-fortably on these serried rows of 'folding chairs,' which folded sometimes, and let down the visitor in scarlet confusion to the floor.

She sighed as she remembered those vivid days and glittering nights. She used to steal downstairs in her little pink wrapper and listen to the eloquence. It delighted her young soul to see her father rising on his toes, coming down sharply on his heels, hammering one hand upon the other; and then to hear the fusilade of applause.

Here were the chairs, often borrowed for weddings, funerals, and church affairs, somewhat worn and depleted, but still numerous. She mused upon them. Chairs – hundreds of chairs. They would sell for very little.

She went through her linen room. A splendid stock in the old days; always carefully washed by Sally; surviving even the boarders. Plenty of bedding, plenty of towels, plenty of napkins and tablecloths. 'It would make a good hotel – but I *can't* have it so – I *can't!* Besides, there's no need of another hotel here. The poor little Haskins House is never full.'

The stock in the china closet was more damaged than some other things, naturally; but she inventoried it with care. The countless cups of crowded church receptions were especially prominent. Later additions these, not very costly cups, but numerous, appallingly.

When she had her long list of assets all in order, she sat and studied it with a clear and daring mind. Hotel – boarding-house – she could think of nothing else. School! A girls' school! A boarding school! There was money to be made at that, and fine work done. It was a brilliant thought at first, and she gave several hours, and much paper and ink, to its full consideration. But she would need some capital for advertising; she must engage teachers – adding to her definite obligation; and to establish it, well, it would require time.

Mr Butts, obstinate, pertinacious, oppressively affectionate, would give her no time. He meant to force her to marry him for her own good – and his. She shrugged her fine shoulders with a little shiver. Marry Peter Butts! Never! Mrs Morrison still loved her husband. Some day she meant to see him again – God willing – and she did not wish to have to tell him that at fifty she had been driven into marrying Peter Butts.

Better live with Andrew. Yet when she thought of living with Andrew, she shivered again. Pushing back her sheets of figures and lists of personal property, she rose to her full graceful height and began to walk the floor. There was plenty of floor to walk. She considered, with a set deep thoughtfulness, the town and the townspeople, the surrounding country, the hundreds upon hundreds of women whom she knew and liked, and who liked her.

It used to be said of Senator Welcome that he had no ene-
mies; and some people, strangers, maliciously disposed,
thought it no credit to his character. His daughter had no ene-
mies, but no one had ever blamed her for her unlimited
friendliness. In her father's wholesale entertainments the whole
town knew and admired his daughter; in her husband's popular
church she had come to know the women of the countryside
about them. Her mind strayed off to these women, farmers'
wives, comfortably off in a plain way, but starving for companionship, for occasional stimulus and pleasure. It was one of her
joys in her husband's time to bring together these women – to
teach and entertain them.

Suddenly she stopped short in the middle of the great high-
ceiled room, and drew her head up proudly like a victorious
queen. One wide, triumphant, sweeping glance she cast at the
well-loved walls – and went back to her desk, working swiftly,
excitedly, well into the hours of the night.

Presently the little town began to buzz, and the murmur ran
far out into the surrounding country. Sunbonnets wagged
over fences; butcher carts and pedlar's wagon carried the
news farther; and ladies visiting found one topic in a thousand houses.

Mrs Morrison was going to entertain. Mrs Morrison had
invited the whole feminine population, it would appear, to
meet Mrs Isabelle Carter Blake, of Chicago. Even Haddleton
had heard of Mrs Isabelle Carter Blake. And even Haddleton
had nothing but admiration for her.

She was known the world over for her splendid work for
children – for the school children and the working children of
the country. Yet she was known also to have lovingly and

wisely reared six children of her own – and made her husband happy in his home. On top of that she had lately written a novel, a popular novel, of which everyone was talking; and on top of that she was an intimate friend of a certain conspicuous Countess – an Italian.

It was even rumored, by some who knew Mrs Morrison better than others – or thought they did – that the Countess was coming, too! No one had known before that Delia Welcome was a school-mate of Isabel Carter, and a life-long friend; and that was ground for talk in itself.

The day arrived, and the guests arrived. They came in hundreds upon hundreds, and found ample room in the great white house.

The highest dream of the guests was realized – the Countess had come, too. With excited joy they met her, receiving impressions that would last them for all their lives, for those large widening waves of reminiscence which delight us the more as years pass. It was an incredible glory – Mrs Isabelle Carter Blake, *and* a Countess!

Some were moved to note that Mrs Morrison looked the easy peer of these eminent ladies, and treated the foreign nobility precisely as she did her other friends.

She spoke, her clear quiet voice reaching across the murmuring din, and silencing it.

'Shall we go into the east room? If you will all take chairs in the east room, Mrs Blake is going to be so kind as to address us. Also perhaps her friend—'

They crowded in, sitting somewhat timorously on the unfolded chairs.

Then the great Mrs Blake made them an address of memorable power and beauty, which received vivid sanction from that imposing presence in Parisian garments on the platform by her side. Mrs Blake spoke to them of the work she was interested in, and how it was aided everywhere by the women's clubs. She gave them the number of these clubs, and described with contagious enthusiasm the inspiration of their great meetings. She spoke of the women's club houses, going up in city after city, where many associations meet and help one another. She was winning and convincing and most entertaining – an extremely attractive speaker.

Had they a women's club there? They had not.

Not *yet*, she suggested, adding that it took no time at all to make one.

They were delighted and impressed with Mrs Blake's speech, but its effect was greatly intensified by the address of the Countess.

'I, too, am American,' she told them; 'born here, reared in England, married in Italy.' And she stirred their hearts with a vivid account of the women's clubs and associations all over Europe, and what they were accomplishing. She was going back soon, she said, the wiser and happier for this visit to her native land, and she should remember particularly this beautiful, quiet town, trusting that if she came to it again it would have joined the great sisterhood of women, 'whose hands were touching around the world for the common good.'

It was a great occasion.

The Countess left next day, but Mrs Blake remained, and spoke in some of the church meetings, to an ever widening circle of admirers. Her suggestions were practical.

'What you need here is a "Rest and Improvement Club,"' she said. 'Here are all you women coming in from the country to do your shopping – and no place to go to. No place to lie down if you're tired, to meet a friend, to eat your lunch in peace, to do your hair. All you have to do is organize, pay some small regular due, and provide yourselves with what you want.'

There was a volume of questions and suggestions, a little opposition, much random activity.

Who was to do it? Where was there a suitable place? They would have to hire someone to take charge of it. It would only be used once a week. It would cost too much.

Mrs Blake, still practical, made another suggestion. 'Why not combine business with pleasure, and make use of the best place in town, if you can get it? I *think* Mrs Morrison could be persuaded to let you use part of her house; it's quite too big for one woman.

Then Mrs Morrison, simple and cordial as ever, greeted with warm enthusiasm by her wide circle of friends.

'I have been thinking this over,' she said. 'Mrs Blake has been discussing it with me. My house is certainly big enough for all of you, and there am I, with nothing to do but entertain you. Suppose you formed such a club as you speak of – for Rest and Improvement. My parlors are big enough for all manner of meetings; there are bedrooms in plenty for resting. If you form such a club I shall be glad to help with my great, cumbersome house, shall be delighted to see so many friends there so often; and I think I could furnish accommodations more cheaply than you could manage in any other way.'

Then Mrs Blake gave them facts and figures, showing how much clubhouses cost – and how little this arrangement would cost. 'Most women have very little money, I know,' she said, 'and they hate to spend it on themselves when they have; but even a little money from each goes a long way when it is put together. I fancy there are none of us so poor we could not squeeze out, say ten cents a week. For a hundred women that would be ten dollars. Could you feed a hundred tired women for ten dollars, Mrs Morrison?'

Mrs Morrison smiled cordially. 'Not on chicken pie,' she said. 'But I could give them tea and coffee, crackers and cheese for that, I think. And a quiet place to rest, and a reading room, and a place to hold meetings.'

Then Mrs Blake quite swept them off their feet by her wit and eloquence. She gave them to understand that if a share in the palatial accommodation of the Welcome House, and as good tea and coffee as old Sally made, with a place to meet, a place to rest, a place to talk, a place to lie down, could be had for ten cents a week each, she advised them to clinch the arrangement at once before Mrs Morrison's natural good sense had overcome her enthusiasm.

Before Mrs Isabelle Carter Blake had left, Haddleton had a large and eager women's club, whose entire expenses, outside of stationery and postage, consisted of ten cents a week *per capita*, paid to Mrs Morrison. Everybody belonged. It was open at once for charter members, and all pressed forward to claim that privileged place.

They joined by hundreds, and from each member came this tiny sum to Mrs Morrison each week. It was very little money, taken separately. But it added up with silent speed. Tea and coffee, purchased in bulk, crackers by the barrel, and whole cheeses – these are not expensive luxuries. The town was full of Mrs Morrison's ex-Sunday-school boys, who furnished her with the best they had – at cost. There was a good deal of work, a good deal of care, and room for the whole supply of Mrs

Morrison's diplomatic talent and experience. Saturdays found the Welcome House as full as it could hold, and Sundays found Mrs Morrison in bed. But she liked it.

A busy, hopeful year flew by, and then she went to Jean's for Thanksgiving.

The room Jean gave her was about the same size as her haven in Andrew's home, but one flight higher up, and with a sloping ceiling. Mrs Morrison whitened her dark hair upon it, and rubbed her head confusedly. Then she shook it with renewed determination.

The house was full of babies. There was little Joe, able to get about, and into everything. There were the twins, and there was the new baby. There was one servant, over-worked and cross. There was a small, cheap, totally inadequate nursemaid. There was Jean, happy but tired, full of joy, anxiety and affection, proud of her children, proud of her husband, and delighted to unfold her heart to her mother.

By the hour she babbled of their cares and hopes, while Mrs Morrison, tall and elegant, in her well-kept old black silk, sat holding the baby or trying to hold the twins. The old silk was pretty well finished by the week's end. Joseph talked to her also, telling her how well he was getting on, and how much he needed capital, urging her to come and stay with them; it was such a help to Jeannie; asking questions about the house.

There was no going visiting here. Jeannie could not leave the babies. And few visitors; all the little suburb being full of similarly overburdened mothers. Such as called found Mrs Morrison charming. What she found them, she did not say. She bade her daughter an affectionate good-bye when the week was up, smiling at their mutual contentment.

'Goodbye, my dear children,' she said. 'I am so glad for all your happiness. I am thankful for both of you.'

But she was more thankful to get home.

Mr Butts did not have to call for his interest this time, but he called none the less.

'How on earth'd you get it, Delia?' he demanded. 'Screwed it out o' these club-women?'

'Your interest is so moderate, Mr Butts, that it is easier to meet than you imagine,' was her answer. 'Do you know the average interest they charge in Colorado? The women vote there, you know.'

He went away with no more personal information than that; and no nearer approach to the twin goals of his desire than the passing of the year.

'One more year, Delia,' he said; 'then you'll have to give in.'

'One more year!' she said to herself, and took up her chosen task with renewed energy.

The financial basis of the undertaking was very simple, but it would never have worked so well under less skilful management. Five dollars a year these country women could not have faced, but ten cents a week was possible to the poorest. There was no difficulty in collecting, for they brought it themselves; no unpleasantness in receiving, for old Sally stood at the receipt of custom and presented the covered cash box when they came for their tea.

On the crowded Saturdays the great urns were set going, the mighty array of cups arranged in easy reach, the ladies filed by, each taking her refection and leaving her dime. Where the effort came was in enlarging the membership and keeping up the attendance; and this effort was precisely in the line of Mrs Morrison's splendid talents.

Serene, cheerful, inconspicuously active, planning like the born statesman she was, executing like a practical politician, Mrs Morrison gave her mind to the work, and thrived upon it. Circle within circle, and group within group, she set small classes and departments at work, having a boys' club by and by in the big room over the woodshed, girls' clubs, reading clubs, study clubs, little meetings of every sort that were not held in churches, and some that were – previously.

For each and all there was, if wanted, tea and coffee, crackers and cheese; simple fare, of unvarying excellence, and from each and all, into the little cashbox, ten cents for these refreshments. From the club members this came weekly; and the club members, kept up by a constant variety of interests, came every week. As to numbers, before the first six months was over The Haddleton Rest and Improvement Club numbered five hundred women.

Now, five hundred times ten cents a week is twenty-six hundred dollars a year. Twenty-six hundred dollars a year would not be very much to build or rent a large house, to furnish five hundred people with chairs, lounges, books and magazines, dishes and service; and with food and drink even of the simplest. But if you are miraculously supplied with a club-house, furnished, with a manager and servant on the spot, then that amount of money goes a long way.

On Saturdays Mrs Morrison hired two helpers for half a day, for half a dollar each. She stocked the library with many magazines for fifty dollars a year. She covered fuel, light, and small miscellanies with another hundred. And she fed her multitude with the plain viands agreed upon, at about four cents apiece.

For her collateral entertainments, her many visits, the various new expenses entailed, she paid as well; and yet at the end of the first year she had not only her interest, but a solid thousand dollars of clear profit. With a calm smile she surveyed it, heaped in neat stacks of bills in the small safe in the wall behind her bed. Even Sally did not know it was there.

The second season was better than the first. There were difficulties, excitements, even some opposition, but she rounded out the year triumphantly. 'After that,' she said to herself, 'they may have the deluge if they like.'

She made all expenses, made her interest, made a little extra cash, clearly her own, all over and above the second thousand dollars.

Then did she write to son and daughter, inviting them and their families to come home to Thanksgiving, and closing each letter with joyous pride: 'Here is the money to come with.'

They all came, with all the children and two nurses. There was plenty of room in the Welcome House, and plenty of food on the long mahogany table. Sally was as brisk as a bee, brilliant in scarlet and purple; Mrs Morrison carved her big turkey with queenly grace.

'I don't see that you're over-run with club women, mother,' said Jeannie.

'It's Thanksgiving, you know; they're all at home. I hope they are all as happy, as thankful for their homes as I am for mine,' said Mrs Morrison.

Afterward Mr Butts called. With dignity and calm unruffled, Mrs Morrison handed him his interest – and principal.

Mr Butts was almost loath to receive it, though his hand automatically grasped the crisp blue check.

'I didn't know you had a bank account,' he protested, somewhat dubiously.

'Oh, yes; you'll find the check will be honored, Mr Butts.'

'I'd like to know how you got this money. You *can't* 'a' skinned it out o' that club of yours.'

'I appreciate your friendly interest, Mr Butts; you have been most kind.'

'I believe some of these great friends of yours have lent it to you. You won't be any better off, I can tell you.'

'Come, come, Mr Butts! Don't quarrel with good money. Let us part friends.'

And they parted.

THE COTTAGETTE

'Why not?' said Mr Mathews. 'It is far too small for a house, too pretty for a hut, too – unusual – for a cottage.'

'Cottagette, by all means,' said Lois, seating herself on a porch chair. 'But it is larger than it looks, Mr Mathews. How do you like it, Malda?'

I was delighted with it. More than delighted. Here this tiny shell of fresh unpainted wood peeped out from under the trees, the only house in sight except the distant white specks on far off farms, and the little wandering village in the river-threaded valley. It sat right on the turf, – no road, no path even, and the dark woods shadowed the back windows.

'How about meals?' asked Lois.

'Not two minutes' walk,' he assured her, and showed us a little furtive path between the trees to the place where meals were furnished.

We discussed and examined and exclaimed, Lois holding her pongee skirts close about her – she needn't have been so careful, there wasn't a speck of dust, – and presently decided to take it.

Never did I know the real joy and peace of living, before that blessed summer at 'High Court.' It was a mountain place, easy enough to get to, but strangely big and still and far away when you were there.

The working basis of the establishment was an eccentric woman named Caswell, a sort of musical enthusiast, who had a summer school of music and the 'higher thought.' Malicious persons, not able to obtain accommodations there, called the place 'High C.'

I liked the music very well, and kept my thoughts to myself, both high and low, but 'The Cottagette' I loved unreservedly. It was so little and new and clean, smelling only of its fresh-planed boards – they hadn't even stained it.

There was one big room and two little ones in the tiny thing, though from the outside you wouldn't have believed it, it looked so small; but small as it was it harbored a miracle – a real bathroom with water piped from mountain springs. Our windows opened into the green shadiness, the soft brownness, the bird-inhabited quiet flower-starred woods. But in front we looked across whole counties – over a far-off river – into another state. Off and down and away – it was like sitting on the roof of something – something very big.

The grass swept up to the door-step, to the walls – only it wasn't just grass of course, but such a procession of flowers as I had never imagined could grow in one place.

You had to go quite a way through the meadow, wearing your own narrow faintly marked streak in the grass, to reach the town-connecting road below. But in the woods was a little path, clear and wide, by which we went to meals.

For we ate with the highly thoughtful musicians, and highly musical thinkers, in their central boarding-house nearby. They didn't call it a boarding-house, which is neither high nor musical; they called it 'The Calceolaria.' There was plenty of that growing about, and I didn't mind what they called it so long as the food was good – which it was, and the prices reasonable – which they were.

The people were extremely interesting – some of them at least; and all of them were better than the average of summer boarders.

But if there hadn't been any interesting ones it didn't matter while Ford Mathews was there. He was a newspaper man, or rather an ex-newspaper man, then becoming a writer for magazines, with books ahead.

He had friends at High Court – he liked music – he liked the place – and he liked us. Lois liked him too, as was quite natural. I'm sure I did.

He used to come up evenings and sit on the porch and talk.

He came daytimes and went on long walks with us. He established his workshop in a most attractive little cave not far beyond us, – the country there is full of rocky ledges and hollows, – and sometimes asked us over to an afternoon tea, made on a gipsy fire.

Lois was a good deal older than I, but not really old at all, and she didn't look her thirty-five by ten years. I never blamed her for not mentioning it, and I wouldn't have done so, myself, on any account. But I felt that together we made a safe and reasonable household. She played beautifully, and there was a piano in our big room. There were pianos in several other little cottages about – but too far off for any jar of sound. When the wind was right we caught little wafts of music now and then; but mostly it was still – blessedly still about us. And yet that Calceolaria was only two minutes off – and with raincoats and rubbers we never minded going to it.

We saw a good deal of Ford and I got interested in him, I couldn't help it. He was big. Not extra big in pounds and inches, but a man with big view and a grip – with purpose and real power. He was going to do things. I thought he was doing them now, but he didn't – this was all like cutting steps in the ice-wall, he said. It had to be done, but the road was long ahead. And he took an interest in my work too, which is unusual for a literary man.

Mine wasn't much. I did embroidery and made designs.

It is such pretty work! I like to draw from flowers and leaves and things about me; conventionalize them sometimes, and sometimes paint them just as they are, – in soft silk stitches.

All about up here were the lovely small things I needed; and not only these, but the lovely big things that make one feel so strong and able to do beautiful work.

Here was the friend I lived so happily with, and all this fairy land of sun and shadow, the free immensity of our view, and the dainty comfort of the Cottagette. We never had to think of ordinary things till the soft musical thrill of the Japanese gong stole through the trees, and we trotted off to the Calceolaria.

I think Lois knew before I did.

We were old friends and trusted each other, and she had had experience too.

'Malda,' she said, 'let us face this thing and be rational.' It was a strange thing that Lois should be so rational and yet so musical – but she was, and that was one reason I liked her so much.

'You are beginning to love Ford Mathews – do you know it?'

I said yes, I thought I was.

'Does he love you?'

That I couldn't say. 'It is early yet,' I told her. 'He is a man, he is about thirty I believe, he has seen more of life and probably loved before – it may be nothing more than friendliness with him.'

'Do you think it would be a good marriage?' she asked. We had often talked of love and marriage, and Lois had helped me to form my views – hers were very clear and strong.

'Why yes – if he loves me,' I said. 'He has told me quite a bit about his family, good western farming people, real Americans. He is strong and well – you can read clean living in his eyes and mouth.' Ford's eyes were as clear as a girl's, the whites of them were clear. Most men's eyes, when you look at them critically, are not like that. They may look at you very expressively, but when you look at them, just as features, they are not very nice.

I liked his looks, but I liked him better.

So I told her that as far as I knew it would be a good marriage – if it was one.

'How much do you love him?' she asked.

That I couldn't quite tell, – it was a good deal, – but I didn't think it would kill me to lose him.

'Do you love him enough to do something to win him – to really put yourself out somewhat for that purpose?'

'Why – yes – I think I do. If it was something I approved of. What do you mean?'

Then Lois unfolded her plan. She had been married, – unhappily married, in her youth; that was all over and done with years ago; she had told me about it long since; and she said she did not regret the pain and loss because it had given her experience. She had her maiden name again – and freedom. She was so fond of me she wanted to give me the benefit of her experience – without the pain.

'Men like music,' said Lois; 'they like sensible talk; they like beauty of course, and all that,—'

'Then they ought to like you!' I interrupted, and, as a matter of fact they did. I knew several who wanted to marry her, but she said 'once was enough.' I don't think they were 'good marriages' though.

'Don't be foolish, child,' said Lois, 'this is serious. What they care for most after all is domesticity. Of course they'll fall in love with anything; but what they want to marry is a home-maker. Now we are living here in an idyllic sort of way, quite conducive to falling in love, but no temptation to marriage. If I were you – if I really loved this man and wished to marry him, I would make a home of this place.'

'Make a home? – why it *is* a home. I never was so happy any-where in my life. What on earth do you mean, Lois?'

'A person might be happy in a balloon, I suppose,' she replied, 'but it wouldn't be a home. He comes here and sits talk-ing with us, and it's quiet and feminine and attractive – and then we hear that big gong at the Calceolaria, and off we go slopping through the wet woods – and the spell is broken. Now you can cook.' I could cook. I could cook excellently. My esteemed Nara had rigorously taught me every branch of what is now called 'domestic science;' and I had no objection to the work, except that it prevented my doing anything else. And one's hands are not so nice when one cooks and washes dishes, – I need nice hands for my needlework. But if it was a question of pleasing Ford Mathews—

Lois went on calmly. 'Miss Caswell would put on a kitchen for us in a minute, she said she would, you know, when we took the cottage. Plenty of people keep house up here, – we can if we want to.'

'But we don't want to,' I said, 'we never have wanted to. The very beauty of the place is that it never had any housekeeping about it. Still, as you say, it would be cosy on a wet night, we could have delicious little suppers, and have him stay—'

'He told me he had never known a home since he was eighteen,' said Lois.

That was how we came to install a kitchen in the Cottagette. The men put it up in a few days, just a lean-to with a window, a sink and two doors. I did the cooking. We had nice things, there is no denying that; good fresh milk and vegetables particularly, fruit is hard to get in the country, and meat too, still we managed nicely; the less you have the more you have to manage – it takes time and brains, that's all.

Lois likes to do housework, but it spoils her hands for practicing, so she can't; and I was perfectly willing to do it – it was all in the interest of my own heart. Ford certainly enjoyed it. He dropped in often, and ate things with undeniable relish. So I was pleased, though it did interfere with my work a good deal. I always work best in the morning; but of course housework has to be done in the morning too; and it is astonishing how much work there is in the littlest kitchen. You go in for a minute, and you see this thing and that thing and the other thing to be done, and your minute is an hour before you know it.

When I was ready to sit down the freshness of the morning was gone somehow. Before, when I woke up, there was only the clean wood smell of the house, and then the blessed out-of-doors: now I always felt the call of the kitchen as soon as I woke. An oil stove will smell a little, either in or out of the house; and soap, and – well you know if you cook in a bedroom how it makes the room feel differently? Our house had been only bedroom and parlor before.

We baked too – the baker's bread was really pretty poor, and Ford did enjoy my whole wheat, and brown, and especially hot rolls and gems. It was a pleasure to feed him, but it did heat up the house, and me. I never could work much – at my work – baking days. Then, when I did get to work, the people would come with things, – milk or meat or vegetables, or children with berries; and what distressed me most was the wheelmarks on our meadow. They soon made quite a road – they had to of course, but I hated it – I lost that lovely sense of being on the last edge and looking over – we were just a bead on a string like other houses. But it was quite true that I loved this man, and would do more than this to please him. We couldn't go off so freely on excursions as we used, either; when meals are to be prepared someone has to be there, and to take in things when they come. Sometimes Lois stayed in, she always asked to, but mostly I did. I couldn't let her spoil her summer on my account. And Ford certainly liked it.

He came so often that Lois said she thought it would look better if we had an older person with us; and that her mother could come if I wanted her, and she could help with the work of course. That seemed reasonable, and she came. I wasn't very fond of Lois's mother, Mrs Fowler, but it did seem a little conspicuous, Mr Mathews eating with us more than he did at the Calceolaria. There were others of course, plenty of them dropping in, but I didn't encourage it much, it made so much more work. They would come in to supper, and then we would have musical evenings. They offered to help me wash dishes, some of them, but a new hand in the kitchen is not much help, I preferred to do it myself; then I knew where the dishes were.

Ford never seemed to want to wipe dishes; though I often wished he would.

So Mrs Fowler came. She and Lois had one room, they had to, – and she really did a lot of the work, she was a very practical old lady.

Then the house began to be noisy. You hear another person in a kitchen more than you hear yourself, I think, – and the walls were only boards. She swept more than we did too. I don't think much sweeping is needed in a clean place like that; and she dusted all the time; which I know is unnecessary. I still did most of the cooking, but I could get off more to draw, out-of-doors; and to walk. Ford was in and out continually, and, it seemed to me, was really coming nearer. What was one summer of interrupted work, of noise and dirt and smell and constant meditation on what to eat next, compared to a lifetime of love? Besides – if he married me – I should have to do it always, and might as well get used to it.

Lois kept me contented, too, telling me nice things that Ford said about my cooking. 'He does appreciate it so,' she said.

One day he came around early and asked me to go up Hugh's Peak with him. It was a lovely climb and took all day. I demurred a little, it was Monday, Mrs Fowler thought it was cheaper to have a woman come and wash, and we did, but it certainly made more work.

'Never mind,' he said, 'what's washing day or ironing day or any of that old foolishness to us? This is walking day – that's what it is.' It was really, cool and sweet and fresh, – it had rained in the night, – and brilliantly clear.

'Come along!' he said. 'We can see as far as Patch Mountain I'm sure. There'll never be a better day.'

'Is anyone else going?' I asked.

'Not a soul. It's just us. Come.'

I came gladly, only suggesting – 'Wait, let me put up a lunch.'

'I'll wait just long enough for you to put on knickers and a short skirt,' said he. 'The lunch is all in the basket on my back. I know how long it takes for you women to "put up" sandwiches and things.'

We were off in ten minutes, light-footed and happy: and the day was all that could be asked. He brought a perfect lunch, too, and had made it all himself. I confess it tasted better to me than my own cooking; but perhaps that was the climb.

When we were nearly down we stopped by a spring on a broad ledge, and supped, making tea as he liked to do out-of-doors. We saw the round sun setting at one end of a world view, and the round moon rising at the other; calmly shining each on each.

And then he asked me to be his wife.—

We were very happy.

'But there's a condition!' said he all at once, sitting up straight and looking very fierce. 'You mustn't cook!'

'What!' said I. 'Mustn't cook?'

'No,' said he, 'you must give it up – for my sake.'

I stared at him dumbly.

'Yes, I know all about it,' he went on, 'Lois told me. I've seen a good deal of Lois – since you've taken to cooking. And since I would talk about you, naturally I learned a lot. She told me how you were brought up, and how strong your domestic instincts were – but bless your artist soul dear girl, you have some others!' Then he smiled rather queerly and murmured, 'surely in vain the net is spread in the sight of any bird.'

'I've watched you, dear, all summer;' he went on, 'it doesn't agree with you.

'Of course the things taste good – but so do my things! I'm a good cook myself. My father was a cook, for years – at good wages. I'm used to it you see.

'One summer when I was hard up I cooked for a living – and saved money instead of starving.'

'O ho!' said I, 'that accounts for the tea – and the lunch!'

'And lots of other things,' said he. 'But you haven't done half as much of your lovely work since you started this kitchen business, and – you'll forgive me, dear – it hasn't been as good. Your work is quite too good to lose; it is a beautiful and distinctive art, and I don't want you to let it go. What would you think of me if I gave up my hard long years of writing for the easy competence of a well-paid cook!'

I was still too happy to think very clearly. I just sat and looked at him. 'But you want to marry me?' I said.

'I want to marry you, Malda, – because I love you – because you are young and strong and beautiful – because you are wild and sweet and – fragrant, and – elusive, like the wild flowers you love. Because you are so truly an artist in your special way, seeing beauty and giving it to others. I love you because of all this, because you are rational and high-minded and capable of friendship, – and in spite of your cooking!'

'But – how do you want to live?'

'As we did here – at first,' he said. 'There was peace, exquisite silence. There was beauty – nothing but beauty. There were the dean wood odors and flowers and fragrances and sweet wild wind. And there was you – your fair self, always delicately dressed, with white firm fingers sure of touch in delicate true work. I loved you then. When you took to cooking it jarred on me. I have been a cook, I tell you, and I know what it is. I hated it – to see my wood-flower in a kitchen. But Lois told me about how you were brought up to it and loved it, and I said to myself, "I love this woman; I will wait and see if I love her even as a cook." And I do, Darling: I withdraw the condition. I will love you always, even if you insist on being my cook for life!'

'O I don't insist!' I cried. 'I don't want to cook – I want to draw! But I thought – Lois said – How she has misunderstood you!'

'It is not true, always, my dear,' said he, 'that the way to a man's heart is through his stomach; at least it's not the only way. Lois doesn't know everything, she is young yet! And perhaps for my sake you can give it up. Can you sweet?'

Could I? Could I? Was there ever a man like this?

WHEN I WAS A WITCH

If I had understood the terms of that one-sided contract with Satan, the Time of Witching would have lasted longer – you may be sure of that. But how was I to tell? It just happened, and has never happened again, though I've tried the same preliminaries as far as I could control them.

The thing began all of a sudden, one October midnight – the 30th, to be exact. It had been hot, really hot, all day, and was sultry and thunderous in the evening; no air stirring, and the whole house stewing with that ill-advised activity which always seems to move the steam radiator when it isn't wanted.

I was in a state of simmering rage – hot enough, even without the weather and the furnace – and I went up on the roof to cool off. A top-floor apartment has that advantage, among others – you can take a walk without the mediation of an elevator boy!

There are things enough in New York to lose one's temper over at the best of times, and on this particular day they seemed to all happen at once, and some fresh ones. The night before, cats and dogs had broken my rest, of course. My morning paper was more than usually mendacious, and my neighbor's morning paper – more visible than my own as I went down town – was more than usually salacious. My cream wasn't cream – my egg was a relic of the past. My 'new' napkins were giving out.

Being a woman, I'm supposed not to swear; but when the motorman disregarded my plain signal, and grinned as he rushed by; when the subway guard waited till I was just about to step on board and then slammed the door in my face – standing behind it calmly for some minutes before the bell rang to warrant his closing – I desired to swear like a mule-driver.

At night it was worse. The way people paw one's back in the crowd! The cow-puncher who packs the people in or jerks them out – the men who smoke and spit, law or no law – the women whose saw-edged cart-wheel hats, swashing feathers and deadly pins, add so to one's comfort inside.

Well, as I said, I was in a particularly bad temper, and went up on the roof to cool off. Heavy black clouds hung low overhead, and lightning flickered threateningly here and there.

A starved, black cat stole from behind a chimney and mewed dolefully. Poor thing! She had been scalded.

The street was quiet for New York. I leaned over a little and looked up and down the long parallels of twinkling lights. A belated cab drew near, the horse so tired he could hardly hold his head up.

Then the driver, with a skill born of plenteous practice, flung out his long-lashed whip and curled it under the poor beast's belly with a stinging cut that made me shudder. The horse shuddered too, poor wretch, and jingled his harness with an effort at a trot.

I leaned over the parapet and watched that man with a spirit of unmitigated ill-will.

'I wish,' said I, slowly – and I did wish it with all my heart 'that every person who strikes or otherwise hurts a horse unnecessarily, shall feel the pain intended – and the horse not feel it!'

It did me good to say it, anyhow, but I never expected any result. I saw the man swing his great whip again, and lay on heartily. I saw him throw up his hands – heard him scream – but I never thought what the matter was, even then.

The lean, black cat, timid but trustful, rubbed against my skirt and mewed.

'Poor Kitty', I said; 'Poor Kitty! It is a shame!' And I thought tenderly of all the thousands of hungry, hunted cats who stink and suffer in a great city.

Later, when I tried to sleep, and up across the stillness rose the raucous shrieks of some of these same sufferers, my pity turned cold. 'Any fool that will try to keep a cat in a city!' I muttered, angrily.

Another yell – a pause – an ear-torturing, continuous cry. 'I wish,' I burst forth, 'that every cat in the city was comfortably dead!'

A sudden silence fell, and in course of time I got to sleep.

Things went fairly well next morning, till I tried another egg. They were expensive eggs, too.

'I can't help it!' said my sister, who keeps house.

'I know you can't,' I admitted. 'But somebody could help it. I wish the people who are responsible had to eat their old eggs, and never get a good one till they sold good ones!'

'They'd stop eating eggs, that's all,' said my sister, 'and eat meat.'

'Let 'em eat meat!' I said, recklessly. 'The meat is as bad as the eggs! It's so long since we've had a clean, fresh chicken that I've forgotten how they taste!'

'It's cold storage,' said my sister. She is a peaceable sort; I'm not.

'Yes, cold storage!' I snapped. 'It ought to be a blessing – to tide over shortages, equalize supplies, and lower prices. What does it do? Corner the market, raise prices the year round, and make all the food bad!'

My anger rose. 'If there was any way of getting at them!' I cried. 'The law don't touch 'em. They need to be cursed somehow! I'd like to do it! I wish the whole crowd that profit by this vicious business might taste their bad meat, their old fish, their stale milk – whatever they ate. Yes, and feel the prices as we do!'

'They couldn't you know; they're rich,' said my sister.

'I know that,' I admitted, sulkily. 'There's no way of getting at 'em. But I wish they could. And I wish they knew how people hated 'em, and felt that, too – till they mended their ways!'

When I left for my office I saw a funny thing. A man who drove a garbage cart took his horse by the bits and jerked and wrenched brutally. I was amazed to see him clap his hands to his own jaws with a moan, while the horse philosophically licked his chops and looked at him.

The man seemed to resent his expression, and struck him on the head, only to rub his own poll and swear amazedly, looking around to see who had hit him. The horse advanced a step, stretching a hungry nose toward a garbage pail crowned with cabbage leaves, and the man, recovering his sense of proprietorship, swore at him and kicked him in the ribs. That time he had to sit down, turning pale and weak. I watched with growing wonder and delight.

A market wagon came clattering down the street; the

hard-faced young ruffian fresh for his morning task. He gathered the ends of the reins and brought them down on the horse's back with a resounding thwack. The horse did not notice this at all, but the boy did. He yelled!

I came to a place where many teamsters were at work hauling dirt and crushed stone. A strange silence and peace hung over the scene where usually the sound of the lash and sight of brutal blows made me hurry by. The men were talking together a little, and seemed to be exchanging notes. It was too good to be true. I gazed and marvelled, waiting for my car.

It came, merrily running along. It was not full. There was one not far ahead, which I had missed in watching the horses; there was no other near it in the rear.

Yet the coarse-faced person in authority who ran it, went gaily by without stopping, though I stood on the track almost, and waved my umbrella.

A hot flush of rage surged to my face. 'I wish you felt the blow you deserve,' said I, viciously, looking after the car. 'I wish you'd have to stop, and back to here, and open the door and apologize. I wish that would happen to all of you, every time you play that trick.'

To my infinite amazement, that car stopped and backed till the front door was before me. The motorman opened it, holding his hand to his cheek. 'Beg your pardon, madam!' he said.

I passed in, dazed, overwhelmed. Could it be? Could it possibly be that – that what I wished came true. The idea sobered me, but I dismissed it with a scornful smile. 'No such luck!' said I.

Opposite me sat a person in petticoats. She was of a sort I particularly detest. No real body of bones and muscles, but the contours of grouped sausages. Complacent, gaudily dressed, heavily wigged and ratted, with powder and perfume and flowers and jewel – and a dog.

A poor, wretched, little, artificial dog – alive, but only so by virtue of man's insolence; not a real creature that God made. And the dog had clothes on – and a bracelet! His fitted jacket had a pocket – and a pocket-handkerchief! He looked sick and unhappy.

I meditated on his pitiful position, and that of all the other poor chained prisoners, leading unnatural lives of enforced celibacy, cut off from sunlight, fresh air, the use of their limbs; led forth at stated intervals by unwilling servants, to defile our streets; over-fed, under-exercised, nervous and unhealthy.

'And we say we love them!' said I, bitterly to myself 'No wonder they bark and howl and go mad. No wonder they have almost as many diseases as we do! I wish—' Here the thought I had dismissed struck me again. 'I wish that all the unhappy dogs in cities would die at once!'

I watched the sad-eyed little invalid across the car. He dropped his head and died. She never noticed it till she got off; then she made fuss enough.

The evening papers were full of it. Some sudden pestilence had struck both dogs and cats, it would appear. Red headlines struck the eye, big letters, and columns were filled out of the complaints of those who had lost their 'pets', of the sudden labors of the board of health, and interviews with doctors.

All day, as I went through the office routine, the strange sense of this new power struggled with reason and common knowledge. I even tried a few furtive test 'wishes' – wished that the waste basket would fall over, that the inkstand would fill itself; but they didn't.

I dismissed the idea as pure foolishness, till I saw those newspapers, and heard people telling worse stories.

One thing I decided at once – not to tell a soul. 'Nobody'd believe me if I did,' said I to myself 'And I won't give 'em the chance. I've scored on cats and dogs, anyhow – and horses.'

As I watched the horses at work that afternoon, and thought of all their unknown sufferings from crowded city stables, bad air and insufficient food, and from the wearing strain of asphalt pavements in wet and icy weather, I decided to have another try on horses.

'I wish,' said I, slowly and carefully, but with a fixed intensity of purposes, 'that every horse owner, keeper, hirer and driver or rider, might feel what the horse feels, when he suffers at our hands. Feel it keenly and constantly till the case is mended.'

I wasn't able to verify this attempt for some time; but the effect was so general that it got widely talked about soon, and this 'new wave of humane feeling' soon raised the status of horses in our city. Also it diminished their numbers. People began to prefer motor drays – which was a mighty good thing.

Now I felt pretty well assured in my own mind, and kept my assurance to myself. Also I began to make a list of my cherished grudges, with a fine sense of power and pleasure.

'I must be careful,' I said to myself; 'very careful; and, above all things, make the punishment fit the crime.'

The subway crowding came to my mind next; both the people who crowd because they have to, and the people who make them. 'I mustn't punish anybody, for what they can't help,' I mused. 'But when it's pure meanness!' Then I bethought me of the remote stockholders, of the more immediate directors, of the painfully prominent officials and insolent employees – and got to work.

'I might as well make a good job of it while this lasts,' said I to myself 'It's quite a responsibility, but lots of fun.' And I wished that every person responsible for the condition of our subways might be mysteriously compelled to ride up and down in them continuously during rush hours.

This experiment I watched with keen interest, but for the life of me I could see little difference. There were a few more well-dressed persons in the crowds, that was all. So I came to the conclusion that the general public was mostly to blame, and carried their daily punishment without knowing it.

For the insolent guards and cheating ticket-sellers who give you short change, very slowly, when you are dancing on one foot and your train is there, I merely wished that they might feel the pain their victims would like to give them, short of real injury. They did, I guess.

Then I wished similar things for all manner of corporations and officials. It worked. It worked amazingly. There was a sudden conscientious revival all over the country. The dry bones rattled and sat up. Boards of directors, having troubles enough of their own, were aggravated by innumerable communications from suddenly sensitive stockholders.

In mills and mints and railroads, things began to mend. The country buzzed. The papers fattened. The churches sat up and took credit to themselves. I was incensed at this, and, after brief consideration, wished that every minister would preach to his congregation exactly what he believed and what he thought of them.

I went to six services the next Sunday – about ten minutes each, for two sessions. It was most amusing. A thousand pulpits were emptied forthwith, refilled, re-emptied, and so on, from week to week. People began to go to church; men largely –

women didn't like it as well. They had always supposed the ministers thought more highly of them than now appeared to be the case.

One of my oldest grudges was against the sleeping-car people; and now I began to consider them. How often I had grinned and borne it – with other thousands submitting helplessly.

Here is a railroad – a common carrier – and you have to use it. You pay for your transportation, a good round sum.

Then if you wish to stay in the sleeping car during the day, they charge you another two dollars and a half for the privilege of sitting there, whereas you have paid for a seat when you bought your ticket. That seat is now sold to another person – twice sold! Five dollars for twenty-four hours in a space six feet by three by three at night, and one seat by day; twenty-four of these privileges to a car – $120 a day for the rent of the car – and the passengers to pay the porter besides. That makes $44,800 a year.

Sleeping cars are expensive to build, they say. So are hotels; but they do not charge at such a rate. Now, what could I do to get even? Nothing could ever put back the dollars into the millions of pockets; but it might be stopped now, this beautiful process.

So I wished that all persons who profited by this performance might feel a shame so keen that they would make public avowal and apology, and, as partial restitution, offer their wealth to promote the cause of free railroads!

Then I remembered parrots. This was lucky, for my wrath flamed again. It was really cooling, as I tried to work out responsibility and adjust penalties. But parrots! Any person who wants to keep a parrot should go and live on an island alone with their preferred conversationalist!

There was a huge, squawky parrot right across the street from me, adding its senseless, rasping cries to the more necessary evils of other noises.

I had also an aunt with a parrot. She was a wealthy, ostentatious person, who had been an only child and inherited her money.

Uncle Joseph hated the yelling bird, but that didn't make any difference to Aunt Mathilda.

I didn't like this aunt, and wouldn't visit her, lest she think I was truckling for the sake of her money; but after I had wished this time, I called at the time set for my curse to work; and it did work with a vengeance. There sat poor Uncle Joe, looking thinner and meeker than ever, and my aunt, like an overripe plum, complacent enough.

'Let me out!' said Polly, suddenly. 'Let me out to take a walk!'

'The clever thing!' said Aunt Mathilda. 'He never said that before.'

She let him out. Then he flapped up on the chandelier and sat among the prisms, quite safe.

'What an old pig you are, Mathilda!' said the parrot.

She started to her feet – naturally.

'Born a Pig trained a Pig – a Pig by nature and education!' said the parrot. 'Nobody'd put up with you, except for your money; unless it's this long-suffering husband of yours. He wouldn't, if he hadn't the patience of Job!'

'Hold your tongue!' screamed Aunt Mathilda. 'Come down from there! Come here!'

Polly cocked his head and jingled the prisms. 'Sit down, Mathilda!' he said, cheerfully. You've got to listen. You are fat and homely and selfish. You are a nuisance to everybody about you. You have got to feed me and take care of me better than ever – and you've got to listen to me when I talk. Pig!'

I visited another person with a parrot the next day. She put a cloth over his cage when I came in.

'Take it off!' said Polly. She took it off.

'Won't you come into the other room?' she asked me, nervously.

'Better stay here!' said her pet. 'Sit still – sit still!'

She sat still.

'Your hair is mostly false,' said pretty Poll. 'And your teeth – and your outlines. You eat too much. You are lazy. You ought to exercise, and don't know enough. Better apologize to this lady for backbiting! You've got to listen.'

The trade in parrots fell off from that day; they say there is no call for them. But the people who kept parrots, keep them yet – parrots live a long time.

Bores were a class of offenders against whom I had long borne undying enmity. Now I rubbed my hands and began on them, with this simple wish: that every person whom they bored should tell them the plain truth.

There is one man whom I have specially in mind. He was blackballed at a pleasant club, but continues to go there. He isn't a member – he just goes; and no one does anything to him.

It was very funny after this. He appeared that very night at a meeting, and almost every person present asked him how he came there. 'You're not a member, you know,' they said. 'Why do you butt in? Nobody likes you.'

Some were more lenient with him. 'Why don't you learn to be more considerate of others, and make some real friends?' they said. 'To have a few friends who do enjoy your visits ought to be pleasanter than being a public nuisance.'

He disappeared from that club, anyway.

I began to feel very cocky indeed.

In the food business there was already a marked improvement; and in transportation. The hubbub of reformation waxed louder daily, urged on by the unknown sufferings of all the profiters by iniquity.

The papers thrived on all this; and as I watched the loud-voiced protestations of my pet abomination in journalism, I had a brilliant idea, literally.

Next morning I was down town early, watching the men open their papers. My abomination was shamefully popular, and never more so than this morning. Across the top was printing in gold letters:

All intentional lies, in adv., editorial, news, or any other column . . . Scarlet

All malicious matter . . . Crimson

All careless or ignorant mistakes . . . Pink

All for direct self-interest of owner . . . Dark green

All mere bait – to sell the paper . . . Bright green

All advertising, primary or secondary . . . Brown

All sensational and salacious matter . . . Yellow

All hired hypocrisy . . . Purple

Good fun, instruction and entertainment . . . Blue

True and necessary news and honest editorials . . . Ordinary print

You never saw such a crazy quilt of a paper. They were bought like hot cakes for some days; but the real business fell off very soon. They'd have stopped it all if they could; but the papers looked all right when they came off the press. The color scheme flamed out only to the bona-fide reader.

I let this work for about a week, to the immense joy of all the other papers; and then turned it on to them, all at once. Newspaper reading became very exciting for a little, but the trade fell off. Even newspaper editors could not keep on feeding a market like that. The blue printed and ordinary printed matter grew from column to column and page to page. Some papers – small, to be sure, but refreshing began to appear in blue and black alone.

This kept me interested and happy for quite a while; so much so that I quite forgot to be angry at other things. There was such a change in all kinds of business, following the mere printing of truth in the newspapers. It began to appear as if we had lived in a sort of delirium – not really knowing the facts about anything. As soon as we really knew the facts, we began to behave very differently, of course.

What really brought all my enjoyment to an end was women. Being a woman, I was naturally interested in them, and could see some things more clearly than men could. I saw their real power, their real dignity, their real responsibility in the world; and then the way they dress and behave used to make me fairly frantic. 'Twas like seeing archangels playing jack-straws – or real horses only used as rocking-horses. So I determined to get after them.

How to manage it! What to hit first! Their hats, their ugly, inane, outrageous hats – that is what one thinks of first. Their silly, expensive clothes – their diddling beads and jewelry – their greedy childishness – mostly of the women provided for by rich men.

Then I thought of all the other women, the real ones, the vast majority, patiently doing the work of servants without even a servant's pay – and neglecting the noblest duties of mother-hood in favor of house-service; the greatest power on earth, blind, chained, untaught, in a treadmill. I thought of what they might do, compared to what they did do, and my heart swelled with something that was far from anger.

Then I wished – with all my strength – that women, all women, might realize Womanhood at last; its power and pride and place in life; that they might see their duty as mothers of the world – to love and care for everyone alive; that they might see their duty to men – to choose only the best, and then to bear and rear better ones; that they might see their duty as human beings, and come right out into full life and work and happiness!

I stopped, breathless, with shining eyes. I waited, trembling, for things to happen.

Nothing happened.

You see, this magic which had fallen on me was black magic – and I had wished white.

It didn't work at all, and, what was worse, it stopped all the other things that were working so nicely.

Oh, if I had only thought to wish permanence for those lovely punishments! If only I had done more while I could do it, had half appreciated my privileges when I was a Witch!

AN HONEST WOMAN

'There's an honest woman if ever there was one!' said the young salesman to the old one, watching their landlady whisk inside the screen door and close it softly without letting in a single fly – those evergreen California flies not mentioned by real estate men.

'What makes you think so?' asked Mr Burdock, commonly known as 'Old Burdock,' wriggling forward, with alternate jerks, the two hind legs which supported his chair, until its backward tilt was positively dangerous.

'Think!' said young Abramsonwith extreme decision, 'I happen to know. I've put up here for three years past, twice a year; and I know a lot of people in this town – sell to 'em right along.'

'Stands well in the town, does she?' inquired the other with no keen interest. He had put up at the Main House for eight years, and furthermore he knew Mrs Main when she was a child; but he did not mention it. Mr Burdock made no pretense of virtue, yet if he had one in especial it lay in the art of not saying things.

'I should say she does!' the plump young man replied, straightening his well-curved waistcoat. 'None better. She hasn't a bill standing – settles the day they come in. Pays cash for everything she can. She must make a handsome thing of this house; but it don't go in finery – she's as plain as a hen.'

'Why, I should call Mrs Main rather a good-looking woman,' Burdock gently protested.

'Oh yes, good-looking enough; but I mean her style – no show – no expense – no dress. But she keeps up the house all right – everything first class, and reasonable prices. She's got good money in the bank they tell me. And there's a daughter – away at school somewhere – won't have her brought up in a hotel. She's dead right, too.'

'I dunno why a girl couldn't grow up in a hotel – with a nice mother like that,' urged Mr Burdock.

'Oh come! You know better 'n that. Get talked about in any case – probably worse. No sir! You can't be too careful about a girl, and her mother knows it.'

'Glad you've got a high opinion of women. I like to see it,' and Mr Burdock tilted softly backward and forward in his chair, a balancing foot thrust forth. He wore large, square-toed, rather thin shoes with the visible outlines of feet in them.

The shoes of Mr Abramson, on the other hand, had pronounced outlines of their own, and might have been stuffed with anything – that would go in.

'I've got a high opinion of good women,' he announced with finality. 'As to bad ones, the less said the better!' and he puffed his strong cigar, looking darkly experienced.

'They're doin' a good deal towards reformin' 'em, nowadays, ain't they?' ventured Mr Burdock.

The young man laughed disagreeably. 'You can't reform

spilled milk,' said he. 'But I do like to see an honest, hard-working woman succeed.'

'So do I, boy,' said his companion, 'so do I,' and they smoked in silence.

The hotel bus drew up before the house, backed up creakingly, and one passenger descended, bearing a large, lean suitcase showing much wear. He was an elderly man, tall, well-built, but not well-carried; and wore a long, thin beard. Mr Abramson looked him over, decided that he was neither a buyer nor a seller, and dismissed him from his mind.

Mr Burdock looked him over and brought the front legs of his chair down with a thump.

'By Heck!' said he softly.

The newcomer went in to register. Mr Burdock went in to buy another cigar.

Mrs Main was at the desk alone, working at her books. Her smooth, dark hair curved away from a fine forehead, both broad and high; wide-set, steady gray eyes looked out from under level brows with a clear directness. Her mouth, at thirty-eight, was a little hard.

The tall man scarcely looked at her, as he reached for the register book; but she looked at him, and her color slowly heightened. He signed his name as one of considerable importance, 'Mr Alexander E. Main, Guthrie, Oklahoma.'

'I want a sunny room,' he said. 'A south room, with a fire when I want it. I feel the cold in this climate very much.'

'You always did,' remarked Mrs Main quietly.

Then he looked; the pen dropping from his fingers and rolling across the untouched page, making a dotted path of lessening blotches.

Mr Burdock made himself as small as he could against the

cigar stand, but she ruthlessly approached, sold him the cigar he selected, and waited calmly till he started out, the tall man still staring.

Then she turned to him.

'Here is your key,' she said. 'Joe, take the gentleman's grip.'

The boy moved off with the worn suitcase, but the tall man leaned over the counter towards her.

Mr Burdock was carefully closing the screen door – so carefully that he could still hear.

'Why Mary! Mary! I must see you,' the man whispered.

'You may see me at any time,' she answered quietly. 'Here is my office.'

'This evening!' he said excitedly. 'I'll come down this evening when it's quiet. I have so much to tell you, Mary.'

'Very well,' she said. 'Room 27, Joe,' and turned away.

Mr Burdock took a walk, his cigar still unlighted.

'By Heck!' said he. 'By – Heck! – And she as cool as a cucumber – That confounded old skeezicks! – Hanged if I don't happen to be passin'.'

A sturdy, long-legged little girl was Mary Cameron when he first did business with her father in a Kansas country store. Ranch born and bred, a vigorous, independent child, gravely selling knives and sewing silk, writing paper and potatoes 'to help father.'

Father was a freethinker – a man of keen, strong mind, scant education, and opinions which ran away with him. He trained her to think for herself, and she did; to act up to her beliefs, and she did; to worship liberty and the sacred rights of the individual, and she did.

But the store failed, as the ranch had failed before it. Perhaps 'old man Cameron's' arguments were too hot for the store loafers; perhaps his free thinking scandalized them. When Burdock saw Mary again, she was working in a San Francisco restaurant. She did not remember him in the least; but he knew one of her friends there and learned of the move to California – the orange failure, the grape failure, the unexpected death of Mr Cameron, and Mary's self-respecting efficiency since.

'She's doin' well already – got some money ahead – and she's just as straight!' said Miss Josie. 'Want to meet her?'

'Oh no,' said Mr Burdock, who was of a retiring disposition 'No, she wouldn't remember me at all.'

When he happened into that restaurant again a year later, Mary had gone, and her friend hinted dark things.

'She got to goin' with a married man!' she confided. 'Man from Oklahoma – name o' Main. One o' these Healers – great man for talkin'. She's left here, and I don't know where she is.'

Mr Burdock was sorry, very sorry – not only because he knew Mary, but because he knew Mr Main. First – where had he met that man first? When he was a glib young phrenologist in Cincinnati. Then he'd run against him in St Louis – a palmist this time, and then in Topeka – 'Dr Alexander,' some sort of an 'opaththist.' Dr Main's system of therapy varied, it appeared, with circumstances; he treated brains or bones as it happened, and here in San Francisco had made quite a hit; had lectured, had written a book on sex.

That Mary Cameron, with her hard sense and high courage, should take up with a man like that!

But Mr Burdock continued to travel, and some four years later, coming to a new hotel in San Diego, he had found Mary again, now Mrs Mary Main, presiding over the affairs of the house, with a small daughter going to school sedately.

Nothing did he say, to or about her; she was closely attending to her business, and he attended to his; but the next time he was in Cincinnati he had no difficulty in hearing of Mrs Alexander Main – and her three children – in very poor circumstances indeed.

Of Main he had heard nothing for many years – till now.

He returned to the hotel, and walked near the side window of the office. No one there yet. Selecting chewing gum for solace, as tobacco might betray him, he deliberately tucked a camp stool under the shadow of the overhanging rose bush and sat there, somewhat thornily, but well hidden.

'It's none o' my business, but I mean to get the rights o' this,' said Mr Burdock.

She came in about a quarter of ten, as neat, as plain, as quiet as ever, and sat down under the light with her sewing. Many pretty things Mrs Main made lovingly, but never wore.

She stopped after a little, folded her strong hands in her lap, and looking straight before her.

'If I could only see what she's looking at, I'd get the hang of it,' thought Mr Burdock, occasionally peering.

What she was looking at was a woman's life – and she studied it calmly and with impartial justice.

A fearless, independent girl, fond of her father but recognizing his weaknesses, she had taken her life in her own hands at about the age of twenty, finding in her orphanhood mainly freedom. Her mother she hardly remembered. She was not attractive to such youths as she met in the course of business, coldly repellent to all casual advances, and determined inwardly not to marry, at least not till she had made something of herself. She had worked hard, kept her health, saved money, and read much of the 'progressive literature' her father loved.

Then came this man who also read – studied – thought; who felt as she felt, who shared her aspirations, who 'understood her.' (Quite possibly he did – he was a person of considerable experience.)

Slowly she grew to enjoy his society, to depend upon it. When he revealed himself as lonely, not over-strong, struggling with the world, she longed to help him; and when, at last, in a burst of bitter confidence, he had said he must leave her, that she had made life over for him but that he must tear himself away, that she was life and hope to him, but he was not free – she demanded the facts.

He told her a sad tale, seeming not to cast blame on any but himself; but the girl burned deep and hot with indignation at the sordid woman, older than he, who had married him in his inexperienced youth, drained him of all he could earn, blasted his ideals, made his life an unbearable desert waste. She had – but no, he would not blacken her who had been his wife.

'She gives me no provable cause for divorce,' he told her. 'She will not loosen her grip. I have left her, but she will not let me go.'

'Were there any – children?' she asked after a while.

'There was one little girl—' he said with a pathetic pause. She died—'

He did not feel it necessary to mention that there were three little boys – who had lived, after a fashion.

Then Mary Cameron made a decision which was more credit to her heart than to her head, though she would have warmly denied such a criticism.

'I see no reason why your life – your happiness – your service to the community – should all be ruined and lost because you were foolish as a boy.'

'I was,' he groaned. 'I fell under temptation. Like any other sinner, I must bear my punishment. There is no escape.'

'Nonsense.' said Mary. 'She will not let you go. You will not live with her. You cannot marry me. But I can be your wife – if you want me to.'

It was nobly meant. She cheerfully risked all, gave up all, to make up to him for his 'ruined life'; to give some happiness to one so long unhappy; and when he vowed that he would not take advantage of such sublime unselfishness, she said that it was not in the least unselfish – for she loved him. This was true – she was quite honest about it.

And he? It is perfectly possible that he entered into their 'sacred compact' with every intention of respecting it. She made him happier than anyone else ever had, so far.

There were two happy years when Mr and Mrs Main – they took themselves quite seriously – lived in their little flat together and worked and studied and thought great thoughts for the advancement of humanity. Also there was a girl child born, and their contentment was complete.

But in time the income earned by Mr Main fell away more and more; till Mrs Main went forth again and worked in a hotel, as efficient as ever, and even more attractive.

Then he had become restless and had gone to Seattle to look for employment – a long search, with only letters to fill the void.

And then – the quiet woman's hands were clenched together till the nails were purple and white – then The Letter came.

She was sitting alone that evening, the child playing on the floor. The woman who looked after her in the daytime had gone home. The two 'roomers' who nearly paid the rent were out. It was a still, soft evening.

She had not had a letter for a week – and was hungry for it. She kissed the envelope – where his hand had rested. She squeezed it tight in her hands – laid her cheek on it – pressed it to her heart.

The baby reached up and wanted to share in the game. She gave her the envelope.

He was not coming back – ever . . . It was better that she should know at once . . . She was a capable woman – independent – he need not worry about her in that way . . . They had been mistaken . . . He had found one that was more truly his . . . She had been a Great Boon to him . . . Here was some money for the child . . . Good-bye.

She sat there, still, very still, staring straight before her, till the child reached up with a little cry.

Then she caught that baby in her arms, and fairly crushed her with passionate caresses till the child cried in good earnest and had to be comforted. Stony-eyed, the mother soothed and rocked her till she slept, and laid her carefully in her little crib. Then she stood up and faced it.

'I suppose I am a ruined woman,' she said.

She went to the glass and lit the gas on either side, facing herself with fixed gaze and adding calmly, 'I don't look it!'

She did not look it. Tall, strong, nobly built, softer and richer for her years of love, her happy motherhood; the woman she saw in the glass seemed as one at the beginning of a splendid life, not at the end of a bad one.

No one could ever know all that she thought and felt that night, bracing her broad shoulders to meet this unbelievable blow.

If he had died she could have borne it better; if he had disappeared she would at least have had her memories left. But now she had not only grief but shame. She had been a fool – a plain, ordinary, old-fashioned, girl fool, just like so many others she had despised. And now?

Under the shock and torture of her shattered life, the brave, practical soul of her struggled to keep its feet, to stand erect. She was not a demonstrative woman. Possibly he had never known how much she loved him, how utterly her life had grown to lean on his.

This thought struck her suddenly and she held her head higher. 'Why should he ever know?' she said to herself, and then, 'At least I have the child!' Before that night was over her plans were made.

The money he had sent, which her first feeling was to tear and burn, she now put carefully aside. 'He sent it for the child,' she said. 'She will need it.' She sublet the little flat and sold the furniture to a young couple, friends of hers, who were looking for just such a quiet home. She bought a suit of mourning, not too cumbrous, and set forth with little Mollie for the South.

In that fair land to which so many invalids come too late, it is not hard to find incompetent women, widowed and penniless, struggling to make a business of the only art they know – emerging from the sheltered harbor of 'keeping house' upon the troubled sea of 'keeping boarders.'

Accepting moderate terms because of the child, doing good work because of long experience, offering a friendly sympathy out of her own deep sorrow, Mrs Main made herself indispensable to such a one.

When her new employer asked her about her husband, she would press her handkerchief to her eyes and say, 'He has left me. I cannot bear to speak of him.'

This was quite true.

In a year she had saved a little money, and had spent it for a ticket home for the bankrupt lady of the house, who gladly gave her 'the goodwill of the business' for it.

Said goodwill was lodged in an angry landlord, a few discontented and largely delinquent boarders, and many unpaid tradesmen. Mrs Main called a meeting of her creditors in the stiff boarding house parlor.

She said, 'I have bought this business, such as it is, with practically my last cent. I have worked seven years in restaurants and hotels and know how to run this place better than it has been done so far. If you people will give me credit for six months, and then, if I make good, for six months more, I will assume these back debts – and pay them. Otherwise I shall have to leave here, and you will get nothing but what will come from a forced sale of this third-hand furniture. I shall work hard, for I have this fatherless child to work for.' She had the fatherless child at her side – a pretty thing, about three years old.

They looked the house over, looked her over, talked a little with the boarder of longest standing, and took up her offer.

She made good in six months; at the end of the year had begun to pay debts; and now—

Mrs Main drew a long breath and came back to the present.

Mollie, dear Mollie, was a big girl now, doing excellently well at a good school. The Main House was an established success – had been for years. She had some money laid up – for Mollie's college expenses. Her health was good, she liked her work, she was respected and esteemed in the town, a useful member of a liberal church, of the Progressive Woman's Club, of the City Improvement Association. She had won Comfort, Security, and Peace.

His step on the stairs – restrained – uncertain – eager.

Her door was open. He came in and closed it softly behind him. She rose and opened it.

'That door stands open,' she said. 'You need not worry. There's no one about.'

'Not many, at any rate,' thought the unprincipled Burdock.

She sat down again quietly. He wanted to kiss her, to take her in his arms; but she moved back to her seat with a decided step, and motioned him to his.

'You wanted to speak to me, Mr Main. What about?'

Then he poured forth his heart as he used to, in a flow of strong, convincing words.

He told of his wanderings, his struggles, his repeated failures; of the misery that had overwhelmed him in his last fatal mistake.

'I deserve it all,' he said with the quick smile and lift of the head that once was so compelling. 'I deserve everything that has come to me . . . Once to have had you . . . and to be so blind a fool as to let go your hand! I needed it, Mary, I needed it.'

He said little of his intermediate years as to facts; much as to the waste of woe they represented.

'Now I am doing better in my business,' he said. 'I have an established practice in Guthrie, but my health is not good and I have been advised to come to a warmer climate at least for a while.'

She said nothing but regarded him with a clear and steady eye. He seemed an utter stranger, and an unattractive one. That fierce leap of the heart, which, in his presence, at his touch, she recalled so well – where was it now?

'Will you not speak to me, Mary?'

'I have nothing to say.'

'Can you not – forgive me?'

She leaned forward, dropping her forehead in her hands. He waited breathless; he thought she was struggling with her heart.

In reality she was recalling their life together, measuring its further prospects in the light of what he had told her, and comparing it with her own life since. She raised her head and looked him squarely in the eye.

'I have nothing to forgive,' she said.

'Ah, you are too generous, too noble!' he cried. 'And I? The burden of my youth is lifted now. My first wife is dead – some years since – and I am free. You are my real wife, Mary, my true and loving wife. Now I can offer you the legal ceremony as well.'

'I do not wish it,' she answered.

'It shall be as you say,' he went on. 'But for the child's sake – I wish to be a father to her.'

'You are her father,' said she. 'That cannot be helped.'

'But I wish to give her my name.

'She has it. I gave it to her.'

'Brave, dear woman! But now I can give it to you.'

'I have it also. It has been my name ever since I – according to my conscience – married you.'

'But – but – you have no *legal* right to it, Mary.'

She smiled, even laughed.

'Better read a little law, Mr Main I have used that name for twelve years, am publicly and honorably known by it; it is mine, legally.'

'But Mary, I want to help you.'

'Thank you. I do not need it.'

'But I want to do for the child – my child – our little one!'

'You may,' said she. 'I want to send her to college. You may help if you like. I should be very glad if Mollie could have some pleasant and honorable memories of her father.' She rose suddenly. 'You with to marry me now, Mr Main?'

'With all my heart I wish it, Mary. You will?—'

He stood up – he held out his arms to her.

'No,' said she, 'I will not. When was twenty-four I loved you. I sympathized with you. I was willing to be your wife – truly and faithfully your wife; even though you could not legally marry me – because I loved you. Now I will not marry you because I do not love you. That is all.'

He glanced about the quiet, comfortable room; he had already estimated the quiet, comfortable business; and now, from some forgotten chamber of his honey-combed heart, welled up a fierce longing for this calm, strong, tender woman whose power of love he knew so well.

'Mary! You will not turn me away! I love you – I love you as I never loved you before!'

'I'm sorry to hear it,' she said. 'It does not make me love you again.'

His face darkened.

'Do not drive me to desperation,' he cried. 'Your whole life here rests on a lie, remember. I could shatter it with a word.'

She smiled patiently.

'You can't shatter facts, Mr Main. People here know that you left me years ago. They know how I have lived since. If you try to blacken my reputation here I think you will find the climate of Mexico more congenial.'

On second thought, this seemed to be the opinion of Mr Main, who presently left for that country.

It was also agreed with by Mr Burdock, who emerged later, a little chilly and somewhat scratched, and sought his chamber.

'If that galoot says anything against her in this town, he'll find a hotter climate than Mexico – by Heck!' said Mr Burdock to his boots as he set them down softly. And that was all he ever said about it.

TURNED

In her soft-carpeted, thick-curtained, richly furnished chamber, Mrs Marroner lay sobbing on the wide, soft bed.

She sobbed bitterly, chokingly, despairingly; her shoulders heaved and shook convulsively; her hands were tight-clenched; she had forgotten her elaborate dress, the more elaborate bed-cover; forgotten her dignity, her self-control, her pride. In her mind was an overwhelming, unbelievable horror, an immeasurable loss, a turbulent, struggling mass of emotion.

In her reserved, superior, Boston-bred life she had never dreamed that it would be possible for her to feel so many things at once, and with such trampling intensity.

She tried to cool her feelings into thoughts; to stiffen them into words; to control herself – and could not. It brought vaguely to her mind an awful moment in the breakers at York Beach, one summer in girlhood, when she had been swimming under water and could not find the top.

In her uncarpeted, thin-curtained, poorly furnished chamber on the top floor, Gerta Petersen lay sobbing on the narrow, hard bed.

She was of larger frame than her mistress, grandly built and strong; but all her proud, young womanhood was prostrate now, convulsed with agony, dissolved in tears. She did not try to control herself. She wept for two.

If Mrs Marroner suffered more from the wreck and ruin of a longer love – perhaps a deeper one; if her tastes were finer, her ideals loftier; if she bore the pangs of bitter jealousy and outraged pride, Gerta had personal shame to meet, a hopeless future, and a looming present which filled her with unreasoning terror.

She had come like a meek young goddess into that perfectly ordered house, strong, beautiful, full of good will and eager obedience, but ignorant and childish – a girl of eighteen.

Mr Marroner had frankly admired her, and so had his wife. They discussed her visible perfections and as visible limitations with that perfect confidence which they had so long enjoyed. Mrs Marroner was not a jealous woman. She had never been jealous in her life – till now.

Gerta had stayed and learned their ways. They had both been fond of her. Even the cook was fond of her. She was what is called 'willing,' was unusually teachable and plastic; and Mrs Marroner, with her early habits of giving instruction, tried to educate her somewhat.

'I never saw anyone so docile,' Mrs Marroner had often commented. 'It is perfection in a servant, but almost a defect in character. She is so helpless and confiding.'

She was precisely that; a tall, rosy-cheeked baby; rich womanhood without, helpless infancy within. Her braided wealth of dead-gold hair, her grave blue eyes, her mighty shoulders, and long, firmly moulded limbs seemed those of a primal earth spirit; but she was only an ignorant child, with a child's weakness.

When Mr Marroner had to go abroad for his firm, unwillingly, hating to leave his wife, he had told her he felt quite safe to leave her in Gerta's hands – she would take care of her.

'Be good to your mistress, Gerta,' he told the girl that last morning at breakfast. 'I leave her to you to take care of. I shall be back in a month at latest.'

Then he turned, smiling, to his wife. 'And you must take care of Gerta, too,' he said. 'I expect you'll have her ready for college when I get back.'

This was seven months ago. Business had delayed him from week to week, from month to month. He wrote to his wife, long, loving, frequent letters; deeply regretting the delay, explaining how necessary, how profitable it was; congratulating her on the wide resources she had; her well-filled, well-balanced mind; her many interests.

'If I should be eliminated from your scheme of things, by any of those "acts of God" mentioned on the tickets, I do not feel that you would be an utter wreck,' he said. 'That is very comforting to me. Your life is so rich and wide that no one loss, even a great one, would wholly cripple you. But nothing of the sort is likely to happen, and I shall be home again in three weeks – if this thing gets settled. And you will be looking so lovely, with that eager light in your eyes and the changing flush I know so well – and love so well! My dear wife! We shall have to have a new honeymoon – other moons come every month, why shouldn't the mellifluous kind?'

He often asked after 'little Gerta,' sometimes enclosed a picture postcard to her, joked his wife about her laborious efforts to educate 'the child'; was so loving and merry and wise—

All this was racing through Mrs Marroner's mind as she lay there with the broad, hemstitched border of fine linen sheeting crushed and twisted in one hand, and the other holding a sodden handkerchief.

She had tried to teach Gerta, and had grown to love the patient, sweet-natured child, in spite of her dullness. At work with her hands, she was clever, if not quick, and could keep small accounts from week to week. But to the woman who held a Ph.D., who had been on the faculty of a college, it was like baby-tending.

Perhaps having no babies of her own made her love the big child the more, though the years between them were but fifteen.

To the girl she seemed quite old, of course; and her young heart was full of grateful affection for the patient care which made her feel so much at home in this new land.

And then she had noticed a shadow on the girl's bright face. She looked nervous, anxious, worried. When the bell rang she seemed startled, and would rush hurriedly to the door. Her peals of frank laughter no longer rose from the area gate as she stood talking with the always admiring tradesmen.

Mrs Marroner had labored long to teach her more reserve with men, and flattered herself that her words were at last effective. She suspected the girl of homesickness; which was denied. She suspected her of illness, which was denied also. At last she suspected her of something which could not be denied.

For a long time she refused to believe it, waiting. Then she had to believe it, but schooled herself to patience and understanding. 'The poor child,' she said. 'She is here without a mother – she is so foolish and yielding – I must not be too stern with her.' And she tried to win the girl's confidence with wise, kind words.

But Gerta had literally thrown herself at her feet and begged her with streaming tears not to turn her away. She would admit nothing, explain nothing; but frantically promised to work for Mrs Marroner as long as she lived – if only she would keep her.

Revolving the problem carefully in her mind, Mrs Marroner thought she would keep her, at least for the present. She tried to repress her sense of ingratitude in one she had so sincerely tried to help, and the cold, contemptuous anger she had always felt for such weakness.

'The thing to do now,' she said to herself, 'is to see her through this safely. The child's life should not be hurt any more than is unavoidable. I will ask Dr Bleet about it – what a comfort a woman doctor is! I'll stand by the poor, foolish thing till it's over, and then get her back to Sweden somehow with her baby. How they do come where they are not wanted – and don't come where they are wanted!' And Mrs Marroner, sitting along in the quiet, spacious beauty of the house, almost envied Gerta.

Then came the deluge.

She had sent the girl out for needed air toward dark. The late mail came; she took it in herself. One letter for her – her husband's letter. She knew the postmark, the stamp, the kind of typewriting. She impulsively kissed it in the dim hall. No one would suspect Mrs Marroner of kissing her husband's letters – but she did, often.

She looked over the others. One was for Gerta, and not from Sweden. It looked precisely like her own. This struck her as a little odd, but Mr Marroner had several times sent messages and cards to the girl. She laid the letter on the hall table and took hers to her room.

'My poor child,' it began. What letter of hers had been sad enough to warrant that?

'I am deeply concerned at the news you send.' What news to so concern him had she written? 'You must bear it bravely, little girl. I shall be home soon, and will take care of you, of course. I hope there is no immediate anxiety – you do not say. Here is money, in case you need it. I expect to get home in a month at latest. If you have to go, be sure to leave your address at my office. Cheer up – be brave – I will take care of you.'

The letter was typewritten, which was not unusual. It was unsigned, which was unusual. It enclosed an American bill – fifty dollars. It did not seem in the least like any letter she had ever had from her husband, or any letter she could imagine him writing. But a strange, cold feeling was creeping over her, like a flood rising around a house.

She utterly refused to admit the ideas which began to bob and push about outside her mind, and to force themselves in. Yet under the pressure of these repudiated thoughts she went downstairs and brought up the other letter – the letter to Gerta. She laid them side by side on a smooth dark space on the table; marched to the piano and played, with stern precision, refusing to think, till the girl came back. When she came in, Mrs Marroner rose quietly and came to the table. 'Here is a letter for you,' she said.

The girl stepped forward eagerly, saw the two lying together there, hesitated, and looked at her mistress.

'Take yours, Gerta. Open it, please.'

The girl turned frightened eyes upon her.

'I want you to read it, here,' said Mrs Marroner.

'Oh, ma'am No! Please don't make me!'

'Why not?'

There seemed to be no reason at hand, and Gerta flushed more deeply and opened her letter. It was long; it was evidently puzzling to her; it began 'My dear wife.' She read it slowly.

'Are you sure it is your letter?' asked Mrs Marroner. 'Is not this one yours? Is not that one – mine?'

She held out the other letter to her.

'It is a mistake,' Mrs Marroner went on, with a hard quietness. She had lost her social bearings somehow; lost her usual keen sense of the proper thing to do. This was not life, this was a nightmare.

'Do you not see? Your letter was put in my envelope and my letter was put in your envelope'. Now we understand it.'

But poor Gerta had no antechamber to her mind; no trained forces to preserve order while agony entered. The thing swept over her, resistless, overwhelming. She cowered before the outraged wrath she expected; and from some hidden cavern that wrath arose and swept over her in pale flame.

'Go and pack your trunk,' said Mrs Marroner. 'You will leave my house tonight. Here is your money.'

She laid down the fifty-dollar bill. She put with it a month's wages. She had no shadow of pity for those anguished eyes, those tears which she heard drop on the floor.

'Go to your room and pack,' said Mrs Marroner. And Gerta, always obedient, went.

Then Mrs Marroner went to hers, and spent a time she never counted, lying on her face on the bed.

But the training of the twenty-eight years which had elapsed before her marriage; the life at college, both as student and teacher; the independent growth which she had made, formed a very different background for grief from that in Gerta's mind.

After a while Mrs Marroner arose. She administered to herself a hot bath, a cold shower, a vigorous rubbing. 'Now I can think,' she said.

First she regretted the sentence of instant banishment. She

went upstairs to see if it had been carried out. Poor Gerta! The tempest of her agony had worked itself out at last as in a child, and left her sleeping, the pillow wet, the lips still grieving, a big sob shuddering itself off now and then.

Mrs Marroner stood and watched her, and as she watched she considered the helpless sweetness of the face; the defenseless, unformed character; the docility and habit of obedience which made her so attractive – and so easily a victim. Also she thought of the mighty force which had swept over her; of the great process now working itself out through her; of how pitiful and futile seemed any resistance she might have made.

She softly returned to her own room, made up a little fire, and sat by it, ignoring her feelings now, as she had before ignored her thoughts.

Here were two women and a man. One woman was a wife; loving, trusting, affectionate. One was a servant; loving, trusting, affectionate: a young girl, an exile, a dependent; grateful for any kindness; untrained, uneducated, childish. She ought, of course, to have resisted temptation; but Mrs Marroner was wise enough to know how difficult temptation is to recognize when it comes in the guise of friendship and from a source one does not suspect.

Gerta might have done better in resisting the grocer's clerk; had, indeed, with Mrs Marroner's advice, resisted several. But where respect was due, how could she criticize? Where obedience was due, how could she refuse – with ignorance to hold her blinded – until too late?

As the older, wiser woman forced herself to understand and extenuate the girl's misdeed and foresee her ruined future, a new feeling rose in her heart, strong, clear, and overmastering; a sense of measureless condemnation for the man who had done this thing. He knew. He understood. He could fully foresee and measure the consequences of his act. He appreciated to the full the innocence, the ignorance, the grateful affection, the habitual docility, of which he deliberately took advantage.

Mrs Marroner rose to icy peaks of intellectual apprehension, from which her hours of frantic pain seemed far indeed removed. He had done this thing under the same roof with her – his wife. He had not frankly loved the younger woman, broken with his wife, made a new marriage. That would have been heartbreak pure and simple. This was something else.

That letter, that wretched, cold, carefully guarded, unsigned letter: that bill – far safer than a check – these did not speak of affection. Some men can love two women at one time. This was not love.

Mrs Marroner's sense of pity and outrage for herself, the wife, now spread suddenly into a perception of pity and outrage for the girl. All that splendid, clean young beauty, the hope of a happy life, with marriage and motherhood; honorable independence, even – these were nothing to that man. For his own pleasure he had chosen to rob her of her life's best joys.

He would 'take care of her' said the letter? How? In what capacity?

And then, sweeping over both her feelings for herself, the wife, and Gerta, his victim, came a new flood, which literally lifted her to her feet. She rose and walked, her head held high. 'This is the sin of man against woman,' she said. 'The offense is against womanhood. Against motherhood. Against – the child.'

She stopped.

The child. His child. That, too, he sacrificed and injured – doomed to degradation.

Mrs Marroner came of stern New England stock. She was not a Calvinist, hardly even a Unitarian, but the iron of Calvinism was in her soul: of that grim faith which held that most people had to be damned 'for the glory of God.'

Generations of ancestors who both preached and practiced stood behind her; people whose lives had been sternly moulded to their highest moments of religious conviction. In sweeping bursts of feeling they achieved 'conviction,' and afterward they lived and died according to that conviction.

When Mr Marroner reached home, a few weeks later, following his letters too soon to expect an answer to either, he saw no wife upon the pier, though he had cabled; and found the house closed darkly. He let himself in with his latch-key, and stole softly upstairs, to surprise his wife.

No wife was there.

He rang the bell. No servant answered it.

He turned up light after light; searched the house from top to bottom; it was utterly empty. The kitchen wore a clean, bald, unsympathetic aspect. He left it and slowly mounted the stair, completely dazed. The whole house was clean, in perfect order, wholly vacant.

One thing he felt perfectly sure of – she knew.

Yet was he sure? He must not assume too much. She might have been ill. She might have died. He started to his feet. No, they would have cabled him. He sat down again.

For any such change, if she had wanted him to know, she would have written. Perhaps she had, and he, returning so suddenly, had missed the letter. The thought was some comfort. It must be so. He turned to the telephone, and again hesitated. If she had found out – if she had gone – utterly gone, without a word – should he announce it himself to friends and family?

He walked the floor; he searched everywhere for some letter, some word of explanation. Again and again he went to the telephone – and always stopped. He could not bear to ask: 'Do you know where my wife is?'

The harmonious, beautiful rooms reminded him in a dumb, helpless way of her; like the remote smile on the face of the dead. He put out the lights; could not bear the darkness; turned them all on again.

It was a long night—

In the morning he went early to the office. In the accumulated mail was no letter from her. No one seemed to know of anything unusual. A friend asked after his wife – 'Pretty glad to see you, I guess?' He answered evasively.

About eleven a man came to see him; John Hill, her lawyer. Her cousin, too. Mr Marroner had never liked him. He liked him less now, for Mr Hill merely handed him a letter, remarked, 'I was requested to deliver this to you personally,' and departed, looking like a person who is called on to kill something offensive.'

'I have gone. I will care for Gerta. Goodbye. Marion.'

That was all. There was no date, no address, no postmark; nothing but that.

In his anxiety and distress he had fairly forgotten Gerta and all that. Her name aroused in him a sense of rage. She had come between him and his wife. She had taken his wife from him. That was the way he felt.

At first he said nothing, did nothing; lived on alone in his house, taking meals where he chose. When people asked him about his wife he said she was traveling – for her health. He would not have it in the newspapers. Then, as time passed, as no enlightenment came to him, he resolved not to bear it any longer, and employed detectives. They blamed him for not having put them on the track earlier, but set to work, urged to the utmost secrecy.

What to him had been so blank a wall of mystery seemed not to embarrass them in the least. They made careful inquiries as to her 'past,' found where she had studied, where taught, and on what lines; that she had some little money of her own, that her doctor was Josephine L. Bleet, M.D., and many other bits of information.

As a result of careful and prolonged work, they finally told him that she had resumed teaching under one of her old professors; lived quietly, and apparently kept boarders; giving him town, street, and number, as if it were a matter of no difficulty whatever.

He had returned in early spring. It was autumn before he found her.

A quiet college town in the hills, a broad, shady street, a pleasant house standing in its own lawn, with trees and flowers about it. He had the address in his hand, and the number showed clear on the white gate. He walked up the straight gravel path and rang the bell. An elderly servant opened the door.

'Does Mrs Marroner live here?'

'No, sir.'

'This is number twenty-eight?'

'Yes, sir.'

'Who does live here?'

'Miss Wheeling, sir.'

Ah! Her maiden name. They had told him, but he had forgotten.

He stepped inside. 'I would like to see her,' he said.

He was ushered into a still parlor, cool and sweet with the scent of flowers, the flowers she had always loved best. It almost brought tears to his eyes. All their years of happiness rose in his mind again; the exquisite beginnings; the days of eager longing before she was really his; the deep, still beauty of her love.

Surely she would forgive him – she must forgive him. He would humble himself; he would tell her of his honest remorse – his absolute determination to be a different man.

Through the wide doorway there came in to him two women. One like a tall Madonna, bearing a baby in her arms.

Marion, calm, steady, definitely impersonal; nothing but a clear pallor to hint of inner stress.

Gerta, holding the child as a bulwark, with a new intelligence in her face, and her blue, adoring eyes fixed on her friend – not upon him.

He looked from one to the other dumbly.

And the woman who had been his wife asked quietly:

'What have you to say to us?'

MAKING A CHANGE

'Wa-a-a-a! Waa-a-a-aaa!'

Frank Gordins set down his coffee cup so hard that it spilled over into the saucer.

'Is there no way to stop that child crying?' he demanded.

'I do not know of any,' said his wife, so definitely and politely that the words seemed cut off by machinery.

'*I do*,' said his mother with even more definiteness, but less politeness.

Young Mrs Gordins looked at her mother-in-law from under her delicate level brows, and said nothing. But the weary lines about her eyes deepened; she had been kept awake nearly all night, and for many nights.

So had he. So, as a matter of fact, had his mother. She had not the care of the baby – but lay awake wishing she had.

'There's no need at all for that child's crying so, Frank. If Julia would only let me—'

'It's no use talking about it,' said Julia. 'If Frank is not satisfied with the child's mother he must say so – perhaps we can make a change.'

This was ominously gentle. Julia's nerves were at the breaking point. Upon her tired ears, her sensitive mother's heart, the grating wail from the next room fell like a lash – burnt in like fire. Her ears were hypersensitive, always. She had been an ardent musician before her marriage, and had taught quite successfully on both piano and violin. To any mother a child's cry is painful; to a musical mother it is torment.

But if her ears were sensitive, so was her conscience. If her nerves were weak her pride was strong. The child was her child, it was her duty to take care of it, and take care of it she would. She spent her days in unremitting devotion to its needs, and to the care of her neat flat; and her nights had long since ceased to refresh her.

Again the weary cry rose to a wail.

'It does seem to be time for a change of treatment,' suggested the older woman acidly.

'Or a change of residence,' offered the younger, in a deadly quiet voice.

'Well, by Jupiter! There'll be a change of some kind, and p. d. q.!' said the son and husband, rising to his feet.

His mother rose also, and left the room, holding her head high and refusing to show any effects of that last thrust.

Frank Gordins glared at his wife. His nerves were raw, too. It does not benefit any one in health or character to be continuously deprived of sleep. Some enlightened persons use that deprivation as a form of torture.

She stirred her coffee with mechanical calm, her eyes sullenly bent on her plate.

'I will not stand having Mother spoken to like that,' he stated with decision.

'I will not stand having her interfere with my methods of bringing up children.'

'Your methods! Why, Julia, my mother knows more about taking care of babies than you'll ever learn! She has the real love of it – and the practical experience. Why can't you *let* her take care of the kid – and we'll all have some peace!'

She lifted her eyes and looked at him; deep inscrutable wells of angry light. He had not the faintest appreciation of her state of mind. When people say they are 'nearly crazy' from weariness, they state a practical fact. The old phrase which describes reason as 'tottering on her throne,' is also a clear one.

Julia was more near the verge of complete disaster than the family dreamed. The conditions were so simple, so usual, so inevitable.

Here was Frank Gordins, well brought up, the only son of a very capable and idolatrously affectionate mother. He had fallen deeply and desperately in love with the exalted beauty and fine mind of the young music teacher, and his mother had approved. She too loved music and admired beauty.

Her tiny store in the savings bank did not allow of a separate home, and Julia had cordially welcomed her to share in their household.

Here was affection, propriety and peace. Here was a noble devotion on the part of the young wife, who so worshipped her husband that she used to wish she had been the greatest musician on earth – that she might give it up for him! She had given up her music, perforce, for many months, and missed it more than she knew.

She bent her mind to the decoration and artistic management of their little apartment, finding her standards difficult to maintain by the ever-changing inefficiency of her help. The musical temperament does not always include patience; nor, necessarily, the power of management.

When the baby came her heart overflowed with utter devotion and thankfulness; she was his wife – the mother of his child. Her happiness lifted and pushed within till she longed more than ever for her music for the free pouring current of expression, to give forth her love and pride and happiness. She had not the gift of words.

So now she looked at her husband, dumbly, while wild visions of separation, of secret flight – even of self-destruction – swung dizzily across her mental vision. All she said was 'All right, Frank. We'll make a change. And you shall have – some peace.'

'Thank goodness for that, Jule! You do look tired, Girlie – let Mother see to His Nibs, and try to get a nap, can't you?'

'Yes,' she said. 'Yes . . . I think I will.' Her voice had a peculiar note in it. If Frank had been an alienist, or even a general physician, he would have noticed it. But his work lay in electric coils, in dynamos and copper wiring – not in woman's nerves – and he did not notice it.

He kissed her and went out, throwing back his shoulders and drawing a long breath of relief as he left the house behind him and entered his own world.

'This being married – and bringing up children – is not what it's cracked up to be.' That was the feeling in the back of his mind. But it did not find full admission, much less expression.

When a friend asked him, 'All well at home?' he said, 'Yes, thank you – pretty fair. Kid cries a good deal – but that's natural, I suppose.'

He dismissed the whole matter from his mind and bent his faculties to a man's task – how he can earn enough to support a wife, a mother, and a son.

At home his mother sat in her small room, looking out of the window at the ground glass one just across the 'well,' and thinking hard.

By the disorderly little breakfast table his wife remained motionless, her chin in her hands, her big eyes staring at nothing, trying to formulate in her weary mind some reliable reason why she should not do what she was thinking of doing. But her mind was too exhausted to serve her properly.

Sleep – Sleep – Sleep – that was the one thing she wanted. Then his mother could take care of the baby all she wanted to, and Frank could have some peace . . . Oh, dear! It was time for the child's bath.

She gave it to him mechanically. On the stroke of the hour she prepared the sterilized milk, and arranged the little one comfortably with his bottle. He snuggled down, enjoying it, while she stood watching him.

She emptied the tub, put the bath apron to dry, picked up all the towels and sponges and varied appurtenances of the elaborate performance of bathing the first-born, and then sat staring straight before her, more weary than ever, but growing inwardly determined.

Greta had cleared the table, with heavy heels and hands, and was now rattling dishes in the kitchen. At every slam the young mother winced, and when the girl's high voice began a sort of doleful chant over her work, young Mrs Gordins rose to her feet with a shiver, and made her decision.

She carefully picked up the child and his bottle, and carried him to his grandmother's room.

'Would you mind looking after Albert?' she asked in a flat, quiet voice; 'I think I'll try to get some sleep.'

'Oh, I shall be delighted,' replied her mother-in-law. She said it in a tone of cold politeness, but Julia did not notice. She laid the child on the bed and stood looking at him in the same dull way for a little while, then went out without another word.

Mrs Gordins, senior, sat watching the baby for some long moments. 'He's a perfectly lovely child!' she said softly, gloating over his rosy beauty. 'There's not a *thing* the matter with him! It's just her absurd ideas. She's so irregular with him! To think of letting that child cry for an hour! He is nervous because she is. And of course she couldn't feed him till after his bath – of course not!'

She continued in these sarcastic meditations for some time, taking the empty bottle away from the small wet mouth, that sucked on for a few moments aimlessly, and then was quiet in sleep.

'I could take care of him so that he'd *never* cry!' she continued to herself, rocking slowly back and forth. 'And I could take care of twenty like him – and enjoy it! I believe I'll go off somewhere and do it. Give Julia a rest. Change of residence, indeed!'

She rocked and planned, pleased to have her grandson with her, even while asleep.

Greta had gone out on some errand of her own. The rooms were very quiet. Suddenly the old lady held up her head and sniffed. She rose swiftly to her feet and sprang to the gas jet – no, it was shut off tightly. She went back to the dining-room – all right there.

'That foolish girl has left the range going and it's blown out!' she thought, and went to the kitchen. No, the little room was fresh and clean; every burner turned off.

'Funny! It must come in from the hall.' She opened the door. No, the hall gave only its usual odor of diffused basement. Then the parlor – nothing there. The little alcove called by the renting agent 'the music room,' where Julia's closed piano and violin case stood dumb and dusty – nothing there.

'It's in her room – and she's asleep!' said Mrs Gordins, senior; and she tried to open the door. It was locked. She knocked – there was no answer; knocked louder – shook it – rattled the knob. No answer.

Then Mrs Gordins thought quickly. 'It may be an accident, and nobody must know. Frank mustn't know. I'm glad Greta's out. I *must* get in somehow!' She looked at the transom, and the stout rod Frank had himself put up for the portieres Julia loved.

'I believe I can do it, at a pinch.'

She was a remarkably active woman of her years, but no memory of earlier gymnastic feats could quite cover the exercise. She hastily brought the step-ladder. From its top she could see in, and what she saw made her determine recklessly.

Grabbing the pole with small strong hands, she thrust her light frame bravely through the opening, turning clumsily but successfully, and dropping breathlessly and somewhat bruised to the floor, she flew to open the windows and doors.

When Julia opened her eyes she found loving arms around her, and wise, tender words to soothe and reassure.

'Don't say a thing, dearie – I understand. I *understand* I tell you! Oh, my dear girl – my precious daughter! We haven't been half good enough to you, Frank and I! But cheer up now – I've got the *loveliest* plan to tell you about! We *are* going to make a change! Listen now!'

And while the pale young mother lay quiet, petted and waited on to her heart's content, great plans were discussed and decided on.

Frank Gordins was pleased when the baby 'outgrew his crying spells.' He spoke of it to his wife.

'Yes,' she said sweetly. 'He has better care.'

'I knew you'd learn,' said he, proudly.

'I have!' she agreed. 'I've learned – ever so much!'

He was pleased too, vastly pleased, to have her health improve rapidly and steadily, the delicate pink come back to her cheeks, the soft light to her eyes; and when she made music for him in the evening, soft music, with shut doors – not to waken Albert – he felt as if his days of courtship had come again.

Greta the hammer-footed had gone, and an amazing French matron who came in by the day had taken her place. He asked no questions as to this person's peculiarities, and did not know that she did the purchasing and planned the meals, meals of such new delicacy and careful variance as gave him much delight. Neither did he know that her wages were greater than her predecessors. He turned over the same sum weekly, and did not pursue details.

He was pleased also that his mother seemed to have taken a new lease of life. She was so cheerful and brisk, so full of little jokes and stories – as he had known her in his boyhood; and above all she was so free and affectionate with Julia, that he was more than pleased.

'I tell you what it is!' he said to a bachelor friend. 'You fellows don't know what you're missing!' And he brought one of them home to dinner – just to show him.

'Do you do all that on thirty-five a week?' his friend demanded.

'That's about it,' he answered proudly.

'Well, your wife's a wonderful manager – that's all I can say. And you've got the best cook I ever saw, or heard of, or ate of – I suppose I might say – for five dollars.'

Mr Gordins was pleased and proud. But he was neither pleased nor proud when someone said to him, with displeasing frankness, 'I shouldn't think you'd want your wife to be giving music lessons, Frank!'

He did not show surprise nor anger to his friend, but saved it for his wife. So surprised and so angry was he that he did a most unusual thing – he left his business and went home early in the afternoon. He opened the door of his flat. There was no one in it. He went through every room. No wife; no child; no mother; no servant.

The elevator boy heard him banging about, opening and shutting doors, and grinned happily. When Mr Gordins came out Charles volunteered some information.

'Young Mrs Gordins is out, Sir; but old Mrs Gordins and the baby – they're upstairs. On the roof, I think.'

Mr Gordins went to the roof. There he found his mother, a smiling, cheerful nursemaid, and fifteen happy babies.

Mrs Gordins, senior, rose to the occasion promptly.

'Welcome to my baby garden, Frank,' she said cheerfully. 'I'm so glad you could get off in time to see it.'

She took his arm and led him about, proudly exhibiting her sunny roof-garden, her sand-pile, and big, shallow, zinc-lined pool; her flowers and vines, her see-saws, swings, and floor mattresses.

'You see how happy they are,' she said. 'Celia can manage very well for a few moments.' And then she exhibited to him the whole upper flat, turned into a convenient place for many little ones to take their naps or to play in if the weather was bad.

'Where's Julia?' he demanded first.

'Julia will be in presently,' she told him, 'by five o'clock anyway. And the mothers come for the babies by then, too. I have them from nine or ten to five.'

He was silent, both angry and hurt.

'We didn't tell you at first, my dear boy, because we knew you wouldn't like it, and we wanted to make sure it would go well. I rent the upper flat, you see – it is forty dollars a month, same as ours – and pay Celia five dollars a week, and pay Dr Holbrook downstairs the same for looking over my little ones every day. She helped me to get them, too. The mothers pay me three dollars a week each, and don't have to keep a nursemaid. And I pay ten dollars a week board to Julia, and still have about ten of my own.'

'And she gives music lessons?'

'Yes, she gives music lessons, just as she used to. She loves it, you know. You must have noticed how happy and well she is now – haven't you? And so am I. And so is Albert. You can't feel very badly about a thing that makes us all happy, can you?'

Just then Julia came in, radiant from a brisk walk, fresh and cheery, a big bunch of violets at her breast.

'Oh, Mother,' she cried, 'I've got tickets and we'll all go to hear Melba – if we can get Celia to come in for the evening.'

She saw her husband, and a guilty flush rose to her brow as she met his reproachful eyes.

'Oh, Frank!' she begged, her arms around his neck. 'Please don't mind! Please get used to it! Please be proud of us! Just think, we're all so happy, and we earn about a hundred dollars a week – all of us together. You see I have Mother's ten to add to the house money, and twenty or more of my own!'

They had a long talk together that evening, just the two of them. She told him, at last, what a danger had hung over them – how near it came.

'And Mother showed me the way out, Frank. The way to have my mind again – and not lose you! She is a different woman herself now that she has her heart and hands full of babies. Albert does enjoy it so! And *you've* enjoyed it – till you found it out!

'And dear – my own love – I don't mind it now at all! I love my home, I love my work, I love my mother, I love you. And as to children – I wish I had six!'

He looked at her flushed, eager, lovely face, and drew her close to him.

'If it makes all of you as happy as that,' he said, 'I guess I can stand it.'

And in after years he was heard to remark, 'This being married and bringing up children is as easy as can be – when you learn how!'

MRS ELDER'S IDEA

Did you ever repeat a word or phrase so often that it lost all meaning to you?

Did you ever eat at the same table, of the same diet, till the food had no taste to you?

Did you ever feel a sudden over-mastering wave of revolt against the ceaseless monotony of your surroundings till you longed to escape anywhere at any cost?

That was the way Mrs Elder felt on this gray, muggy morning, toward the familiar objects about her dining room, the familiar dishes on the table, even, for the moment, at the familiar figure at the other end of it.

It was Mr Elder's idea of a pleasant breakfast to set up his preferred newspaper against the water pitcher, and read it as long as he could continue eating and drinking. Other people were welcome to do the same, he argued; *he* had no objection. It is true that there was but one newspaper.

Mrs Elder was a woman naturally chatty, but skilled in silence. One cannot long converse with an absorbed opposing countenance which meets one's choicest anecdote, some minutes after the event, with a testy 'What's that?'

She sat still, stirring her cool coffee, waiting to ring for it, hot, when he wanted more, and studying his familiar outlines with a dull fascination. She knew every line and tint, every curve and angle, every wrinkle in the loosefitting coat, every moderate change in expression. They were only moderate, nowadays. Never any more did she see the looks she remembered so well, over twenty years ago; looks of admiration, of approval, of interest, of desire to please; looks with a deep kindling fire in them—

'I would thou wert either cold or hot,' she was half consciously repeating to herself.

O yes, he was kind to her in most things; he was fond of her, even, she could admit that. He missed her, when she was not there, or would miss her – she seldom had a chance to test it. They had no quarrel, no complaint against each other; only a long, slow cooling, as of lava beds; the gradual evaporation of a fine fervor; that process of torpid, tepid, mutual accommodation which is complacently referred to by the wordly wise as 'settling down.'

'Had she no children?' will demand those whose psychological medicine closets hold but a few labels.

'For a Woman: A Husband, Home and Children. Good for whatever ails her.'

'For a Man: Success, Money, A Good Wife.'

'For a Child: Proper Care, Education, A Good Bringing Up.'

There are no other persons to be doctored, and no other remedies.

Now Mrs Elder had had children, four, fulfilling the formula announced by Mr Grant Allen, some years since, that each couple must have four children, merely to preserve the balance of the population; two to replace their parents, and two to die. Two of hers had accordingly; died; and two, living, were now ready to replace their parents; that is they were grown up.

Theodore was of age, and had gone into business already, at a distance. Alice was of age, too; the lesser age allowed the weaker vessel, and also away from home. She was staying with an aunt in Boston, a wealthy aunt who insisted in maintaining her in luxury; but the girl insisted equally upon studying at the Institute of Technology, and threatened an early departure into the proud freedom of self support.

Mrs Elder was fond of children, but these young persons were not children any more. She would have been glad to continue her ministrations; but however motherhood may seek to prolong its period of usefulness, childhood is evanescent; and youth, modern youth, serenely rebellious. The cycle which is supposed to so perfectly round out a woman's life, was closed for the present.

Mr Elder projected a cup, without looking at it, or her; and Mrs Elder rang, poured his coffee, modified it to his liking, and handed it back to him. She even took a fresh cup for herself, but found she did not want it.

There was a heavier shadow than usual between them this morning. As a general thing there was not a real cloud, only the bluish mist of distance in thick air; but now they had had a 'difference,' a decided difference.

Mr Elder's concerns in life had never been similar to his wife's. She had tried, as is held to be the duty of wives, to interest herself in his, but with only a measurable success. Her own preferences had never amounted to more than topics of conversation, to him, and distasteful topics, at that. What was the use of continually talking about things, if you could not have them and ought not to want to?

She loved the city, thick and bustling, the glitter and surge of the big shops with their kaleidoscope exhibition of color and style, that changed even as you looked.

Her fondness for shopping was almost a passion; to her an unending delight; to him, a silly vice.

This attitude was reversed in the matter of tobacco; to him, an unending delight; to her, a silly vice.

They had had arguments upon these lines, but that was years ago.

One of the reasons for Mrs Elder's hard-bitten silence was Mr Elder's extreme dislike of argument. Why argue, when you could not help yourself? that was his position; and not to be able to help herself was hers. How could she shop, to any advantage, when they lived an hour from town, and she had to ask for money to go with, or at least for money to shop with.

Just once in her life had Mrs Elder had an orgy of shopping. A widowed aunt of Mr Elder, who had just paid them a not too agreeable visit, surprised her beyond words with a Christmas present of a hundred dollars. 'It is conditional,' she said grimly, holding the amazing yellow-backed treasure in her bony and somewhat purple hand. 'You're not to tell Herbert a word about it till it's spent. You're to go in town, early in January, some day when the sales are on, and spend it all. And half of it you're to spend on yourself. Promise, now.'

Mrs Elder had promised, but the last condition was a little stretched. She swore she had wanted the movable electric drop light and the little music machine, but Herbert and the children seemed to use them more than she did. Anyhow she had a day's shopping, which was the solace of barren years.

She liked the theatre, too, but that had been so wholly out of the question for so long that it did not trouble her, much.

As for Mr Elder, he had to work in the city to maintain his family, but what he liked above everything else was the country; the real, wild, open country, where you could count your visible neighbors on your fingers, and leave them, visible, but not audible. They had compromised for twenty-two years, by living in Highvale, which was enough like a city to annoy him, and enough like the country to annoy her. She hated the country, it 'got on her nerves.'

Which brings us to the present difference between them.

Theodore being grown up and earning his living; Alice being well on the way to it, and a small expense at present; Mr Elder had concluded that his financial resources would allow of the realization of his fondest hope – retirement. A real retirement, not only officially, from business, and its hated environment; but physically, into the remote and lonely situation which his soul loved. So he had sold his business and bought a farm.

They had talked about it all last evening; at least she had. Mr Elder, as has been stated, was not much of a talker. He had seemed rather more preoccupied than usual during dinner; possibly he did realize in a dim way that the change would be extremely unwelcome to his wife. Then as they settled down to their usual quiet evening, wherein he was supremely comfortable in house-coat; slippers, cigars of the right sort, the books he loved, and a good light at the left back corner of his leather-cushioned chair; and wherein she read as long as she could stand it, sewed as long as she could stand it, and talked as long as he could stand it.

This time, he had, after strengthening himself with a preliminary cigar, heaved a sigh, and faced the inevitable.

'Oh, Grace,' he said, laying down his book, as if this was a minor incident which had just occurred to him, 'I've sold out the business.'

She dropped her work, and looked at him, startled. He went on, wishing to make all clear at once – he did hate discussion.

'Given up for good. It don't cost us much to live, now the children are practically off our hands. You know I've always hated office work; it's a great relief to be done with it, I assure you . . . And I've bought that farm on Warren Hill . . . We'll move out by October. I'd have left it till Spring – but I had a splendid chance to sell – and then I didn't dare wait lest I lose the farm . . . No use keeping up two places . . . Our lease is out in October, you know.'

He had left little gaps of silence between these blows, not longer than those required to heave up the axe for its full swing; and when he finished Mrs Elder felt as if her head verily rolled in the basket. She moistened her lips, and looked at him rather piteously, saying nothing at first. She could not say anything.

He arose from the easy depth of the chair, and came round the table, giving her a cursory kiss, and a reassuring pat on the shoulder.

'I know you won't like it at first, Grace, but it will do you good – good for your nerves – open air – rest – and a garden. You can have a lovely garden – and' (this was a carefully thought out boon, really involving some intent of sacrifice) 'and company, in summer. Have your friends come out!'

He sat down again feeling that the subject had been fully, fairly and finally discussed. She thought differently. There arose in her a slow, boiling flood of long-suppressed rebellion. He could speak like this – he could do a thing like that – and she was expected to say 'Yes, Herbert' to what amounted to penal servitude for life – to her.

But the habit of a score of years is strong, to say nothing of the habit of several scores of centuries, and out of that surging sea of resistance came only fatuous protests, and inefficacious pleas.

Mr Elder had been making up his mind to take this step for many years, and it was now a fact accomplished. He had decided that it would be good for his wife even it she did not like it; and that conviction gave him added strength.

Against this formidable front of fact and theory she had nothing to advance save a pathetic array of likes and dislikes; feeble neglected things, weak from disuse. But he had generously determined to 'let her talk it out' for that one evening; so she had talked from hour to hour – till she had at last realized that all this talk reached nowhere – the thing was done.

A dull cloud oppressed her dreams; she woke with a sense of impending calamity, and as the remembrance grew, into awakening pain. There was constraint between them at the breakfast table; a cold response from her when he went, with a fine effect of being cheerful and affectionate; and then Mrs Elder was left alone to consider her future.

She was a woman of forty-two, in excellent health, and would have been extremely good-looking if she could have 'dressed the part.' Some women look best in evening dress, some in house gowns, some in street suits; the last was her kind.

She gave her orders for the day listlessly, noting with weary patience the inefficiency of the suburban maid, and then suddenly thinking of how much worse the servant question would become on Warren Hill.

'Perhaps he expects me to do the housework,' she grimly remarked to herself. 'And have company. Company!'

As a matter of fact, Mrs Elder did not enjoy household visitors. They were to her a care, an added strain upon her housekeeping skill. Her idea of company was 'seeing people'; the chance meeting in the street, the friendly face in a theatre crowd, the brisk easily-ended chatter of a 'call,' and now and then a real party – where one could dance. Should she ever dance again?

Mrs Elder always considered it a special providence that brought Mrs Gaylord, a neighbor, in to see her that day; and with her a visiting friend, Mrs MacAvelly, rather a silent person, but sympathetic and suggestive. Mrs Gaylord was profusely interested and even angry at Mr Elder's heartlessness, as she called it; but Mrs MacAvelly had merely assisted in the conversation, by gentle references to this and that story, book and play. Had she seen this? Had she read that? Did she think so and so was right to do what she did?

After they left, Mrs Elder went down town, and bought a magazine or two which had been mentioned, and got a book from the little library.

She read, she was amazed, shocked, fascinated; she read more, and after a week of this inoculation, a strange light dawned upon her mind, quite suddenly and clearly.

'Why not?' she said to herself. And again, 'Why not?' Even in the night she woke and lay smiling, while heavy breathing told of sleep beside her; saying inwardly, 'Why not?'

It was only the end of August; there was a month yet.

She made plans, rapidly but quietly; consulting at length with several of her friends in Highvale, women with large establishments, large purses, and profoundly domestic tastes.

Mrs Gaylord was rapturously interested, introducing her to other friends, and Mrs MacAvelly wrote a little note from the city, mentioning several more; from more than one of these came large encouragement.

She wrote to her daughter also, and her son, whose business brought him to Boston that season. They had a talk in the soft-colored little parlor; Mrs Elder smiling, flushed, eager and excited as a girl, as she announced her plans, under pledge of strictest secrecy.

'I don't care whether you agree or not!' she stoutly proclaimed. 'But I'm going to do it. And you mustn't say one word. He never said a word till it was all done.'

None the less she looked a little anxiously at Theodore. He soon reassured her. 'Bully for you, Mama,' he said. 'You look about sixteen! Go ahead – I'll back you up.'

Alice was profoundly pleased.

'How perfectly splendid, Mama! I'm so proud of you! What glorious times we'll have, won't we just?' And they discussed her plans with enthusiasm and glee.

Toward the middle of September Mr Elder, immersed though he was in frequent visits to that idol of his heart, the farm, began to notice the excitement in his wife's manner. 'I hope you're not tiring yourself too much, packing,' he said, and added, quite affectionately, 'You won't hate it so much after a while, my dear.'

'No, I won't,' she admitted, with an ambiguous smile. 'I think I might even like it, a little while, in Summer.'

About the twentieth of the month she made up her mind to tell him, finding it harder than she had anticipated in the first proud moments of determination.

It was evening again, and he had settled luxuriously into his big chair, surrounded by The Country Gentleman, The Fruit-Grower, and The Breeder and Sportsman. She let him have one cigar, and then – 'Herbert.'

He was a moment or two in answering – coming up from the depths of his studies in 'The Profits of Making Honey' with appropriate slowness. 'Yes, Grace, what is it?'

'I am not going with you to the farm.'

He smiled a little wearily. 'Oh, yes you are, my dear; don't make a fuss about the inevitable.'

She flushed at that and gathered courage. 'I have made other arrangements,' she said calmly. 'I am going to board in Boston. I've rented a furnished floor. Theodore is going to hire one room, and Alice one. And we take our meals out. She is to have a position this year. They both approve—' She hesitated a moment, and added breathlessly, 'I'm to be a professional shopper! I've got a lot of orders ahead. I can see my way half through the season already!'

She paused. So did he. He was not good at talking. 'You seem to have it all arranged,' he said drily.

'I have,' she eagerly agreed. 'It's all planned out.'

'Where do I come in?' he asked, after a little.

She took him seriously. 'There is plenty of room for you, dear, and you'll always be welcome. You might like it awhile – in Winter.'

This time it was Mr Elder who spent some hours in stating his likes and dislikes, but she explained how easily he could hire some one to pack and move for him – and how much happier he would be, when once well settled on the farm.

'You can get a nice housekeeper you see – for I shan't be costing you *anything* now!'

'I'm going to town next week,' she added, 'and we hope to see you by Christmas, at latest.'

They did.

They had an unusually happy Christmas, and an unusually

happy Summer following. From sullen rage, Mr Elder, in serene rural solitude, simmered down to a grieved state of mind. When he did come to town, he found an eagerly delighted family; and a wife so roguishly young, so attractively dressed, so vivacious and happy and amusing, that the warmth of a sudden Indian Summer fell upon his heart.

Alice and Theodore chuckled in corners. 'Just see Papa making love to Mama! Isn't it impressive?'

Mrs Elder was certainly much impressed by it; and Mr Elder found that two half homes and half a happy wife, were really more satisfying than one whole home, and a whole unhappy wife, withering in discontent.

In her new youth and gaiety of spirit, and her half-remorseful tenderness for him, she grew ever more desirable, and presently the Elder family maintained a city flat and a country home; and spent their happy years between them.

THEIR HOUSE

Mr Waterson's house was small, owing to the smallness of his income, but it was clean, most violently and meticulously clean, owing to the proficiency of Mrs Waterson as a housekeeper

Mrs Waterson, in Mr Waterson's house, presented at times the appearance of an Admiral commanding a catboat; at other times she resembled that strictly localized meteorological disturbance, a tempest in a teapot. While her children were young they had furnished something of an outlet for her energies. They were nice children, quiet like their father, conscientious like their mother, of good constitutions, and not difficult to 'raise.' But she had 'raised' them by main force none the less, and during their nonage Mr Waterson had some peace in his house. He had no room of course, nor thought of claiming any, but in such small space as was temporarily allowed him he could read – sometimes.

Now the youngest boy had gone into business, and the youngest girl had suddenly married, using discretion in choice, and developing unexpected obstinacy in carrying out her decision. It is difficult to enforce authority upon a captive whose disobedience means escape.

'You were married at sixteen yourself, mother,' said Jennie junior, and took herself off.

So Mrs Waterson at the age of thirty-nine was left to concentrate her abundant efficiency upon her home and her husband. The house submitted perforce, wearing a cowed and submissive look, with its window-shades drawn to the line, its parlor darkened, its floors scrubbed, swept, or drastically washed, according to their nature. Mr Waterson also submitted – one cannot blame one's wife for being a good housekeeper, even a too good housekeeper.

He was a just man, and a kind one, and so thoroughly imbued with the conviction that woman's place is the home that he never dreamed of criticizing the way in which his wife filled it. Yet if ever a man was unhappy without knowing it, it was John Waterson. His was a studious soul, with the scholar's love of quiet and indifference to dust. He was fitted for high-ceilinged, long-windowed, book-walled libraries, looking out on peaceful lawns, deep-shaded. He liked plenty of room about him, not only for books and papers, but for his personal collections and instruments, and for certain small experiments. Secretly he fostered ambitions for scientific research. Yet all the room he had at his command was one bookcase in the parlor, an oak desk in the attic, and the somewhat begrudged use of the dining-room table after the red cloth was on and the lamp lit, with the condition that he must clean up before going to bed. As for bedroom space, he had his half the bed, less than half the closet, and two drawers in the bureau, the under ones. As Mrs Waterson liked the window shut and he liked it open, as she wanted more bedclothing than he by a pair of blankets, as she liked to go to bed early and he late, they compromised by half-opening the window, dividing the blankets longitudinally, one lying awake or the other being waked up – and were both patiently uncomfortable.

Now that the children were gone, there was really room for him if either of them had thought of having separate apartments, but they never did. The long-cramped Mrs Waterson eagerly arranged her daughter's chamber as a 'spare room,' decked it with all their best, and shut it up. The boys' room was only an attic anyhow and now became a much needed place of storage for Mr Waterson's 'clutter,' as she called it. He called it, in his secret heart, his 'study,' but it was only an attic, hot in summer and cold in winter.

'We ought to have a bigger house, Jennie,' he observed one night, as he had done many times before.

'Well,' said Mrs Waterson, faithfully inserting the *we* to take the edge off her remark, 'when we can afford a bigger house we'll have it.'

She was standing by the bureau combing her thick brown hair, while he lay there, wide awake and a little rebellious, watching her. Of course he could have sat up later, but there were so many directions to remember about the lamp and the stove and the window and to put up all his papers, and not to stumble on the stairs and waken her – which he knew he should infallibly do – that he preferred to come to bed and be done with it.

Hair is beautiful upon the head, smooth-coiled or softly flowing, and Mrs Waterson had 'a fine suit of hair,' but he never quite enjoyed the prosaic motions, swift and monotonous, with which she combed out the tangles, brushed it smooth, and braided it neatly for the night. When she cleaned the comb and wound the thin wisp of loose hairs around her fingers he always felt a sense of distaste – though he had never admitted it to himself. If she felt somewhat the same when he set his lean jaw askew to meet the razor, and masked his features in lather, or when the human form divine was in the ignominious attitude of pulling on a shirt, she never admitted it either. They had no complaint to make of one another, these good people. She was an irreproachable wife, albeit somewhat wearing, as good women often are; he was a model husband, though not pre-eminently successful as a 'provider,' which also is apt to occur. And they had loved each other for twenty-three years.

That they still loved each other neither doubted, but the friction of personal dissimilarity in a too close intimacy had worn and bitten away that golden cord to the merest thread, all unobserved.

Mr Waterson lay still and revolved his secret. Yes, he had better tell her now. The oldest boy, his father's special pride, who had been graduated at twenty and stepped into congenial employment at once with a scientific institution, had sent home a letter with a startling proposition. Couldn't father sell out his business, or let it temporarily, and go with an exploring expedition now forming? He, the son, could get him a small place, he thought, and he would so love to have Dad along. He knew it would be hard on mother, but couldn't mother go to Jennie's, now Jennie had a home?

Mr Waterson had carried the letter in his pocket for some days, pondering hopelessly on this golden opportunity. All his life he had longed for such a chance. It meant a period of freedom, and his patient soul expanded at the thought – time to think, men to talk with who were interested in the same things, growth, study, perhaps some real discovery. But duty held him in his place. He must support his wife, maintain his home, carry on his business.

Before answering, however, he meant to broach the subject to his wife. Perhaps he had a faint, unspoken hope that she might see a way for him to go. Perhaps he felt rather the need of her strong good sense to strengthen him in the way of duty and help him to refuse.

So now, while she stood there, holding her hair in a firm clutch and dragging the comb through it with smart, tearing strokes – he always wondered that she had any hair left – he told her of Jack's letter.

She listened quietly, saying nothing till he had quite finished. Then, when her braid was plaited down to the thin diminishing end, she wrapped her blue kimono close about her and sat down on the edge of the bed, looking at him more lovingly than usual.

'Why don't you do it?' she said, with her brisk smile. 'It would do you good!'

He was much surprised. 'But, my dear – how can I? Here are you – and the house – and the business. If I could sell it—' he added, with a flicker of hope.

Mr Waterson kept a dry goods store, a quiet, reliable old-fashioned dry goods store, which brought in just enough from year to year, and never any more.

'I can sell the business for you,' said his wife cheerfully. 'I'll run it awhile, and sell it – to advantage. Just you try me!'

He believed she could if she set her mind to it.

'But the house – the expenses.'

'I can manage the house, too. Just you try me, John. You put everything in my name and go! It's the chance you've always wanted, isn't it?'

It was, without doubt, and he wanted it so much that her cheerful energy and determined optimism wrought him to the pitch of enthusiasm necessary for so great a step.

He put all his property in his wife's name, gave her power of attorney to attend to his affairs, drew half of their savings and started off on the expedition.

He felt like a lad of twenty instead of a man of forty-five. The years rolled off from him with his responsibilities. Eager, clear-minded, full of hope and courage, more like a brother than a father with his son, he set forth with his face to the future.

He had thought himself an elderly man. He felt now like a young one. He had thought himself in duty bound to work always for his wife and family. To his sudden amazement he found that the family cares he had carried for so long rolled off him like a forgotten burden. House, store, business obligations – they had disappeared.

He did think a good deal about his wife at first. So ingrained was his conviction that women should stay at home that it did not seem right to think of her as running a store, and yet he knew she could do it, and do it well. That summer that he had broken his leg she had carried on the business for him most successfully. He wrote some letters of advice, growing shorter and farther apart as the weeks passed. Letters were always difficult and unsatisfying to him. They were even more so to her. She was a woman of deeds rather than words, even spoken ones, and written language was not at all her medium of expression. So she wrote presently to this effect:

'Now, my dear husband, you really can't advise from that distance. I've undertaken the business and it's going nicely. You're off on your expedition and that's going nicely, I judge. Just dismiss this end from your mind, dear. Let's make an agreement right now that if either one of us is sick or injured or needs the other in any way, we'll write or wire at once, but so long as things go all right we won't bother to write unless we feel like it. I know you love me, and I love you, and we'll be glad to see each other again, but for now – just go and play!'

So with a sense of deep though hardly recognized relief, John Waterson let all his personal ties fall loose, and only at rare intervals did he send brief, cheerful letters home, to tell of some wonderful new find they had made, some book he had read, some fruitful talk with other scholars, some work he contemplated. Scant as his opportunities had been, so earnest had been his study along the lines which interested him that he was able to hold his own among these scientists and even to contribute something to their discussions. Now and then he sent her newspaper reports in which the achievements of the expedition were recorded, and in which his own name occasionally appeared.

As he receded from her daily sight, as his always rather perfunctory letters grew few and far between, and as she read of his doings and what others thought of him, he began to loom larger and more attractive in her mind. He would have been surprised indeed to know how she treasured those scant letters now, though far too proud to ask for more after she herself had proposed the lightening of their correspondence. From the first years of their marriage she had not loved her husband as she loved him now.

Then when he wrote to her that there was a chance for him to go still farther, on a long voyage with explorations in another country, which might keep him away another year or two, it took all her strength to send just the right kind of a letter to ensure his going.

'That's *fine*, John,' she said; 'simply *fine*. I am so glad for you. I wouldn't have you miss it for anything. Of course I hate to lose you for so long, but we've had twenty-three years together, and will have all the rest of our lives together; this is perhaps the only time you'll ever have to go where you want to. It's fine for Jack, too, and for you to be together. Don't miss it on my account. Things are going on well here: the business is looking up; my health is fine. I may be able to sell the house – if I don't hear from you to the contrary.'

He really felt a little ashamed to leave her so long, but she seemed so happy, and so – well, he was almost nettled by her serene assurance that she could run the business as well as he could.

Jack was eager to have him go.

'Oh, come on, Dad! Mother's all right. She's having the time of her life. Jennie's there, you know, in case anything should happen, but mother's never sick. And Walter's doing well in the city; he'd help out if she got in trouble with the business. Come along!'

So Mr Waterson, already strengthened and stimulated by congenial occupation, went over seas with the party. He wrote few letters, but he did find time to write a monograph on the single branch of the single subject of which he now really knew as much as any one man, and when this monograph was read at a great international convention, and printed, and praised far and wide by those who knew enough to appreciate it, he sent the accounts of it, with the paper itself, to his wife, and felt that he had not lived in vain.

It was four years before he returned to his home city. Two feelings strove within him, making him alternately happy and miserable. One was a homesick longing for his wife, his house

even – almost his store. The other was a shuddering disinclination to go back to what, in this light, looked like a prison. He,
who had been a man among men for so long, to go back and be
told to shut windows and lock doors and wind clocks – things
he always forgot to do, unless so told; he, who had strayed for
thousands of miles, with his own luggage and accumulating
papers and specimens – he wondered ruefully where he should
put them – now dreaded with a real horror to reconfine himself
to the bookcase in the parlor, the desk in the attic, the two
bureau drawers.

Mrs Waterson meanwhile had had four years to work in, at
work which, to her sincere surprise, she had found more congenial than that of forever recooking similar food and reclearing
the same rooms, clothes and dishes.

She ran the store a few months on its old lines, then sent for
an efficiency expert and spent several days in close consultation
with him. She was not content with his report on the store, but
asked him his opinion on other businesses in the town, and
paid for it.

'Rather an expensive young man, wasn't he?' a conservative
friend inquired.

'The most profitable visitor I ever had,' she replied with
decision.

She drew more profit from his visit than his direct advice.
Hers was a mind that saw the principle of things. She grasped
the simple secret of 'efficiency' and proceeded to apply it.

If Mr Waterson had left his business behind him as one dropping a burden, Mrs Waterson left her housekeeping as one
escaping from a treadmill. Her natural energies had now for the
first time room for full action. Her store blossomed with sudden
changes, wisely planned. She enlarged here, altered there,

added new features. It became, in a modest way, a department store. To the 'gents' furnishing' department she added a hand laundry – a laundry so safe and sanitary, so quick and clean, that it doubled her trade in that line. If the laundry itself was no great profit – and it was not at first – it added greatly to the profits of the business. With the laundry went naturally a mending bureau; that grew swiftly into a plain-sewing, and that into a dressmaking establishment, all in connection with the background of dry goods.

Exulting in her new freedom, proving her power and finding it increase with use, Mrs Waterson used her first year's profits to add to her building and to acquire an interest in a grocery store next door. The second year she bought out a small hotel which had utterly failed to pay. She made it pay. She knew the kind of manager to hire, and how to manage him, she had her own house-furnishing department to draw on, her grocery business, and her laundry, now solidly flourishing.

The third year saw her department store and her hotel paying handsomely, with a bank account rolling up steadily. She had sold their house, in the second year of her husband's absence, to good advantage, and bought a larger lot, rather on the outskirts of the town, with a long slope down to a quiet river and numbers of old trees. The house on it was of no value, and as soon as she saw her way clear she had it torn down and began to build.

Never in her life had she been so happy, not even when love's fulfillment had for a while stilled that insistent urge within her which always had demanded more to do. Doubtless if she had not had her pleasant family life to look back on, her satisfactory children to be proud of, and her husband – for whom she longed increasingly – to look forward to, all this joyful exertion and new pride would have had its empty side, and left her often lonely. But her domestic conscience was clean; her woman's heart had given and taken to the full, and she found time to enjoy Jennie's baby almost as much as any other grandmother.

Jennie's husband she learned fully to approve of. He was now a general manager in her big store, doing excellent work, and drawing a much higher salary than he had before. The business ran on well, with only such risks and difficulties as roused her to fresh courage and resource.

The house rose with speed. She had been slow and careful in its planning, and now urged the work to completion. He was coming – she wanted it ready for him.

Mr Waterson had not written since announcing the probable date of their return. Why should he? He was coming as fast as letters could, and, if he was delayed here and there, why so would the letters have been. He was coming as fast as he could, and as the slow miles passed, the thoughts of home, the thoughts of her, grew steadily sweeter.

When at last he was on the steamer, with only the ocean between them, the thoughts grew into keen longings. He wanted to see home again, the pleasant town where he had so many friends, where he felt now he could hold his head higher after his scientific honors. He wanted to see his daughter, and his new granddaughter, described as a wonder of the world. Most of all he wanted to see his wife.

Two things he did not long for, though they seemed more endurable as he neared them – his store and the cramped quarters of his home. He wondered if she had sold it, and where they should live.

She met him at the station with a neat electric brougham.

'Ours!' she said. In its seclusion they sat close and held one another so tightly that it hurt.

'Oh, my dear, my dear!' she breathed occasionally. And then he would kiss her again.

How young she looked! How pretty she looked! How cheery and how – smooth! She seemed some way sweeter, less peremptory.

'I've got a surprise for you, John – a big one!'

'I'm not surprised at anything you do, my darling,' he protested. But he was.

The wide grounds, the curving driveway, the tall trees, the glowing banks of flowers, they all surprised him. Then the wide-winged, handsome house, its hospitable hall with the open fire, the big parlors, the dining-room all rich with panelled wood, the pantry and kitchen and laundry – all on one side.

She took him across the hall again, and through a little passage, double-doored. 'The library,' she said. Back of its shelf-lined calm a smaller room. 'Your study, dear!' A little iron stair ran upward. She led him to the floor above. 'Your bedroom, darling.' A roomy bathroom and big closets, with another little passage. 'And this is mine.'

He looked about and caught his breath a little.

'You've done all this,' he said, 'while I was just playing!'

'While you were beginning your real work, dear heart – the work you're going to carry on. While you were making the whole town proud of you – yes, the whole country, if they knew enough. *And* your wife! Why, John!' she held him off and looked at him with wet, shining eyes, 'John, darling, I never appreciated you before. To think of the man you are burying yourself in that old store – just for our sakes! You built the business, John, honest and strong; I've followed your steps. Now you shall really work at what you love – and so will I!

'Surely it's a woman's business to make the home! We ought to have thirty years yet to love each other in!

'This is Our House, John!'

BEE WISE

'It's a queer name,' said the man reporter.

'No queerer than the other,' said the woman reporter. 'There are two of them, you know – Beewise and Herways.'

'It reminds me of something,' he said, 'some quotation – do you get it?'

'I think I do,' she said. 'But I won't tell. You have to consider for yourself.' And she laughed quietly. But his education did not supply the phrase.

They were sent down, both of them, from different papers, to write up a pair of growing towns in California which had been built up so swiftly and yet so quietly that it was only now after they were well established and prosperous that the world had discovered something strange about them.

This seems improbable enough in the land of most unbridled and well-spurred reporters, but so it was.

One town was a little seaport, a tiny sheltered nook, rather cut off by the coast hills from previous adoption. The other lay up beyond those hills, in a delightful valley all its own with two most precious streams in it that used to tumble in roaring white during the rainy season down their steep little canyons to the sea, and trickled there, unseen, the rest of the year.

The man reporter wrote up the story in his best descriptive vein, adding embellishments where they seemed desirable, withholding such facts as appeared to contradict his treatment, and doing his best to cast over the whole a strong sex-interest and the glamor of vague suspicions.

The remarkable thing about the two towns was that their population consisted very largely of women and more largely of children, but there were men also, who seemed happy enough, and answered the questions of the reporters with good-will. They disclaimed, these men residents, anything peculiar or ultra-feminine in the settlements, and one hearty young Englishman assured them that the disproportion was no greater than in England. 'Or in some of our New England towns,' said another citizen, 'where the men have all gone west or to the big cities, and there's a whole township of withering women-folks with a few ministers and hired men.'

The woman reporter questioned more deeply perhaps, perhaps less offensively; at any rate she learned more than the other of the true nature of the sudden civic growth. After both of them had turned in their reports, after all the other papers had sent down representatives, and later magazine articles had been written with impressive pictures, after the accounts of permitted visitors and tourists had been given, there came to be a fuller knowledge than was possible at first, naturally, but no one got a clearer vision of it all than was given to the woman reporter that first day, when she discovered that the Mayor of Herways was an old college mate of hers.

The story was far better than the one she sent in, but she was a lady as well as a reporter, and respected confidence.

It appeared that the whole thing started in that college class, the year after the reporter had left it, being suddenly forced to drop education and take to earning a living. In the senior class was a group of girls of markedly different types, and yet so similar in their basic beliefs and ultimate purposes that they had grown through the four years of college life into a little 'sorority' of their own. They called it 'The Morning Club,' which sounded innocent enough, and kept it secret among themselves. They were girls of strong character, all of them, each with a definite purpose as to her life work.

There was the one they all called 'Mother,' because her whole heart and brain were dominated by the love of children, the thought of children, the wish to care for children; and very close to her was the 'Teacher,' with a third, the 'Nurse,' forming a group within a group. These three had endless discussions among themselves, with big vague plans for future usefulness.

Then there was the 'Minister,' the 'Doctor,' and the far-seeing one they called the 'Statesman.' One sturdy, square-browed little girl was dubbed 'Manager' for reasons frankly prominent, as with the 'Artist' and the 'Engineer.' There were some dozen or twenty of them, all choosing various professions, but all alike in their determination to practice those professions, married or single, and in their vivid hope for better methods of living. 'Advanced' in their ideas they were, even in an age of advancement, and held together in especial by the earnest words of the Minister, who was always urging upon them the power of solidarity.

Just before their graduation something happened. It happened to the Manager, and she called a special meeting to lay it before the club.

The Manager was a plain girl, strong and quiet. She was the one who always overflowed with plans and possessed the unusual faculty of carrying out the plans she made, a girl who had always looked forward to working hard for her own living of choice as well as necessity, and enjoyed the prospect.

'Girls!' said she, when they were all grouped and quiet. 'I've news for you – splendid news! I wouldn't spring it on you like this, but we shall be all broken and scattered in a little while – it's just in time!' She looked around at their eager faces, enjoying the sensation created.

'Say – look here!' she suddenly interjected. 'You aren't any of you engaged, are you?'

One hand was lifted, modestly.

'What does he *do*?' pursued the speaker. 'I don't care who he is, and I know he's all right or you wouldn't look at him – but what does he *do*?'

'He isn't sure yet,' meekly answered the Minister, 'but he's to be a manufacturer, I think.'

'No objection to your preaching, of course.' This was hardly a question.

'He says he'll hear me every Sunday – if I'll let him off at home on weekdays,' the Minister replied with a little giggle.

They all smiled approval.

'He's all right,' the Manager emphatically agreed. 'Now then girls – to put you out of your misery at once – what has happened to me is ten million dollars.'

There was a pause, and then a joyous clapping of hands.

'Bully for you!'

'Hurrah for Margery!'

'You deserve it!'

'Say, you'll treat, won't you?'

They were as pleased as if the huge and sudden fortune were common property.

'Long lost uncle – or what, Marge?'

'Great uncle – my grandmother's brother. Went to California with the 'forty-niners – got lost, for reasons of his own, I suspect. Found some prodigious gold mine – solid veins and nuggets, and spent quiet years in piling it up and investing it.'

'When did he die?' asked the Nurse softly.

'He's not dead – but I'm afraid he soon will be,' answered the Manager slowly. 'It appears he's hired people to look up the family and see what they were like – said he didn't propose to ruin any feeble-minded people with all that money. He was pleased to like my record. Said—' she chuckled, 'said I was a man after his own heart! And he's come on here to get acquainted and to make this over before he's gone. He says no dead man's bequest would be as safe as a live man's gift.'

'And he's *given* you all that!'

'Solid and safe as can be. Says he's quite enough left to end his days in peace. He's pretty old . . . Now then, girls—' She was all animation. 'Here's my plan. Part of this property is land, land and water, in California. An upland valley, a little port on the coast – an economic base, you see – and capital to develop it. I propose that we form a combination, go out there, settle, build, manage – make a sample town – set a new example to the world – a place of woman's work and world-work too . . . What do you say?'

They said nothing for the moment. This was a large proposition.

The Manager went on eagerly: 'I'm not binding you to anything; this is a plain business offer. What I propose to do is to develop that little port, open a few industries and so on, build a reservoir up above and regulate the water supply – use it for power – have great gardens and vineyards. Oh, girls – it's California! We can make a little Eden! And as to Motherhood—' she looked around with a slow, tender smile, 'there's no place better for babies!'

The Mother, the Nurse, and the Teacher all agreed to this.

'I've only got it roughly sketched out in my mind,' pursued the speaker eagerly. 'It will take time and care to work it all out right. But there's capital enough to tide us over first difficulties, and then it shall be just as solid and simple as any other place, a practical paying proposition, a perfectly natural little town, planned, built, and managed—' her voice grew solemn, 'by women – for women – and *children*! A place that will be of real help to humanity. – Oh girls, it's such a chance!'

That was the beginning.

The woman reporter was profoundly interested. 'I wish I could have stayed that year,' she said soberly.

'I wish you had, Jean! But never mind – you can stay now. We need the right kind of work on our little local paper – not just reporting – you can do more than that, can't you?'

'I should hope so!' Jean answered heartily. 'I spent six months on a little country paper – ran the whole thing nearly, except editorials and setting up. If there's room here for me I can tell you I'm coming – day before yesterday!' So the Woman Reporter came to Herways to work, and went up, o'nights, to Beewise to live, whereby she gradually learned in completeness what this bunch of women had done, and was able to prepare vivid little pamphlets of detailed explanations which paved the way for so many other regenerated towns.

And this is what they did:

The economic base was a large tract of land from the sea-coast hills back to the high rich valley beyond. Two spring-fed brooks ran from the opposite ends of the valley and fell steeply to the beach below through narrow canyons.

The first cash outlay of the Manager, after starting the cable line from beach to hill which made the whole growth possible, was to build a reservoir at either end, one of which furnished drinking water and irrigation in the long summer, the other a swimming pool and a steady stream of power. The powerhouse in the canon was supplemented by wind-mills on the heights and tide-mill on the beach, and among them they furnished light, heat, and power – clean, economical electric energy. Later they set up a solar engine which furnished additional force, to minimize labor and add to their producing capacity.

For supporting industries, to link them with the world, they had these: First a modest export of preserved fruits, exquisitely prepared, packed in the new fibre cartons which are more sanitary than tin and lighter than glass. In the hills they raised Angora goats, and from their wool supplied a little mill with high-grade down-soft yarn, and sent out fluffy blankets, flannels and knitted garments. Cotton too they raised, magnificent cotton, and silk of the best, and their own mill supplied their principal needs. Small mills, pretty and healthful, with bright-clad women singing at their looms for the short working hours. From these materials the designers and craftswomen, helped by the Artist, made garments, beautiful, comfortable, easy and lasting, and from year to year the demand for 'Beewise' gowns and coats increased.

In a windy corner, far from their homes, they set up a tannery, and from the well-prepared hides of their goats they made various leather goods, gloves and shoes, – 'Beewise' shoes, that came to be known at last through the length and breadth of the land – a shoe that fitted the human foot, allowed for free action, and was pleasant to the eye. Many of the townspeople wore sandals and they were also made for merchandise.

Their wooded heights they treasured carefully. A forestry service was started, the whole area studied, and the best rate of planting and cutting established. Their gardens were rich and beautiful; they sold honey, and distilled perfumes.

'This place is to grow in value, not deteriorate,' said the Manager, and she planted for the future.

At first they made a tent city, the tents dyed with rich colors, dry-floored and warm. Later, the Artist and the Architect and the Engineer to the fore, they built houses of stone and wood and heavy sheathing paper, making their concrete of the dead palm leaves and the loose bark of swift-growing eucalyptus, which was planted everywhere and rose over night almost, like the Beanstalk – houses beautiful comfortable, sea-shell clean.

Steadily the Manager held forth to her associates on what she called 'the business end' of their enterprise. 'The whole thing must pay,' she said, 'else it cannot stand – it will not be imitated. We want to show what a bunch of women can do successfully. Men can help, but this time we will manage.'

Among their first enterprises was a guest house, planned and arranged mainly for women and children. In connection with this was a pleasure garden for all manner of games, gymnastics and dancing, with wide courts and fields and roofed places for use in the rainy season.

There was a sanitarium, where the Doctor and the Nurse gathered helpers about them, attended to casual illness, to the needs of child-birth, and to such visitors who came to them as needed care.

Further there was a baby-garden that grew to a kindergarten, and that to a school, and in time the fame of their educational work spread far and wide, and there was a constantly increasing list of applicants. For 'Beewise' was a Residence Club; no one could live there without being admitted by the others.

The beach town, Herways, teemed with industry. At the little pier their small coast steamer landed, bringing such supplies as they did not make, leaving and taking passengers. Where the beach was level and safe they bathed and swam, having a water-pavilion for shelter and refreshment. From beach to hill-top ran a shuttle service of light cars; 'Jacob's Ladder,' they called it.

The broad plan of the Manager was this: with her initial capital to develop a working plant that would then run itself at a profit, and she was surprised to find how soon that profit appeared, and how considerable it was.

Then came in sufficient numbers, friends, relatives, curious strangers. These women had no objection to marrying on their own terms. And when a man is sufficiently in love he sees no serious objection to living in an earthly paradise and doing his share in building up a new community. But the men were carefully selected. They must prove clean health – for a high grade of motherhood was the continuing ideal of the group.

Visitors came, increasing in numbers as accommodations increased. But as the accommodations, even to land for tenting must be applied for beforehand, there was no horde of gaping tourists to vulgarize the place.

As for the working people – there were no others. Everyone in Herways and Beewise worked, especially the women – that was the prime condition of admission; every citizen must be clean physically and morally as far as could be ascertained, but no amount of negative virtues availed them if they were not valuable in social service. So they had eager applications from professional women as fast as the place was known, and some they made room for – in proportion. Of doctors they could maintain but a few; a dentist or two, a handful of nurses, more teachers, several artists of the more practical sort who made beauty for the use of their neighbors, and a few far-reaching world servants, who might live here, at least part of the time, and send their work broadcast, such as poets, writers and composers.

But most of the people were the more immediately necessary workers, the men who built and dug and ran the engines, the women who spun and wove and worked among the flowers, or vice versa if they chose, and those who attended to the daily wants of the community.

There were no servants in the old sense. The dainty houses had no kitchens, only the small electric outfit where those who would might prepare coffee and the like. Food was prepared in clean wide laboratories, attended by a few skilled experts, highly paid, who knew their business, and great progress was made in the study of nutrition, and in the keeping of all the people well. Nevertheless the food cost less than if prepared by many unskilled, ill-paid cooks in imperfect kitchens.

The great art of child-culture grew apace among them with the best methods now known. Froebelian and Montessorian ideas and systems were honored and well used, and with the growing knowledge accumulated by years of observation and experience the right development of childhood at last became not merely an ideal, but a commonplace. Well-born children grew there like the roses they played among, raced and swam and swung, and knew only health, happiness and the joy of unconscious learning.

The two towns filled to their normal limits.

'Here we must stop,' said the Manager in twenty years' time. 'If we have more people here we shall develop the diseases of cities. But look at our financial standing – every cent laid out is now returned, the place is absolutely self-supporting and will grow richer as years pass. Now we'll swarm like the bees and start another – what do you say?'

And they did, beginning another rational paradise in another beautiful valley, safer and surer for the experience behind them.

But far wider than their own immediate increase was the spread of their ideas, of the proven truth of their idea, that a group of human beings could live together in such wise as to decrease the hours of labor, increase the value of the product, ensure health, peace and prosperity, and multiply human happiness beyond measure.

In every part of the world the thing was possible; wherever people could live at all they could live to better advantage. The economic base might vary widely, but wherever there were a few hundred women banded together their combined labor could produce wealth, and their combined motherhood ensure order, comfort, happiness, and the improvement of humanity.

'Go to the ant, thou sluggard, consider her ways and be wise.'

FULFILMENT

Two women rocked slowly in the large splint chairs on a breezy corner of the hotel piazza. One sat as if she grew there, as if a rocking-chair were her natural habitat, as if she passed her life occupying rocking-chairs, merely eating and sleeping in the necessary intervals between one sitting and the next; as if, without a rocking-chair, she lacked explanation, missing it as a sailor his ship, or a cowboy his horse.

The other looked comfortable enough, and rocked appreciatively, but her air and her garments suggested other seats: desk-chairs, parlor-car chairs, and no chairs at all – long erect standing, brisk continued walking. There was about her even a subtle suggestion of one running easily, and this in spite of pleasant relaxation, such as one sees in the lines of a sleeping hound.

Mrs Edgar Maxwell, she of the soul affinity to rocking-chairs, was daintily engaged with some bright fancy work, a graceful wildrose wreath on a large linen centerpiece. Her white fingers were dexterously busy, but her eyes were placid pools of contentment.

Her sister, Irma Russell, did nothing. Her vigorous supple hands were quiet, though carrying their clear suggestion of active power, but her eyes were vividly alive.

They talked freely, with increasing intimacy, with a clear view of two long empty stretches of verandah, and neither of them thought that the closed slats of the long green-blinded window beside them concealed a conscienceless novelist. They did not know he was in the hotel, as indeed he intended no one should. He was only waiting over a day to meet a friend, and carefully avoiding the crowds of female admirers, toward whom decent courtesy and business principles compelled some politeness when unescapable.

The term 'conscienceless' is perhaps too severe to describe him; he had an artistic conscience, deep, broad, accurate, relentless, but refused to be bound by the standards of most people.

Mrs Maxwell held her work off from her approving eyes, and drew a happy little sigh of admiration. Her glance dwelt briefly on the green slopes and blue heights about them, then long and tenderly on her boy and girl, playing tennis with the other young folks in the near distance.

'Oh, Irma!' she said. 'If only you were as happy as I am!'

'How do you know I'm not. You haven't seen me for twenty years, you know. Do I look unhappy?'

'Oh, no! I think you look wonderfully well, and you have certainly done well out there.'

'Out there' was California. It seemed the end of the earth to Mrs Maxwell.

Irma smiled. 'You are a dear girl – you always were, Elsie. It's a treat to see you. We haven't had a chance at a good talk for all this while – about half our lives. Pitch in now – tell me about your happiness.

Elsie laid down her work for a moment and looked lovingly at her sister.

'You always were – different,' she said. 'I remember just as well how we used to talk – just girls! And now we're both forty and over – and here we are together again! But I've nothing to tell – that you don't know.'

'I know the facts, of course,' her sister agreed. 'You wrote me of your engagement, sent wedding cards and baby-cards, and all – and photographs of everybody. But you never were much of a letter-writer – you always did talk better than you wrote, Elsie. What I want you to talk about is first your happiness – and, second, your superiority.'

'My superiority! Why, Irma! What do you mean?'

'Just a little air of "Poor Irma" I detect about you – that's all. I'm perfectly well; I'm doing nicely with my prunes and apricots; I want to know why you think you're happier than I am.'

Elsie met the affectionate quizzical gray eyes with the peaceful conviction of her own soft blue ones. 'You certainly know that, Irma. You've seen Hugh – and the children.'

'Yes, I've seen Hugh and the children – they are dears – I cheerfully agree to that. But what I want is the story of your life. Come – I've been a day at your house and here a week, getting acquainted all over again – and this is the first clear safe quiet time we've had together. You're just as sweet as ever, and I love to see you so contented – you haven't changed a bit, for all your "Hugh and the children."'

'There isn't anything to tell, Irma, but what you know. Hugh came the year you left. It helped me not to miss you so cruelly. We couldn't marry for some time – he had to save, and I waited. But I was glad to – I'd have waited till now for Hugh . . . Then we had to struggle along for a good while – you knew that, too, and often helped, bless you! The children came pretty soon – and then we lost little Bobby . . . and the dear baby that never even lived to be named.' The blue eyes filled, but she looked at the gay young tennis players again and turned bravely back to her sister. 'There was waiting, and work, and going without – there always has been a lot of planning and some sacrifices, of course. But there has been love, always, and the blessed children . . . even the grief – we had *together* . . . It is life, Irma, it is living – and if I seem to say, "Poor Irma!" – which I deny, it is only on that account. A woman who hasn't married, who isn't a mother – I don't care how successful she is – she hasn't *lived*.'

'I see,' said Irma, somewhat drily. 'I thought as much. I wanted you to say it, that's all. And now will you answer me a few questions. How do you spend your time?'

'My time?' Elsie looked at her perplexedly. 'Spend my time? Why, as any woman does.'

'Yes, but specify, please – what do you *do*? Hour by hour – what does your day mean to you?'

The conscienceless novelist behind the green slats had been half dozing on the little hard sofa in the corner, and carrying on a half-hearted skirmish with the rudiments of ordinary people's principles. Now he trampled on those principles, kicked them out entirely, drew forth a worn little note-book, and devoted himself with whole-hearted enthusiasm to the business of listening. 'Invaluable material!' he murmured inaudibly.

'I don't know as I ever thought of it that way,' Elsie said slowly.

'Well – think of it that way now,' her sister urged. 'You get up at – shall we say seven? What do you do – with brain and hand and heart, all day?'

'I – why, I keep house. You know!' protested Elsie.

'Do you make the fire? Get breakfast? Wash and iron?'

'No indeed – of course not. That was one reason Hugh waited. He said his wife was not to be his servant,' quoted Mrs Maxwell proudly.

'I see. Well – what *do* you do?'

'Why – when the children were little there was more to do than there is now – of course, night and day too.'

'You had no nurse?'

'No – we couldn't afford that. Besides, I preferred to care for my children myself – it is a mother's sacred duty, I think. And a pleasure,' she added carefully.

Irma looked at her sister with tender sympathy. She loved her far too much to suggest that for this sacred duty she had never prepared herself by either study or practice, and that in performance of it she had lost fifty per cent of her children. That would have been cruel – and useless.

'We'll skip the babies, Elsie. Your youngest is fifteen. You haven't had to spend many hours a day on them for ten years or so, now have you? Come – what do you *do* with your time? Twenty-four hours a day; eight out for sleep, one for toilet activities, two for three meals – that leaves thirteen. What do you do for a day's work in thirteen hours?'

'Oh, I'm sure it's not that!' protested Elsie. 'It can't be!'

'Irma produced pencil and paper. 'What time do you get up – seven?'

'Ye – es—' agreed her sister, rather faintly.

'Seven-thirty,' wrote Irma. 'Breakfast at eight?'

'Yes.'

'An hour to eat it?'

'Oh, no – half an hour – the children have to get off – and Hugh. We're always through by eight-thirty.'

'What time is lunch?'

'One o'clock – that doesn't take long either – the children have to hurry – say half an hour.'

'And dinner?'

'Dinner's at seven – Hugh is so often late. I'd like it at six-thirty – on account of the cook – but it's seven.'

'Well, now, my dear sister. I'll give you your evening to play in; but you have from eight-thirty to one, and one-thirty to seven to account for – ten hours. A good working day – what do you do with it?'

'Ten hours!' Elsie would not admit it.

'Ten hours – your own figures. I'll give you another half-hour after breakfast, and after lunch – just to dawdle, read the paper, and so on, but that leaves nine. Now then, Elsie – speak up!'

Elsie spoke up, a little warmly.

'You can't measure housekeeping that way – by hours. Sometimes it's one thing and sometimes another. There is always something to do – always! And then there's one thing you forget – people coming in – and my going out.'

'Exercise – we'll allow an hour for exercise – you don't walk more than an hour a day, do you, sister?'

'I don't mean just walking – one hasn't time to walk much. I mean calling – and shopping.'

'And you haven't any idea how many hours a day – or a week – you call – or shop?'

'No, I haven't. I tell you it's impossible to figure it out that way. And then when the children come home I have to *be there*.' She grasped a thought, and lifted her head rather defiantly. 'That's what housekeeping is,' she said proudly. 'It's being there!'

'I see,' said Irma, and wrote it down. (So did the novelist.)

'I'll stop quizzing you as to hours, child – it's evident you never made a time-schedule in your life – much less kept one. Did you ever make a budget? Do you know, as a matter of fact, if your housekeeping is more or less efficient, more or less expensive, than your neighbors?'

Elsie drew herself up, a little hurt. 'I am sure nobody could be more economical than I am. Hugh always says I am such a good manager. I often make my house-dresses myself, and Betty's; and I watch the sales.'

'But you don't know – nor Hugh – anything definite about it? Comparing with other families of the same size – on a similar amount?'

'I'd like to know what you're driving at, Irma. No – we neither of us has made any such calculation. No two families are alike. Each one is a law to itself – has to be. If I am satisfied – and Hugh is – whose business is it besides?'

'Not mine,' agreed Irma cheerfully. 'Excuse me, dear, if I've offended you. I wanted to get at the real working of your life if I could, to compare with mine. Let's take a new tack. Tell me – have you kept up your physical culture?'

'I have not,' said Elsie, a little sharply. 'Motherhood interferes with gymnastics.'

'Are you as strong and active as you used to be?'

'I am not,' still a little sharply. 'You don't seem to understand, Irma – I suppose you can't, not being a mother – that if you have children you can't have everything else.'

'Have you kept up your music? Or your languages?'

'No – for the same reason.'

'Have you learned anything new? Now, Elsie, don't be angry – what I'm getting at is this: You have spent twenty years in one way, I in another. You have certain visible possessions and joys which I have not. You have also had experiences – griefs – cares – which I have not. I'm just trying to see if besides these you have other gains, or if these are the only gains to offset what I may show.'

'I'm not angry with you, Irma – how could I be? You are my only sister, and you've always been good to me. I'll make you all the concessions you wish. Marriage is a mutual compromise, dear. A man gives up his freedom and a woman gives up hers. They have their love – their home – their children. But nobody can have everything.'

'That's a fact – I'll grant you that, Elsie. But tell me one more thing – what do you look forward to?'

'I don't look forward,' protested Elsie stoutly. 'I don't believe in it. "Sufficient unto the day—"'

'"Is the evil thereof"?' asked Irma. 'Please do look forward. You are forty-two. You'll live, I hope, to be twice that. What do you expect to accomplish in the next forty years?' There was a deeper note in her voice.

Elsie dropped her work and looked at her, a little shaken.

'As long as you have lived before – and no preliminary childhood to wade through! From now on, full grown, experienced, with your home, your happiness, your motherhood achieved; with your housekeeping surely no great burden by this time. With no more children coming and these two fairly grown – they'll be off your hands entirely soon – college – business – marriage. Then you won't have to "be there" so much, will you? What are you going to do – with forty years of life?'

'I may not live—' suggested Elsie, rather as if it were an agreeable alternative.

'And you may. We're a long-lived lot, all of us. And you know motherhood really adds to the chances of longevity – if you don't die at it. I'll excuse you from the last ten though; after seventy you can rock all the time. Call it thirty years, ten hours a day – or nine – or eight – why Elsie – don't you even *want* to do anything?'

Elsie gave a little nervous laugh. 'I feel like quoting from *Potash and Perlmutter*,' she said, '"Whadda y' mean do anything?" Come, you leave off questioning me and let's hear all the fine things you've been doing – you never would write about yourself.'

Irma rose and walked softly, smoothly, up and down the piazza, watched with slanting eagerness by the eyes behind the slats. She came back and stood near her sister, leaning against the railing.

'All right – I'll make up for it now. And in the first place, Elsie, I don't want you to think I minimize your happiness – it is a great big splendid slice of life that you've had and I haven't. I'm sorry I've missed it – I'd like to have had that too. Well – here's my record:

'I went to California as you know at twenty-one. Sort of governess-companion. All of our people protested – but I *was* twenty-one – they couldn't stop me. I went because I wanted to grow – and I have grown. I studied the place, the people, the opportunities. I kept at work, saved my salary, added to my capacities. Took that chance to go to Europe with the Cheeseboro kids – saw a lot – learned a lot – got three languages, a world of experience – and a good bit of money. That was at twenty-four.

'Came back to the coast and invested my money in a small private school business.'

'You gave me some of it, you dear thing,' Elsie interrupted, affectionately.

'Oh, well – that was natural. I had enough left to start. I did well with the school, and set up a sort of boarding-school – a health-and-educational stunt, up in the foot-hills. Bought land up there – a fine breezy mesa it is, with an artesian well of its own.

'I worked – but it's work I love. Built on, enlarged my staff, cautiously. Added a sort of winter camp for adults – not invalids. By the time I was thirty I had quite a place up there, a lovely home of my own all by itself on a sort of promontory – with such a garden! O Elsie – you're coming out to see me some day – all of you!

'Then I went very cautiously, used my accumulating experience, invested wisely and slowly. Things move rather quickly out there, but common sense keeps on being useful. As to money I'm very comfortable indeed, and may be rich – rich enough. All sweet, safe, honestly-earned money – my own.

'But that's the least of it. What I'm gladdest of is the *living*. The kind of work I've done has helped people – lots of people – especially children. I've been a sort of foster-mother to hundreds of them, you see, some fifteen years, averaging twenty new ones a year – that's three hundred, besides those in the first five beginning years.

'Also – I adopted some.'

Elsie started. 'And never said a word about it!'

'No – I wanted to see how it would turn out. But I've got four I call my own – took 'em as babies, you know. They're a splendid lot. Two about the age of Tom and Betty – two younger – I'll show you their pictures presently.

'Personally, physically, I mean, I'm a hundred per cent. stronger and more efficient than I used to be. I've trained – years and years of it – in sunlight and mountain air. It's not just strength, but skill. I can climb mountains, ride, shoot, fence, row, swim, play golf, tennis, billiards, dance like a youngster – or a professional. I'm more *alive*, literally, than I was at twenty. I have a good car and can run it as well as the man.

'Then I know more – I've had plenty of time to study. The town is only a half-hour run – the city about an hour.

'I belong to clubs, classes, societies. I'm a citizen, too – I can vote now. I begin to have ambitions of *bigger* service by and by – widening and deepening as I get older. I have plans for when I'm fifty – sixty – seventy.

'As to prunes and apricots – they are growing well – pay well, too. I have a little cannery of my own – and a little settlement of working people near it, and a *crêche* there for the women to tuck the babies in while they work – a jewel of a *crêche*, mind you. And I'm promoting all manner of industries among the women. I've got plans – oh, I couldn't begin to tell you of my plans!'

'You never did,' said Elsie slowly. 'I – I never dreamed you had spread out so. How splendid of you, Irma!'

'It isn't what I've done that keeps me so happy,' mused her sister. 'It's the things I'm going to do! The widening horizon! Every year I feel stronger, braver, see things more clearly. Life is so – glorious!

'You see, Elsie dear, I have had the babies to love and care for, even if not mine born – they were babies – and I do love them. I have a home, too, a lovely one, with comfort and beauty and peace – and space, too. The one thing I haven't got is the husband – there you are ahead. But I'm not wearing the willow, sister. Life is big enough to bring endless happiness, even without that. Don't you ever show me that "Poor Irma!" look again – now, will you?'

'No—' said Elsie, sitting very quiet, 'I never will.'

There was a hop at the Hotel that night.

Elsie sat among the matrons, watching her son and daughter frisk with the young people.

Irma, dressed to quiet perfection, danced; danced so well that girls, half her age, were envious of her partners.

'What a woman!' said the unprincipled novelist to himself before he danced with her.

'Which is the quickest route to Southern California?' he inquired, after he had danced with her.

IF I WERE A MAN

That was what pretty little Mollie Mathewson always said when Gerald would not do what she wanted him to – which was seldom.

That was what she said this bright morning, with a stamp of her little high-heeled slipper, just because he had made a fuss about that bill, the long one with the 'account rendered,' which she had forgotten to give him the first time and been afraid to the second – and now he had taken it from the postman himself.

Mollie was 'true to type.' She was a beautiful instance of what is reverentially called 'a true woman.' Little, of course – no true woman may be big. Pretty, of course – no true woman could possibly be plain. Whimsical, capricious, charming, changeable, devoted to pretty clothes and always 'wearing them well,' as the esoteric phrase has it. (This does not refer to the clothes – they do not wear well in the least; but to some special grace of putting them on and carrying them about, granted to but few, it appears.)

She was also a loving wife and a devoted mother; possessed

of 'the social gift' and the love of 'society' that goes with it, and, with all these was fond and proud of her home and managed it as capably as – well, as most women do.

If ever there was a true woman it was Mollie Mathewson, yet she was wishing heart and soul she was a man.

And all of a sudden she was!

She was Gerald, walking down the path so erect and square-shouldered, in a hurry for his morning train, as usual, and, it must be confessed, in something of a temper.

Her own words were ringing in her ears – not only the 'last word,' but several that had gone before, and she was holding her lips tight shut, not to say something she would be sorry for. But instead of acquiescence in the position taken by that angry little figure on the veranda, what she felt was a sort of superior pride, a sympathy as with weakness, a feeling that 'I must be gentle with her,' in spite of the temper.

A man! Really a man; with only enough subconscious memory of herself remaining to make her recognize the differences.

At first there was a funny sense of size and weight and extra thickness, the feet and hands seemed strangely large, and her long, straight, free legs swung forward at a gait that made her feel as if on stilts.

This presently passed, and in its place, growing all day, wherever she went, came a new and delightful feeling of being *the right size*.

Everything fitted now. Her back snugly against the seat-back, her feet comfortably on the floor. Her feet? . . . His feet! She studied them carefully. Never before, since her early school days, had she felt such freedom and comfort as to feet – they were firm and solid on the ground when she walked; quick, springy, safe – as when, moved by an unrecognizable impulse, she had run after, caught, and swung aboard the car.

Another impulse fished in a convenient pocket for change – instantly, automatically, bringing forth a nickel for the conductor and a penny for the newsboy.

These pockets came as a revelation. Of course she had known they were there, had counted them, made fun of them, mended them, even envied them; but she never had dreamed of how it *felt* to have pockets.

Behind her newspaper she let her consciousness, that odd mingled consciousness, rove from pocket to pocket, realizing the armored assurance of having all those things at hand, instantly get-at-able, ready to meet emergencies. The cigar case gave her a warm feeling of comfort – it was full; the firmly held fountain-pen, safe unless she stood on her head; the keys, pencils, letters, documents, notebook, checkbook, bill folder – all at once, with a deep rushing sense of power and pride, she felt what she had never felt before in all her life – the possession of money, of her own earned money – hers to give or to withhold; not to beg for, tease for, wheedle for – hers.

That bill – why if it had come to her – to him, that is, he would have paid it as a matter of course, and never mentioned it – to her.

Then, being he, sitting there so easily and firmly with his money in his pockets, she wakened to his life-long consciousness about money. Boyhood – its desires and dreams, ambitions. Young manhood – working tremendously for the wherewithal to make a home – for her. The present years with all their net of cares and hopes and dangers; the present moment, when he needed every cent for special plans of great importance, and this bill, long overdue and demanding payment, meant an amount of inconvenience wholly unnecessary if it had been given him when it first came; also, the man's keen dislike of that 'account rendered.'

'Women have no business sense!' she found herself saying, 'and all that money just for hats – idiotic, useless, ugly things!'

With that she began to see the hats of the women in the car as she had never seen hats before. The men's seemed normal, dignified, becoming, with enough variety for personal taste, and with distinction in style and in age, such as she had never noticed before. But the women's—

With the eyes of a man and the brain of a man; with the memory of a whole lifetime of free action wherein the hat, close-fitting on cropped hair, had been no handicap; she now perceived the hats of women.

Their massed fluffed hair was at once attractive and foolish, and on that hair, at every angle, in all colors, tipped, twisted, tortured into every crooked shape, made of any substance chance might offer, perched these formless objects. Then, on their formlessness the trimmings – these squirts of stiff feathers, these violent outstanding bows of glistening ribbon, these swaying, projecting masses of plumage which tormented the faces of bystanders.

Never in all her life had she imagined that this idolized millinery could look, to those who paid for it, like the decorations of an insane monkey.

And yet, when there came into the car a little woman, as foolish as any, but pretty and sweet-looking, up rose Gerald Mathewson and gave her his seat; and, later, when there came in a handsome red-cheeked girl, whose hat was wilder, more violent in color and eccentric in shape than any other; when she stood near by and her soft curling plumes swept his cheek once and again, he felt a sense of sudden pleasure at the intimate tickling touch – and she, deep down within, felt such a wave of shame as might well drown a thousand hats forever.

When he took his train, his seat in the smoking car, she had a new surprise. All about him were the other men, commuters too, and many of them friends of his.

To her, they would have been distinguished as 'Mary Wade's husband' – 'the man Belle Grant is engaged to' – 'that rich Mr Shopworth' – or 'that pleasant Mr Beale.' And they would all have lifted their hats to her, bowed, made polite conversation if near enough – especially Mr Beale.

Now came the feeling of open-eyed acquaintance, of knowing men – as they were. The mere amount of this knowledge was a surprise to her; the whole background of talk from boyhood up, the gossip of barber-shop and club, the conversation of morning and evening hours on trains, the knowledge of political affiliation, of business standing and prospects, of character – in a light she had never known before.

They came and talked to Gerald, one and another. He seemed quite popular. And as they talked, with this new memory and new understanding, an understanding which seemed to include all these men's minds, there poured in on the submerged consciousness beneath a new, a startling knowledge – what men really think of women.

Good average American men were there; married men for the most part, and happy – as happiness goes in general. In the minds of each and all there seemed to be a two-story department, quite apart from the rest of their ideas, a separate place where they kept their thoughts and feelings about women.

In the upper half were the tenderest emotions, the most exquisite ideals, the sweetest memories, all lovely sentiments as to 'home' and 'mother,' all delicate admiring adjectives, a sort of sanctuary, where a veiled statue, blindly adored, shared place with beloved yet commonplace experiences.

In the lower half – here that buried consciousness woke to keen distress – they kept quite another assortment of ideas. Here, even in this clean-minded husband of hers, was the memory of stories told at men's dinners, of worse ones overheard in street or car, of base traditions, coarse epithets, gross experiences – known, though not shared.

And all these in the department 'woman,' while in the rest o the mind – here was new knowledge indeed.

The world opened before her. Not the world she had been, reared in; where Home had covered all the map, almost, and the rest had been 'foreign,' or 'unexplored country;' but the world as it was, man's world, as made, lived in, and seen, by men.

It was dizzying. To see the houses that fled so fast across the car window, in terms of builders' bills, or of some technical insight into materials and methods; to see a passing village with lamentable knowledge of who 'owned it' – and of how its Boss was rapidly aspiring to State power, or of how that kind of paving was a failure; to see shops, not as mere exhibitions of desirable objects, but as business ventures, many mere sinking ships, some promising a profitable voyage – this new world bewildered her.

She – as Gerald – had already forgotten about that bill, over which she – as Mollie – was still crying at home. Gerald was 'talking business' with this man, 'talking politics' with that; and now sympathizing with the carefully withheld troubles of a neighbor.

Mollie had always sympathized with the neighbor's wife before.

She began to struggle violently, with this large dominant masculine consciousness. She remembered with sudden clearness things she had read – lectures she had heard; and resented with increasing intensity this serene masculine preoccupation with the male point of view.

Mr Miles, the little fussy man who lived on the other side of the street, was talking now. He had a large complacent wife; Mollie had never liked her much, but had always thought him rather nice – he was so punctilious in small courtesies.

And here he was talking to Gerald – such talk!

'Had to come in here,' he said. 'Gave my seat to a dame who was bound to have it. There's nothing they won't get when they make up their minds to it – eh?'

'No fear!' said the big man in the next seat, 'they haven't much mind to make up, you know – and if they do, they'll change it.'

'The real danger,' began the Revd Alfred Smythe, the new Episcopal clergyman, a thin, nervous, tall man, with a face several centuries behind the times, 'is that they will overstep the limits of their God-appointed sphere.'

'Their natural limits ought to hold 'em, I think,' said cheerful Dr Jones. 'You can't get around physiology, I tell you.'

'I've never seen any limits, myself, not to what they want, anyhow;' said Mr Miles, 'merely a rich husband and a fine house and no end of bonnets and dresses, and the latest thing in motors, and a few diamonds – and so on. Keeps us pretty busy.'

There was a tired gray man across the aisle. He had a very nice wife, always beautifully dressed, and three unmarried daughters, also beautifully dressed – Mollie knew them. She knew he worked hard too, and looked at him now a little anxiously.

But he smiled cheerfully.

'Do you good, Miles,' he said. 'What else would a man work for? A good woman is about the best thing on earth.'

'And a bad one's the worst, that's sure,' responded Miles.

'She's a pretty weak sister, viewed professionally,' Dr Jones averred with solemnity, and the Revd Alfred Smythe added: 'She brought evil into the world.'

Gerald Mathewson sat up straight. Something was stirring in him which he did not recognize – yet could not resist.

'Seems to me we all talk like Noah,' he suggested drily. 'Or the ancient Hindu scriptures. Women have their limitations, but so do we, God knows. Haven't we known girls in school and college just as smart as we were?'

'They cannot play our games,' coldly replied the clergyman.

Gerald measured his meager proportions with a practiced eye.

'I never was particularly good at football myself,' he modestly admitted, 'but I've known women who could outlast a man in all-round endurance. Besides – life isn't spent in athletics!'

This was sadly true. They all looked down the aisle where a heavy ill-dressed man with a bad complexion sat alone. He had held the top of the columns once, with headlines and photographs. Now he earned less than any of them.

'It's time we woke up,' pursued Gerald, still inwardly urged to unfamiliar speech. 'Women are pretty much *people*, seems to me. I know they dress like fools – but who's to blame for that? We invent all those idiotic hats of theirs, and design their crazy fashions, and, what's more, if a woman is courageous enough to wear common sense clothes – and shoes – which of us wants to dance with her?

'Yes, we blame them for grafting on us, but are we willing to let our wives work? We are not. It hurts our pride, that's all. We are always criticizing them for making mercenary marriages, but what do we call a girl who marries a chump with no money? Just a poor fool, that's all. And they know it.

'As for those physical limitations, Dr Jones, I guess our side of the house has some responsibility there, too – eh?

'And for Mother Eve – I wasn't there and can't deny the story, but I will say this, if she brought evil into the world we men have had the lion's share of keeping it going ever since – how about that?'

They drew into the city, and all day long in his business, Gerald was vaguely conscious of new views, strange feelings, and the submerged Mollie learned and learned.

MR PEEBLES'S HEART

He was lying on the sofa in the homely, bare little sitting room; an uncomfortable stiff sofa, too short, too sharply upcurved at the end, but still a sofa, whereon one could, at a pinch, sleep.

Thereon Mr Peebles slept, this hot still afternoon; slept uneasily, snoring a little, and twitching now and then, as one in some obscure distress.

Mrs Peebles had creaked down the front stairs and gone off on some superior errands of her own; with a good palm-leaf fan for a weapon, a silk umbrella for a defense.

'Why don't you come too, Joan?' she had urged her sister, as she dressed herself for departure.

'Why should I, Emma? It's much more comfortable at home. I'll keep Arthur company when he wakes up.'

'Oh, Arthur! He'll go back to the store as soon as he's had his nap. And I'm sure Mrs Older's paper'll be real interesting. If you're going to live here you ought to take an interest in the club, seems to me.'

'I'm going to live here as a doctor – not as a lady of leisure, Em. You go on – I'm contented.'

So Mrs Emma Peebles sat in the circle of the Ellsworth Ladies' Home Club, and improved her mind, while Dr J. R. Bascom softly descended to the sitting room in search of a book she had been reading.

There was Mr Peebles, still uneasily asleep. She sat down quietly in a cane-seated rocker by the window and watched him awhile; first professionally, then with a deeper human interest.

Baldish, grayish, stoutish, with a face that wore a friendly smile for customers, and showed grave, set lines that deepened about the corners of his mouth when there was no one to serve; very ordinary in dress, in carriage, in appearance was Arthur Peebles at fifty. He was not 'the slave of love' of the Arab tale, but the slave of duty.

If ever a man had done his duty – as he saw it – he had done his, always.

His duty – as he saw it – was carrying women. First his mother, a comfortable competent person, who had run the farm after her husband's death, and added to their income by Summer boarders until Arthur was old enough to 'support her.' Then she sold the old place and moved into the village to 'make a home for Arthur,' who incidentally provided a hired girl to perform the manual labor of that process.

He worked in the store. She sat on the piazza and chatted with her neighbors.

He took care of his mother until he was nearly thirty, when she left him finally; and then he installed another woman to make a home for him – also with the help of the hired girl. A pretty, careless, clinging little person he married, who had long made mute appeal to his strength and carefulness, and she had continued to cling uninterruptedly to this day.

Incidentally a sister had clung until she married, another

until she died; and his children – two daughters, had clung also. Both the daughters were married in due time, with sturdy young husbands to cling to in their turn; and now there remained only his wife to carry, a lighter load than he had ever known – at least numerically.

But either he was tired, very tired, or Mrs Peebles' tendrils had grown tougher, tighter, more tenacious, with age. He did not complain of it. Never had it occurred to him in all these years that there was any other thing for a man to do than to carry whatsoever women came within range of lawful relationship.

Had Dr Joan been – shall we say – carriageable – he would have cheerfully added her to the list, for he liked her extremely. She was different from any woman he had ever known, different from her sister as day from night, and, in lesser degree, from all the female inhabitants of Ellsworth.

She had left home at an early age, against her mother's will, absolutely ran away; but when the whole countryside rocked with gossip and sought for the guilty man – it appeared that she had merely gone to college. She worked her way through, learning more, far more, than was taught in the curriculum; became a trained nurse, studied medicine, and had long since made good in her profession. There were even rumors that she must be 'pretty well fixed' and about to 'retire'; but others held that she must have failed, really or she never would have come back home to settle.

Whatever the reason, she was there, a welcome visitor; a source of real pride to her sister, and of indefinable satisfaction to her brother-in-law. In her friendly atmosphere he felt a stirring of long unused powers; he remembered funny stories, and how to tell them; he felt a revival of interests he had thought quite outlived, early interests in the big world's movements.

'Of all unimpressive, unattractive, *good* little men –' she was thinking, as she watched, when one of his arms dropped off the slippery side of the sofa, the hand thumped on the floor, and he awoke and sat up hastily with an air of one caught off duty.

'Don't sit up as suddenly as that, Arthur, it's bad for your heart.'

'Nothing the matter with my heart, is there?' he asked with his ready smile.

'I don't know – haven't examined it. Now – sit still – you know there's nobody in the store this afternoon – and if there is, Jake can attend to 'em.'

'Where's Emma?'

'Oh, Emma's gone to her "club" or something – wanted me to go, but I'd rather talk with you.'

He looked pleased but incredulous, having a high opinion of that club, and a low one of himself.

'Look here,' she pursued suddenly, after he had made himself comfortable with a drink from the swinging ice-pitcher, and another big cane rocker, 'what would you like to do if you could?'

'Travel!' said Mr Peebles, with equal suddenness. He saw her astonishment. 'Yes, travel! I've always wanted to – since I was a kid. No use! We never could, you see. And now – even if we could – Emma hates it.' He sighed resignedly

'Do you like to keep store?' she asked sharply.

'*Like* it?' He smiled at her cheerfully, bravely, but with a queer blank hopeless background underneath. He shook his head gravely. 'No, I do not, Joan. Not a little bit. But what of that?'

They were still for a little, and then she put another question. 'What would you have chosen – for a profession – if you had been free to choose?'

His answer amazed her threefold; from its character, its sharp promptness, its deep feeling. It was in one word – 'Music!'

'Music!' she repeated. 'Music! Why I didn't know you played – or cared about it.'

'When I was a youngster,' he told her, his eyes looking far off through the vine-shaded window, 'father brought home a guitar – and said it was for the one that learned to play it first. He meant the girls of course. As a matter of fact I learned it first – but I didn't get it. That's all the music I ever had,' he added. 'And there's not much to listen to here, unless you count what's in church. I'd have a Victrola – but—' he laughed a little shamefacedly, 'Emma says if I bring one into the house she'll smash it. She says they're worse than cats. Tastes differ you know, Joan.'

Again he smiled at her, a droll smile, a little pinched at the corners. 'Well – I must be getting back to business.'

She let him go, and turned her attention to her own business, with some seriousness.

'Emma,' she proposed, a day or two later. 'How would you like it if I should board here – live here, I mean, right along.'

'I should hope you would,' her sister replied. 'It would look nice to have you practising in this town and not live with me – all the sister I've got.'

'Do you think Arthur would like it?'

'Of course he would! Besides – even if he didn't – you're my sister – and this is my house. He put it in my name, long ago.'

'I see,' said Joan, 'I see.'

Then after a little – 'Emma – are you contented?'

'Contented? Why, of course I am. It would be a sin not to be. The girls are well married – I'm happy about them both. This is a real comfortable house, and it runs itself – my Matilda is a jewel if ever there was one. And she don't mind company – likes to do for 'em. Yes – I've nothing to worry about.'

'Your health's good – that I can see,' her sister remarked, regarding with approval her clear complexion and bright eyes.

'Yes – I've nothing to complain about – that I know of,' Emma admitted, but among her causes for thankfulness she did not even mention Arthur, nor seem to think of him till Dr Joan seriously inquired her opinion as to his state of health.

'His health? Arthur's? Why he's always well. Never had a sick day in his life – except now and then he's had a kind of a break-down,' she added as an afterthought.

Dr Joan Bascom made acquaintances in the little town, both professional and social. She entered upon her practise, taking it over from the failing hands of old Dr Braithwaite – her first friend, and feeling very much at home in the old place. Her sister's house furnished two comfortable rooms downstairs, and a large bedroom above. 'There's plenty of room now the girls are gone,' they both assured her.

Then, safely ensconced and established, Dr Joan began a secret campaign to alienate the affections of her brother-in law. Not for herself – oh no! If ever in earlier years she had felt the need of some one to cling to, it was long, long ago. What she sought was to free him from the tentacles – without re-entanglement.

She bought a noble gramophone with a set of first-class records, told her sister smilingly that she didn't have to listen, and Emma would sit sulkily in the back room on the other side of the house, while her husband and sister enjoyed the music.

She grew used to it in time, she said, and drew nearer, sitting on the porch perhaps; but Arthur had his long denied pleasure in peace.

It seemed to stir him strangely. He would rise and walk, a new fire in his eyes, a new firmness about the patient mouth, and Dr Joan fed the fire with talk and books and pictures with study of maps and sailing lists and accounts of economical tours.

'I don't see what you two find so interesting in all that stuff about music and those composers,' Emma would say. 'I never did care for foreign parts – musicians are all foreigners, anyway.'

Arthur never quarrelled with her; he only grew quiet and lost that interested sparkle of the eye when she discussed the subject.

Then one day, Mrs Peebles being once more at her club, content and yet aspiring, Dr Joan made bold attack upon her brother-in-law's principles.

'Arthur.' she said. 'Have you confidence in me as a physician?'

'I have,' he said briskly. 'Rather consult you than any doctor I ever saw.'

'Will you let me prescribe for you if I tell you you need it?'

'I sure will.'

'Will you take the prescription?'

'Of course I'll take it – no matter how it tastes.'

'Very well. I prescribe two years in Europe.'

He stared at her, startled.

'I mean it. You're in a more serious condition than you think. I want you to cut clear – and travel. For two years.'

He still stared at her. 'But Emma—'

'Never mind about Emma. She owns the house. She's got

enough money to clothe herself – and I'm paying enough board
to keep everything going. Emma don't need you.'

'But the store—'

'Sell the store.'

'Sell it! That's easy said. Who'll buy it?'

'I will. Yes – I mean it. You give me easy terms and I'll take
the store off your hands. It ought to be worth seven or eight
thousand dollars, oughtn't it – stock and all?'

He assented, dumbly.

'Well, I'll buy it. You can live abroad for two years, on a
couple of thousand, or twenty-five hundred – a man of your
tastes. You know those accounts we've read – it can be done
easily. Then you'll have five thousand or so to come back to –
and can invest it in something better than that shop. Will you
do it—?'

He was full of protests, of impossibilities.

She met them firmly. 'Nonsense! You can too. She doesn't
need you, at all – she may later. No – the girls don't need you –
and they may later. Now is your time – *now*. They say the
Japanese sow their wild oats after they're fifty – suppose you do!
You can't be so *very* wild on that much money, but you can
spend a year in Germany – learn the language – go to the
opera – take walking trips in the Tyrol – in Switzerland; see
England, Scotland, Ireland, France, Belgium, Denmark – you
can do a lot in two years.'

He stared at her fascinated.

'Why not? Why not be your own man for once in your life –
do what *you* want to – not what other people want you to?'

He murmured something as to 'duty' – but she took him up
sharply.

'If ever a man on earth has done his duty, Arthur Peebles,

you have. You've taken care of your mother while she was perfectly able to take care of herself; of your sisters, long after they were; and of a wholly able-bodied wife. At present she does not need you the least bit in the world.'

'Now that's pretty strong,' he protested. 'Emma'd miss me – I know she'd miss me—'

Dr Bascom looked at him affectionately. 'There couldn't a better thing happen to Emma – or to you, for that matter – than to have her miss you, real hard.'

'I know she'd never consent to my going,' he insisted, wistfully.

'That's the advantage of my interference,' she replied serenely. 'You surely have a right to choose your doctor, and your doctor is seriously concerned about your health and orders foreign travel – rest – change – and music.'

'But Emma—'

'Now, Arthur Peebles, forget Emma for awhile – I'll take care of her. And look here – let me tell you another thing – a change like this will do her good.'

He stared at her, puzzled.

'I mean it. Having you away will give her a chance to stand up. Your letters – about those places – will interest her. She may want to go, sometime. Try it.'

He wavered at this. Those who too patiently serve as props sometimes underrate the possibilities of the vine.

'Don't discuss it with her – that will make endless trouble. Fix up the papers for my taking over the store – I'll draw you a check, and you get the next boat for England, and make your plans from there. Here's a banking address that will take care of your letters and checks—'

The thing was done! Done before Emma had time to protest. Done, and she left gasping to upbraid her sister.

Joan was kind, patient, firm as adamant.

'But how it *looks*, Joan – what will people think of me! To be left deserted – like this!'

'People will think according to what we tell them and to how you behave, Emma Peebles. If you simply say that Arthur was far from well and I advised him to take a foreign trip – and if you forget yourself for once, and show a little natural feeling for him – you'll find no trouble at all.'

For her own sake the selfish woman, made more so by her husband's unselfishness, accepted the position. Yes – Arthur had gone abroad for his health – Dr Bascom was much worried about him – chance of a complete breakdown, she said. Wasn't it pretty sudden? Yes – the doctor hurried him off. He was in England – going to take a walking trip – she did not know when he'd be back. The store? He'd sold it.

Dr Bascom engaged a competent manager who ran that store successfully, more so than had the unenterprising Mr Peebles. She made it a good paying business, which he ultimately bought back and found no longer a burden.

But Emma was the principal charge. With talk, with books, with Arthur's letters followed carefully on maps, with trips to see the girls, trips in which travelling lost its terrors, with the care of the house, and the boarder or two they took 'for company,' she so ploughed and harrowed that long fallow field of Emma's mind that at last it began to show signs of fruitfulness.

Arthur went away leaving a stout, dull woman who clung to him as if he was a necessary vehicle or beast of burden – and thought scarcely more of his constant service.

He returned younger, stronger, thinner, an alert vigorous man, with a mind enlarged, refreshed, and stimulated. He had found himself.

And he found her, also, most agreeably changed; having developed not merely tentacles, but feet of her own to stand on.

When next the thirst for travel seized him she thought she'd go too, and proved unexpectedly pleasant as a companion.

But neither of them could ever wring from Dr Bascom any definite diagnosis of Mr Peebles' threatening disease. 'A dangerous enlargement of the heart' was all she would commit herself to, and when he denied any such trouble now, she gravely wagged her head and said 'it had responded to treatment.'

MRS MERRILL'S DUTIES

Grace Leroy in college, was quite the most important member of the class. She had what her professors proudly pointed out as the rarest thing among women – a scientific mind. The arts had no charms for her; she had no wish to teach, no leaning toward that branch of investigation and alleviation in social pathology we are so apt to call 'social service.'

Her strength was in genuine research work, and, back of that, greatest gift of all, she showed high promise in 'the scientific imagination,' the creative synthesizing ability which gives new discoveries to the world.

In addition to these natural advantages a merciful misfortune saved her from the widespread silvery quicksand which so often engulfs the girl graduate. Instead of going home to decorate the drawing-room and help her mother receive, she was obliged to go to work at once, owing to paternal business difficulties.

Her special teacher, old Dr Welsch, succeeded in getting a laboratory position for her; and for three years she worked side by side with a great chemist and physicist, Dr Hammerton, his most valued assistant.

She was very happy.

Happy, of course, to be useful to her family at once, instead of an added burden. Happy in her sense of independence and a real place in the world; happy in the feeling of personal power and legitimate pride of achievement. Happiest of all in the brightening dawn of great ideas, big glittering hopes of a discovery that should lighten humanity's burdens. Hardly did she dare to hope for it, yet it did seem almost possible at times. Being of a truly religious nature she prayed earnestly over this; to be good enough to deserve the honor; to keep humble and not overestimate her powers; to be helped to do the Great Work.

Then Life rolled swiftly along and swept her off her feet.

Her father recovered his money and her mother lost her health. For a time there seemed absolute need of her at home.

'I must not neglect plain duty,' said the girl, and resigned her position.

There was a year of managing the household, with the care of younger brothers and sisters; a year of travel with the frail mother, drifting slowly from place to place, from physician to physician, always hoping, and always being disappointed.

Then came the grief of losing her, after they had grown so close, so deeply, tenderly intimate.

'Whatever happens,' said Grace to herself, 'I shall always be glad of these two years. No outside work could justify me in neglecting this primal duty.'

What did happen next was her father's turning to her for comfort. She alone could in any degree take her mother's place to him. He could not bear to think of her as leaving the guidance of the family. His dependence was touching.

Grace accepted the new duty bravely.

There was the year of deep mourning, both in symbolic garments and observances and in the real sorrow; and she found
herself learning to know her father better than she ever had,
and learning how to somewhat make up to him for the companionship he had lost. There was the need of mothering the
younger ones, of managing the big house.

Then came the next sister's debut, and the cares and responsibilities involved. Another sister was growing up, and the
young brother called for sympathetic guidance. There seemed
no end to it.

She bowed her head and faced her duty.

'Nothing can be right,' she said, 'which would take me away
from these intimate claims.'

Everyone agreed with her in this.

Her father was understanding and tender in his thoughtfulness.

'I know what a sacrifice you are making, daughter, in giving
up your chemistry, but what could I do without you! . . .' You
are so much like your mother . . .'

As time passed she did speak once or twice of a housekeeper,
that she might have some free hours during the day-time, but
he was so hurt at the idea that she gave it up.

Then something happened that proved with absurd ease the
fallacy of the fond conclusion that nothing could be right
which would take her away. Hugh Merrill took her away, and
that was accepted by everyone as perfectly right.

She had known him a long time, but had hardly dared let
herself think of marrying him – she was so indispensable at
home. But when his patience and his ardor combined finally
swept her off her feet; when her father said: 'Why, of course, my
child! Hugh is a splendid fellow! We shall miss you – but do
you think I would stand in the way of your happiness!' – she

consented. She raised objections about the housekeeping, but her father promptly met them by installing a widowed sister, Aunt Adelaide, who had always been a favorite with them all.

She managed the home quite as well, and the children really better, than had Grace; and she and her brother played cribbage and backgammon in the evenings with pleasant reversion to their youthful comradeship – he seemed to grow younger for having her there.

Grace was so happy, so relieved by the sudden change from being the mainstay of four other people and a big house to being considered and cared for in every way by a strong resourceful affectionate man, that she did not philosophize at all at the easy dispensibility of the indispensable.

With Hugh she rested; regained her youth, bloomed like a flower. There was a long delightful journey; a pleasant home-coming; the setting up of her very own establishment; the cordial welcome from her many friends.

In all this she never lost sight of her inner hope of the Great Work.

Hugh had profound faith in her. They talked of it on their long honeymoon, in full accord. She should have her labora-tory, she should work away at her leisure, she would do wonderful things – he was sure of it.

But that first year was so full of other things, so crowded with invitations, so crowded with careful consideration of clothes and menus and servants, the duties of a hostess, or a guest – that the big room upstairs was not yet a laboratory.

An unexpected illness with its convalescence took another long period; she needed rest, a change. Another year went by.

Grace was about thirty now.

Then the babies came – little Hugh and Arnold – splendid

boys. A happier, prouder mother one would not wish to see. She thanked God with all her heart; she felt the deep and tender oneness with her husband that comes of parentage, with reverent joy.

To the task of education she now devoted her warmly loving heart, her clear strong mind. It was noble work. She neglected nothing. This duty was imperative. No low-grade nursemaid should, through ignorance, do some irremediable injury to opening baby minds.

With the help of a fully competent assistant, expensive, but worth all she cost, Mrs Merrill brought up those boys herself, and the result should have satisfied even the most exacting educator. Hearty, well-grown, unaffected, with clear minds and beautiful manners, they grew up to sturdy boyhood, taking high places when they went to school; loved by their teachers, comrades and friends, and everyone said: 'What a lovely mother she is!'

She did not admit to anyone that even in this period of lovely mothering, even with the home happiness, the wife happiness, the pleasant social position, there was still an aching want inside. She wanted her laboratory, her research, her work. All her years of education, from the first chemistry lessons at fourteen to the giving up of her position at twenty-four, had made her a chemist, and nature had made her a discoverer.

She had not read much during these years; it hurt her – made her feel an exile. She had shut the door on all that side of her life, and patiently, gladly fulfilled the duties of the other side, neglecting nothing.

Not till ten more years had passed did she draw a long breath and say: 'Now I will have my laboratory!'

She had it. There was the big room, all this time a nursery; now at last fitted up with all the mysterious implements and supplies of her chosen profession.

The boys were at school – her husband at his business – now she could concentrate on the Great Work.

And then Mrs Merrill began to realize 'the defects of her qualities.'

There is such a thing as being too good.

We all know that little one-handed tool combination which carries in its inside screw-driver, gouge and chisel, awl and file – a marvellously handy thing to have in the house. Yes – but did you ever see a carpenter use one? The real workman, for real work, must have real tools, of which the value is, not that they will all fit one hollow and feeble handle, but that each will do what it is meant for, well.

We have seen in Grace Leroy Merrill the strength of mind and character, Christian submission, filial duty, wifely love, motherly efficiency. She had other qualities also, all pleasant ones. She was a pre-eminently attractive woman, more than pretty – charming. She was sweet and cordial in manner, quick and witty, a pleasure to talk with for either man or woman. Add to these the possession of special talent for dress, and a gentle friendliness that could not bear to hurt anyone, and we begin to feel 'this is too much. No person has a right to be so faultless, so universally efficient and attractive.'

Social psychology is a bit complicated. We need qualities, not only valuable for personal, but for social relation. In the growing complexity of a highly specialized organization the law of organic specialization calls for a varying degree of sacrifice in personal fulfillment. It is quite possible, indeed it is usual, to find individuals whose numerous good qualities really stand in the way of their best service to society. The best tools are not those of the greatest 'all round' variety of usefulness.

When the boys were grown up enough to be off her mind for many hours a day; when the house fairly ran itself in the hands of well-trained servants; when, at last, the laboratory was installed and the way seemed open; Mrs Merrill found herself fairly bogged in her own popularity. She had so many friends; they were so unfailingly anxious to have her at their dinners, their dances, their continuous card parties; they came to her so confidingly, so frequently – and she could never bear to hurt their feelings.

There were, to be sure, mornings. One is not required to play bridge in the morning, or dance, or go to the theatre. But even the daily ordering for a household takes some time, and besides the meals there are the supplies in clothing, linen, china; and the spring and fall extras of putting things away with mothballs, having rugs cleaned and so on – and so on.

Then – clothes; her own clothes. The time to think about them; the time to discuss them; the time to buy them; the time to stand up and be fitted – to plan and struggle with the dressmaker – a great deal of time – and no sooner is the feat accomplished than – presto! – it must be done all over.

Day after day she mounted the stairs to her long looked-for work-room, with an hour – or two – or three – before her. Day after day she was called down again; friends at the telephone, friends at the door; friends who were full of cheerful apology and hopes that they did not disturb her; and tradesmen who were void of either.

'If only I could get something *done!*' she said, as she sat staring at her retorts. 'If once I could really accomplish a piece of good work, that should command public acknowledgement – then they would understand. Then I could withdraw from all this—'

For she found that her hours were too few, and too broken, to allow of that concentration of mind without which no great work is possible.

But she was a strong woman, a patient woman, and possessed of a rich fund of perseverance. With long waiting, with careful use of summer months when her too devoted friends were out of town, she managed in another five years, to really accomplish something. From her little laboratory, working alone and under all distractions, she finally sent out a new formula; not for an explosive of deadly power, but for a safe and simple sedative, something which induced natural sleep, with no ill results.

It was no patented secret. She gave it to the world with the true scientific spirit, and her joy was like that of motherhood. She had at last achieved! She had done something – something of real service to thousands upon thousands. And back of this first little hill, so long in winning, mountain upon mountain, range on range, rose hopefully tempting before her.

She was stronger now. She had gotten back into the lines of study, of persistent work. Her whole mind stirred and freshened with new ideas, high purposes. She planned for further research, along different lines. Two Great Ones tempted her; a cheap combustible fluid; and that biggest prize of all – the mastering of atomic energy.

And now, now that she had really made this useful discovery, which was widely recognized among those who knew of such matters, she could begin to protect herself from these many outside calls!

What did happen?

She found herself quite lionized for a season – name in the papers, pictures, interviews, and a whole series of dinners and receptions where she was wearied beyond measure by the well-meant comments on her work.

Free? Respected? Let alone?

Her hundreds of friends, who had known her so long and so well, as a charming girl, a devoted daughter, an irreproachable wife, a most unusually successful mother, were only the more cordial now.

'Have you heard about Grace Merrill? Isn't it wonderful! She always had ability – I've always said so.'

'Such a service to the world! A new anesthetic!'

'Oh, it's not an anesthetic – not really.'

'Like the Twilight Sleep, I imagine.'

'It's splendid of her anyway. I've asked her to dinner Thursday, to meet Professor Andrews – he's an authority on dietetics, you know, and Dr North and his wife – they are such interesting people!'

Forty-six! Still beautiful, still charming, still exquisitely gowned. Still a happy wife and mother, with Something Done – at last.

And yet—

Her next younger sister, who had lost her husband and was greatly out of health, now wanted to come and live with her; their father had followed his wife some years back and the old home was broken up.

That meant being tied up at home again. And as to the social engagements, she was more hopelessly popular than ever.

Then one day there came to see her Dr Hammerton. His brush of hair was quite white, but thick and erect as ever. His keen black eyes sparkled portentously under thick white eyebrows.

'What's this you've been doing, Child? Show me your shop.'

She showed him, feeling very girlish again in the presence of her early master. He looked the place over in silence, told her he had read about her new product, sat on the edge of a table and made her take a chair.

'Now tell me about it!' he said.

She told him – all about it. He listened, nodding agreeably as she recounted the steps.

'Mother? Yes. Father? Yes – for awhile at least. Husband? Yes. Boys? Of course – and you've done well. But what's the matter now?'

She told him that too – urging her hope of forcing some acknowledgment by her proven ability.

He threw back his big head and laughed.

'You've got the best head of any woman I ever saw,' he said; 'you've done what not one woman in a thousand does – kept a living Self able to survive family relations. You've proven, now, that you are still in the ring. You ought to do – twenty – maybe thirty years of worthwhile work. Forty-six? I was forty-eight when you left me, have done my best work since then, am seventy now, and am still going strong. You've spent twenty-two years in worthwhile woman-work that's *done* – now you have at least as much again to do human work. I daresay you'll do better because of all this daughtering and mothering – women are queer things. Anyhow you've plenty of time. But you must get to work.

'Now, see here – if you let all these childish flub-dubs prevent you from doing what God made you for – you're a Criminal Fool!'

Grace gave a little gasp.

'I mean it. You know it. It's all nonsense, empty nonsense. As for your sister – let her go to a sanitarium – she can afford it, or live with her other sister – or brother. You've earned your freedom.

'As to clothes and parties – Quit!'

She looked at him.

'Yes, I know. You're still pretty and attractive, but *what of it?* Suppose Spencer or Darwin had wasted their time as parlor ornaments – supposing they could have – would they have had a right to?'

She caught at the names. 'You think I could do something – Great?' she asked. 'You think I am – big enough – to try?'

He stood up. She rose and faced him.

'I think you are great, to have done what you have – a task no man could face. I think you will be greater – perhaps one of the big World Helpers.' Then his eyes shot fire – and he thundered: 'How Dare you hinder the World's Work by wasting your time with these idle women? It is Treason – High Treason – to Humanity.'

'What can I do?' she asked at last.

'That's a foolish question, child. Use your brain – you've got plenty. Learn to assert yourself and stand up to it, that's all. Tell your sister you can't. Disconnect the telephone. Hire some stony-faced menial to answer the door and say: "Mrs Merrill is engaged. She left orders not to be disturbed."'

'Decide on how many evenings you can afford to lose sleep, and decline to go out on all others. It's simple enough.'

'But you've got to *do* it. You've got to plan it and stand by it. It takes Courage – and it takes Strength.'

'But if it is my duty –' said Grace Merrill.

The old man smiled and left her. 'Once that woman sees a Duty!' he said to himself.

SELECTIONS FROM THE AUTHOR'S AUTOBIOGRAPHY

The Living of Charlotte Perkins Gilman
(1935)

From CHAPTER 1
BACKGROUND

The immediate line I am really proud of is the Beecher family. Dr Lyman Beecher was my father's grandfather, his twelve children were world-servers. It is the fashion of late among juveniles of quite different origins to contemptuously dismiss the settlers and builders of New England as 'Puritanic.' One needs more historical perspective than is possessed by these persons to appreciate the physical and moral courage of those Great Adventurers; their energy and endurance; their inventive progressiveness. The 'Blue Laws' of Connecticut, so widely sneered at, were a great advance in liberality from the English laws behind them.

As characters broadened with the spread of the growing nation new thinkers appeared, the urge toward heaven was humanized in a widening current of social improvement, making New England a seed-bed of progressive movements, scientific, mechanical, educational, humanitarian as well as religious. Into this moving world the Beechers swung forward, the sons all ministers, the daughters as able. Harriet Beecher Stowe is best known, but Catherine Beecher, who so scandalized the German theologian by her answer to 'Edwards on the Will,' is still honored in the middle west for her wide influence in promoting the higher education of women; and Isabella Beecher Hooker was one of the able leaders in the demand for equal suffrage.

Mary Beecher, my grandmother, the only daughter not doing public work, married Thomas C. Perkins, a lawyer of Hartford, Connecticut, and had four children, Frederick, Emily, Charles and Katherine. Emily married Edward Everett Hale, the distinguished Unitarian divine, author and lecturer; Katherine married William C. Gilman; Charles followed his father's footsteps in the Hartford law office; and Frederick, the oldest, my father, took to books as a duck to water. He read them, he wrote them, he edited them, he criticized them, he became a librarian and classified them. Before he married he knew nine languages, and continued to learn others afterward.

As an editor he helped to found, or worked on, the *Independent*, the *Christian Union* (later the *Outlook*), the *Galaxy*, Old and New, and various other papers and magazines. As a librarian he introduced the decimal system of classification, and his reference book, *The Best Reading*, was for long the standard. When I first visited the British Museum, Dr Garnett was most polite to me for my father's sake. In those days, when scholarship could still cover a large proportion of the world's good books, he covered them well. Uncle E. E. Hale told me that he never asked my father a question that he could not immediately answer, or tell him where to find the answer.

But – with all these abilities went certain marked characteristics which prevented assured success. While a student in Yale he thrashed a professor, who had, he said, insulted him; which exhibition of temper cut short his college attendance. He was keen to feel injustice and quick to resent it; impatient of any dictation, careless of consequences when aroused. In an Irish riot in New York, during the Civil War, a Negro was being chased through the streets by a mob. Down rushed Mr Perkins from his office, dragged the Negro into the hallway and faced the mob, but was himself pulled into safety by friends. A courageous man and a good boxer, but unwise. He did not, be it noted, enlist. When about thirty-one he married Mary Fitch Westcott of Providence, Rhode Island, and they had three children in three years, of whom I was the third.

The doctor said that if my mother had another baby she would die. Presently my father left home. Whether the doctor's dictum was the reason or merely a reason I do not know. What I do know is that my childhood had no father. He was an occasional visitor, a writer of infrequent but always amusing letters with deliciously funny drawings, a sender of books, catalogues of books, lists of books to read, and also a purchaser of books with money sadly needed by his family.

Once I remember him holding me by the heels when I had casually swallowed a pin. 'It *cannot* be a pin!' protested my mother, but I managed to explain that I had put it in the bread and milk myself – why, I cannot imagine.

Once he brought some black Hamburg grapes to mother, and would not let her give them to us as her heart desired. There was a game of chess at which I beat him, or thought I did – being but nine I now doubt the genuineness of that victory; one punishment, half-hearted, and never repeated, at the same age; and a visit some two years later, when we lived in the country and he brought my twelve-year-old brother a gun; these are the sum of my memories of my father in childish years.

There must have been other visits. I think he used to come at Christmas when possible, but nothing else has stayed in my mind. He made no official separation, said his work kept him elsewhere. No word of criticism did I ever hear, mother held him up to us as a great and admirable character. But he was a stranger, distant and little known. The word Father, in the sense of love, care, one to go to in trouble, means nothing to me, save indeed in advice about books and the care of them – which seems more the librarian than the father.

By heredity I owe him much; the Beecher urge to social service, the Beecher wit and gift of words and such small sense of art as I have; but his learning he could not bequeath, and far more than financial care I have missed the education it would have been to have grown up in his society.

A profound believer in the divine right of mothers once stated, in answer to some suggestion of mine as to the need of expert assistance in child-culture, that the mother was in any case the best person to bring up her children; if she was a good mother she was an example to be followed, if a bad one, an example to be avoided.

If unswerving love, tireless service, intense and efficient care, and the concentrated devotion of a lifetime that knew no other purpose make a good mother, mine was of the best. To appraise the story of that motherhood needs a background.

Her father, Henry Westcott, was descended from Stukely Westcott, one of Roger Williams's deacons and fellow-settler of 'Providence Plantations' in days when being a Baptist took some courage, and he, my grandfather, was a Unitarian when being a Unitarian took even more. I remember him dimly, a mild, gray man, whom I horrified by crawling downstairs face foremost at an early age. Mother told me lovely tales of his tenderness and benevolence. He would start for home with a well-filled market-basket and give most of the contents to needy persons on the way. Grandmother's reaction she did not mention. In that characteristic bit of Irish rebellion, the Dorr War, grandfather had to stand guard with a musket, but he saw to it that it was not loaded – killed he might be, but he did not propose to kill any one else.

He was a widower with a little girl of four when he married Clarissa Fitch Perkins, a child of fifteen. A small child too; I have a little dress she made and wore, the softest finest muslin, scanty and short as some of our recent abbreviated garments, with a tiny Empire waistlet and short sleeves, mere shoulder-bits. Deeply embroidered is this frail garment, with inset lace in the big Persian pattern figures, all the work of those slim fingers.

At seventeen she had a baby, which died, and another at eighteen, Mary Fitch Westcott, my mother. I remember grandmother as up and about, visiting us, but before I was eight she became bedridden – of arthritis I suppose – and was the object of my childish prayers and sympathetic letters. She was cared for, almost to her death, by her mother, who was Clarissa Fitch, of Windham, Connecticut. Clarissa married Edward Perkins, cousin of my paternal grandfather. Great-grandma was a handsome stiff-backed old lady, wearing a brown 'front' and a cap, and managing those about her with swift competence.

Mary Westcott, darling of an elderly father and a juvenile mother, petted, cossetted and indulged, grew up in frail health. She was 'given up' by one physician, who said she had consumption and could not survive a date he set. She did, but he signified his displeasure by not recognizing her afterward. Delicate and beautiful, well educated, musical, and what was then termed 'spiritual minded,' she was femininely attractive in the highest degree.

Her adventures and sorrows in this field began when she was a school-girl of fifteen in pantalettes, and an admiring gentleman, named Wilder, asked permission of the thirty-three-year-old mother to 'pay his addresses' to her daughter. From that time there were always lovers, various and successive. The still child-like Mary, even at seventeen, used to excuse herself from callers and go upstairs to put her dolls to bed.

Engagements were made, broken and renewed, and re-broken. One sudden adorer proposed to her at first sight. The penultimate engagement – with a Mr Glazier, a theological student in the strongly Baptist city of Providence – was broken on account of his faith; but he saw another light and became a Unitarian. They were again betrothed, and he was visiting at the house immediately before their approaching marriage, when he contracted typhoid fever and died. Poor mother!

In course of time she met her mother's second cousin, Frederick Beecher Perkins of Hartford. They were engaged, that engagement also was broken, but finally, at the extreme old maidenhood of twenty-nine, she married him.

Of those three swiftly appearing babies the first died from some malpractice at birth; the second, Thomas A. Perkins, is still living, and in fourteen months I followed, on the afternoon of July third, 1860. If only I'd been a little slower and made it the glorious Fourth! This may be called the first misplay in a long game that is full of them.

There now follows a long-drawn, triple tragedy, quadruple perhaps, for my father may have suffered too; but mother's life was one of the most painfully thwarted I have ever known. After her idolized youth, she was left neglected. After her flood of lovers, she became a deserted wife. The most passionately domestic of home-worshiping housewives, she was forced to move nineteen times in eighteen years, fourteen of them from one city to another. After a long and thorough musical education, developing unusual talent, she sold her piano when I was two, to pay the butcher's bill, and never owned another. She hated debt, and debts accumulated about her, driving her to these everlasting moves. Absolutely loyal, as loving as a spaniel which no ill treatment can alienate, she made no complaint, but picked up her children and her dwindling furniture and traveled to the next place. She lived with her husband's parents, with her own parents, with his aunts, in various houses here and there when he so installed her, fleeing again on account of debt.

My childish memories are thick with railroad journeys, mostly on the Hartford, Providence and Springfield; with occasional steamboats; with the smell of 'hacks' and the funny noise the wheels made when little fingers were stuck in little ears and withdrawn again, alternately. And the things we had to wear! When I protested, mother said it was the easiest way to carry them. This I long resented, not in the least realizing how many things she must have had to carry, with two small children to convoy.

After some thirteen years of this life, mother, urged by friends, and thinking to set my father free to have another wife if he would not live with her, divorced him. This he bitterly resented, as did others of the family. So long as 'Mary Fred' was a blameless victim they pitied her and did what they could to help, but a divorce was a disgrace. Divorced or not she loved him till her death, at sixty-three. She was with me in Oakland, California, at the time, and father was then a librarian in San Francisco, just across the bay. She longed, she asked, to see him before she died. As long as she was able to be up, she sat always at the window watching for that beloved face. He never came. That's where I get my implacable temper.

This tragic life carried another grief, almost equal to loss of home and husband – the perplexed distress of the hen who hatched ducks. My mother was a baby-worshiper, even in her own childhood, always devoted to them, and in her starved life her two little ones were literally all; all of duty, hope, ambition, love and joy. She reared them with unusual intelligence and effectiveness, using much of the then new Kindergarten method, and so training herself with medical books that the doctor said he could do no better by us.

But as these children grew they grew away from her, both of them. The special gift for baby-care did not apply so well to large youngsters; the excellent teaching in first steps could not cope with the needs of changing years; and the sublime devotion to duty, the unflinching severity of discipline made no allowance for the changing psychology of children whose characters were radically different from her own. She increasingly lost touch with them, wider and wider grew the gulf between; it reminds one of that merciless old text: 'From him who hath not shall be taken away even that which he hath.'

There is a complicated pathos in it, totally unnecessary. Having suffered so deeply in her own list of early love affairs, and still suffering for lack of a husband's love, she heroically determined that her baby daughter should not so suffer if she could help it. Her method was to deny the child all expression of affection as far as possible, so that she should not be used to it or long for it. 'I used to put away your little hand from my cheek when you were a nursing baby,' she told me in later years; 'I did not want you to suffer as I had suffered.' She would not let me caress her, and would not caress me, unless I was asleep.

This I discovered at last, and then did my best to keep awake till she came to bed, even using pins to prevent dropping off, and sometimes succeeding. Then how carefully I pretended to be sound asleep, and how rapturously I enjoyed being gathered into her arms, held close and kissed.

If love, devotion to duty, sublime self-sacrifice, were enough in child-culture, mothers would achieve better results; but there is another requisite too often lacking – knowledge. Yet all the best she had, the best she knew, my mother gave, at any cost to herself.

Note. A fourth child was born some years later and died in infancy.

CHAPTER 2
BEGINNINGS

Of infant achievements I have by hearsay this: at about three years old, being summoned to the parlor, I appeared with the announcement, 'Here I come, doll in hand, to obey my mother's command.' Further, evidently having heard tobacco condemned, and finding a visiting relative in the act of using it, the four-year-old reformer sternly remarked to him: 'I disgust you Uncle Charles!'

I taught myself to read during an illness of mother's, having been brought almost to that point by her, but remember much greater pride in putting the last touch on ability to dress myself by buttoning my little frock all up the back, at five.

Great-aunt Catherine Beecher visited us in the old house in Apponaug, Rhode Island, which fact I happen to remember because of a shock felt by the whole nation, by the world. The newspaper was outlined in black. Aunt Catherine, with her little gray curls, and my mother facing her, sat speechless – Lincoln was dead! They took me in town that day, to Providence, and the streets were hung with black.

Mother, to us children, was mainly the disciplinarian, but all her conscientious severity was unable to anticipate the varied mischief of two lively-minded youngsters without sufficient occupation. She taught us, admirably; *Object Lessons* were our delight, and Hooker's *Child's Book of Nature*.

We took *Our Young Folks*, in which some pleasant papers on natural science made an indelible impression on me, and one story, 'Andy's Adventures,' convinced me forever of the essential folly of lying. It occurred to me even then, that whereas mother taught us that lying was very wrong, evidently much more wrong than other misdemeanors, yet when it came to punishment we were whipped just as severely for less offenses – that this was unjust. Once, having done something for which whipping was due, I humbled my proud spirit and confessed, begging mother to forgive me. She said she would, but whipped me just the same. This gave me a moral 'set-back' in the matter of forgiveness – I've never been good at it.

Often during life has the first waking hour brought ideas, percepts, often of wide reach, and even in those baby years I woke once with a vast concept my inadequate vocabulary utterly failed to describe. It only provoked laughter when I said: 'It felt like having the whole world on my toes' . . . an enormous sense of social responsibility with power to handle it.

Our many movings we children took as a matter of course; to us the stays here and there seemed long, a six months' visit is a little lifetime to a child. We were most lovingly entertained by my father's aunts, Charlotte and Anna Perkins, for both of whom I was named. Those pious ladies, who used rags for handkerchiefs in order to send more to the missionaries, used to pick out the best from clothing contributed to give us children. They lived in Hartford in a square old house on the corner of Main Street and College – now Capitol Avenue.

Here mother had a little school for us, with some other children; she was a phenomenally good teacher for the very young. To one of those early schoolmates a tale belongs, funny enough to repeat. There were two little boys, let us call them Harry and Johnny Blake. Harry was a dark, handsome boy, and polite to me – a new experience. Mother took me to the Blakes' to dinner one day, a dinner so good I remember it yet – boiled salmon, egg sauce, green peas. Mrs Blake was most kind, but the main attraction was Harry, a most courteous young host. So I gave my seven-year-old heart to Harry – and after that summer never saw him again for some fifty years. Then, in New York, joining some friends for a theater party, a tall, dark, handsome man was introduced to me as Mr Blake, of Hartford. 'Harry Blake!' I cried, unbelievingly, but he it was. We sat down together and dropped those fifty years completely, went back to 1868, my mother's little school, the other children, and I told him of that visit and how good his mother was to me. While completely immersed in childish reminiscences a tall, handsome, gray-haired lady was brought up and introduced to me as 'Mrs Blake.' I sprang to my feet and greeted her with affectionate enthusiasm – 'Harry's mother!' I cried . . . and it was his wife . . .

I was taught to sew before five, little patchwork squares, in the tiniest of 'over-and-over' stitches. When about eight, button-hole-stitch was added to my accomplishments, and here occurred my first invention, genuine enough, though slight. As taught, the thread was looped about the needle before pulling it through, and I discovered that the same effect could be produced by pulling it through first and then picking up the thread in a certain way, with the advantage of being able to use up a shorter end.

We children were so violently well brought up that we cherished an Ishmaelitish resentment against 'grown-ups'. Young women we called 'proudies,' and for young men I found a lovely name in a book – 'fops.' Of all the record of malicious mischief which distinguishes those early years the utter worst is this: we would roll our hoops in mud and trundle them against the voluminous crinolines of the period. When angry ladies turned on the aggressors they were met by such sweet-faced, polite apologies as abated their wrath instantly

In a New York boarding-house, for description of which see Henry Alden's *Old New York* – he even mentions 'little Charlotte Perkins' – we established a record for infant iniquity, but it lacked the Machiavellian quality of those apologies. In later school-life my brother remained a source of ingenious misdemeanors, while I was well behaved, so I truly think that he, the older, was mainly responsible for our pranks, but one crowning outrage there in New York was wholly mine. The house was one of those tall, narrow ones with a four-story staircase winding back and forth in pinched loops scarcely a foot wide. Down this slit one could look, or drop things, from the top floor to the basement. To Mrs Swift, the landlady, doubtless a worthy soul, we imps had taken a dislike. She had reproved us as we well deserved, for our sins against the boarders. We objected also to her little red-eyed poodle, Pinky, and did horrid things to his food.

On one sad occasion I, looking over the banisters on the top floor, perceived Mrs Swift similarly leaning over on the ground floor, directly below me . . . If you were a mischievous child – she had the beginning of a bald spot on the crown of her head –

what would you have done? Or at least wanted to do? I did it. It was too tempting – Down softly from story to story sailed the little white drop, and landed, spat! exactly on that bald spot . . .

That was the time when a distracted mother insisted that my father, who happened to call that evening, should whip me. He did, with a small whip she had purchased for our chastisement.

'Hold out your hand!'

I held it out, as flatly stretched as I could make it.

He struck the little hand several times, told mother that he would never do that again, and never did.

Among our pleasantest visits were those at the new big house of Aunt Harriet Stowe in Hartford. She had built it, to suit her eager fancy, out of the proceeds of *Uncle Tom's Cabin*. There was a two-story conservatory in the rear, the great entrance hall opened on it, the back parlor, and the dining-room; upstairs a gallery on three sides allowed access from bedrooms and hall. Aunt Harriet used to sit at a small table in that back parlor, looking out on the flowers and ferns and little fountain while she painted in water-colors. From her dainty flower pictures I got my first desire to paint, and an eager love for Windsor & Newton's little china dishes.

One splendid memory of those years stands out above all others. We were with the aunts in Hartford, at the time of the Grant and Colfax election. There was a torch-light procession, houses were illuminated, much money was spent in decoration by those who had it to spend. We had not, but determined to make as good a show as we could. In every one of our tiny window-panes we stuck a candle, making a many-faceted glitter more effective than fewer lights in larger panes.

'The Stowe girls,' Hattie and Eliza, came to help us. Across the front door we placed a large table, and behind the narrow windows on either side set a large lamp. In the full light of those lamps stood a Goddess of Liberty – eight years old! A white dress, a liberty cap, a liberty pole (which was a new mop-handle with a red-white-and-blue sash tied on it and a cornucopia of the same colors on its top), and a great flag draped around me – there I stood – Living. One crowded hour of glorious life, that was, to a motionless, glorified child.

The procession seemed to go on forever. I think it took at least an hour to pass a given point, but to that fixed little figure at one given point it was none too long. They were soldiers, real soldiers in uniform, who had been in the war but three years since, who cared passionately about the General they wished to elect. As each company passed a specially illuminated house the leader would turn and march backward, keeping time with his sword, and it was: 'ONE! TWO! THREE! U! S! G! HURRAH!' . . .

I can hear them now.

Might not our educators consider if such a soul-expanding experience is not of lasting value to a child; and if, some day, we may not learn how to accustom our children to large feelings instead of keeping them always among little ones . . .

If I was a pretty child no hint of it was allowed to enter my mind. Mother cut off the fat little brown curls at an early age, lest I should be vain – and kept them as long as she lived.

My passion for beauty dates far back; in picture books the one or two that were really beautiful; in the colors of the worsted mother used, loving some and hating others; in bits of silk and ribbon, buttons – children used to collect strings of buttons in those days; I keenly recall my delight in specially beautiful things. There was a little cloak of purple velvet, deep pansy-purple, made over from something of mother's, that enraptured my soul.

Dolls were never lovely enough, most of them were mere babies, china heads and flat-jointed, sawdust-stuffed bodies; I wanted people, boy and man dolls as well as girls, and named my favorites Lady Geraldine, Lady Isabel, and so on. I wanted queens, and thrones to play with, murmuring a little jingle about 'Burnished brass and polished glass' – I did not see why dolls could not be like the kings and princesses I read about. Their meager bodies especially distressed me. 'Why don't they make them like little statues?' I demanded. Only once, calling somewhere with mother, did I find a girl who played as I did – an unforgettable pleasure. And once I conceived a devoted affection for a schoolmate, a pale, long-haired Sunday-school-ish child – Etta Talcott was her name. When we as usual moved away, I sent her a sacrificial offering, a box adorned with decalcomania which I thought lovely, and in it my dearest toys.

For real growth there were two notable steps during a brief school period, when I was eight – my total schooling covered four years, among seven different schools, ending when I was fifteen. This little patch was in a public school in Hartford, quite a big one it seemed to us. Floods of children I remember, going down some stairs, and beauty – a girl with a rich mane of wavy chestnut hair. There was a carrot-headed Irish boy who read in a halting sing-song about 'the yellow catkins hanging on the willows in the spring,' and gave a touching version of 'Lo, the poor Indian's' speech thus: 'Then came the timid white-man, asking to lie down on the Indian's bare skin.' We thought the white men far from timid.

I had reached long division, and learned how to prove the

examples, a keen delight to the rational mind. Taking the slate to be marked by the teacher, she said, 'This one is wrong.' 'I have proved it,' I replied confidently. Then she showed me her book with the answers. 'See, here is the answer, yours is wrong.' To which I still replied, 'But I have proved it.' Then she did the example herself, and proved it, and I was right – the book was wrong! This was a great lesson; science, law, was more to be trusted than authority.

Then, one day when that big light room was quiet save for the soft buzz of many hushed voices muttering over their lessons, the speculative Charlotte said to herself: 'I wonder why we all have to keep still . . . I wonder what would happen if any one spoke out loud . . . I'm going to find out.' But I was cautious as well as experimental, and selected the shortest word I could think of. Across the low-murmuring room arose a clear, child-ish voice remarking, 'It.' 'Who said that?' Up went my hand. 'Come here.' I went there. The teacher put her arm around me (my brother and I usually stood well with our teachers on account of general information and decorum). 'Why did you do that?' she asked.

'I wanted to see what would happen,' I truthfully replied.

Nothing happened. She said I must not do it again, for which indeed there was no occasion. So I learned another great lesson, long remembered and acted on – that things debarred may sometimes be done – in safety.

Of all those childish years the most important step was this, I learned the use of a constructive imagination. Under mother's careful regimen we children had a light and early supper, and then were read to for a while, too short a while, inexorably cut off by bedtime. The reading was interesting, sometimes thrilling, *Oliver Twist* for instance, to an eight-year-old. But that painfully early bed hour stopped the story, perhaps in the middle of a chapter; off we went, dumbly, but with inward rebellion.

You may lead a horse to water but you cannot make him drink. Bed is one thing, sleep is another. Exciting literature after supper is not the best digestive. Lying there, not a bit sleepy, full of eager interest in the unfinished chapter, following the broken adventure to possible developments, I learned the joy of brain-building. Balboa was not more uplifted by his new ocean.

Beauty and splendor were mine at last to pile and change at will. The stern restrictions, drab routine, unbending discipline that hemmed me in, became of no consequence. I could make a world to suit me. All that inner thirst for glorious loveliness could be gratified now, at will, unboundedly. Not all this was clear to me at the time, but one thing was – this was so delightful that it must be wrong.

Fine blunderers in ethics we are, so generally conveying to children the basic impression that pleasantness must be wrong, and right doing unpleasant!

I arranged it with my conscience thus: every night I would think only of pleasant things that really might happen; once a week I would think of lovelier, stranger things, once a month of wonders, and once a year of anything I wanted to! This program was probably soon forgotten, but it shows conscience wrestling with fancy at an early age.

The dream world grew apace. Sometimes it was 'having my wishes.' Here with sagacity I avoided all those foolish mistakes made by the misguided persons in the fairy-tales, who had their wishes and made a mess of them. My first one was: 'I wish that everything I wish may be Right!' To be Right was the main thing in life.

Most of the wishing was childish pleasure in having things of glittering gorgeousness, but what comes up most clearly was the laying in of copious materials to work with, as paper, pencils, paints. There was a stationer's store in Hartford then, Geer & Pond's, wherein was a big sample case of Windsor & Newton's water-colors – I wished for the whole case! They had also a pen of unparalleled beauty, a gold pen with a handle of pink pearl – that never-attained pen lasted me for years as a type of beauty.

Soon, among the delights of having things, grew the greater delight of doing things. In the attic were piles of *Harper's Weeklys* with the powerful cartoons of Nast. I browsed among them, became deeply impressed with civic crime and the difficulty of stopping it, and when my school-mates would crowd around me at recess and say 'Let's tell,' my preferred topic was the capture and punishment of Boss Tweed – this at about ten. I did not compose, make stories like Frances Hodgson in her childhood, but was already scheming to improve the world.

In 1870 we went to live in the country near Rehoboth, Massachusetts. After a summer with friends mother took a house by herself, and there we lived, for about three years, on what I do not know. Clothing was mostly given to us, though mother made the brown-checked gingham dresses and drawers in which I played untrammeled, and knitted long woolen stockings and mittens for us both. We ran barefoot in summer, reveled in snow-drifts in winter. My brother kept hens, from which he made enough to buy himself an overcoat, besides furnishing us with eggs and fowls to eat.

There were memorably delicious meals, new potatoes boiled in their jackets, all peeling and mealy, with a bowl of hot milk with butter and salt in it; and a whole dinner of 'hasty pudding,' first with milk, then with butter and molasses, then with milk again and so till we could no more. These were pure delight at the time, but now look strongly like bed-rock necessities.

Three years of this country life, healthy but barren. No playmates, save two children of the farmer who lived opposite. No school, though mother still gave us lessons, and once a schoolteacher came – possibly boarded a while, and taught us some arithmetic. This letter (probably fall of 1872) – I was doubtless told to make a better copy – illuminates the period.

DEAR FATHER

Will you please send the money for July, August and September. You told me to remind you of The Princess and Goblin if you forgot it. My three kits are getting large and fat. Thomas drowned the old cat for she killed four chicks. Thomas has got a nice garden and furnishes us with potatoes, tomatoes, melons, corn, beans and squashes and pumpkins. We have apples and pears in plenty. Please write a real long letter to me. This morning Thomas found a chimney swallow in the dining room. He had come down the parlor chimney, the fireplace of which was open. I wish you would write to me often; Willie Judd and Thomas Lord write to Thomas and he to them but nobody writes to me but you. Thomas caught a little turtle about an inch big. Thomas has got his snares set again, and caught a partridge this morning. I inclose two pictures in hopes you will do the same. Your affectionately

with my little monogram for signature.

My brother, with his garden, hens and hunting had a somewhat fuller life, outside, but no one had a richer, more glorious life than I had, inside. It grew into fairy-tales, one I have yet; it spread to limitless ambitions. With 'my wishes' I modestly chose to be the most beautiful, the wisest, the best person in the world; the most talented in music, painting, literature, sculpture – why not, when one was wishing?

But no personal wealth or glory satisfied me. Soon there developed a Prince and Princess of magic powers, who went about the world collecting unhappy children and taking them to a guarded Paradise in the South Seas. I had a boundless sympathy for children, feeling them to be suppressed, misunderstood.

It speaks volumes for the lack of happiness in my own actual life that I should so industriously construct it in imagination. I wanted affection, expressed affection. My brother was really very fond of me, but his teasing hid it from me entirely. Mother loved us desperately, but her tireless devotion was not the same thing as petting, her caresses were not given unless we were asleep, or she thought us so.

My dream world was no secret. I was but too ready to share it, but there were no sympathetic listeners. It was my life, but lived entirely alone. Then, influenced by a friend with a pre-Freudian mind, alarmed at what she was led to suppose this inner life might become, mother called on me to give it up. This was a command. According to all the ethics I knew I must obey, and I did . . .

Just thirteen. This had been my chief happiness for five years. It was by far the largest, most active part of my mind. I was called upon to close off the main building as it were and live in the 'L.' No one could tell if I did it or not, it was an inner fortress, open only to me . . .

But obedience was Right, the thing had to be done, and I did it. Night after night to shut the door on happiness, and hold it shut. Never, when dear, bright, glittering dreams pushed hard, to let them in. Just thirteen . . .

From CHAPTER 4
BUILDING A RELIGION

Out of much consideration I finally came to a definite decision as to my duty. The old condition of compelled obedience was gone forever. I was a free agent, but as such I decided that until I was twenty-one I would still obey. I saw that mother was probably wiser than I, that she had nothing to live for but us two children and would probably suffer much if we were rebellious, and that, furthermore, she had a right to her methods of education, while we were minors. So I told her that I would obey her until I was of age, and then stop. Dismissing this matter, I then marked out a line of work.

In my seventeenth year I wrote to my father, saying that I wished to help humanity, that I realized I must understand history, and where should I begin. He was always effective in book advice, none better, and sent me a fine list of reliable works. I have the little scrap of paper yet, in his handwriting—

Rawlinson's   Five Great Empires
   "   "   Sixth Great Empire
   "   "   Seventh   "   "

Dawkins,	Cave Hunting
Fergusson,	Rude Stone Monuments
Lubbock,	Prehistoric Times and Origins of Civilization
Tylor,	Early History of Mankind
"	Primitive Culture

Also he sent a large number of *Popular Science Monthlies*, a valuable magazine then, in the hands of the Youmans, carrying the still fresh discussion of evolution, such works as Andrew White's *Warfare of Religion and Science*, the general new urge in studies of natural law.

This was the beginning of a real education, always allowing for the excellent foundation laid by mother in early years. I now read connectedly, learning the things I most wanted to know, in due order and sequence, none of them exhaustively but all in due relation; enough of astronomy to get a clear idea of the whirling wonder of the earth's formation, enough of geology to grasp the visible age of this small world and the fossil evidence of evolution.

Humanity was always the major interest, the sciences held useful as they showed our origin, our lines of development, the hope and method of further progress. Here the path was clear; biology, anthropology, ethnology, sociology. History soon showed itself as an amusingly limited and partial account of what had happened; Lecky was helpful here. I presently joined 'The Society for the Encouragement of Studies at Home,' headed by Miss Tichnor of Boston. My courses were in Ancient History, a year with the Ancient Hebrews, one on Egypt, another with several early peoples, all intensely interesting. At one of our annual meetings, in the house still standing on the corner of Park and Beacon streets, Boston, we were addressed by Oliver Wendell Holmes, a small, delightful man.

In none of these studies could I have passed a college examination, I suppose, but the result of studying from a strong desire to know, and in orderly sequence and relation, was to give me a clear, connected general outline of the story of life on earth, and of our own nature and progress, which has proved lastingly useful.

Soon I realized the importance of religion as a cultural factor, but also the painfully conspicuous absurdities and contradictions of the world's repeated attempts in this line. As I followed the evolution of religion, saw it still dominated by some of its earliest errors, and universally paralyzed by the concept of a fixed revelation, the view was somewhat discouraging. But as clearly I saw the universal need of it, the functional demand of the brain for a basic theory of life, for a conscious and repeated connection with the Central Power, and for 'sailing orders,' a recognized scale of duties. I perceived that in human character there must be 'principles,' something to be depended on when immediate conditions did not tend to produce right conduct. James Freeman Clark's *Ten Great Religions* was a long step in this field of study, with much besides, and with wide illustration from both real life and fiction.

One may have a brain specialized in its grasp of ethics, as well as of mechanics, mathematics or music. Even as a child I had noted that the whole trouble and difficulty in a story was almost always due to lying or deceit. 'He must never know,' she cries, or 'She must never know,' he insists, and the mischief begins. Also, I observed a strange disproportion in the order of virtues, the peculiar way in which they vary in the order of their importance, by race, class, age, sex.

So I set about the imperative task of building my own religion, based on knowledge. This, to the 'believer,' is no satisfactory foundation. All religions of the past have rested on someone's say so, have been at one in demanding faith as the foremost virtue. Understanding was never required, nor expected, in fact it was forbidden and declared impossible, quite beyond 'the poor human intellect.'

'It may be poor,' said young Charlotte to herself, 'but it is all the intellect there is. I know of none better. At any rate it is all I have, and I'll use it.' As this religion of mine underlies all my Living, is the most essential part of my life, and began in these years, it will have to go in.

'Here I am,' said I, 'in the world, conscious, able to do this or that. What is it all about? How does it work? What is my part in it, my job – what ought I to do?' Then I set to work calmly and cheerfully, sure that the greatest truths were the simplest, to review the story of creation and see what I could see. The first evident fact is action, something doing, this universe is a going concern.

'Power,' said I. 'Force. Call it God. Now then, is it one, or more?' There are various forces at work before us, as centripetal and centrifugal, inertia and others, but I was trying to get a view of the whole show, to see if there was any dominant underlying power.

Looking rapidly along the story of the world's making and growing, with the development of life upon it, I could soon see that in spite of all local variations and back-sets, the process worked all one way – up. This of course involves deciding on terms, as to what is better or worse, higher or lower, but it seemed to me mere sophistry to deny that vegetable forms and activities are higher than mineral; animal higher than vegetable:

and of animal life man the highest form and still going on. This long, irresistible ascent showed a single dominant force. 'Good!' said I. 'Here's God – One God and it Works!'

The next question was of the character of this Force and its effect on the growing world, was it Good? Or Bad?

Here loomed before me the problem of evil, long baffling so many. But I knew that mighty thinkers had thought for ages without discovering some of the most patent facts; their failure did not prove the facts difficult to discover, it merely showed that they had not thought of them. Also, I was strengthened by an innate incredulity which refused to accept anybody's say-so, even if it had been said for a thousand years. If a problem was said to be insoluble, I forthwith set out to solve it. So I sat me down before the problem of evil, thus:

'I will go back to the period of a molten world, where we can call nothing right or wrong, and follow carefully up the ages – see where it comes in.' So I followed the process until the earth was cool enough to allow the formation of crystals, each square or pentagonal or whatever was its nature, and then if one was broken or twisted, I pounced upon the fact – 'here it is! It is right for this to be a hexagon, wrong for it to be squeezed flat.' Following this thought in vegetable and animal growth, I was soon able to make my first ethical generalization: 'That is right for a given organism which leads to its best development.'

It is told that Buddha, going out to look on life, was greatly daunted by death. 'They all eat one another!' he cried, and called it evil. This process I examined, changed the verb, said, 'They all feed one another,' and called it good. Death? Why this fuss about death? Use your imagination, try to visualize a world *without* death! The first form of life would be here yet, miles deep by this time, and nothing else; a static world. If birth is allowed, without death, the resulting mass would leave death as a blessed alternative. Death is the essential condition of life, not an evil.

As to pain——? I observed that the most important continuous functions of living are unconsciously carried on within us; that the most external ones, involving a changing activity on our part, as in obtaining food, and mating, are made desirable by pleasure; that just being alive is a pleasure; that pain does not come in unless something goes wrong. 'Fine!' said I. 'An admirable world. God is good.'

As to the enormous suffering of our humankind, that we make, ourselves, by erroneous action – and can stop it when we choose.

Having got thus far, there remained to study the two main processes of religion, the Intake and the Output. (The phrasing of all this is of more recent years, but the working out of it was done in those years of early girlhood from sixteen to twenty.)

The Intake; the relation of the soul to God. All manner of religions have wandered around this point, and in spite of wide difference in terminology, the fact is established that the individual can derive renewed strength, peace and power from inner contact with this Central Force. They *do it*, Christian, Hebrew, Moslem, Buddhist. It is evident that this Force does not care what you call it, but flows in, as if we had tapped the reservoir of the universe.

However, one cannot put a quart in a pint cup. Sucking away on this vast power and not doing anything with it, results in nothing, unless it may be a distention of the mind, unfitting it for any practical contacts. So we sometimes see the most profoundly religious persons accomplishing the least good, while more is done by some who spend less time in prayer.

Seeking to clarify my mind on this point I deliberately put myself in God's place, so to speak, tried to imagine how I should feel toward my creatures, what I should expect of them. If that Power is conscious we may assume it to be rational, surely, and in no way *less* than we! If not conscious, we must simply find out how it works. What does God want of the earth? To whirl and spin and keep its times and seasons. What of the vegetable world? To blossom and bear fruit. Of the animals? The same fulfilment of function. Of us? The same and more. We, with all life, are under the great law, Evolution.

I figured it out that the business of mankind was to carry out the evolution of the human race, according to the laws of nature, adding the conscious direction, the telic force, proper to our kind – we are the only creatures that can assist evolution; that we could replenish our individual powers by application to the reservoir; and the best way to get more power was to use what one had.

Social evolution I easily saw to be in human work, in the crafts, trades, arts and sciences through which we are related, maintained and developed. Therefore the first law of human life was clear, and I made my second ethical generalization: 'The first duty of a human being is to assume right functional relation to society' – more briefly, to find your real job, and do it. This is the first duty, others accompany and follow it, but not all of them together are enough without this.

This I found perfectly expressed in a story read in later years, of a noted English engineer, whose personal life was open to much criticism, and who was about to die of heart disease. His nurse, a redoubtable Nova Scotian, annoyed him by concern about his soul, his approaching Judgment and probable damnation.

'My good woman,' said he, 'when I die, if I come to judgment, I believe that I shall be judged by the bridges I have built.'

Life, duty, purpose, these were clear to me. God was Real. under and in and around everything, lifting lifting. We, conscious of that limitless power, were to find our places, our special work in the world, and when found, do it, do it at all costs.

There was one text on which I built strongly: 'Whoso doeth the will shall know of the doctrine.' 'Good,' said I. 'That's *provable*; I'll try it.' And I set to work, with my reliable system of development, to 'do the will' as far as I could see it.

From CHAPTER 5
GIRLHOOD – IF ANY

Sixteen, with a life to build. My mother's profound religious tendency and implacable sense of duty; my father's intellectual appetite; a will power, well developed, from both; a passion of my own for scientific knowledge, for real laws of life; an insatiable demand for perfection in everything, and that proven process of mine for acquiring habits – instead of 'Standing with reluctant feet where the brook and river meet,' I plunged in and swam.

I am giving the girlhood which I remember, the dominant feelings, the most earnest efforts. As I look over the diaries of the time, the first one is for 1876, the records are trivial enough, hardly anything is shown of the desperately serious 'living' which was going on. It was my definite aim that there should be nothing in my diary which might not be read by anyone; I find in these faintly scribbled pages most superficial accounts of small current events, an unbaked girlishness of no special promise.

Very occasionally some indication of the inner difference appears, as once while seventeen: 'Am going to try hard this winter to see if I cannot enjoy myself like other people.' This shows the growing stoicism which was partly forced on me by repeated deprivations, then consciously acquired. The local life in which we moved seemed to me petty in the extreme. The small routine of our housekeeping, the goings and comings of friends and relatives, and the rare opportunities for small entertainment, have left almost no impression.

What I do remember, indelibly, is the cumulative effort toward a stronger, nobler character. At the end of the eighteen-year-old diary is written: 'Goodby old Year! It has been one of much progress and considerable improvement. My greatest fault now is inordinate egotism.' A persistent characteristic, this.

Our living was of the simplest, mother and I doing the little housework, washing and all. There were coal stoves to care for, and I, 'in the vicious pride of my youth,' could take a hod of anthracite coal in both hands and run up two flights of stairs with it, singing all the way. Also, I could lift a full water-pail in one hand up to the level of my ear.

I improved in painting my little water-color portraits of flowers, and began to get small orders for them. Mrs C. C. Smith, a friend of both my parents, a Boston woman, high in educational circles, visited us, and was not pleased to see a girl of my age so untrained. She suggested that I attend The School of Design, about to be opened in Providence. Mother objected to this on the ground that it would take me out of her influence and management; she held that a girl should, as she put it, 'remain in her mother's sphere until she entered her husband's.' This was somehow derived from her Swedenborgianism. My natural query, 'Does a girl never have a sphere of her own?' was ignored. But the good lady from Boston was a friend of father's as well as mother's; she doubtless represented to him that I had talent, he was willing to pay the fees, and the matter seemed to me so important that I decided to stretch my determined obedience for once.

We sat at our little dining-table, mother and Aunt Caroline and I. Calmly I stated the advantages offered, improvement in my work, means of earning a living, a chance to make friends and connections, ending: 'If you command me not to go I shall obey you, but do you dare refuse such an opportunity?' She didn't. So I went to the Rhode Island School of Design, and learned much.

The school was on the top floor of a five-story building on Westminster Street, about a mile from our house. There was an elevator, but I was always looking for additional exercise, and walked up. At first slowly and sedately, then I ran one flight and walked three, then ran two and presently all, then began again with two steps at a time, and in a month or so I was running up the whole four flights two steps at a time and beating the elevator, to my immense satisfaction.

I was no artist, but a skilled craftsman. My flower-portraiture was perfect of its kind, but not 'art.' The study in free-hand drawing I liked, the charcoal work, even the beginnings in oil, but chiefly delightful was perspective, which just fitted some corner of my mind. When the exercises were given I had the example done before the description was hardly finished, and then it was hung on the wall as a specimen of class-work.

Which calls to mind a story about another specimen and a discomfited young man. We were taught modelling, and I had a medallion to copy, a head of Couture by William M. Hunt. The copy was a good one and was kept among the school exhibits. Years later another principal of the school, a young man and cocky, passed it around at an artist's club supper as

Hunt's own, expatiating dictatorially on its merits. But a friend of mine present saw my monogram on it, and pointed out that it was done by C. A. Perkins while a student, to the chagrin of the exhibitor.

One odd result of the art school experience was temporary employment in a monument shop. They wanted some student to assist in their drawing work, and I got the job. All I remember of that effort is how to put on a 'flat wash' – to tint evenly a large surface, and the shape of an 'ogee curve.'

Another was to teach drawing in a small private school. There I encountered the only child I ever saw who really could not draw. She was 'form blind,' could not distinguish between a square and a circle, as it were.

One amusing source of income was the painting of advertising cards for Kendall's Soap Company. Cousin Robert Brown was in that business, and the fashion of distributing small lithographed cards to attract customers had just begun. Robert had a fertile imagination, he devised the pictures he wanted and I drew and colored them. I did not know how, did not do them well, but neither of us minded that. One of their established figures was 'The Soapine Whale,' this animal I labored with repeatedly. Another of his involved a big gray-dappled horse which used to lead in pulling freight-cars through the city, and with much effort I drew him, my first horse.

Little by little I added to my earning capacity, selling the little cardboard panels with groups of flowers on them, and giving lessons both in school and privately. This flower-painting developed to a sort of limited perfection. I was told later by a competent judge that if I would give myself to it I could paint still life as well as any one on earth. But this seemed to me a poor ambition, not conducive to my object – the improvement of the human race.

Some lasting friendships were contracted during these years, one, somewhat unique in its character, with a gentle, lovely, intellectual girl, Martha Luther by name. She was sixteen, I seventeen. We liked each other immensely. Said I to her: 'We seem to be on the brink of what they call "A schoolgirl friendship," which so often breaks up in foolish quarrel or misunderstanding. Let's make ours safe and permanent.'

So we undertook to be always utterly frank with each other in word and deed, never to pretend anything we did not fully feel. I explained, furthermore, that I was irregular in fervor, that for a time I should want to see her continually, and that there would be spaces when affection seemed to wane, but if she would understand and be patient it would well up warmly again. We earnestly entered into this compact of mutual understanding, kept its agreements, enjoyed years of perfect companionship, and as grandmothers are still friends. This was my first deep personal happiness.

The Hazards, one of the 'noble families' of Rhode Island, were extremely kind to me in these years of girlhood. There was the grandfather, Rowland Hazard I, the son, Rowland Hazard II, the grandson, Rowland Hazard III, later came a fourth, and there may be a fifth of the dynasty by now.

Mrs Rowland II was like some beneficent duchess. There chanced to be a strong resemblance between me and her sister, Mrs Blake, who was dead; also to her daughter, Ada Blake, and to Mrs Hazard's daughter Helen. There was no connection between our families, but the resemblance was so marked that I was repeatedly taken for one or the other of the girls even in her own house.

Mrs Hazard engaged me to give lessons to her youngest

daughter, which never struck me at the time as pure benevolence. She invited me occasionally to parties, and to visit them at their lovely home in Peacedale, Rhode Island. I recall now with the keenest appreciation how wisely kind they were to me, all of them, trying to help this obstinate young stoic, to ameliorate somewhat the hard conditions in which I lived.

My mother was anxious as to my conduct in all this grandeur. 'Does Charlotte know how to behave?' she asked, and gracious Mrs Hazard answered: 'If she does not know what to do, she does something of her own that is just as good.'

I had no suitable clothes for such society, which distressed me not a whit. On my way home from giving lessons I would stop at their splendid home for an afternoon tea or something, wearing what was practically my only dress, hanging up what was practically my only hat in the hall, perfectly unconcerned in the matter of clothes. If, hatless, I was taken for one of the family, why that was a compliment.

More formative and valuable was friendship with the family of Dr William F. Channing, son of William Ellery Channing, the great Unitarian divine. Here I found broad free-thinking, scientific talk, earnest pro motion of great causes – life. There were two beautiful daughters, lifelong friends, one closer than a sister to this day.

The handsomest girls of all I knew were Helen Hazard, Nellie Sharpe, and Jessie Luther, the last two still alive and lovely; the most utterly charming was May Diman, cut off by an accident in her rich youth. Another kind and helpful friend of my youth, somewhat older than I and appreciative of my strenuous efforts at well doing, was Miss Kate Bucklin, who used to take me to the theater and buy me books. Dear woman! she is still sending me presents.

Among other benefactions she took me to Ogunquit, Maine, for vacation visits, with other friends. We stayed at the Cliff House, successor to which still stands on that sheer cliff, about which is a turmoil of rock delightful to geologists. One deep, narrow chasm they named Charlotte Perkins's Leap, because I jumped across it. It was not really very wide, but looked dangerous enough if one was not clear-headed and surefooted.

One year there was a handsome Harvard boy in the party, who invited me out to sit on the rocks in the moonlight. Thus romantically placed, he confided to me that he had kissed more than one girl for what he was sure was the first time. Replying, I soberly inquired if he did not expect to marry some day, which he admitted. 'When you first kiss the girl you mean to marry, don't you wish that to be her "first time"?' Yes, he did. 'Then don't you see that every time you kiss these other girls first you are robbing some other man of that dear pleasure?' He saw. Our conversation continued on a most friendly and confidential basis, but I noticed that next night he took one of the pretty waitresses out on the rocks – they were nice neighborhood girls.

Some months after, that fine young fellow shot himself. His parents were sternly pious people and thought he would be damned, for committing suicide, and I was most happily able to lift that load from their hearts by repeating to them what he had told me of black misery of mind, of how he often thought of suicide, but intended not to use the pistol his father gave him, lest such a use of it hurt his feelings! The indication of growing melancholia was so clear that the agonized parents felt sure he was insane, and even the kind of God they believed in would hardly damn a lunatic.

From CHAPTER 6
POWER AND GLORY

Among our immediate associates I heard nothing of the larger movements of the time, but with the Channing family and their friends was a larger outlook, while in my steady reading I lived in the world as a whole. This world seemed to be suffering from many needless evils, evils for which some remedies seemed clear to me even then. I was deeply impressed with the injustices under which women suffered, and still more with the ill effects upon all mankind of this injustice; but was not in close touch with the suffrage movement. Once I went to a meeting of some earnest young temperance workers, but was not at all at home in that atmosphere of orthodox religion and strong emotion. My method was to approach a difficulty as if it was a problem in physics, trying to invent the best solution.

It was a period of large beginnings in many lines. 'Strong-minded' girls were going to college under criticism and ridicule, the usual curriculum in those days was held quite beyond 'the feminine mind.' Some thirty years later, an editor, sadly impressed by the majority of prize-takers being girls, protested

that these same curricula were 'evidently too feminine.' I recall
part of a bit of newspaper wit at the time, about 1880:

> She'd a great and varied knowledge she'd picked up at a
> woman's college,
> Of quadratics, hydrostatics and pneumatics very vast;
> She'd discuss, the learned charmer, the theology of
> Brahma,
> All the 'ologies of the colleges and the knowledges of the
> past.
>
> She knew all the forms and features of the prehistoric
> creatures,
> Icthyosaurus, megliosaurus, plestosaurus, and many more,
> She could talk about the Tuscans and the Greeks and the
> Etruscans,
> All the scandals of the Vandals and the sandals that they
> wore.
>
> But she couldn't get up a dinner for a gaunt and starving
> sinner,
> Or concoct a simple supper for her poor old hungry
> Poppa,
> For she never was constructed on the old domestic plan.

The 'charmer' before marriage and the cook afterward were the
prevailing ideas at the time, as indeed they still are in some places.
But things began to change, women appeared in stores and
offices – I once met a man from Maine who told me how he was
severely criticized for employing saleswomen – so unwomanly!
such a public occupation! Doubtless our Civil War, like this last

one, drove women to do what men had done before. Clothing changed, there appeared the 'tailored suit,' even made by men! made for street wear, plain and serviceable. Ideas began to change. Mona Caird in England produced that then much talked of book, *Is Marriage a Failure?*

Education was advancing, the kindergarten making slow but sure impression. Far-seeing mothers were beginning to give their children information about sex. There was a start toward an equal standard in chastity, equal *up*, not down as at present. A little paper called *The Alpha* was brought out in Washington to urge this ideal. The first poem I had published was in this tiny paper. It was called 'One Girl of Many,' a defense of what was then termed the 'fallen' woman.

In the present-day lowering of standards of behavior one exhibition of ignorance and meanness of spirit is the charge, 'You did the same in your day, only you were secretive about it.' Any one whose memory covers fifty years knows better. There were plenty of young men who were 'fast,' and some girls who were called 'pretty gay,' but even at that the words had different meanings.

For instance there was just one damsel in all my acquaintance who was certainly 'gay.' She was so proud of the 'wasp-waist' admired at the time, that she tied her corset-laces to the bedpost and pulled, to draw them tight enough. Her behavior with young men was so much discussed that I determined to learn something of her.

'You know I am not "in society,"' I told her. 'I am interested as a student, and I wish you would tell me just what the game is – what it is that you are trying to do.' She recognized my honest interest, and was quite willing to explain. Considering thoughtfully she presently replied, 'It is to get a fellow so he cannot keep his hands off you – and then not let him touch you.'

This was bad enough in all conscience, but she was the only one out of scores. Among the more daring girls there was some discussion of whether, when a fellow came home with you, he might also claim a kiss. But there was also discussion, quite popular, of this question of Emerson's, 'Does the soul underlie a condition of infinite remoteness?' I remember coming to the conclusion that it did.

On sleighing-parties and 'straw-rides' there was a good deal of holding hands and some kissing, all in cheerful, giggling groups; and I do not doubt that going to ride with what livery-stable men called a 'courtin' horse' involved a good deal of hugging.

But the standards and general behavior of 'nice girls' – and most of them were nice – are shown clearly in the books of Louisa M. Alcott and Mrs A. D. T. Whitney.

Among the many splendid movements of the late nine-teenth century was one dear to my heart, that toward a higher physical culture. In Europe and then here the impulse was felt, building gymnasiums, practice of calisthenics even for girls, and the rapid development of college athletics. In this line of improvement I was highly ambitious. With right early training I could easily have been an acrobat, having good nervous coordination, strength, courage, and excellent balanc-ing power . . .

Needless to say that I never wore corsets, that my shoes were 'common sense' (and more people seemed to have common sense at the time), that all my clothing 'hung from the shoul-der' – the custom being to drag all those heavy skirts from the waist. I devised a sort of side-garter suspender, to which skirts were buttoned, and, not a flat bandage to make a woman look like a boy, but after many trials evolved a species of brassiere which supported the breasts without constriction anywhere. It had elastic over the shoulder and under the arm, allowing perfect freedom for breathing and arm-motion, while snug and efficient as a support.

Textile construction always delighted me, inventing, composing, making suitable and if possible lovely garments. There has been plenty of it to do. During all my youth I had to wear other people's clothes, gifts from friends and relatives. Mother bought my first new dress when I was thirteen or fourteen. Later I had some pretty frocks for those Boston visits, and enjoyed them like any girl.

Never in my life have I been able to dress as I would like to. That requires one or more of three things I never had enough of, time, strength, or money. And since I would not wear what others did if against my principles of hygiene, truth, beauty, comfort or humanity – as for instance the use of feathers for trimming, or unnecessary furs – the result has left much to be desired. Real beauty I cared for intensely, fashion I despised.

In the fall of 1891 I wanted a gymnasium for women. There was none in Providence. I went to Dr Brooks, who had taught calisthenics in my last school, and who had a man's gymnasium, and asked him why he did not have one for women. He said not enough women wanted it. 'How many would you need?' He said about thirty. Then I set forth, visited every girl I knew and many that I didn't, and got up a class, not thirty indeed, but enough to encourage him to begin. He opened a high-grade woman's gymnasium, beautifully fitted, and let me design a stencil for the wall-border! Thanks to Mrs Hazard's patronage some of the 'first families' were represented among the pupils, which ensured success.

For three years I had the use of this well-appointed place, free, and found it a joy indeed. Aside from its initial purpose it provided social pleasure. There were a lot of nice girls, and I even learned some dancing, for we had polka-races, the witchy 'slide and kick, slide and kick, slide and slide and slide and kick' of the racquet, and long lines of high-swinging legs in the 'Patience step,' from the then new opera.

My special efforts were not toward anything spectacular, but directed to the building up of a sound physique. Going twice a week, each day I ran a mile, not for speed but wind, and can still run better than many a younger woman. I could vault and jump, go up a knotted rope, walk on my hands under a ladder, kick as high as my head, and revel in the flying rings. But best of all were the traveling rings, those wide-spaced single ones, stirrup-handled, that dangle in a line the length of the hall.

To mount a table with one of those in one hand, well drawn back, launch forth in a long swing and catch the next with the other, pull strongly on the first to get a long swing back, carefully letting go when it hung vertically so that it should be ready for the return, and go swinging on to the next, down the whole five and back again – that is as near flying as one gets, outside of a circus. I could do it four times in those days.

Life does not offer many opportunities for this exercise, but I had a chance at it when about thirty-six, again when somewhat over fifty, and last, lecturing in Oklahoma University, I did it once, the whole row and back, at sixty-five. Whereby it is apparent that a careful early training in physical culture lasts a lifetime. I never was vain of my looks, nor of any professional achievements, but am absurdly vain of my physical strength and agility.

Five little rules of health I devised: 'Good air and plenty of it, good exercise and plenty of it, good food and plenty of it, good sleep and plenty of it, good clothing and as little as possible.' How I should have delighted in the short, light garments of to-day! But I would have made mine wide enough to walk in, this pinched pillow-case effect is far from freedom. The result of all this training was to establish a cheerful vigor that enjoyed walking about five miles a day, with working hours from six a.m. to ten p.m. except for meals.

We moved, April, 1881, to a better house, on the north-west corner of Manning and Ives Streets. Ours was the ground floor, Aunt Caroline took the second, and I had a little room on the third, where the little landlady kept three for herself. That little chamber of mine, with its one arched window facing south, was hot in summer and cold in winter, but I enjoyed it hugely – thus celebrating its prospect:

My View

From my high window the outlooker sees
    The whole wide southern sky;
Fort Hill is in the distance, always green,
With ordinary houses thick between,
    And scanty passers by.

Our street is flat, ungraded, little used,
    The sidewalks grown with grass;
And, just across, a fenceless open lot,
Covered with ash-heaps, where the sun shines hot
    On bits of broken glass.

It's hard on Nature, blotting her fair face
　　With such discourteous deeds;
But one short season gives her time enough
To softly cover all the outlines rough
　　With merciful thick weeds.

Then numerous most limited back-yards,
　　One thick with fruit trees, overgrown with vines,
But most of them are rather bare and small,
With board and picket fences, running all
　　In parallel straight lines.

Hardly a brilliant prospect, you will think,
　　The common houses, scanty passers by,
Bare lot thick strewn with cinder-heaps and shards,
And small monotonous township of backyards –
　　Ah! You forget the sky!

The window I promptly took out of the casing, it stayed out for the three years we lived there. In very stormy weather I used to stand one of the spare leaves from the dining-table against it; that and closed blinds kept out most of the snow. There was no bathroom in this house, that luxury I never possessed till living in Oakland in 1891, but I took my daily cold bath from the wash-bowl until the ice in the water-pail was so thick I could not break it with my heel. A rough facecloth, a triple scrub – it used to leave me steaming.

'Oct. 5th, 1881. Ice! Up at six, cold as I ever want to be. Warm up with bath and do chores as usual.' Rising hours were early, '6:10,' '6:50,' '5:55,' '6,' '6:05' they run. The day began with three coal-stoves to attend to, in winter; get breakfast, do chamberwork, be ready for pupils at nine. These were two girls who came to the house for tutoring; in the afternoons there were others in different parts of the city to whom I went, teaching drawing, painting, gymnastics, and ordinary branches with cheerful enthusiasm.

I gave drawing lessons to a boy and girl, the girl died, and the lonely little brother begged to have me come and stay with him. So I tried governessing, for ten weeks, and learned more about the servant question in that time than most of us ever find out.

No long-tutored heir to a kingdom ever came to the throne with a more triumphant sense of freedom and power than mine when I reached my twenty-first birthday. I had lived six steady years of self-enforced obedience to management I heartily disapproved of, and which was in some ways lastingly injurious; submission to a tutelage so exacting that even the letters I wrote were read, as well as those I received; an account was always demanded of where I had been, whom I had seen, and what they had said – there was no unhandled life for me.

Afterward mother used to grieve because I did not give her my confidence. One does not readily give what was so long a compelled tribute. Naturally a confiding child, it required many years of misunderstanding and enforced exhibition to teach me complete reserve. For instance, at sixteen, I wrote the first bit of verse that seemed to me real poetry, a trifling thing about white violets. I went with it at once to mother. She listened with no apparent interest, and as soon as I had finished said, 'Go and put on the tea-kettle.' As a matter of fact she thought the verses beautiful, and kept them carefully, but at the time the tea-kettle was vividly in mind and the sensitiveness of a budding poetess was not. A trifling incident, but it hurt so that it was never forgotten, and I did not go to her so readily with later verses.

Twenty-one. My own mistress at last. No one on earth had a right to ask obedience of me. I was self-supporting of course, a necessary base for freedom which the young revolters of today often overlook. This freedom never meant self-indulgence. From sixteen I had not wavered from that desire to help humanity which underlay all my studies. Here was the world, visibly unhappy and as visibly unnecessarily so; surely it called for the best efforts' of all who could in the least understand what was the matter, and had any rational improvements to propose.

It is the fashion today for our alien critics and their imitators to ridicule the American urge toward improvement, personal or social. Why it should seem absurd for human beings to try to improve their conditions, physical, mental, moral, mechanical, industrial, economic, ethical or social, I cannot see. There certainly is room for it.

The nature of the work which loomed so large in my mind was by no means definite at that time. Painting, drawing, teaching, these were but means of support; though I did look forward to being a cartoonist as one form of influence. Writing was expected to be mainly didactic and gratuitous, and lecturing never came into my range 'til ten years later. But there was a tremendous sense of power, clean glorious power, of ability to do whatever I decided to undertake.

I contemplated much further study, meaning to spend time in various countries and learn each language like a native; much more in the sciences, a wide outline knowledge of history, economics, politics, there was no field of knowledge applicable to human need which was outside my purpose. Astronomy I never cared for; it seemed so definitely apart from social progress.

My health was splendid, I never tired, with a steady cheerfulness which external discomforts or mishaps could not dim. When asked, 'How do you do?' it was my custom to reply, 'as well as a fish, as busy as a bee, as strong as a horse, as proud as a peacock, as happy as a clam.'

As to looks, if I had been sex-conscious and dressed the part I think I should have been called beautiful. But one does not call a philosophic steam-engine beautiful. My dress was not designed to allure. When from Lily Langtry came the lovely and sensible 'Jersey' I seized upon it with delight, and wore it, with a plain, and for those days, markedly short skirt, and a neckerchief, continuously. Clothes were still given me, to make over. I spent little. In one eleven months my total outlay was $5.11 – including shoes! But a pair of 'button boots,' kid, cost only three dollars then.

This tremendous surge of free energy at twenty-one had no result in misbehavior. It found expression mainly in locking my door, actually and metaphorically. Once I sat up all night, just to see how it felt after having been sent to bed so inexorably from infancy; no revelry, just reading and working. Once I slept on the floor; once with a friend, on her roof – an unforgettable experience to me, to look up at the stars – to wake in the night with a soft breath of pure air on one's face and look straight up into that deep, glittering sky – if ever I build a house of my own (which becomes increasingly doubtful), it shall have a habitable roof.

One new indulgence was to go out evenings alone. This I worked out carefully in my mind, as not only a right but a duty. Why should a woman be deprived of her only free time, the time allotted to recreation? Why must she be dependent on some man, and thus forced to please him if she wished to go anywhere at night?

A stalwart man once sharply contested my claim to this freedom to go alone. 'Any true man,' he said with fervor, 'is always ready to go with a woman at night. He is her natural protector.' 'Against what?' I inquired. As a matter of fact, the thing a woman is most afraid to meet on a dark street is her natural protector. Singular.

Personally I have never known fear, except in dreams, that paralyzing terror born of indigestion. But if the streets were not safe for women they should be made so. In the meantime, if there is real danger, let them carry a pistol. So far, in forty-five years of free movement at night, from San Francisco to London, I have never met danger, and almost never the slightest impertinence.

As mother could no longer forbid my going, she tried to prevent me by saying that it made her feel badly. This I considered carefully. What I had decided was right she thought wrong. I was not afraid but she was. There did not seem to be any real danger, her fear was not based on present facts but on the way she had been brought up, for which I was not in the least responsible. Mothers and other relatives would always feel badly about it until it became habitual, a custom. Customs have to be made. I was sorry that mother should worry, but the reason lay in earlier standards, not in my conduct. So out I went.

Ever since the beginning of the character-building, I had established the inflexible habit of doing what I had decided to be right, unmoved by any further consideration. This inflexibility of youthful judgment becomes more malleable with passing years. One is not so certain of ethical values. With all my stern devotion to duty as I saw it, I was still painfully sensitive to the opinion of others. An old friend of mother's came to visit us, and was shocked at my independence. She strove to rebuke and improve my conduct, and I cried like a child being scolded – but did not change.

So far there was a good record of health, strength, cheerfulness and patience, and constant industry. Within, the splendid sense of power, the high though indefinite purpose, the absolute consecration to coming service. Regarding consequences I had no illusions. No one who sets out to make the world better should expect people to enjoy it, all history shows what happens to would-be improvers.

In ancient times such persons were promptly killed, I noticed; later they were persecuted, ostracized. What I had to expect was mostly misunderstanding, and the ceaseless opposition of that old enemy, General Apathy. Emerson's remark, 'Misunderstood! It is a right fool's word!' pleased me much. So I looked ahead to a steady lifetime of social study and service, with no reward whatever, on the theory that one should face life giving all and asking nothing.

One day in the gymnasium during a rest period, the girls were discussing what age they would rather be, for life. Most of them agreed on eighteen, which many of them were at the time. When they asked me I said fifty. They didn't believe it. 'Why?' they demanded. 'Because,' I explained, 'when I'm fifty, people will respect my opinions if they are ever going to, and I shall not be too old to work.'

This I remembered when starting the *Forerunner* at fifty.

From CHAPTER 7
LOVE AND MARRIAGE

In January 1882, I met Charles Walter Stretson, the painter. He was quite the greatest man, near my own age, that I had ever known. He stood alone, true to his art, in that prosaic mercantile town, handicapped with poverty, indifference and misunderstanding. His genius was marked; although largely self-taught, his work was already so remarkable for its jeweled color that a dishonest dealer tried to suborn him to paint Diazes for him – in vain.

In a very minor way I had been painting, drawing and teaching the same for years, and was able in some small degree to appreciate his splendid work, and wholly to sympathize with his gallant determination. In courage, in aspiration, in ideals, in bitter loneliness, we were enough alike to be drawn together.

Very promptly he asked me to marry him. Very promptly I declined. Then, reviewing the occurrence with that cold philosophy of mine, I asked myself, 'Is it right so lightly to refuse what after all may be the right thing to do?' This is a vivid commentary on my strenuous youth. Between deprivation and denial from outside, and intensive self-denial from within, there was no natural response of inclination or desire, no question of, 'Do I love him?' only, 'Is it right?'

So I took up the matter again, said that I had no present wish to marry him, but that it was possible that I might in time, and that if he so desired he might come to see me for a year and we would find out – which he was very willing to do.

Followed a time of what earlier novelists used to call 'conflicting emotions.' There was the pleasure of association with a noble soul, with one who read and studied and cared for real things, of sharing high thought and purpose, of sympathy in many common deprivations and endurances. There was the natural force of sex-attraction between two lonely young people, the influence of propinquity.

Then, on my part, periods of bitter revulsion, of desperate efforts to regain the dispassionate poise, the balanced judgment I was used to. My mind was not fully clear as to whether I should or should not marry. On the one hand I knew it was normal and right in general, and held that a woman should be able to have marriage and motherhood, and do her work in the world also. On the other, I felt strongly that for me it was not right, that the nature of the life before me forbade it, that I ought to forego the more intimate personal happiness for complete devotion to my work.

Having lived so long on clear convictions, on definite well-reasoned decisions, there was something ignominious in feeling myself slip and waver in uncertainty. Once I demanded a year's complete separation, to recover clear judgment, but could not secure it. It was a terrible two years for me, and must have been wearing for him, but he held on. Then, at one time when he had met a keen personal disappointment, I agreed to marry him. After that, in spite of reactions and misgivings, I kept my word, but the period of courtship was by no means a happy one.

There are poems of this time which show deep affection, and high hopes, also doubt and uncertainty.

On the opening of the year of my wedding appears this cheerful inscription:

1883–1884. Midnight – Morning. With no pride, with little hope, with uncertain occasional happiness, with no glad energy and living power, with no faith or nearly none, but still, thank God! with firm belief in what is right and wrong, I begin the new year. Let me recognize fully that I do not look forward to happiness, that I have no decided hope of success. So long must I live. One does not die young who so desires it. Perhaps it was not meant for me to work as I intended. Perhaps I am not to be of use to others. I am weak. I anticipate a future of failure and suffering. Children sick and unhappy. Husband miserable because of my distress, and I—

I think sometimes that it may be the other way, bright and happy – but this comes oftenest, holds longest. But this life is marked for me. I will not withdraw, and let me at least learn to be uncomplaining and unselfish. Let me do my work and not fling my pain on others. Let me keep at least this ambition, to be good and a pleasure to *some* one, to some others, no matter what I feel myself.

More of this, and then:

And let me not forget to be grateful for what I have, some strength, some purpose, some design, some progress, some esteem, respect and affection. And some Love. Which I can neither see, feel nor believe in when the darkness comes. I mean this year to try hard for somewhat of my former force and courage. As I remember it was got by practice.

This was evidently a very black hour. Succeeding days show more cheer and vigor, as March 24th, 'Then gym. enjoying it *intensely* and doing more than usual. Carried a girl on *one arm* and hip – easily!'

We were married in May, 1884 . . .

Mr Stetson's father, a Baptist minister, married us, in the house on the corner of Manning and Ives Streets, and then, with some last things to carry, we walked down to Wayland Avenue, where our three rooms awaited us. We had the whole second floor, big corner rooms every one, and the young artist had made it beautiful.

'Do it just as you choose,' I told him. 'I have no tastes and no desires. I shall like whatever you do.'

The house stood on a high bank, looking southward over the chimneys of a few small buildings below to the broad basin of the Seekonk, ringed at night with golden lights. White ducks drifted like magnolia petals along the still margins. Opposite us was a grove of tall pines – a pleasant place to walk and sit.

The housework for two in this tiny place was nothing to me, then some time I definitely devoted to deliberately breaking the regular habits of doing things on set days and hours in which I had been trained, repudiating the rigid New England schedule. Orderly habits of working are good, and later I established my own, but the immutable submission of the dutiful housewives I know, bred rebellion in me.

I determined to learn to cook. 'I won't have a cook-book in

the house,' quoth I. 'I'm going to learn how.' Knowing already the ordinary needful dishes, I began to alter the relative amount of ingredients, in small degree, and note the results, as of a little more sugar or less flour. Soon I learned the reaction of the different materials, and then was able to compose. The common method of merely following recipes is like studying music by learning a collection of tunes.

One of the most pleasing compliments of later years was that of a New York club man who told me I could command a high salary as chef in his club. During the period of experimentation no harm was done, I had enough practical knowledge to keep things edible, they merely varied from time to time, as indeed 'home-cooking' frequently does.

Two instances were funny, however. Our first pair of chickens were in the oven. Walter went out to see how they were getting along. He sat down on the floor in front of the stove and laughed loud and long. I presently joined him in the position and the laughter. There lay the poor dears, their legs sticking out at casual angles, simply wreathed in stiff ringlets of slowly exuding stuffing, crisping as it oozed. I had made that stuffing too soft, the stitches wherewith it was sewed in too wide, the oven was too slow, and I had not tied their legs. But they tasted just as good.

The other experiment we gave to the neighbor's children; it was harmless but peculiar. Mother used to make a plain cake flavored with almond, of which I was fond. I made one, and in the course of my researches I put in more flour than was usual. The result was a meritorious cake, a solid cake of sterling character, a cake which would have gone well among lumbermen in winter, or lost in the woods with no other food. It lingered, that cake, growing no softer.

Then said I, 'I will make "trifle" of this cake.' One might as well have undertaken to make a ballet dancer of a Swedish servant girl. 'First it must be soaked in wine,' I mused. I had no wine, and was a total abstainer at that. 'Wine is a fruit juice,' quoth I, and having no fruit at hand but apples and lemons, I made a thin apple-sauce, seasoned as usual with nutmeg, and vivified with a little lemon juice. In this I soaked the slices of cake, and up to that time the dish was good. I ate a piece and enjoyed it. Then came the soft custard, and never did I make a smoother one, flavoring it as I liked best, with cinnamon.

This in a tall glass dish, the piled slices of softened and enriched cake, the perfect custard flowing over all. My husband gazed upon it with a happy smile, and put some of the almond-apple-lemon-nutmeg-cinnamon mixture into his mouth. As many expressions chased across his countenance as were the tastes encountered, and with amazing discernment he unraveled the combination and named them all. It was a noble confection, but too composite, and served as a wholly sufficient lesson in the art of flavoring.

We were really very happy together. There was nothing to prevent it but that increasing depression of mine. My diary is full of thankfulness for happiness and prayers for deserving it, full of Walter's constant kindness and helpfulness in the work when I was not well – the not-wellness coming oftener and oftener.

The record dwells on delectable meals in full enumeration, as if I was a schoolboy. As a note on current prices this: 'Dinner vilely expensive, chops, six little chops, .50 cts.!' 'Walter home about five. Brings me flowers. Dear boy!' 'Walter gets most of the breakfast.' 'Amuse ourselves in the evenings with funny drawings.' These were works of art of an unusual nature, a head and body to the waist being drawn by one of us and the paper folded back at the waistline leaving the sides indicated; and then the other finished the legs, not knowing in the least what the other part was like. The results are surprising.

I think Walter was happy. A most successful exhibition in Boston had established him more favorably and enabled him to meet domestic expenses; and an order for a set of large etchings was added.

A lover more tender, a husband more devoted, woman could not ask. He helped in the housework more and more as my strength began to fail, for something was going wrong from the first. The steady cheerfulness, the strong, tireless spirit sank away. A sort of gray fog drifted across my mind, a cloud that grew and darkened.

'Feel sick and remain so all day.' 'Walter stays home and does everything for me.' 'Walter gets breakfast.' October 10th: 'I have coffee in bed mornings while Walter briskly makes fires and gets breakfast.' 'O dear! That I should come to this!' By October 13th the diary stops altogether, until January 1, 1885. 'My journal has been long neglected by reason of ill-health. This day has not been a successful one as I was sicker than for some weeks. Walter also was not very well, and stayed at home, principally on my account. He has worked for me and for us both, waited on me in every tenderest way, played to me, read to me, done all for me as he always does. God be thanked for my husband.'

February 16th: 'A well-nigh sleepless night. Hot, cold, hot, restless, nervous, hysterical. Walter is love and patience personified, gets up over and over, gets me warm wintergreen, bromide, hot foot-bath, more bromide – all to no purpose.'

Then, with impressive inscription: 'March 23rd, 1885. This

day, at about five minutes to nine in the morning, was born my child, Katharine.'

> Brief ecstasy. Long pain.
> Then years of joy again.

Motherhood means giving . . .

We had attributed all my increasing weakness and depression to pregnancy, and looked forward to prompt recovery now. All was normal and ordinary enough, but I was already plunged into an extreme of nervous exhaustion which no one observed or understood in the least. Of all angelic babies that darling was the best, a heavenly baby. My nurse, Maria Pease of Boston, was a joy while she lasted, and remained a lifelong friend. But after her month was up and I was left alone with the child I broke so fast that we sent for my mother, who had been visiting Thomas in Utah, and that baby-worshiping grandmother came to take care of the darling, I being incapable of doing that – or anything else, a mental wreck.

Presently we moved to a better house, on Humboldt Avenue nearby, and a German servant girl of unparalleled virtues was installed. Here was a charming home; a loving and devoted husband; an exquisite baby, healthy, intelligent and good; a highly competent mother to run things; a wholly satisfactory servant – and I lay all day on the lounge and cried.

CHAPTER 8
THE BREAKDOWN

In those days a new disease had dawned on the medical horizon. It was called 'nervous prostration.' No one knew much about it, and there were many who openly scoffed, saying it was only a new name for laziness. To be recognizably ill one must be confined to one's bed, and preferably in pain.

That a heretofore markedly vigorous young woman, with every comfort about her, should collapse in this lamentable manner was inexplicable. 'You should use your will,' said earnest friends. I had used it, hard and long, perhaps too hard and too long; at any rate it wouldn't work now.

'Force some happiness into your life,' said one sympathizer. 'Take an agreeable book to bed with you, occupy your mind with pleasant things.' She did not realize that I was unable to read, and that my mind was exclusively occupied with unpleasant things. This disorder involved a growing melancholia, and that, as those know who have tasted it, consists of every painful mental sensation, shame, fear, remorse, a blind oppressive confusion, utter weakness, a steady brain-ache that fills the conscious mind with crowding images of distress.

The misery is doubtless as physical as a toothache, but a brain, of its own nature, gropes for reasons for its misery. Feeling the sensation fear, the mind suggests every possible calamity; the sensation shame – remorse – and one remembers every mistake and misdeeds of a lifetime, and grovels to the earth in abasement.

'If you would get up and do something you would feel better,' said my mother. I rose drearily, and essayed to brush up the floor a little, with a dustpan and small whiskbroom, but soon dropped those implements exhausted, and wept again in helpless shame.

I, the ceaselessly industrious, could do no work of any kind. I was so weak that the knife and fork sank from my hands – too tired to eat. I could not read nor write nor paint nor sew nor talk nor listen to talking, nor anything. I lay on that lounge and wept all day. The tears ran down into my ears on either side. I went to bed crying, woke in the night crying, sat on the edge of the bed in the morning and cried – from sheer continuous pain. Not physical, the doctors examined me and found nothing the matter.

The only physical pain I ever knew, besides dentistry and one sore finger, was having the baby, and I would rather have had a baby every week than suffer as I suffered in my mind. A constant dragging weariness miles below zero. Absolute incapacity. Absolute misery. To the spirit it was as if one were an armless, legless, eyeless, voiceless cripple. Prominent among the tumbling suggestions of a suffering brain was the thought, 'You did it yourself! You did it yourself! You had health and strength and hope and glorious work before you – and you threw it all away. You were called to serve humanity, and you cannot serve yourself. No good as a wife, no good as a mother, no good at anything. And you did it yourself!' . . .

The baby? I nursed her for five months. I would hold her close – that lovely child! – and instead of love and happiness, feel only pain. The tears ran down on my breast . . . Nothing was more utterly bitter than this, that even motherhood brought no joy.

The doctor said I must wean her, and go away, for a change. So she was duly weaned and throve finely on Mellins' Food, drinking eagerly from the cup – no bottle needed. With mother there and the excellent maid I was free to go.

Those always kind friends, the Channings, had gone to Pasadena to live, and invited me to spend the winter with them. Feeble and hopeless I set forth, armed with tonics and sedatives, to cross the continent. From the moment the wheels began to turn, the train to move, I felt better. A visit to my brother in Utah broke the journey.

He had gone west as a boy of nineteen, working as a surveyor in Nevada, and later, finding Utah quite a heaven after Nevada, had settled in Ogden and married there. At one time he was City Engineer. His wife knew of my coming, but it was to be a surprise to my brother, and succeeded.

He came to the door in his shirt-sleeves, as was the local custom, holding a lamp in his hand. There stood the sister he had not seen in eight years, calmly smiling.

'Good evening,' said I with equanimity. This he repeated, nodding his head fatuously, 'Good evening! Good evening! Good evening!' It was a complete success.

As I still bore a grudge for the teasing which had embittered my childish years, I enjoyed this little joke, already feeling so much better that I could enjoy. There was another little joke, too. He took me to ride in that vast, shining, mile-high valley, and pointing to some sharply defined little hills which looked about five or ten miles away, asked me how far I thought they were. But I had read stories of that dry, deceiving air, and solemnly replied, 'Three hundred miles.' They were forty, but that didn't sound like much.

Society in Ogden at that time was not exacting; the leading lady, I was told, was the wife of a railroad conductor. We went to a species of ball in a hotel. The bedrooms were all occupied by sleeping babies, as described in *The Virginian*. Among the dancers there was pointed out to me a man who had killed somebody – no one seemed to hold it against him; and another who had been scalped three times – the white patches were visible among the hair. I had thought scalping a more exhaustive process. At that rate a disingenuous savage could make three triumphant exhibits from one victim. As I did not dance we had a game of whist, and I was somewhat less than pleased to see each of the gentlemen playing bring a large cuspidor and set it by his side. They needed them.

From Utah to San Francisco – on which trip I first met the San Francisco flea. Long since he has been largely overcome, but then was what the newspapers call 'a force to be reckoned with' – not California newspapers, of course.

My father was then at the head of the San Francisco Public Library. He met me on the Oakland side, and took me across to a room he had engaged for me for a day or two. Here he solemnly called on me, as would any acquaintance, and went with me across the ferry again when I started south.

'If you ever come to Providence again I hope you will come to see me,' said I politely, as we parted, to which he courteously replied, 'Thank you. I will bear your invitation in mind.'

So down the great inland plain of California, over the Mojave Desert, and to heaven.

Pasadena was then but little changed from the sheep-ranch it used to be. The Channings had bought a beautiful place by the little reservoir at the corner of Walnut Street and Orange Avenue. Already their year-old trees were shooting up unbelievably, their flowers a glory.

The Arroyo Seco was then wild and clean, its steep banks a tangle of loveliness. About opposite us a point ran out where stood a huge twin live oak, still to be seen, but not to be reached by strangers. There was no house by them then, callas bloomed by the hydrant, and sweet alyssum ran wild in the grass.

Never before had my passion for beauty been satisfied. This place did not seem like earth, it was paradise. Kind and congenial friends, pleasant society, amusement, out-door sports, the blessed mountains, the long, unbroken sweep of the valley, with snow-peaks at the far eastern end – with such surroundings I recovered so fast, to outward appearance at least, that I was taken for a vigorous young girl. Hope came back, love came back, I was eager to get home to husband and child, life was bright again.

The return trip was made a little sooner than I had intended because of a railroad war of unparalleled violence which drove prices down unbelievably. It seemed foolish not to take advantage of it, and I bought my ticket from Los Angeles to Chicago, standard, for $5.00. If I had waited for a few days more it could have been bought for $1. The eastern end was unchanged, twenty dollars from Chicago to Boston, but that cut-throat competition was all over the western roads, the sleepers had every berth filled, often two in each.

So many traveled that it was said the roads made quite as much money as usual.

Leaving California in March, in the warm rush of its rich spring, I found snow in Denver, and from then on hardly saw the sun for a fortnight. I reached home with a heavy bronchial cold, which hung on long, the dark fog rose again in my mind, the miserable weakness – within a month I was as low as before leaving . . .

This was a worse horror than before, for now I saw the stark fact – that I was well while away and sick while at home – a heartening prospect! Soon ensued the same utter prostration, the unbearable inner misery, the ceaseless tears. A new tonic had been invented, Essence of Oats, which was given me, and did some good for a time. I pulled up enough to do a little painting that fall, but soon slipped down again and stayed down. An old friend of my mother's, dear Mrs Diman, was so grieved at this condition that she gave me a hundred dollars and urged me to go away somewhere and get cured.

At that time the greatest nerve specialist in the country was Dr S. W. Mitchell of Philadelphia. Through the kindness of a friend of Mr Stetson's living in that city, I went to him and took 'the rest cure'; went with the utmost confidence, prefacing the visit with a long letter giving 'the history of the case' in a way a modern psychologist would have appreciated. Dr Mitchell only thought it proved self-conceit. He had a prejudice against the Beechers. 'I've had two women of your blood here already,' he told me scornfully. This eminent physician was well versed in two kinds of nervous prostration; that of the business man exhausted from too much work, and the society woman exhausted from too much play. The kind I had was evidently beyond him. But he did reassure me on one point – there was no dementia, he said, only hysteria.

I was put to bed and kept there. I was fed, bathed, rubbed, and responded with the vigorous body of twenty-six. As far as he could see there was nothing the matter with me, so after a month of this agreeable treatment he sent me home, with this prescription:

'Live as domestic a life as possible. Have your child with you all the time.' (Be it remarked that if I did but dress the baby it left me shaking and crying – certainly far from a healthy companionship for her, to say nothing of the effect on me.) 'Lie down an hour after each meal. Have but two hours' intellectual life a day. And never touch pen, brush or pencil as long as you live.'

I went home, followed those directions rigidly for months, and came perilously near to losing my mind. The mental agony grew so unbearable that I would sit blankly moving my head from side to side – to get out from under the pain. Not physical pain, not the least 'headache' even, just mental torment, and so heavy in its nightmare gloom that it seemed real enough to dodge.

I made a rag baby, hung it on a doorknob and played with it. I would crawl into remote closets and under beds – to hide from the grinding pressure of that profound distress . . .

Finally, in the fall of '87, in a moment of clear vision, we agreed to separate, to get a divorce. There was no quarrel, no blame for either one, never an unkind word between us, unbroken mutual affection – but it seemed plain that if I went crazy it would do my husband no good, and be a deadly injury to my child.

What this meant to the young artist, the devoted husband,

the loving father, was so bitter a grief and loss that nothing would have justified breaking the marriage save this worse loss which threatened. It was not a choice between going and staying, but between going, sane, and staying, insane. If I had been of the slightest use to him or to the child, I would have 'stuck it,' as the English say. But this progressive weakening of the mind made a horror unnecessary to face; better for that dear child to have separated parents than a lunatic mother.

We had been married four years and more. This miserable condition of mind, this darkness, feebleness and gloom, had begun in those difficult years of courtship, had grown rapidly worse after marriage, and was now threatening utter loss; whereas I had repeated proof that the moment I left home I began to recover. It seemed right to give up a mistaken marriage.

Our mistake was mutual. If I had been stronger and wiser I should never have been persuaded into it. Our suffering was mutual too, his unbroken devotion, his manifold cares and labors in tending a sick wife, his adoring pride in the best of babies, all coming to naught, ending in utter failure – we sympathized with each other but faced a bitter necessity. The separation must come as soon as possible, the divorce must wait for conditions.

If this decision could have been reached sooner it would have been much better for me, the lasting mental injury would have been less. Such recovery as I have made in forty years, and the work accomplished, seem to show that the fear of insanity was not fulfilled, but the effects of nerve bankruptcy remain to this day. So much of my many failures, of misplay and misunderstanding and 'queerness' is due to this lasting weakness, and kind friends so unfailingly refuse to allow for it, to believe it, that I am now going to some length in stating the case.

That part of the ruin was due to the conditions of childhood I do not doubt, and part to the rigid stoicism and constant effort in character-building of my youth; I was 'over-trained,' had wasted my substance in riotous – virtues. But that the immediate and continuing cause was mismarriage is proved by the instant rebound when I left home and as instant relapse on returning.

After I was finally free, in 1890, wreck though I was, there was a surprising output of work, some of my best. I think that if I could have had a period of care and rest then, I might have made full recovery. But the ensuing four years in California were the hardest of my life. The result has been a lasting loss of power, total in some directions, partial in others; the necessity for a laboriously acquired laziness foreign to both temperament and conviction, a crippled life.

But since my public activities do not show weakness, nor my writings, and since brain and nerve disorder is not visible, short of lunacy or literal 'prostration,' this lifetime of limitation and wretchedness, when I mention it, is flatly disbelieved. When I am forced to refuse invitations, to back out of work that seems easy, to own that I cannot read a heavy book, apologetically alleging this weakness of mind, friends gibber amiably, 'I wish I had your mind!' I wish they had, for a while, as a punishment for doubting my word. What confuses them is the visible work I have been able to accomplish. They see activity, achievement, they do not see blank months of idleness; nor can they see what the work would have been if the powerful mind I had to begin with had not broken at twenty-four.

A brain may lose some faculties and keep others; it may be potent for a little while and impotent the rest of the time. Moreover, the work I have done has never been 'work' in the sense of consciously applied effort. To write was always as easy to me as to talk. Even my verse, such as it is, flows as smoothly as a letter, is easier in fact. Perhaps the difficulty of answering letters will serve as an illustration of the weakness of mind so jocosely denied by would-be complimenters.

Here are a handful of letters – I dread to read them, especially if they are long – I pass them over to my husband – ask him to give me only those I must answer personally. These pile up and accumulate while I wait for a day when I feel able to attack them. A secretary does not help in the least, it is not the manual labor of writing which exhausts me, it is the effort to understand the letter, and make intelligent reply. I answer one, two, the next is harder, three – increasingly foggy, four – it's no use, I read it in vain, I *don't know what it says*. Literally, I can no longer understand what I read, and have to stop, with my mind like a piece of boiled spinach.

Reading is a simple art, common to most of us. As a child I read eagerly, greedily; as a girl I read steadily, with warm interest, in connected scientific study. No book seemed difficult. One of my Harvard boy friends told me no girl could read Clifford and understand him. Of course I got Clifford at once – and found him clear and easy enough.

After the debacle I could read nothing – instant exhaustion preventing. As years passed there was some gain in this line; if a story was short and interesting and I was feeling pretty well I could read a little while. Once when well over forty I made a test, taking a simple book on a subject I was interested in – Lucy Salmon on the servant question. I read for half an hour with ease; the next half-hour was harder, but I kept on. At the end of the third I could not understand a word of it.

That surely is a plain instance of what I mean when I say my mind is weak. It is precisely that, weak. It cannot hold attention, cannot study, cannot listen long to anything, is always backing out of things because it is tired. A library, which was once to me as a confectioner's shop to a child, became an appalling weariness just to look at.

This does not involve loss of clear perception, lack of logic, failure to think straight when able to think at all. The natural faculties are there, as my books and lectures show. But there remains this humiliating weakness, and if I try to drive, to compel effort, the resulting exhaustion is pitiful.

To step so suddenly from proud strength to contemptible feebleness, from cheerful stoicism to a whimpering avoidance of any strain or irritation for fear of the collapse ensuing, is not pleasant, at twenty-four. To spend forty years and more in the patient effort of learning how to carry such infirmity so as to accomplish something in spite of it is a wearing process, full of mortification and deprivation. To lose books out of one's life, certainly more than ninety per cent of one's normal reading capacity, is no light misfortune.

'But you write books!' Yes, I have written enough to make a set of twenty-five, including volumes of stories, plays, verse, and miscellany; besides no end of stuff not good enough to keep. But this was all the natural expression of thought, except in the stories, which called for composition and were more difficult – especially the novels, which are poor. The power of expression remained, fortunately for me, and the faculty of inner perception, of seeing the relation of facts and their consequences.

I am not skilled in mental disorders, and cannot say what it was which paralyzed previous capacities so extensively, while leaving some in working order. Perhaps another instance will be indicative. For nearly all these broken years I could not look down an index. To do this one must form the matrix of a thought or word and look down the list until it fits. I could not hold that matrix at all, could not remember what I was looking for. To this day I'd rather turn the pages than look at the index.

Worst of all was the rapid collapse of my so laboriously built-up hand-made character. Eight years of honest conscientious nobly-purposed effort lost, with the will power that made it. The bitterness of that shame will not bear reviving even now.

All progress in definite study stopped completely. Even so light a subject as a language I have tried in vain – and I meant to learn so many! Lucky for me that the foundation laid in those years of selected study was broad and sound; and lucky again that with such a background, what I have been able to gather since has fitted in reliably.

In periods of special exhaustion, and those first years which should have meant recovery were such as to involve endless exhaustion, this feeble-mindedness often meant an almost infantile irresponsibility in what I said. At one of those times, in 1891, when I was so far below zero that I should have been in a sanitarium, but instead was obliged to meet people, there bustled up a brisk young woman to greet me. She told me her name, and added, perhaps noticing my empty eyes, 'You don't remember me, do you!'

I looked at her and groped slowly about in that flaccid vacant brain of mine for some association. One memory arose, one picture of where I had seen her and with whom, but no saving grace of politeness, of common decency, of any consideration for her feelings. I spoke like a four-year-old child, because I thought of it and thought of nothing else – 'Why yes, I remember you. I don't like your mother.' It was true enough, but never in the world would I have said such a thing if I had been 'all there.'

There have been other offenses. My forgetfulness of people, so cruel a return for kindness; an absent-mindedness often working harm; many a broken engagement; unanswered letters and neglected invitations; much, very much of repeated failure of many kinds is due wholly to that continuing weakness of mind.

The word 'exhaustion' is a loose term, carrying to most minds merely the idea of being tired, of which we all know something. There is a physical weariness when it 'feels good to sit down'; the first two weeks of gymnasium work used to bring that lovely feeling.

Exhaustion of wilted nerves is quite another matter. There is no 'appetite' in the mind, no interest in anything. To see, to hear, to think, to remember, to do anything, is incredible effort, as if trying to rise and walk under a prostrate circus tent, or wade in glue. It brings a heavy darkness, every idea presenting itself as a misfortune; an irritable unease which finds no rest, and an incapacity of decision which is fairly laughable.

For all the years in which I have had to pack a suitcase and start on a trip, that packing is dreaded; and often finds me at midnight, after several hours' attempt, holding up some article and looking at it in despair, utterly unable to make up my mind whether to take it or not. In one of the worst times, in 1896, I stood on a street corner for fifteen minutes, trying in vain to decide whether or not to take the car home.

As to the work accomplished in spite of all this. The lecturing is a perfectly natural expression of as natural clear thinking. It never has been felt as an effort, save when the audience was dull or combative. Yet at that I can only do so much of it; in regular Chautauqua work, for instance, I'm a failure.

The writing similarly is easy and swift expression, running at the rate of about a thousand words an hour for three hours – then it stops, no use trying to squeeze out any more. Any attempt at forced work stops everything for days. At that ordinary output the work I have accomplished would have required far less time, had I kept the natural power of my mind. All the writing, in easy five-day weeks, between four and five years; all the lectures, a thousand or more, with necessary traveling, another five years. All other work, as organizing, helping in club-work, every possible activity I can remember, including dressmaking and cooking and gardening, might be stretched to fill another five. There are fifteen years accounted for, out of, to date, forty-two.

That leaves twenty-seven years, a little lifetime in itself, taken out, between twenty-four and sixty-six, which I have lost. Twenty-seven adult years, in which, with my original strength of mind, the output of work could have been almost trebled. Moreover, this lifetime lost has not been spent in resting. It was always a time of extreme distress, shame, discouragement, misery.

Is a loss like this, suffering like this, to be met with light laughter and compliments? To be waved aside as if I were imagining it? It is true that the persistence of a well-trained physique is confusing to the average observer. A sympathetic lady once remarked, 'Yes, it is a sad thing to see a strong mind in a weak body.' Whereat I promptly picked her up and carried her around the room. 'Please understand,' said I, 'that what ails me is a weak mind in a strong body.' But she didn't understand, they never do. Only those near enough to watch the long, blank months of idleness, the endless hours of driveling solitaire, the black empty days and staring nights, know.

An orthodox visible disease that sends one to bed, as scarlet fever or mumps, is met by prompt sympathy. A broken arm, a sprained ankle, any physical mutilation, is a recognized misfortune. But the humiliating loss of a large part of one's brain power, of more than half one's working life, accompanied with deep misery and anguish of mind – this when complained of is met with amiable laughter and flat disbelief.

What is the psychology of it? Do these friends think it is more polite to doubt my word than to admit any discredit to my brain? Do they think I have been under some delusion as to all those years of weakness and suffering, or that I am pretending something in order to elicit undeserved commiseration? Or do they not think at all?

I try to describe this long limitation, hoping that with such power as is now mine, and such use of language as is within that power, this will convince any one who cares about it that this 'Living' of mine had been done under a heavy handicap . . .

That summer of 1887 was so dreadful, as I have said, that it drove me to the final decision that our marriage must end. Once the decision was made I breathed a little easier, there was a remote glimmer of hope. But we must wait till arrangements could be made, proper provision for the child, and so on.

All that winter Grace Channing kept my spirits up with her letters, with talk and plans for work, and in the summer of '88 she came east, and we spent some months together in Bristol, Rhode Island. There we wrote a play, in collaboration, and there gathered background for later work; and I revived with such companionship and interest. We came back to the city September 1st. She was to return to Pasadena on October 8th, and I planned to go with her.

For possible assets, there was my quarter interest in the old place in Hartford, still undivided, and half of which must be returned to my brother, who had earlier borrowed on his quarter for family use. With this for my one resource and a month to work in I promptly engaged carpenters to make the crates and boxes for such furniture as I meant to take.

'How can you engage them when you have no money?' asked Walter.

'I shall get the money by selling my property.'

'How do you know you can?'

'I shall have to, to pay the carpenters.'

And I did. Good Rowland Hazard II bought it for two thousand dollars, and I'm sure he got fully that when the place was sold, later. There were debts to pay, clothes to be made, the men to pay – all the work of breaking up housekeeping and packing for the journey.

Our pretty little home was dismantled. Mother was to go back to my brother in Utah. Mr Stetson went to live in his studio. There was an elderly dressmaker well known to us, who had a desire to see California. She undertook to go with me, help with little Katharine and otherwise, and pay her own way back, if I furnished her fare going.

So I set forth on October 8th, with Katharine, Grace, this inadequate dressmaker, a large lunch-basket, my tickets, and all my remaining money in my pocket – ten dollars.

'What will you do when you get there?' asked anxious friends.

'I shall earn my own living.'

'How do you know you can?'

'I shall have to when I get there.'

From CHAPTER 9
PASADENA

With Pasadena begins my professional 'living.' Before that there was no assurance of serious work. To California, in its natural features, I owe much. Its calm sublimity of contour, richness of color, profusion of flowers, fruit and foliage, and the steady peace of its climate were meat and drink to me.

Dr Channing, always kind, had engaged for my coming a small cottage near his place, on the corner of Orange Grove Avenue and Arroyo Drive, right opposite 'Carmelita,' then the home of Dr and Mrs Carr, now a park. Today that corner lot is worth a fortune. In 1888 I rented that little wood-and-paper four-room house for $10.00 a month.

It stood in a neglected grove of orange trees rich with fragrant blossoms, roses ran over the roof, tall oleanders stood pink against the sky. There was a lemon verbena in the border by the front path; one day I broke off a new shoot to give a visitor from the east – it was six feet long. When the Channings gave roses to tourist friends, they brought them in a trunk tray.

Everywhere there was beauty, and the nerve-rest of steady windless weather. Living was cheap in all local supplies. A man came to the door one day, selling white grapes from a wagon-load. These seemed to me a luxury, but I said I'd take ten cents' worth if he'd give me that. He did, about a peck. The 'vegetable Chinaman' came often, with his dainty bundles of green things tied with long grass. For ten cents I could buy a rambling collop they called a mutton chop, big enough to make two meals for an invalid woman and a small child.

Long, long hours in a hammock under the roses. Occasional times when I could write. I felt like a drowned thing, drifting along under water and sometimes bobbing to the surface.

At first my tiny house was encumbered and my nerves wrung by the incubus I brought from Providence as 'mother's helper.' She had been a fairly capable dressmaker, in a dull, slow way, taking a week to make a dress. That was not so extreme a time as it looks now, one day for cutting out – the skirt with its lining and facing; the overskirt, to be elaborately draped; the 'five-seamed-basque' with its careful fitting, and all the binding and boning, buttons and buttonholes which went to make a dress in those days. But now she proved in all ways useless.

With the child – and a more amenable darling never was, with intelligent treatment – she failed utterly. She could not cook, she would not sweep nor dust nor wash dishes – said it coarsened her hands! Her density was such that any direction had to be given with a slow explicitness suitable to the under-witted. When unpacking crates and arranging furniture I asked this unpromising Irish woman, picking my words with care, 'Have you seen a long wooden shelf with iron brackets?' She answered, 'Do you mean a small marble slab?' This she could not have seen, as I did not own such a thing.

Summing up the wide variety of things she would not do, I

finally told her I would ask but one service – that she mend and put away the clean clothes. And that moron would roll up and put in the drawer unmended hose! She stayed on, in the face of clearest suggestions of departure, until one day when these became direct and urgent requests with directions about trains, she burst into tears and quaveringly protested: 'I do believe you are trying to get rid of me!' I was.

Then I had a boarder for a while, an anachronism. She was the daughter of a country clergyman of the old school, brought up on Addison and Dr Johnson. Her ideal of social ecstasy was Conversation with the largest of C's . . . She had it too, at the Channings.

By Christmas Mr Stetson joined me, hoping that the change might have so bettered my condition that we might even yet reconsider; but it was no use, a dragging year followed, and in January, 1890, he finally left me, called suddenly to the bedside of his dying mother. This was the definite open separation, following the decision of the fall of 1887.

As the mutual agreement of two rational adults who have found by experience that they cannot live together is not 'ground for divorce' as it should be, but is termed 'collusion' and prevents it; as my wrecked health could not be traced to any fault of a devoted husband; and as neither of us would lie; it was necessary to conform to some legal requirement as a 'cause.' Desertion and non-support was agreed upon, and after a year of this I brought suit.

The lawyer I went to was a courteous gentleman, and made his inquiries with every consideration for my feelings. I found that 'failure to provide' was nugated by the California law of community property; whatever either party earned belonged to both, so if I lived on my own earnings half the sum was still contributed by the absent one. As to desertion – 'Does your husband write to you?' 'Yes.' 'About how often?' 'Two or three times a week.' And the case was off.

The more immediate problem was how to provide, even in that land of low prices, for self and child. I had to start with a present of a hundred dollars, highly appreciated. For the rest I depended on teaching and writing, with the preliminary necessity of getting strong enough to do any steady work.

The utter failure and loss of my marriage was bitter enough, but compensated by the blessed child; the loss of health was worse, the weakness, the dark, feeble mind. But my religion remained, and my social philosophy, that perception of the organic unity of the group which so dwarfs all individual pain. When able to think clearly I faced the situation thus:

'Thirty years old. Made a wrong marriage – lots of people do. Am heavily damaged, but not dead. May live a long time. It is intellectually conceivable that I may recover strength enough to do some part of my work. I will assume this to be true, and act on it.' And I did.

One of the Grand Old Women of California, Mrs Caroline B. Severance, was so impressed by my sad case, that she wrote a pathetic letter about my lack of any special capacity to earn my bread, to my great-aunt, Isabella Beecher Hooker, who forwarded it to Uncle Edward Everett Hale, who referred it to Mr Stetson, who sent it to me.

This letter I never mentioned to the dear old lady, who was afterward deeply impressed by my achievements and remained a warm friend as long as she lived, which was to be well over ninety. I went with her once, when she was ninety-three, to call on Mrs Rebecca Spring, who was ninety-nine – a memorable experience.

Shriveled and shrunken was the almost centenarian, her eyes mere buttonholes. I felt as helpless before her as a man with a baby. 'What do you do with your time?' I ventured. In a high, thin, squeaky voice she replied, 'I read novels. When I was young they would not let me read them, and now I read them all the time.'

In that first year of freedom I wrote some thirty three short articles, and twenty-three poems, besides ten more child-verses. Almost all the poems were given to various progressive papers, the one or two sold brought but two or three dollars. The same with the articles, though I did sell more of them, at prices like ten dollars or six dollars and seventy-five cents.

Except for two or three bits published before marriage, I had written in six years only a half-dozen or so, as 'Nature's Answer,' and 'The Ship' while at home, and two good ones while away, 'A Nevada Desert,' and 'The Rock and the Sea.' That one was begun on Bass Rock, Narragansett Pier, and finished on the floor after I was at home again. Almost all of my descriptive poetry is about California. To this day, when in that lovely country, the verses come of themselves. The little 'Nevada Desert' is good of its kind, though T. B. Aldrich sent it back from the *Atlantic*, with the remark that it needed the spot of color without which no picture was perfect. He had not seen Nevada.

With Grace I wrote plays. Our collaboration was fluently happy. One day, entering perfectly into the characters, we simply talked the dialogue, writing it down as fast as spoken. Not only did we write plays, we acted in them, most successfully. There was an admirable group of amateur actors in Pasadena. Somewhat to my surprise I was usually cast in comic parts – being always willing to make a fool of myself.

One of the oddest jobs ever offered me was during Pasadena days. A new Opera House, fruit of a 'boom' time, awaited final decoration, the selection of seat-coverings, curtains, etc. Grace and I went to see it, I said it was a pity Mr Stetson was not there to finish the decoration, and lo! they asked me to do it. Never in my life had I done anything of the sort, but on that established precept of mine – 'Always accept an opportunity unless it's wrong' – I undertook this. It was fun too, selecting materials, winding ropes and covering large wooden balls with plush like the hangings, and ornamenting the curtains to the box-entrances with impressive Turkish characters copied from a scarf I had – perhaps some Oriental visitor may have been astonished by what he read.

In this theater we gave plays for the benefit of local needs, and in one of them I was a too-affectionate old maid, dressed in a costume of elaborate absurdity. To this day I remember the ripple of laughter which greeted my entrance, as I tipped up the huge hoopskirt to get through, and how that laughter continued all the time I was on. It is a fascinating art, acting. Once I was Lady Teazle and had to wear a corset – the only time in my life; and I almost fainted.

One of our plays was afterward almost accepted by Mr Frohman; he meant to bring out in it young Mrs Blaine, and had it all cast, with penciled names of Georgia Cayvan, Herbert Kelsey and other notables of the period. But, not knowing this we asked for it, and he sent it back.

The first real success, in that first year, was my poem 'Similar Cases,' concerning which I received this unforgettable letter from William Dean Howells:

BOSTON, June 9th., 1890.

DEAR MADAM,

I have been wishing ever since I first read it – and I've read it many times with unfailing joy – to thank you for your poem in the April *Nationalist*. We have nothing since the Biglow Papers half so good for a good cause as 'Similar Cases.'

And just now I've read in *The Woman's Journal* your 'Women of Today.' It is as good almost as the other, and dreadfully true.

Yours sincerely,
WM. DEAN HOWELLS.

That was a joy indeed. I rushed over to show Grace and the others. There was no man in the country whose good opinion I would rather have had. I felt like a real 'author' at last.

There were classes of some kind among friendly ladies, there were pupils of sorts; I remember one group of small children to whom I taught drawing. Children draw by nature, as do savages, but these had had their powers paralyzed in school. They declared they could not draw, 'Can't you draw *anything*?' 'No, Ma'am.' 'Can't you draw a horse?' 'No, Ma'am.'

Then I proceeded to develop a system which works well. 'Oh, come on, let's draw something. Can you draw a cow?' 'No, Ma'am,' 'Do you know the difference between a horse and a cow?' They emphatically did and could mention some of the distinctions.

'Now we'll draw the horse, anyway, we'll make his body first, a horse's body is three-cornered isn't it?' Loud denial. 'Well, it's square then – no? Is it kind of long like a barrel?' To this they agreed, and we all made a longish roundish body on our various pieces of brown paper. I used wrapping paper and very soft pencils, and we threw away our sketches – 'You're not making pictures to take home,' I told them, 'you are just drawing, like dancing or singing.'

Then the horse's head: 'It's round like an apple, isn't it?' It wasn't, not at all, nor was it, as I further suggested, stuck tight to his body; nor did he have a neck like a swan, not in the least. Those youngsters knew perfectly well what a horse looked like, that his ears stood up and his tail hung down, and presently they all had a shaky sort of a sketch which any one could instantly tell was a horse.

Then came the triumphant sense of power, of achievement, they could draw! Pursuing this triumph, I continually set them amusing copies, as of hopping hobgoblins, or something of like appeal to the child mind, with such glaring peculiarities of outline and proportion as it was impossible to miss; and they drew them, recognizably. With enough practice of such easy and entertaining sort, their powers of perception and execution quickly developed and the road was open to better work.

In the scrappy little two-by-four diary I tried to keep that first year, I find but very occasional notes, as 'Class, rained, no one came but Mrs Mitchel.' 'Did two cards for Mr Taylor, charged $3.00.' 'Rose Rowley, paid for two lessons, this and next.' 'Mrs Crank calls about giving her son lessons.' 'Lessons to Mary Wood, Paint on Mrs K's cards. Get extremely tired over them.'

'Tired' always means that ghastly below-zero weariness, and it was a frequent item, as – 'Jan. 26. Tired.' 'Mon. 27. Very tired.' 'Tues. 28. Tired.' 'Wed. 29. Very tired.' 'Thurs. 30. Awfully tired.' 'Fri. 31. Still tired, weak and sad.' And so on. Again Feb. 22nd, 'Am pretty miserable just along here.' '23. Am really miserable.' Then gradually, '25. Sad enough.' '27.

Feel better. Arrange ms. to send off.' 'March 5. Work with Grace on new play.' '8th. A fine busy day. Am feeling better. Write by myself in the evening.' A comment on lack of strength – 'Sweep parlor, proud.'

There are plenty of blanks in this diary, and mistakes, two weeks with nothing down but two days' lessons, eight weeks absolutely blank, more with only one lesson set down. The blanks were the drowned time, not even sense to make those scanty notes.

Yet there was much of pleasantness all along – the dear Channings always good to me – Mrs Channing had me give her lessons in painting and did well at it; other kind friends, games of whist, and entertainments of various sorts. The Channings had a masquerade, and I made for Harold, Grace's brother, a zany's costume, for which I had no pattern. It was the kind having a hood fitting around face and head, neck and shoulders, and with two horns. All this in alternate red and green, tunic, hose and pointed long-toed shoes. I remember my pride in this difficult piece of construction, but do not at all remember what I wore.

Fortunately for my poor efforts it cost but little to live, I think twenty-five dollars a month would have covered it all for little Katharine and myself. Our small housework I managed except washing, and an occasional day's cleaning. The little house stood on an exposed corner, Mexicans lived in tiny shacks down in the Arroyo, more than once things were stolen from me if left outside, a rug from the porch, a step-ladder that stood against the house.

But I refused to worry. 'There is little to steal and I am quite willing to be killed,' was my attitude. When tramps came for food I devised a special reception, giving them, not charity but hospitality. 'Could you give me something to eat, Ma'am?' 'Certainly, I can, come in,' and I set a place at the table with us. When, as was often the case, the man was a decent person, honestly looking for work, this was welcome and appreciated; if he was a hobo he didn't like it as well. But no one ever presumed on it. Only once did a man come back for more, and he apologetically explained, 'You know I chopped wood for you before.'

On one of those long useless afternoons during the first months in that cottage there came an opportunity for the execution of a long-cherished scheme of revenge, an amusing instance of impersonal resentment and enduring vindictiveness. As a child I had read stories of the shameless persistent intrusion of book-agents, how they refused to take no for an answer, but continued to press their wares regardless of protest, wasting their victim's time. It had always seemed to me that something might be done in retaliation, now after many years, here was the opportunity.

Two pests were continuous in California, flies and agents – there was no way of freezing them out. The agents usually came in vehicles, this one did. He dismounted, tied his horse, and approached. It was about two o'clock, the afternoon stretched before me, empty and useless, mine enemy was delivered into my hand.

First I told him definitely that I should not buy his book. These people are trained to pay no attention to a 'prospect's' refusal, which disregard is an insult to begin with; however, I cleared my skirts before starting. Down he sat and began on his task.

I let him talk and he talked a long time, the invalid in the hammock making a good listener. More than once I told him I should not buy, which did not daunt him in the least. If, after some time, he paused for a bit, seemed a trifle discouraged, then a question would set him going again. If, upon long effort to no purpose, he really seemed to think of departure, I asked to look at his volume, or made some further inquiry. When he finally seemed to weary of his monologue and gathered up his things to go, then I began to talk – and I was a good entertainer in those days.

In this particular case the 'prospect' could afford to waste an afternoon, it was wasted anyway. But the agent's time was probably of some value to him, and he spent three hours of it, entirely in vain. 'I told you I should not buy the book,' I gently reminded him, on his departure about five o'clock.

There is another tale of that time more amusing, and, in intention at least, more creditable. The place was owned by two poor old people – it was their only remaining bit of property. They sold the orange crop on the trees to another shabby old party, who came one morning with horse and wagon, to gather it. He worked all day, but could not quite finish, so he came to me and asked, 'Could I put my horse in your barn, Ma'am, and sleep on the porch – I hate to go nine miles home and back just for that little jag?'

This was something of a poser. I was alone there with my small daughter, and already quite open to gossip and criticism. But principles were strong. 'This is a Christian duty,' I decided. 'It is in no way wrong.' So I told him the barn was not mine but I had no doubt my neighbor would allow him to stable his horse there, and he might sleep on my porch or in the little lean-to kitchen, as he preferred.

That kitchen by the way was a sort of joke, built from the big boxes and crates my furniture came in, with windows supplied by some large pieces of glass found on the place. It cost me only some nails and carpenter work, about thirteen dollars as I remember.

The old fellow washed his hands at the hydrant and came in to supper with us. Then I sought to get rid of him, as Grace was coming as usual to work with me on a play. No proposed place of entertainment attracted him however, not even the Y. M. C. A. So he sat around while I read to Katharine, and then I helped him move my hard little lounge out into the kitchen.

'If you should git skeered in the night don't be afraid to call on me,' he gallantly urged, and I said nothing of the risk I was taking. Grace came, we worked as usual, and the night passed without event. In the morning my undesired guest again made his toilet at the hydrant, and came to breakfast. While eating a thought struck him, a misgiving, possibly.

'Where is your husband, Ma'am?' he asked.

'In Providence, Rhode Island,' I told him.

He thumped down both fists on the table, knife and fork upheld. 'If I'd 'a known that,' quoth he with decision, 'nothin' would have induced me to stay here!'

So that's what I got by facing scandal to do a kindness, and it paid richly in amusement.

Another incident of that year was that I was driven to consult a physician, an excellent woman, Dr Follansbee of Los Angeles, and found that there were now certain internal difficulties of a purely physical nature added to my mental ones with ensuing complications and need for prolonged treatment.

Besides 'Similar Cases' the most outstanding piece of work of 1890 was 'The Yellow Wallpaper.' It is a description of a case of nervous breakdown beginning something as mine did, and

treated as Dr S. Weir Mitchell treated me with what I considered the inevitable result, progressive insanity.

This I sent to Mr Howells, and he tried to have the *Atlantic
Monthly* print it, but Mr Scudder, then the editor, sent it back
with this brief card:

> DEAR MADAM
>
> Mr Howells has handed me this story.
>
> I could not forgive myself if I made others as miserable
> as I have made myself!
>
> Sincerely yours,
H.E. SCUDDER.

This was funny. The story was meant to be dreadful, and succeeded. I suppose he would have sent back one of Poe's on the
same ground. Later I put it in the hands of an agent who had
written me, one Henry Austin, and he placed it with the *New
England Magazine*. Time passed, much time, and at length I
wrote to the editor of that periodical to this effect:

> DEAR SIR,
>
> A story of mine, 'The Yellow Wallpaper,' was printed
> in your issue of May, 1891. Since you do not pay on
> receipt of ms. nor on publication, nor within six months
> of publication, may I ask if you pay at all, and if so at
> what rates?

They replied with some heat that they had paid the agent,
Mr Austin. He, being taxed with it, denied having got the
money. It was only forty dollars anyway! As a matter of fact I
never got a cent for it till later publishers brought it out in book

form, and very little then. But it made a tremendous impression. A protest was sent to the Boston *Transcript*, headed 'Perilous Stuff'—

To the Editor of the Transcript:

In a well-known magazine has recently appeared a story entitled 'The Yellow Wallpaper.' It is a sad story of a young wife passing the gradations from slight mental derangement to raving lunacy. It is graphically told, in a somewhat sensational style, which makes it difficult to lay aside, after the first glance, til it is finished, holding the reader in morbid fascination to the end. It certainly seems open to serious question if such literature should be permitted in print.

The story can hardly, it would seem, give pleasure to any reader, and to many whose lives have been touched through the dearest ties by this dread disease, it must bring the keenest pain. To others, whose lives have become a struggle against an heredity of mental derangement, such literature contains deadly peril. Should such stories be allowed to pass without severest censure?

M.D.

Another doctor, one Brummel Jones, of Kansas City, Missouri, wrote me in 1892 concerning this story, saying: 'When I read "The Yellow Wallpaper" I was very much pleased with it; when I read it again I was delighted with it, and now that I have read it again I am overwhelmed with the delicacy of your touch and the correctness of portrayal. From a doctor's standpoint, and I am a doctor, you have made a success. So far as I know, and I am fairly well up in literature, there has been no detailed account of incipient insanity.' Then he tells of an opium addict who refused to be treated on the ground that physicians had no real knowledge of the disease, but who returned to Dr Jones, bringing a paper of his on the opium habit, shook it in his face and said, 'Doctor, you've been there!' To which my correspondent added, 'Have you ever been – er—; but of course you haven't.' I replied that I had been as far as one could go and get back.

One of the *New England Magazine*'s editors wrote to me asking if the story was founded on fact, and I gave him all I decently could of my case as a foundation for the tale. Later he explained that he had a friend who was in similar trouble, even to hallucinations about her wallpaper, and whose family were treating her as in the tale, that he had not dared show them my story till he knew that it was true, in part at least, and that when he did they were so frightened by it, so impressed by the clear implication of what ought to have been done, that they changed her wallpaper and the treatment of the case – and she recovered! This was triumph indeed.

But the real purpose of the story was to reach Dr S. Weir Mitchell, and convince him of the error of his ways. I sent him a copy as soon as it came out, but got no response. However, many years later, I met some one who knew close friends of Dr Mitchell's who said he had told them that he had changed his treatment of nervous prostration since reading 'The Yellow Wallpaper.' If that is a fact, I have not lived in vain.

A few years ago Mr Howells asked leave to include this story in a collection he was arranging – *Masterpieces of American Fiction*. I was more than willing, but assured him that it was no more 'literature' than my other stuff, being definitely written 'with a purpose.' In my judgment it is a pretty poor thing to write, to talk, without a purpose.

All these literary efforts providing but little, it was well indeed that another avenue of work opened to me at this time.

California is a state peculiarly addicted to swift enthusiasms. It is a seed-bed of all manner of cults and theories, taken up, and dropped, with equal speed. In 1890 the countryside was deeply stirred by Bellamy's *Looking Backward*. Everywhere was new interest in economics, in the labor question. The *Nationalist*, in which 'Similar Cases' appeared, was the chief organ of the Bellamy doctrines, and Nationalist clubs sprang up over the land; California, always fertile, blossomed with them.

One day, while riding in the bus, a lady spoke to me, a stranger, and asked me to speak for the Nationalist Club of Pasadena. This was an entirely new proposition. I had never given a public address nor expected to. But here was an opportunity, not wrong, and I accepted it. All I knew of the art of oratory was something I had read in a newspaper when a child – that a public speaker should address the farthest person in the room, then every one could hear. That had struck me as good sense, and I had laid it up, to prove most useful now.

I wrote the lecture, on the main topic of all my work – Human Nature – I have it yet. The meeting was held in a vacant store, the small audience sitting on benches, chairs, whatever they could find, one big fellow on a barrel over against the wall. He was the farthest one, and when he came up, among others to shake hands and make complimentary remarks, I asked him if he could hear me. 'You bet I could hear you,' he cheerfully replied, 'If I couldn't I'd 'a come nearer.'

The lecture was warmly received, others followed, soon I was speaking on alternate Sundays in Los Angeles and Pasadena,

and in neighboring towns occasionally. It was pleasant work –
I had plenty to say and the Beecher faculty for saying it. My
hearers were for the most part rather ignorant, at any rate
uncritical, knowing which, I was saved from undue pride in
their approval.

Their method of financing these lectures was simple. A collection was taken, out of which they paid for the hall and
whatever expenses there were, and they gave me the rest.
'$3.50' I find in that scrappy little diary of mine, and again,
'Collection $3.00.' Once a big, black-bearded working man,
shaking hands after the lecture, cordially urged, 'You come and
talk to us – we'll give you a nickel every time!'

One poor woman was extremely anxious that I should come
to dinner with her, after the lecture in Los Angeles, and I went.
Her husband was a day laborer, her daughter in service, and she
herself worked out by the day. They lived in a henhouse, literally, one of those longish, slant-roofed affairs, divided into three
compartments, bedroom, living-room, kitchen. I rested on a
sagging couch in the middle room and thought, 'Why this isn't
so bad – it's small and shabby, but here are the necessities—'
and then I thought, 'Suppose I could never get out of this henhouse!' and it looked less possible.

CHAPTER 11
MOTHERHOOD

Something of my mother's passion for children I had inherited, but not especially for babies, as with her. My feeling was a deep sympathy for children of all ages, a reverence for them as the world's best hope; a tenderness for these ever-coming strangers, misunderstood, misjudged, mistreated, even when warmly 'loved.' In my own childhood and youth I had well learned that 'love' by no means ensures understanding or appreciation.

In that eager, youthful effort at self-improvement, I had always as one purpose the handing down of a better character, a better constitution, than I had inherited. Quite early I had formulated the dictum: 'The first duty of a mother is to be a mother worth having.' The second is to select a father worth having. Upon that follows all that can be given in the way of environment and education.

Always I loved children and children loved me. In the days of my teaching the pupils were happy, enjoying the verses, stories and pictures with which the lessons were accompanied. Even the atrocious little boy upon whom I once wasted ten weeks of governessing, afterward sent me this sad little note, brought by a servant:

Miss Pirkins
   i am very sick and would like to have you make me sum rimes and pictures on squere pieces of paper the way we did when we were down to maine if you please
   Yours Truly

                                          ————

there is a ancer
   when can I have them

When I looked forward hopefully to marriage I planned to have six children, three of each kind. The coming of my baby was unmeasured joy and hope, with high purposes of wisest, tenderest care.

But the black helplessness into which I fell, with its deadness of heart, its aching emptiness of mind, grievously limited all my usefulness to her. In place of a warm efficient love I could feel nothing but that dull, constant pain. A mother weeping away her days on a lounge is not much good. Yet that lovely child would come 'hitching' – she never crept, but sat up and wiggled along – across the room to bring me a handkerchief because she saw my tears.

Nevertheless, there were some things I could do, and some avoid. From Spencer I learned wisdom and applied it. There is much, very much, that can be done in the first few years of a child's life. This one had, not surprisingly, inherited a pronounced disinclination to 'mind.' A command brought instant opposition. With stern authority and what they used to call 'discipline,' this would have meant a contest of wills, punishments, bitter unhappiness.

On the other hand she was more than willing to oblige, to do anything and everything to be helpful – if not compelled. Children are of all people most open to suggestion. 'Let's' is the magic word with them, from playmate or grown person – if the grown person is honest! Yet this easy and powerful handle by which to move them to the conduct we desire, is ignored by most of us, and we persist in using our superiority to enforce the behavior demanded, with conflict and resentment. Using the method of suggestion, there was never any difficulty in these first years of education.

Another piece of forethought I was able to use, of such marked value to the educator that it is a marvel so few seem to think of it. I call it 'laying pipe.' It is necessary for a child to have confidence in the parent or teacher, to respect his judgment, to rely on his advice. Every time the parent says, 'You'll fall!' or 'You'll catch cold!' and the child does not, his confidence is shaken. I took continuous pains not only to avoid this mistake, as by saying, 'You may fall,' but to take advantage of occasions when I could foretell consequences with certainty, do so, and point out the results.

From her earliest years, I always made a steady habit of mentioning a reason for an action with the act, as 'Please shut the door, I feel the cold air.' There is a reason for every act, and while we cannot always give a child *the* reason, we can give a reason, accustoming the young mind automatically to associate cause and effect. The immeasurable advantage of this training becomes clearer with every year of growth. It soon becomes enough to mention the cause, and the result is produced, as 'I feel the cold air from that door' – and the child shuts it.

When we demand, after some piece of foolishness, 'Why did

you do that?' a child not accustomed to associate reasons with actions has nothing to say. He sees no reason for most of the things we do, or expect him to do, and has none to produce for his own conduct.

Children are naturally reasonable, and, most of them, well meaning. This one of mine was both, and never gave trouble or caused anxiety by her behavior. An incident when she was between three and four will illustrate this: she had gone down the lane to play with the washerwoman's children, a thing not 'forbidden' but advised against. I went after her and led the little sunbonneted figure home.

'Why, Katharine!' I said gravely, 'this is the first time I have known you to do a thing I asked you no to.' Quoth a calm little voice under the sunbonnet, 'All children have to be naughty sometimes.' See me condemned out of my own mouth – the *first time* – and I making a fuss about it!

Another instance of the pipe-laying process consists in looking ahead along the years and their inevitable developments, or to coming events, and telling the child beforehand such things as will comfortably prepare the mind. When that transcontinental journey lay before us I talked about it, repeatedly, speaking of the interesting features and of the unavoidable disadvantages.

'It's rather hard on children, being in the cars so many days,' I explained, 'because they have to keep still. Most of the people are grown up, some are old and some are sick, and they can't bear noisy children Maybe there will be some children you can play quietly with, maybe not. Anyway, I'll carry some things to amuse you.' Then I would dilate on the interesting features of the trip, just casually talking about it as I would to any friend. So when we went there was no shock or disappointment, she was quite prepared to behave as well as anybody, and did – at three and a half.

It is also easy to anticipate some of the questions children are sure to ask, by telling them beforehand many things which will make later answers understandable. All the labored profundity people spend on teaching children what we used solemnly to call 'the mystery of life,' might be resolved to a pleasant, matter-of-fact piece of information, in due proportion to the rest of life, if various simple data as to this chapter of nature's open book had been made familiar beforehand.

Absolute honesty was another thing I could give her, sick or well. She never had cause to doubt my word. If I made a mistake I was quick to acknowledge it, to apologize if necessary, a custom she easily imitated. Children are preternaturally quick to recognize pretense in any form. We are too apt to say: 'Mama is angry,' or 'Mama is hurt,' instead of *being* it. Once when we were playing on the floor together, the child, not meaning any harm, spit at me.

I got up at once, swiftly, and left her. Nothing was said, or done to her, but her playmate was gone, and there was displeasure in the air. Of course she demanded a reason – what was the matter? I replied coldly, 'You have insulted me.' My prompt and noticeable reaction showed what an insult was as no description could have done. She met, not punishment, but consequence, and did not do it again because she did not like the consequence.

Childhood is a transient condition; what we are trying to 'raise' is a competent adult. Just 'minding' under compulsion, does not train the mind to govern conduct by principle or by consequence in later life. As for the more recent method of not training them at all – the visible results are not altogether pleasurable, even to the victims.

Another instance, from that field of conduct in which children are so incessantly 'trained' – table manners. Katharine and I were living in the Pasadena cottage. She was four. As a baby in a high chair, her dainty accuracy in eating had been notable. Now she entered on a phase of really offensive messing. I used the usual methods of reasonable appeal, but the misbehavior seemed a stronger impulse than her reason could master. So I set to work to think out the true causation of the desired conduct, and how to enlist her own desire in acquiring it:

'What is the real reason I am so anxious she should have good table manners?' It was not far to seek, without them she would be cut off from good society when she was grown. This reason was not one which could be effectually presented now. A mental image of what you are told will happen in later years, the predicted loss of something you do not in the least understand or value, has small weight. Somehow I must make good table manners the price of desirable society now.

The next time she joyfully indulged in unpleasantness I said: 'Excuse me,' rose up quietly, with no emotional stress whatever, took my plate and utensils and retired into the kitchen, leaving a conspicuous vacancy. There was no rebuke, no anger, simply a goneness. 'Mama!' 'Yes, Dear?' 'Where are you?' 'In the kitchen.' 'Why?' 'Well, Dear, I hate to speak of it again, perhaps I've spoken too often already, but honestly, when you do things like that it makes me a little sick, and if you don't mind I prefer to eat here.' But she did mind, very much, and to please herself, to secure something she desired, she mended her manners.

These methods were by no means approved by my friends and neighbors. Discipline and obedience were still the ideal then. My ideas looked to them not only wrong in principle but impracticable. They brought up instances of danger, need for prompt action – 'What do you do when you have to catch a train?' they demanded. 'Tell her we have to catch the train,' I answered, 'with several previous experiences, carefully arranged, wherein she learned how bitterly disappointing it is to be too late.'

There arose an occasion for restraint of impulse on her part which called for real strength of character, and found it. Next door lived a friend with small children, nurses, rabbits, a donkey, toys of all kinds, a neighboring heaven for my small lonely one, who played continually and most happily there. Then she had a cough, not a bad one, but Mrs C. feared it was whooping-cough, which was in town, and of which she had had bitter experience; so she asked me to keep my little girl at home until the cough was gone.

This was a very great loss to her, loss of her principal pleasure, a daily habitual joy. She was five years old. There was no fence or hedge between the places, merely a furrow in the plowed ground of the orange grove. I stated the facts, told her of the undoubted danger of the disease, how one of her little playmates had already suffered from it, how contagious it was, and how she surely did not want to carry danger of injury, perhaps death, to her friends; that Mrs C. had begged her to stay away until well over her cough.

She stayed. I can see now that small, disconsolate figure, in its blue apron and little sunbonnet, standing with little bare toes touching the dividing line, looking at Paradise and never going in. It was not 'obedience,' it was understanding and self-control.

Another touching instance; one night she had the earache. I had done all I could for her, but the dull ache went on, and the poor baby naturally cried, a low monotonous dreary cry. We

340

lay in the big bed, by the rose-shaded window, and my wretched nerves broke. One of the results of my ruin, from which I have never recovered, is hyperesthesia of the auditory nerve, noises hurt, even music must be soft and low, a sudden loud sound is worse than a blow, a room full of chattering people is a buzzing torment – so this low, continuous wailing became unbearable anguish. Knowing well the exhaustion which would follow, preventing the work on which we must live, I made the appeal to reason:

'Katharine dear – mother knows you are sick, in pain, and you have a right to cry. I'm not blaming you at all, precious, but you know mother is sick too (poor child, she knew it but too well), and I can't stand some kinds of noises. I've been trying to stand it, but it is beyond me, and if it goes on I'll have to go out and walk about outside. But I think I could stand it a while longer if you could change the sound – cry on a different key."

And that blessed baby did.

The good mamas of Pasadena were extremely critical of my methods. One of them said that she would admit that Katharine was the best child she ever saw, but it was no credit to her mother – she would have ruined any other child by her system! They thought it scandalous that I should so frankly teach her the simple facts of sex, but when one of the piously brought up little boys she played with made proposals which would have been dangerous had they been sixteen instead of six, I felt well repaid by her easy confidence, she did not accede and came at once to tell me about it. I showed no sinister alarm, merely explained again how senseless any such performance was for children, and I was glad she knew better than he did. Self-esteem is an excellent weapon.

I dressed her in little gingham aprons, with bloomers of the same, carefully made not to show, children being naturally conservative. But she asked, 'Why can't I wear boy's clothes *clear*?' Also, she played barefooted in the blessed California sunshine – she grew up with a foot which was the delight of sculptors.

For all this I was harshly blamed, accused of 'neglecting my child.' It gives me much satisfaction today to see the children of equally conservative mamas now 'wearing boy's clothes clear' with full approval.

We shared the one bedroom of the tiny house, sleeping close to a south window shaded with white Lady Banksia roses, and with my condition for the only drawback, were very happy together. One of our morning games I put quite literally in verse, and the editor who published it urged that I give myself to the writing of children's verse – said I had a special talent for it. Here is this one:

THE BAD LITTLE COO-BIRD

In the morning, in the bed,
She hugged her little girl and said,
'You're my little bird and this is our nest,
My little coo-bird that I love the best,
　　Now coo! little coo-bird, coo!'
　　And what did that bad baby do?
　　'Coo,' said the mother soft and still,
　　And the daughter answered loud and shrill,
　　　　'To-who! To-whit, to-whoo!'

'No, no,' said the mother, 'no,
I do not like it so,
Such fowls as owls I do not love—

Where is my little cooing dove?
Now coo, little coo-bird, coo!'
      And what did that bad baby do?
      'Coo!' said the mother, soft and still,
      And the daughter answered loud and shrill,
            'Cock-a-doodle-doo!'

'No, no,' said the mother, 'no,
I do not like it so,
I want no cock-a-biddies in my bed!'
And she brooded her nestling warm and said,
      'Now coo, little coo-bird, coo!'
      And what did that dear baby do?
      'Coo,' said the mother, soft and slow,
      And the daughter answered, sweet and low,
            'Coo-oo, Coo-oo, Coo!'

We had happy years together, nine of them, the last four she
was mine alone. In Oakland she had a safe and quiet street, a
good yard, a friend of mine opposite with a family of children to
play with, and a pleasant little school. When I came home from
my work anywhere, toward supper-time, I could see that little
red-capped figure on the gate-post, watching for me, and she
would come, running . . .

Some unbelievable brute of a woman told the child that her
mother was getting a divorce, that her father would undoubtedly marry again, and then she would have a stepmother! She
came to me in tears. 'Darling,' said I, 'if Papa does marry again
it will be Grace Channing,' and the smiles broke through the
tears like April sunshine. Grace she had known and loved since
babyhood, loved as another mother.

Then came the end of the Oakland effort. My mother was dead. My friend on whom I had so counted, was gone. I was not able to carry the boarding-house, and there was new work opening for me in San Francisco, but in a place unsuitable for a child. It was arranged that she should go to her father for a while, my father, going East, taking her with him.

Since her second mother was fully as good as the first, better in some ways perhaps; since the father longed for his child and had a right to some of her society; and since the child had a right to know and love her father – I did not mean her to suffer the losses of my youth – this seemed the right thing to do. No one suffered from it but myself. This, however, was entirely overlooked in the furious condemnation which followed. I had 'given up my child.'

To hear what was said and read what was printed one would think I had handed over a baby in a basket. In the years that followed she divided her time fairly equally between us, but in companionship with her beloved father she grew up to be the artist that she is, with advantages I could never have given her. I lived without her, temporarily, but why did they think I liked it? She was all I had.

While arranging for her journey I never once let her feel that it was pain, a break, anything unusual. It was time to go and see her dear Papa – and she went, happily enough. A pretty little outfit was prepared, a small alligator hand-bag was a special treasure, and full explanation was given about the old gentlemen she was to travel with – there were three of them, taking a state-room.

I took her to the uptown station in Oakland, where the Overland trains stopped for passengers; her grandfather appeared; she climbed gaily aboard. She hurried to the window and looked out, waving to me. She had long shining golden hair. We smiled and waved and threw kisses to each other. The train went out, farther and farther till I couldn't see her any more . . .

That was thirty years ago. I have to stop typing and cry as I tell about it. There were years, years, when I could never see a mother and child together without crying, or even a picture of them. I used to make friends with any child I could so as to hold it in my arms for a little . . .

What were those pious condemners thinking of? I had lost home and husband, my mother was dead, my father, never close at all, was now removed across the continent. My recent 'best friend' had, as it were, soured on my hands, I had no money at all – I had borrowed again to pay for Katharine's ticket and to move, and left failure behind me, and debt. I explained to the landlady that I would pay her as soon as I could, and moved across the bay.

Some years later, my father was speaking favorably to some one as to my methods in child culture.

'You ought to be able to judge,' said I. 'You took the child all across the continent, leaving her mother; one nine-year-old girl with three old gentlemen – how did she behave?'

'She behaved,' he answered carefully, 'as if she was trying to make it as comfortable as possible for every one she was with.'

She always did. She always has . . .

From CHAPTER 17
OVER THE TOP

The International Council of Women is a federated body, composed of many National Councils and a number of other groups, some of great size, as the W.C.T.U. and the W.S.A. It was an important part of the worldwide stir and getting-together of women which so characterizes the last century, representing millions of women, and the noblest upward movements of the age. Fancy the juvenile ignorance that scorns an age in which half the world woke up!

Women had claimed and won equal education, from the public schools to the universities; professional opportunity, and had made a place in medicine, law, the ministry, and all manner of trades, crafts and businesses; equal suffrage, and had made much progress in that demand. But the most wide-spread and in a way the most important of these various associations was the Woman's Club, which reached almost every one, and brought her out of the sacred selfishness of the home into the broader contact and relationship so essential to social progress. Once in five years this International Council held a Congress, to which came leading women from many nations, of many religions and purposes; they came together from all parts of the world and learned to know each other and their common needs.

London was very kind to us. Great houses were opened, invitations poured in, royalty itself was polite. I went as a freelance, invited personally as a speaker, my visit not limited to the Congress. So I went out to Hammersmith, where my friend May Morris lived, and engaged board in Carnforth Lodge. Miss Starr of Hull House had told me of this place, she stayed there while studying book-binding with 'The Dove' experts.

This was a square old manor house, now a home for nurses, which added to its resources by its 'paying guests.' It stood in a large garden, and bore high upon its stately walls a broad band of white, going all the way around, with this inscription – 'The Hammersmith and Fulham District Association for Nursing the Sick Poor in Their Own Homes Supported by Voluntary Contributions Only.'

I was glad to be in England again, to renew friendships made in 1896 and to make new ones. I've been there five times, and every time I like it better. Furthermore, since the War, when the various nations stood out so sharply in their true colors, England rose higher than ever in my esteem.

People were more than kind. I was made a member of the Sesame Club, an international woman's club of a purely social nature. Of the Fabian Society I was still a member, and saw something of them. Having tea with May Morris, 'J. Ramsay MacDonald calls and invites me to dinner.' 'Feel pretty low,' as but too usual.

On a fine May Sunday I visited Mrs Henry Norman. She was the daughter of my dear Edinburgh friend, Mrs Dowie. 'Very cordial and nice. A lovely country, pure picture. Sleep at Ivy Farm, another picture. I hear and see the skylark, hear the cuckoo too.' Nevertheless, on Monday, 'continue very low and miserable,' and Tuesday, 'lie flat on the daisies and buttercups and weep – very low indeed.'

Again in Carnforth Lodge, there presently appeared as fellow-boarder a distant cousin, Miss Foote by name, also studying book-binding. She was a very pleasant companion. We enjoyed the beauties of England together, and smiled as strangers may, at some of its – differences. There came a spell of extremely hot weather, cruelly hot, horses died in London streets. We two Americans sought for ice, and found none. No ice for sale anywhere. Finally we were told, dubiously, 'You might find some at the fishmongers.'

By the fifth of May I proudly record, 'Women and Economics has come.' Small and Maynard arranged with Putnam's for their English publishing. Mr George Haven Putnam remembered me as a small child in Mrs Swift's boarding-house in New York; he was a friend of my father's. There was a demand for my book, but some inefficiency at the American end delayed its coming. Mr Putnam complained to me that while there were so many books he could not sell it was pretty hard to have a waiting list for mine and not be able to get it.

Meanwhile I was writing, always writing, or trying to; with little visits, dinners, and so on in between working days. Presently I met Dr E.A. Ross, the sociologist, whom I had known at Stanford. He and his pretty wife had a tiny flat in London for a while, and they were intensely interested in *Women and Economics*. He asked why I had not put in a bibliography. I told him I had meant to, but when it came to making a list of the books I had read bearing on the subject, there were only two! One was Geddes's and Thompson's *Evolution of Sex*, the other only an article, Lester F. Ward's, in that 1888 *Forum*.

Then they were anxious to know how long I had been at work on it, said they thought it must have been ever since they had seen me last, some four years. 'If I tell you you will never respect me or the book any more,' I protested. But they were determined to know, and I told him that the first draft, the manuscript the publishers accepted, had been written in seventeen days, while visiting in five different houses. This was a blow to the scientific mind.

The book was warmly received in London, with long, respectful reviews in the papers. What with my former reputation, based on the poems, this new and impressive book, and my addresses at the Congress and elsewhere, I became quite a lion.

The Congress opened on June 26, with its week of many meetings, addresses, reports, and so on. Noted women were gathered there from all quarters of the world – which had any. Other women, as yet distinguished by the interest in progress and the courage that brought them, came in their native costumes; the 'golden lilies' of high-born Chinese ladies, the Hindu sari, the veils of harem women.

The most pressing matters of importance to women, to children, to the home, to the peace, purity and health of the world, all were discussed in stirring papers and speeches, and listened to by great and enthusiastic crowds. Most hospitable entertainment was offered us, large cards of invitation, such as I had never seen before; a reception by Lady Battersea at Surrey House on Park Lane, a garden-party at Fulham Palace – 'Lord Bishop of London and Mrs Creighton,' and another at Gunnersbury Park, Baron Rothschild's place. 'Very gaudy bright and splendid,' says the diary.

The grandest of all was the opening one given at Stafford House by the Duchess of Sutherland. For this, I learned later, our much-impressed American women had prepared with awe, wearing their best and newest, with large outlay. It was an impressive occasion; Stafford House was called the finest private house in London, and as for its Lady – when they asked me, 'What has impressed you most in England?' I promptly answered, 'The Duchess of Sutherland.' She was so big, so progressive and intelligent, so nobly beautiful.

If I had been well – if ever I had had a clear, strong head – all this would have been a vivid and pleasant memory. But I moved through meetings and entertainment with a groping mind, doing what I had to do as well as I could, in my usual dreary twilight. It was always a struggle to get necessary work done, to keep up in some degree with the flood of engagements, to try to recognize and remember people. This last effort I have long since given up. I do not, can not, hold in mind a fraction of the innumerable people I have met. In the everlasting traveling, lecturing and being 'entertained,' it was my custom, after the lecture, to look feebly about and ask, 'Where is the lady I belong to?' Originally a personal limitation, doubtless; added to by the long ruin; made incurable by the professional life.

Came to me one morning during a session a busy Mrs Leo Hunter, eager to have me come to dinner. I looked in my little engagement book— 'Yes, I can come, thank you,' and I asked the place, the hour, the name. 'Don't you know my *name*?' she cried amazedly. I owned that I didn't. 'But how can you come to dinner with me if you don't know my name?' 'You asked me to,' said I. If she had but known how many kind persons were nameless to me!

Before the Congress opened a luncheon was given by the Society of American Women in London, to which I, among many others, was invited. In the waiting-room I saw and admired a particularly English type, tall and generously built, so unlike our slender, nervous American kind, with large blue eyes and glorious hair, heavy golden masses. Presently I learned that she was born in Salem, Massachusetts! The Countess of Warwick was there, and I was warned by a careful lady that this noblewoman 'was not a proper person to meet.' I had heard something of the reasons for criticism, and cheerfully replied that so long as the Prince of Wales was in good society I had no objections to meeting the Countess of Warwick, which presently came to pass.

'*Would* you mind sitting on the other side of the Countess of Warwick?' asked a worried mistress of ceremonies. 'Mrs Frances Hodgson Burnett has taken your place by mistake.' I truthfully told her that I did not care in the least where I sat, but was amused when we passed behind the chairs to see that a very large place-card on the President's left, standing up against a goblet, bearing my name in conspicuous letters, with Mrs Burnett sitting cheerfully in front of it. On the President's right was the Countess, and I sat next beyond, pleased to study so closely 'the most beautiful woman in Europe.'

The President held her in converse, and it worried me to see swift waiters taking away her food before she had time to eat. A particularly good plate of chicken was about to be torn from her and I could not bear it. I touched her arm, with some warm commendation of the chicken and protest that she was not getting anything to eat. This seemed to please her as a matter of good-will, we talked a bit, and she asked me to visit her at Warwick Castle – which I took to be merely a general expression of hospitality.

Next I met her at her sister's reception, which deserves more description, being high-water-mark in the matter of gorgeousness of all I ever attended. Our delegates went to it in all the state they could muster, in jeweled glory. I went alone on a two-penny bus, having to get off in Piccadilly and scuttle around behind St James's Park in the rain and darkness, ducking under the heads of the horses crowding in. Here was mighty Stafford House, here were long lines of knee-breeched liveries, and here was I, giving my waterproof and rubbers to these functionaries as if it were the coatroom at a church fair.

My dress, the only one I had for evening wear, was a dark plum-colored satin which I had made to suit myself, a 'princess dress,' fitted smoothly down the front like a medieval lady's, with a square neck, trimmed with plain bands of velvet of the same rich color. It cost me about fifteen dollars, and at this writing I am still using some of it – I was fond of that dress. One of the reporters, dilating on the glittering costumes, spoke of 'Mrs Stetson in a plain black dress, with no diamonds but her eyes,' a gentleman reporter, that.

In the dressing-rooms I saw a woman I had known in Oakland, rich, elderly, accustomed to social occasions, yet looking strangely timid. She was one of those persons who love to patronize budding celebrities, but apt to drop them suddenly upon disapproval. She had been kind to me during some of my Oakland experiences, had dropped me with sudden violence, and when I left the state considered me a wholly objectionable character. Naturally I did not approach her. To my great astonishment she greeted me with effusion and hung upon my arm, that I might take her about! Circumstances alter cases.

But my most characteristic performance at the reception was as follows: On entrance we were passed along that imposing line of footmen, and our names were cried aloud from man to man as we approached the grand staircase on whose first landing stood the ladies receiving. Drawing near the stairs I saw two members of our Congress, plainly dressed and looking timidly up at the array of tiaras on the landing. They said they had no one to introduce them. 'Come on,' quoth I, serenely, 'tell me your names and I'll introduce you.' One was Susa Young Gates, daughter of Brigham Young, who became a lasting friend, the other Emmiline Wells, I think, another Mormon lady. And so I introduced them to the Duchess of Sutherland, gloriously tall and beautiful, to the Countess of Warwick, her sister; and then, turning to the third, I cheerfully remarked, 'This one I don't remember.'

Which was true, and quite habitual with me, but on this occasion most unfortunate, as the third hostess was Lady Aberdeen, the President of The International Council of Women! She was very pleasant about it but I think not unnaturally displeased – who wouldn't have been!

The most distinguished honor offered to the delegates was an invitation to take tea with the Queen at Windsor Castle. With glowing anticipations the women of all nations prepared for this supreme opportunity. I was as usual very tired, always too tired to meet the demands of these great gatherings; and I shrewdly suspected that this would not be a wholly enjoyable affair, so I did not go. Afterwards I heard that they all had to stand about for two hours in a stone courtyard, which for a woman like Susan B. Anthony and others near her age must have been a serious tax on their strength. At last Victoria appeared, in the carriage named for her, and drove slowly about. Lady Aberdeen knelt on the step and kissed her hand, then presenting one only of the delegates, a lady from Canada who had a title, and the Queen drove out again. After which august spectacle tea was served by flunkies; as a matter of boasting all the others could proudly state that they had been to tea with the Queen, but I could proudly state that I'd been asked and wouldn't go.

They told a somewhat similar story of our Antoinette Sterling, the great contralto, who was a popular favorite in England. Her magnificent voice was so renowned that Victoria summoned her to sing before her. Mrs Sterling, who had arranged to sing for some charity on that day, replied that she had another engagement and could not come. The Queen, who approved her putting charity first, repeated her invitation for another date. The musical Quaker replied that she could not come because she never wore décolleté gowns as required at court, and the patient Queen told her to wear what she pleased. So Antoinette went at last, and sang so gloriously that her majesty gave her a silver tea-set; – I tell the tale as it was told to me.

It appeared the friendly Lady Warwick really meant her invitation. She repeated it at that reception, and somewhat later sent me a telegram three pages long – sixty-three words, a letter, really, urging me to come and address some pen-workers from Birmingham whom she was trying to organize; and to spend the night; so at last I went.

It was but one night, but memorable for the fairytale of that cream-walled castle by the shadowy Avon; the white peacocks on the velvet lawns; the harebells on the battlements – I went up there and picked one so I know. My bedroom was liberally decorated with crests and coronets, on the writing paper, of which there was a plentiful supply; on the chinaware, the towels, the water-cans the sheets and pillow-cases – even the soft, thick rose-colored blankets had a massive one like a inverted soup-plate. It made me think of a steam-boat.

The baronial hall was a revelation in size; three distinct parties might have been held in it without disturbing one another. In the deep embrasure of one window stood a knight in armor on horseback, life-size, – and he made no more impression than a rubber plant.

Any one could visit Warwick for a shilling a head, but when the 'trippers' were being shown about by the austere exhibitor, I felt amusingly superior, being on the other side of the rope! Childishly ignorant among all this gorgeousness was I, and when asked about breakfast in bed cheerfully replied that I preferred to get up. So I came down in the morning to that huge dining-hall, with the great Vandyke – or was it Velásquez? – at one end. It seemed depressingly empty, no one else eating but a remote governess and her charge, the few footmen coldly disapproving. Evidently one was not expected to get up to breakfast. The Earl of Warwick was at home, and also the Countess's mother, Lady Roslyn. She was much pleased with my poems and asked me to visit her at Roslyn Castle. Also Lady Warwick urged me to come to them at their summer cottage, and, later, the Duchess of Sutherland asked me to visit her – that was on account of *Women and Economics*.

None of these things did I do, reasons quite forgotten, but I really wanted to accept the last invitation, because when my Grandmother Perkins had been in England with Aunt Harriet Stowe they had been entertained by the former Duchess of Sutherland, who was a special friend of the Queen. She was unable for reasons of state openly to receive Aunt Harriet as she wished to do, and made this arrangement with her friend instead. However I didn't go.

As an offset to all these grandeurs let me describe my reception by Miss Purdie's maid. Miss Purdie was a fine, liberal-minded Scotch lady, who had me give a parlor lecture in 1896, and now, when entertainment was being planned for the foreign visitors, had asked for me. I had mostly forgotten the former meeting, and went to spy out the land and see if I wanted to be with her.

I never had any impressive clothes, and in England it makes far more difference than it does here. I trotted about in my very ordinary raiment, with my everlasting little black bag, just as I would at home, and so attired rang Miss Purdie's bell. The door was opened by a severe Scotch maid.

'Is Miss Purdie at home?' 'She is.' 'Can I see her?' 'What do you wish to see her for?' 'I wish to call upon her,' and I offered my card. The card mollified her somewhat, but not much, for it had no crest, no name of house or address, not even 'Mrs,' nothing but Charlotte Perkins Stetson.

She let me in, grudgingly, and started up the stairs. I was uncertain of what was expected. 'Shall I come up?' I asked, 'or wait here?' This admission of ignorance she considered most damaging, and sternly replied, 'If you are *really a caller* you may come up!' I came up, was received with open arms by Miss Purdie, and spent a week there very happily. Doubtless that worthy watch-dog took me for an agent – why shouldn't she?

Like a few pictures out of a big book too hastily turned in a dim light, are these memories. There was one urgent luncheon invitation from a Lady – Grove, I think it was. I was torn between my habit of always seeing people who needed me, and increasing weariness, and wrote as much, saying that unless she wished to see me imperatively I could not come. The answering demand was most imperative, so I went; finding a large, handsome lady with two admirers (one of whom was George Eliot's second husband, Mr Cross), who talked with her incessantly, and a spare elderly husband who talked not at all – and myself, evidently only an exhibit.

The Congress over, there remained many friends to see, and always work to do. I wrote an article for *Ainslee's Magazine* and another for the *Arena*, about the Congress, and extremely poor stuff it was. With ease and freedom and some merit, I write thoughts, ideas, reasoning, yes, and feeling too, but descriptive work, such as makes a war correspondent famous, is beyond me.

One delightful visit was with the family of Mrs Bland (Edith Nesbit), at Well Hall, Eltham, Kent. The earlier mansion, built for Margaret Roper by her father, Sir Thomas More, had been burned, and replaced by this one which they said 'was only Georgian.' Behind the house, just across a little vine-walled bridge, was a large rectangular lawn, surrounded by thick grown trees and shrubs, outside which lay the moat that once guarded the older building. Here, in absolute privacy, those lovely children could run barefoot, play tennis and badminton, wear any sort of costume; it was a parlor out of doors. We all joined in merry games, acted little plays and fairy-tales, and took plentiful photographs.

There was another visit to Edinburgh, where I lectured for the Summer School, for the University, on Castle Hill. My dear Mrs Dowie was staying at Levenhall, Musselbirgh, near by, and I spent a few days with her, most happily. From there back to Newcastle, where I renewed friendship with Miss Roecliffe, my kind entertainer of 1896.

In these English travels I found no difficulty whatever either in audiences or in personal contacts. Hearers laughed at my jokes just as they did at home; one man told a friend, 'I'd give half a crown any day just to see that woman smile.' Also, my personal work went on. Strangers confided in me as at home.

One old gentleman with whom I fell into converse on a train in Scotland, pulled himself up at last, protesting in surprise that he never talked with strangers! I explained that I was not a stranger, and I wasn't – people were people anywhere and my service was for all. So they told me their troubles as usual, and I helped as I could, finding always that the losses and sufferings, mistakes and misdeeds of my own life gave me the key to the hearts of others.

While in Newcastle one unexpected amusement was going to the circus – Barnum and Bailey's – in England! Very popular it was, too. Back to London and my favorite Midland Temperance Hotel on Guilford St, a little last shopping and calling, and then I prefaced my departure by trying Brush's Remedy for seasickness. Sailed on August 31, SS. *Menominee*. 'Room 8. Berth 4. Nice sofa bed under porthole. Am not sick.' And next day, 'Blessed be Brush! Am not sick at all.'

As to ocean travel in general, I dislike it intensely. There is no privacy except in bed, and not then unless one has a whole stateroom. Planted in a steamer-chair, the strip of deck before one's face is a promenade, a ceaseless procession of humanity. As to 'sea air' – unless one can get to the very prow, or bear the full blast of the wind, what one gets is *ship air*, and if any beast has a fouler breath than a ship, I have not met it. Anywhere to the leeward it pours out from every door that's open, and from those slow-whirling ventilators which reach down to the very bowels of the ship – and distribute its odors. An ocean steamer is a big, inescapable garden-party, reception, afternoon tea – a constant, swirling crowd. Sorry, but I don't like it.

Landed Monday, September 11th, and back to mother's; one dollar in my pocket. But by Friday came the check from

Ainslee's, $125.00! the most I had ever received up to that time. Things were going well now. There were many 'downs' during the summer, but now the little book says 'Feel fine,' 'Do good morning's work on letters and papers and am not tired.' But by the twenty-first. 'Feel so badly p.m. that I try to take a ride on the cars and have to come back.'

Presently Mr Small, my publisher, called. He came eagerly up the stairs and greeted me warmly, anxious for other books. 'We quite understand,' he said, 'that further arrangements will have to be on a different basis.' *Women and Economics* was a success. The discrepancy between its really enormous vogue and its very meager returns I have never understood. It sold and sold and sold for about twenty-five years. It sold widely in England, so much so that Putnam's brought out a seventh edition with a new introduction in 1911. It was translated into French – but alas! the translator couldn't find a publisher! – into German, Dutch, Italian, Hungarian and Japanese. From none of the translations did I get anything, save the Italian. That was done by the Contessa Pironti, and she sent me $30.00 – noblesse oblige!

The reviews were surprising, numerous, respectful, a most gratifying recognition. So Small agreed to take my next book, *Human Work*, which I proposed to spend the winter in writing. They offered $500.00 down, 15 per cent to 5000 and then 18 per cent; I was launched.

Lecturing also began to go well. For two in Boston I got $87.00, for another $25.00, and from the *Saturday Evening Post*, for several editorials, $48.00; from the *Puritan*, $25.00. By October I record a grand total of $231.56. But next day I sent Katharine $25.00, and to various creditors $50, $38, $30, $50, $20 – there was never much surplus.

From a pleasant Boston visit with the Blackwells, always so good to me, I was off, October 19th for Toledo, staying again with the family of Mayor Jones. Here I did my first 'campaign speaking'; did not take to it much. But there was one funny incident while there. I was hurrying to a down-town meeting when the horse-car was stopped by an altercation between the slender young conductor and a big, elderly man who insisted that his transfer was good, and refused to pay another fare as demanded. The conductor threatened to throw him off, but the passenger got in behind the brake – the back platform was only open at one end – and defied him. The driver looked around grinning, the complacent Americans inside looked on in amusement – but I was in a hurry. So I rose with a most phil-anthropic air and came forward with, 'Let me pay this poor man's fare.' 'Oh no, Madam, no indeed!' protested the insulted disputant, out came his purse and on went the car – it was a mean trick, but the car should not be so delayed.

Then to Indianapolis, October 25th. 'Address Contemporary Club on 'What Work Is.' Rather hard sledding but struck some kindred notes.' Especially in a youth who turns out to be Booth Tarkington. As I delighted in and deeply honored his work, it was a pleasure to find how agreeable he was personally – I called on him next morning and we had a nice talk. Back to Toledo, more speeches, and preached twice on Sunday. Then to St Louis, visiting the Crundens', and speaking for the Pedagogical Society again. 'Big house, went well.' So to Chicago, and dear Mrs Dow.

November 3rd: 'Go down town and see my manager, Mrs Laura D. Pelham.' I had known this lady in Hull House, she and her husband were connected with a lecture bureau. She came to hear me, and then this bureau offered me $250.00 a week, net, if I would work for them. This was large money, but what of that? I felt sure that they overestimated my drawing power, knew that I could not do good work in six lectures a week right along, and also I was on my way to California to spend a quiet winter writing the next book. Furthermore, I had plans for the next year that brooked no postponement. In June I was to marry [George Houghton Gilman], and the chances of a year's time, when one is near forty, are worth more than millions of dollars So that golden opportunity was passed by.

But I lectured 'on my own,' in Chicago, in Milwaukee, in Sioux City, Iowa, and Sheldon – 'Big crowd but it went badly. They don't like it. Hard sledding.' But next day some ladies called. 'They like me and want me again . . . Can't always make a good impression.'

Back to Chicago, more lectures, one in Fond du Lac, Wisconsin, where my title was rendered, 'Our Brains and What's the Matter of 'Em.'

Thursday, November 16th: 'Letter from Russia – a man has translated my book – one Kamensky.'

In Evanston, at the Northwestern University, I had the honor of taking the place of Mr Howells, who could not keep his engagement, and lectured on Ethics. Went well – I was really pleased. So were they, the professors and such. Then in town and take Wisconsin Central at 2:00 a.m. and off to Minneapolis.

There was one occasion in this city when I met what is called 'social attention' in a conspicuous form. I think it was later, but will tell the tale while I remember it. A friend there had arranged a lecture for me. This is no light work, as any one who has done it knows. The tickets were fifty cents. Certain ladies, knowing me by reputation, insisted that I must have some social attention. Pay fifty cents to hear me lecture they would not, but got up a lunch party in my 'honor' at a hotel, where they all paid a dollar for their food, and expected me to address them, for nothing! I arrived about 11:00 a.m. – there was a coal famine, a blizzard and a strike, all at once, and such hindrance and delay that I had had almost no sleep. And here I was taken to this hotel filled with buzzing women, for this luncheon.

'Have you engaged a room for me?' I asked wearily. No, they had not thought to do that. I suggested that I should like a room and a bath, which was presently furnished, to my relief. And all through that chattering lunch I sat thinking how to tell them, without being rude and grossly ungrateful, that to expect a speech for nothing, of a professional speaker, was – well, shall we say unbusinesslike? When women really grow up they will be more fair-minded.

CHAPTER 21
THE LAST TEN

Nearly ten years since writing this book – which ended in hoping. For nine of them I remained in the old house in Norwich.

As to books, I wrote a species of detective story, at least unique, called *Unpunished*. No takers. 'I find your characters interesting,' said one 'reader.' 'That is not necessary in a detective story.' Evidently it is not, but I have often wished it was.

There are two copies of this afloat, buried in manuscript heaps of some agent or publisher. The trouble is that after a year or so I forget their names.

I wrote my *Social Ethics* over and over. That, I hope, will be printed with *Human Work*; social economics and social ethics – on those two I would rest my claim to social service.

Human Work was recently read by a New York publisher. He was surprised to find how few alterations were required, and said he would be glad to reprint it 'if conditions . . .'

As to lecturing – that market has declined before the advance of the radio. I had hoped for some hearing in my native state, where I had spoken in quite recent years; but when

I offered my services to that invaluable association, The League of Women Voters, undertaking to lecture for them anywhere in the state, for expenses only, the total result was one engagement in a neighboring town, audience of ten. Also I had not unreasonably expected to be heard in the Connecticut College for Women, only some twelve miles from Norwich. After so many years of work for the advancement of women, with a fairly worldwide reputation in that work, and with so much that was new and strong to say to the coming generation, it seemed to me a natural opportunity. It did not seem so to the college. Once, for the League of Women Voters, I spoke in their hall – never otherwise.

My happiness in Norwich was in my garden, with Houghton as always, and with a few beloved friends.

There were that admirable minister and more admirable man, Alexander Abbott, and his dear family; and Edwin Higgins – Houghton's close friend and, in time of need, most efficiently mine – and his family. A near neighbor and unfailing comfort, giving restful companionship, was Miss Elizabeth Huntington, and there were others, pleasant and kind.

In January, 1932, I discovered that I had cancer of the breast. My only distress was for Houghton. I had not the least objection to dying. But I did not propose to die of this, so I promptly bought sufficient chloroform as a substitute. Human life consists in mutual service. No grief, pain, misfortune or 'broken heart' is excuse for cutting off one's life while any power of service remains. But when all usefulness is over, when one is assured of unavoidable and imminent death, it is the simplest of human rights to choose a quick and easy death in place of a slow and horrible one.

Public opinion is changing on this subject. The time is

approaching when we shall consider it abhorrent to our civi-lization to allow a human being to die in prolonged agony which we should mercifully end in any other creature. Believing this open choice to be of social service in promoting wiser views on this question, I have preferred chloroform to cancer.

Going to my doctor for definite assurance, he solemnly agreed with my diagnosis and thought the case inoperable.

'Well,' said I cheerfully, 'how long does it take?' He estimated a year and a half. 'How long shall I be able to type?' I asked. 'I must finish my *Ethics*.' He thought I might be quite comfortable for six months. It is now three and a half years and this obliging malady has given me no pain yet.

Then came what was pain – telling Houghton. He wanted an expert opinion, and we got it. No mistake. Then, since I utterly refused a late operation, he urged me to try x-ray treat-ment, which I did with good effects. He suffered a thousand times more than I did – but not for long. On the fourth of May, 1934, he suddenly died, from cerebral hemorrhage.

Whatever I felt of loss and pain was outweighed by gratitude for an instant, painless death for him, and that he did not have to see me wither and die – and he be left alone.

I flew to Pasadena, California, in the fall of 1934, to be near my daughter and grandchildren. Grace Channing, my lifelong friend, has come out to be with me. We two have a little house next door but one to my Katharine, who is a heavenly nurse and companion. Dorothy and Walter, her children, are a delight. Mr Chamberlin, my son-in-law, has made the place into a garden wherein I spend happy afternoons under an orange-tree – the delicious fragrance drifting over me, the white petals lightly falling – in May! Now it is small green oranges occasionally thumping.

One thing I have had to complain of – shingles. *Shingles* – for six weeks. A cancer that doesn't show and doesn't hurt, I can readily put up with; it is easy enough to be sick as long as you feel well – but *shingles!*

People are heavenly good to me. Dear friends write to me, with outrageous praises. I am most unconcernedly willing to die when I get ready. I have no faintest belief in personal immortality – no interest in nor desire for it.

My life is in Humanity – and that goes on. My contentment is in God – and That goes on. The Social Consciousness, fully accepted, automatically eliminates both selfishness and pride. The one predominant duty is to find one's work and do it, and I have striven mightily at that.

The religion, the philosophy, set up so early, have seen me through.

[On August 17, 1935, Mrs Gilman fulfilled her intention to end her life as her malady advanced. The letter, left by her, was a part of the text of this final chapter of her autobiography, beginning: 'Human life consists in mutual service,' and ending 'I have preferred chloroform to cancer.']

MAD, BAD AND SAD

Lisa Appignanesi

'Subtle, textured and enthralling' *Sunday Times*

Mad, bad and sad. From the depression suffered by Virginia Woolf and Sylvia Plath to the mental anguish and addictions of iconic beauties Zelda Fitzgerald and Marilyn Monroe. From Freud and Jung and the radical breakthroughs of psychoanalysis to Lacan's construction of a modern movement and the new women-centred therapies. This is the story of how we have understood mental disorders and extreme states of mind in women over the last two hundred years and how we conceive of them today, when more and more of our inner life and emotions have become a matter for medics and therapists.

'A glittering intellectual history of women, madness and the mind doctors' Melanie McGrath, *Sunday Telegraph*

'Fascinating . . . In this sweeping, humane and formidably researched study Appignanesi does what all the very best investigative writers and journalists do: she raises questions for us to answer' Carmen Callil, *Daily Telegraph*

VIRAGO MODERN CLASSICS

The first Virago Modern Classic, *Frost in May* by Antonia White, was published in 1978. It launched a list dedicated to the celebration of women writers and to the rediscovery and reprinting of their works. Its aim was, and is, to demonstrate the existence of a female tradition in literature, and to broaden the sometimes narrow definition of a 'classic' which has often led to the neglect of interesting books. Published with new introductions by some of today's best writers, the books are chosen for many reasons: they may be great works of literature; they may be wonderful period pieces; they may reveal particular aspects of women's lives; they may be classics of comedy, storytelling, letter-writing or autobiography.

'The Virago Modern Classics list is wonderful. It's quite simply one of the best and most essential things that has happened in publishing in our time. I hate to think where we'd be without it'
Ali Smith

'A continuingly magnificent imprint'
Joanna Trollope

'The Virago Modern Classics have reshaped literary history and enriched the reading of us all. No library is complete without them'
Margaret Drabble

'The writers are formidable, the production handsome. The whole enterprise is thoroughly grand'
Louise Erdrich

'The Virago Modern Classics are one of the best things in Britain today'
Alison Lurie

'Good news for everyone writing and reading today'
Hilary Mantel

'Masterful works'
Vogue